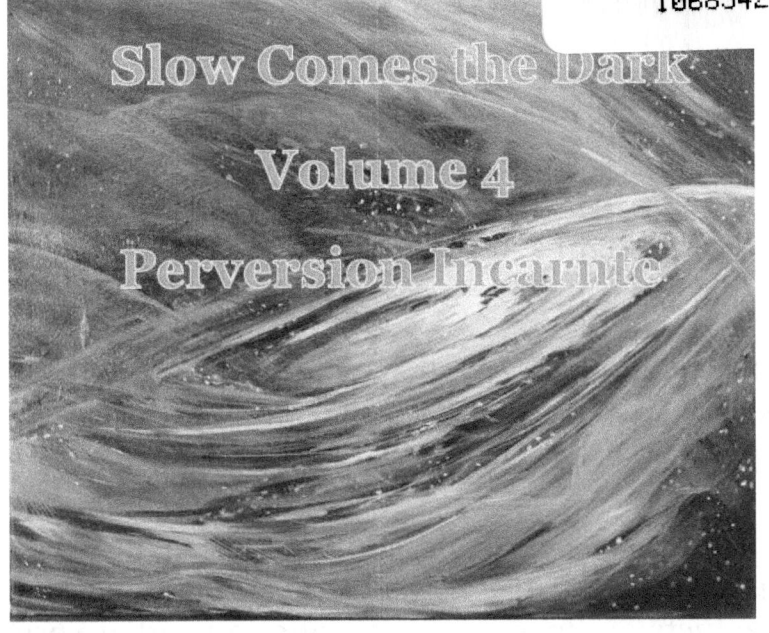

Slow Comes the Dark

Volume 4

Perversion Incarnate

Slow Comes the Dark Volume 4 Perversion Incarnate

Vic Broquard

Slow Comes the Dark Volume 4 Perversion Incarnate

First Edition
ISBN: 978-1-941415-72-6
Copyright ©2013, 2014 by Vic Broquard

This is a work of fiction. All characters, organizations, and events portrayed in this novel are products of the author's imagination and are used fictiously.

http://www.Broquard-ebooks.com
Broquard eBooks
103 Timberlane
East Peoria, IL 61611
author@Broquard-eBooks.com

Artwork by Crooked Willow Studios.

For Morgan and L. Ron Hubbard

Table of Contents

Chapter 1—Arrival of Technology

Blackwell-C, once a Forbidden Planet in the mid-spiral arm, but for half a millennia a full member of the Federation of Planets, was one of the very few worlds within the Federation that was not totally controlled by the major corporations, though they had headquarters on this world and operated out of it. Why? This world had always been more or less a feudal world, run and controlled by the fabulously wealthy and powerful barons. With the arrival of the major corporations some five hundred years ago, the new CEOs soon discovered there wasn't any way to take control of this backwater world from the barons or any real worth in so doing. Rather, they became *dear friends* with the ruling barons, who often carried out the dirty work for these executives. In turn, the executives did other favors for these ruling elites.

Thromstead had grown into one of the top twenty largest cities on Blackwell-C, and at the turn of the century, found itself the primary power brokers for the entire world. In effect, its many barons and counterparts within the major corporations ran the world. However, four men ran the Thromstead Baron's Council and thereby Blackwell-C.

Baron Adler Berthold, forty-six, and Baron Aldric Berringer, forty-seven, tightly controlled the other ten local Thromstead barons. The CEO of Galactic Dynamics, Dederick Kroft, forty-five, and Gerhardt Hagan, the CEO of Galactic Electronics, likewise controlled the other corporations' CEOs, though controlled might be the wrong twist of phrase. They used all manner of subtle means to ensure the loyalty of the other corporation's CEOs. Neither man was innocent of the occasional blackmail. These four men held nearly absolute power at this time.

They were also very close friends, especially so since the two barons played prominent roles in assisting these two CEOs to rise to their power positions. Spying was commonplace, and the two barons were masters of that. Each man was *happily* married, though their use of that qualifier may not be accurate. Sadistic megalomaniacs might be a far more accurate description of these men. And yet sadism had always been a part of what it meant to be a baron of Blackwell-C, had been for over a millennia of recorded history. Until some five hundred-fifty years ago, that sadism had kept this world isolated from the Federation and on its Forbidden list, but that ostracization changed, as all things must. Now this world and its inherent sadism fit like a glove with the new Federation of Planets.

The most above-board visual evidence lay in their ruling baronesses. In ancient times, they had their arms amputated and their tongues cut out. Their breasts were surgically enhanced, and they were forced to wear impossible corsets to obtain tiny waists and to wear six or seven-inch spiked heels. In ancient times, their only means of communication was via a cluck-click language, more or less developed within each family and not understood beyond that confine. With their entry into the Federation and the adoption of modern medical machines, no longer did these baronesses need to have their arms amputated and tongues cut off, rather these medical machines performed the arm removal painlessly, healing them rapidly, and removed voice boxes, a far simpler approach and one that did not so interfere with the baroness's eating and drinking.

In more recent times, the corporations' introduction of the new UFB women made a strong impact here on Blackwell-C, as did the process of genetic mutation. With the exception of voices, the UFB women were nearly perfect candidates for baronesses. Thus, the four wives of these powerful men were local women who had become UFB women. Adler's wife, Baroness Zelda, forty-four, was quite blonde, while Aldric's wife, Verena, forty-five, had light brown hair. Dederick's wife, Athala, forty-three, had light blonde hair, while Gerhardt's wife, Belinda, forty-four, had dark brown hair. All four women's hair reached their knees, as it did with all UFB women. Further, in keeping with tradition, the two baronesses had their voice boxes removed and communicated with their unique cluck-click language, which consisted of possibly twenty nouns and a similar number of verbs, a drastic reduction from the past when over two hundred words could be communicated by adding additional vocal sounds. The CEO's wives, Athala and Belinda, still had their voices, but with their long association with the two baronesses, they understood their cluck-click language.

Thromstead lay in the rocky hills of the Dark Forest. Hence, the city of some ten million had twisting, winding streets, stone homes built on whatever patch of semi-level ground was at hand. Some homes stood above those across the street or behind them. Near the northeastern edge in about the only truly flat land in this entire region lay the bustling, sprawling spaceport, one of the largest on this world, but certainly one of the busiest. Springtime brought a giant burst of colors from the myriad of flowers that thrust up from the melted winter snows, the depths of which sometimes accumulated to three feet. Most all homes were made from stone, including the barons' castles of which there were a dozen in this city alone.

Each castle had a fifteen-foot tall outer wall with one entrance at its heavily fortified gatehouse. These were well guarded and had Grade 10 blast doors that not even a d-gun could completely penetrate. Inside was usually a cobblestone courtyard, a stall for a shuttle, and a motor garage. Yes, these barons prided themselves in maintaining and using exotic automobiles, though they often used the flying shuttles as well. The Manor House was the jewel of each castle.

Constructed of stone, these rose at least three stories tall with an observation deck on its roof. The *dungeons* were in the basements, far underground. It was common for a manor house to have at least fifty rooms, though many were extremely large and used to hold frequent giant balls and parties. Of course, each manor house had a throne room, lavishly decorated, as each baron attempted to display his wealth and power before those who visited them.

The corporation skyscrapers varied from the corporation standard buildings. Why? Three reasons. First, this hilly, rocky area made construction of hundred story skyscrapers difficult. Second, the barons refused to allow anyone to construct buildings taller than their manor houses.

Third, the barons refused to allow unsightly concrete, steel, and glass buildings on their world, claiming they were wholly unsightly and destroyed the native beauty of the stone homes. As a result, the corporation headquarters appeared to be normal manor houses, similar in outward appearance to those of the barons.

These had no outer walls or courtyards and were double the size of the wealthiest baron's manor house. Part of the ground floor was a garage for the occupant's many vehicles. However, in order to meet their space needs, the corporation buildings went far underground. GD and GE headquarters each had twenty subterranean floors, a vast labyrinth of construction. And because these four men were such close friends, an underground tunnel connected Castle Berthold to GD headquarters, on to GE headquarters, and then on to Castle Berringer.

Daily these barons and CEOs used the tunnel to meet with each other, as did their wives who had become far closer friends than their husbands were. Further, the many children of these four couples also darted down the tunnels, playing together from age six onwards. A guard station stood at each underground entrance to the castle or headquarters. Behind them, giant blast doors could be shut, preventing all passage, should the need arise. Since the time of the initial construction, these doors had never been closed, a testimony to just how well these two barons and two CEOs cooperated.

Athala and Belinda had very close ties to their fellow UFB women and baronesses Zelda and Verena. They took the pair under their wings, a deep sympathy for the two blind women who were also unable to speak. While they felt rather helpless, they couldn't imagine how awful the lives of Zelda and Verena were. Hence, they spent much of their day with the two baronesses. Their constant chatting was mostly one-sided, since the two baronesses could only communicate around twenty ideas with their strange cluck-clicking. Nevertheless, their many children played with each other almost daily as they grew up and were a source of pleasure, particularly so for the baronesses, whose main source of information was hearing their children.

Yes, theirs was a dismal, black world filled with unseen terror and fears, far beyond the usual helpless state of the many UFB women, compounded all the more since the barons insisted they move about their castles on their own and unaided by their servants, particularly during the many balls, festive occasions, and daily audiences with their subjects in the throne rooms. Lacking arms, standing and walking precariously on their toe shoes, and unable even to see made these solo walks utterly terrifying for the baronesses, who couldn't even communicate their fright to anyone, though the two CEO wives were only too aware of what they must be going through, but were unable to assist them at those times. Hence, whenever they were with the baronesses, they constantly chatted, giving the blind UFB women some idea of what was going on.

On the other hand, these UFB women and the baronesses always wore the finest clothing and expensive jewelry. Nothing was too good for these prized women. In fact, the barons had expensive earrings made for their baronesses. These prized earrings were elaborate constructions with many dangling lobes made from gold and fitted with rubies and emeralds, and usually the ends rested upon their shoulders, stretching their ear lobes considerably. Over all, these baronesses presented their subjects with a most impressive view. While each was genetically modified to be incredibly beautiful as all UFB women were, these added touches were designed to impress any subject whose eyes gazed upon their baroness. Interchangeable glass eyes were used to heighten the blends with their earrings, fancy gowns, and other jewelry.

One would think that no woman would ever remotely desire to become a baroness, but that would be erroneous. They were revered by their subjects, looked upon with utter amazement. Their young daughters who would ultimately become the next generation of baronesses naively believed that one day they too would hold positions of such honor and respect, and had no idea of the stark terror and patheticness of their mother's lives. Their mothers had no way to communicate this to their daughters, no way to prevent this from happening to their daughters, and no way to encourage them to flee or resist their father's desires to marry then off to become new baronesses.

This isn't to say that these baronesses didn't experience any pleasure in their lives. On the contrary, their husbands understood fully the intense sexual drives that all UFB women had and saw that their wives were satisfied each morning and every night. Failure to provide gratification meant constant problems with the women during the day. Plus, these women received tremendous tactile sensations from each strand of their genetically modified hair. They loved the incredible sensations they received when they used the electrostatic hair machines that so beautifully arranged their knee-length hair— no UFB woman failed to use these machines many times during each day.

At this point in time, a number of critical events were about to take place, events that would ultimately alter the entire world of Blackwell-C. The events centered around their many children who were soon to become official adults and marry, along with the arrival of new genetic modification research and cloning processes, imported from Danforth-C, technology developed by one Dr. Sam Decker who had vanished from history.

"Now finally, we *are* getting somewhere!" exclaimed Dederick, the GD CEO. His two genetic research doctors, Dr. Lanzo Ludwig and Dr. Marko Von Happ, had summoned him to their sub-level twenty laboratory. The new research data and growth cloning machine had finally arrived from GD headquarters on Danforth-C. The two doctors explained to their boss what could now be done, and as expected, Dederick was quite impressed and enthused, granting them unlimited funds to proceed with their experimentations.

"Yes, yes, Dederick," the excited fifty year old Dr. Lanzo continued, "we can now make a clone from anyone. Plus, we should be able to introduce genetic modifications into the new clone as well." Forty-five year old Dr. Marko nodded in complete agreement, thankful his boss was handling the CEO.

"Superb, just superb. We must put this to use at once, doctors. Cost is no object," Dederick added. He and Gerhardt were still trying to find ways and means to take over control of

Blackwell-C from these sadistic barons, but had not found any remote way of doing so, primarily because these barons were even more sadistic and devilish than the corporation CEOs.

Both the CEOs and the barons had rejected the potential offered by creating super-genius sons, the product of a UFBMD man and a normal woman, an action being experimented with on a number of other Federation worlds. Here, that idea was discarded out of hand. For one thing, the barons wouldn't be the genius son's father. Thus, while they would have tremendous IQs, they couldn't become ruling barons, nor would the barons allow such men to exist, seeing them as a direct threat to themselves, rightly so. Similarly, the CEOs wouldn't be these gifted IQ son's fathers and thus did not want them eventually to become CEOs, seeing them as a potential threat to their positions, rightly so once again.

Now with this new cloning technology and the potential genetically to engineer into the clones special properties, Dederick and Gerhardt saw a whole new avenue opening up, one they could use to put these barons in their proper places, subordinate to the corporations and their CEOs. The sons of the barons and the CEOs were exceptionally physically strong, a byproduct of the mating of a normal man and a UFB woman. This, both the barons and the CEOs greatly appreciated. But what if clones of them could be made that were ten times stronger? What if his geneticists could isolate the genetic structure that made the super-geniuses? Could they not then insert those genetic changes into the clones or even themselves, making new super-geniuses? What about cloning themselves? If they could do that, then Dederick and Gerhardt could be immortal in a way, merely cloning a new youthful version of themselves when their current body got too old.

"All right, doctors. You have long studied the DNA of my son and daughter. Use his as a model, but develop for me the ultimate fighter, powerful, strong, and undefeatable. That's goal one. Goal two is to modify my daughter's DNA to see if we can't produce UFB women who lack eyeballs and voice boxes. That will go a long way with these barons, allowing them to make perfect baronesses. Goal three is to isolate what makes these special super-genius sons and create a genetic bio agent to do that to anyone. Goal four is to make a clone of me that is all powerful and with superior intelligence," Dederick outlined his immediate plans for the doctors.

"But we will need many test subjects. Human experimentation is illegal, boss," Dr. Lanzo suggested. Again, Dr. Marko nodded his full agreement, even more thankful his boss was handling the CEO. He doubted he would have had the temerity to have suggested this critical detail. He held his breath in anticipation of Dederick's response. Human experimentation was a verboten topic, one that prevented any real breakthroughs in human genetics, other than the occasional medical cures.

"Sub-levels nineteen and twenty will be sealed off and kept under heavy security. I will provide you with as many test subjects as you desire, doctors. Time is of the essence. We must make these a reality and very soon. A year from now may well be too late. We are at a very critical stage here on Blackwell-C. If we can act within a year, then there is yet hope for the future. So spare no expense, doctors, but get me the results that I must have and soon. I'll bring you six test subjects later this week. You be ready for them. Oh, how old should they be?"

Dr. Lanzo replied, "Teenagers would be best, I believe."

"Good. Now you get to work. I have to bring Gerhardt up to speed on this immediately. We are depending on you, doctors, so don't fail me," Dederick cautioned them both. A few minutes later, he stepped into Gerhardt's top floor office of his GE headquarters.

"Well, the stuff's arrived from Danforth-C. Incredible potential, Gerhardt," he stated.

"Have you given them the goals we agreed upon?" the Galactic Electronics CEO asked calmly.

"Yes. Now it is up to us to provide them with test subjects, teenagers they suggest. I've promised them six within a few days."

Gerhardt nodded. "Timing is critical. Our children are rapidly approaching the marrying age on this world. Quite why they insist on twenty-one is beyond me."

"I know. It's imperative we marry our daughters to the

baron's sons and their daughters to our sons," Dederick replied, "but the barons want to marry their daughters to each other's sons, uniting their two families closer, but we need them closer to us."

Gerhardt laughed. "Quite true, old man, but our daughters have other ideas. So do the baron's daughters, who still continue to romance other young future barons around Thromstead. Well, I guess it won't hurt to allow them their youthful fantasies a while longer, before we marry them off to those of our choosing."

"I suppose you are right. Nadja is making quite a fuss about it. Still, I think the barons have a point. It is time that we insist on preparing our daughters for their future marriages, though I agree with Adler, we dare not blind and dumb them just yet. That can't be undone if the brokered marriages fall through," Dederick suggested.

Gerhardt smiled and noted, "You know, what amazes me the most is the difference in attitude and outlook between our UFB wives and our second-generation UFB daughters. Night and day."

Dederick laughed, "Tell me about it. I'd sooner marry my daughter than my Athala."

"Indeed, same here. It seems that being a second-generation UFB woman brings out the very best in the women, quite unlike those first generation women whom we've genetically modified into UFB women. Incredible difference. I just wish that there were more of these second-generation UFB women around that were slightly older," Gerhardt suggested, "because I'd dump Belinda for one in a heartbeat. Do you suppose their clones will take on the aspects these second-generation UFB women have? A cheerfulness about life, a vitality we don't see in our wives?"

"I doubt it, Gerhardt. Clones are supposed to be a duplicate, so it's unlikely. Come on. We best plan how we're going to get the needed test subjects. I suspect for a time our doctors will be going through a large number of test subjects. We can make use of the Universal Disposal Service to get rid of the failures."

That night, security men from both GD and GE fanned

out into the city of ten million. Masked to hide their identities, they kidnaped three young men and three young women, all between fourteen and eighteen, depositing them drugged and unconsciousness into the sub-level twenty genetic research labs of GD, where the two doctors took over.

First, they took blood samples. Part of the samples was used to test the new growth clone machine. That is, they began producing clones of the six to verify how the machine worked and how well. This way, they expected to have a way to create more test subjects identical to the first set. They had enough blood to make six clones of each of the six. They kept the six captives unconscious for a time.

The next day, Dr. Lanzo began developing his first experimental genetic modification. Long he had been studying the UFB women's DNA and had theoretically invented a new agent, one that would result in a body having no voice box and no eyeballs, as desired by the barons of this strange world. Finally, he had the opportunity to test his proposed modifications, though he had no idea if it would actually work. Hence, the test subjects and the ability to repeat the experiment if it didn't perform as expected.

Four days later, Female Test Subject One awoke, terrified as might be expected. "Subject is attempting to scream. Ah, excellent. No sounds. She is frantically trying to speak or scream or something, but silence is golden. That part is working. Unfortunately, her eyes are still there. Worse, she now has her upper arms. Well, a medical machine could remove those. Progress is being made," Dr. Lanzo spoke into his recorder, documenting the changes. "Otherwise, a perfect UFB woman modification, hair, feet, breasts, waistline. Partial success." He sent for Dederick.

A short while later, Dederick arrived personally to inspect the first results. "Excellent doctor. I can see that she is trying to scream but can't make a sound. So far so good. Say, I do like those upper arms of hers. They are rather attractive. We might be on to a new version of the UFB woman, doctor. Carry on."

"Well, the question now is what do I do with her? I've got her DNA on file and have no further use for her," the doctor explained.

"Well, I'll see that she is properly disposed of, doctor." He left to inform Gerhardt, who also had to come and see for himself how she turned out.

"I agree, Dederick, she's gorgeous. Those little arms do add to her attractiveness. I'd bed her myself. What say we take her to Carsten's? Then of an evening, we can do just that?" Gerhardt suggested.

With the arrival of the corporations years ago, a new, explosive growth industry sprang up on Blackwell-C, one which greatly appealed to the working man and a few women, the escort services and bordellos, which utilized newly made UFB women, compliments of the corporations. Now, the average person could spend an evening with one of these incredibly gorgeous, sexy women, for a modest price, of course. Carsten ran Carsten's Exotic Escorts, where anyone could *rent* one of these beauties for an evening's fun. He didn't want to run a pure bordello, where the men simply paid to have sex with these UFB women. No, his was a more educated, sophisticated clientele.

At this point in time, there were dozens of escort services around the city and double that in pure bordellos. Planet-wide, there were close to ten thousand local women who had been modified into the exotic UFB women. Many poorer local women greatly desired to become stunningly beautiful and earn such top wages. There was a waiting list for these women at this time.

On paper, each such woman was given ten percent of the fee that was charged for her services. Since they didn't appear to age, these women looked twenty-five until around the age of sixty, when age began to become visible. This was the uniformly agreed retirement age for these UFB women. At this time, all would receive a lump sum termination pay, more than enough for them to buy their own cottage and hire servants to attend their many needs until death finally came. The women believed this was an incredible bargain, which is why so many desired to become a UFB woman. What none actually knew was this was mere pretense.

While their bosses agreed to their every demand about

their retirement, when it actually occurred, the women were given a final *inoculation* to prevent any further diseases, theoretically. In fact, the shot terminated their lives. The Universal Disposal Service, or UDS as it was known to those in the know, arrived and disposed of the body. No one was ever the wiser. It was a win-win situation for these owners, who made nice fortunes off of the unsuspecting women. Their only task really was to make sure each woman stayed healthy and did not get pregnant. That and keeping them well supplied with the expensive apparel that they wore and keeping lowly servants to tend to their many needs. This was a highly profitable business on Blackwell-C, where the average person now could have an *encounter* with these, the most beautiful women they'd seen and so closely resembling their own baronesses.

The eighteen year old terrified UFB teen was carried off that night, again by masked men and dropped off at Carsten's. The next day, Carsten called up Dederick. "Thanks for the addition. She is superb! Got her all calmed down now and getting used to everything. Her inability to make any sounds is fantastic. I could use many more of those. Those little short arms of hers are quite exotic indeed, useless, but it adds to her mystique."

"My pleasure, Carsten. I will see what we can do about that," Dederick replied, allowing the man to chat about this stroke of good fortune. That Carsten was so incredibly pleased with this new version UFB woman gave Dederick pause to think. He fully agreed with the barons. *Women should be silent. They only chatter about trivia anyway. It would certainly be pleasant if Athala and Nadja were silent, especially at the supper table. Hell, I only need them to nod yes or no occasionally. I think I will bring this up with Gerhardt and the barons. Perhaps, I've stumbled upon a new and better form for the UFB women all around.* He paid Gerhardt a visit.

After explaining how enthusiastic Carsten was over the addition of the new version UFB teen, he suggested, "What do you think? I know around my place, having completely silent women would be a great benefit. And those little short, but useless, arms are rather exotic."

"Hum, you know, I do believe you are on to something. A silent Belinda and Kirsa would be a blessing. I'm sick and tired of Kirsa carrying on about wanting to marry one of those GE boys, what's his name? I forgot. Doesn't matter. She's going to marry one of the baron's boys when the time comes," Gerhardt commented. "Besides, Adler told me it's time we put our daughters onto the preparatory phase for becoming baronesses."

"I see. What exactly needs to be done? I admit I've not paid close attention to that just yet. Too many more important matters," Dederick asked, trying to recall past conversations with Baron Alder.

"Well, their waists must be cinched smaller. Apparently, that takes a good deal of getting used to. And their bosoms must be enlarged some. The costly part will be the expensive, heavy earrings we'll need to put on them," Gerhardt replied. "You know, if we can convince the barons and/or Carsten and the others to get the UFB women redone this new way, we could make enough funds from that to pay for these mammoth earrings the new baronesses must wear. And that golden veil they must also wear." By that, he meant the ancient tradition of the baronesses wearing a thin golden veil that was attached to their ears and either side of their noses. The veil covered the lower part of their faces, ending below their chin. Both men knew the last step of the conversion process only happened a week before their marriage ceremony. At that time, their eyeballs were replaced with appropriately colored glass eyes. They were given a week to get used to this step before marrying.

"Let's take the barons to see this new one tonight," Dederick suggested and Gerhardt agreed. All four men usually visited one of the local escort services or brothel in the early evening before returning to one of their homes where they shared drinks and sometimes played cards. Of course, at bedtime, they satisfied their wives. There would be no living with their women the following day if they didn't satisfy the women in the morning and at night. Failure drove the women nearly insane with lust and desire. Before the CEOs understood this fully, more than once they had been embarrassed to find their wives rubbing up against bedposts, chairs, whatever they could find, valiantly trying to find some relief. Indeed, the sex drives of the UFB women were powerful and their needs simply had to be met.

This new teen that no one had bothered to get her name before subjecting her to the new genetic bio agent was Anne Becker, and she was terrified, suddenly living a never ending nightmare. However, once under Carsten's roof, servants bathed her and got her cinched up in a tight corset, explaining that her backaches would go away as long as she wore it. She found that to be true, for her back simply couldn't support the weight of her new, massive bosom. When they finally got her fully dressed, Anne finally realized she'd become the one thing she totally detested, a UFB woman. At least, Carsten then explained she would be paid for her work and could collect it when she retired. Funny thing, she'd done a lot of research and had yet to find one of these retired women, though there should have been many by now.

Unable to breathe properly, unable to barely stand, let alone walk, Anne was particularly frightened. That she had somehow lost her voice completely shocked her and added to her misery. Worse, that evening she was forced to walk out to the model display area of the fancy business, where four men seemingly drooled over her, embarrassing her. She hated this whole UFB woman thing but knew she couldn't do anything about it, except try not to faint or fall down. She doubted anyone would help her get back up.

"My God, Dederick, you're right! She's truly giving the word exotic a whole new meaning. Those dainty little upper arms does it. Amazing. I never would have believed it," Baron Adler exclaimed, finding himself highly aroused by Anne.

Likewise, Baron Aldric found her irresistible. "I agree completely. This is fabulous indeed. You say this is an available mutation?"

"Yes, just perfected in GD labs. What do you think? Wouldn't baronesses just love this new look, even though they can't see it?" Gerhardt asked the key question he and Dederick needed answered.

"The Thromstead Baron's Council is next week. We should bring this up at the meeting. Of course, we're going to need sample UFB women to show them. I wonder," Baron Adler hinted, "is the process reversible? Well, not exactly that. If we did our wives and put them on display before the other barons and if they disapproved, could these tiny upper arms be easily removed?"

"Of course, baron. It is a very simple medical operation, healed up in hours," Gerhardt answered. "What about our daughters? I know you've been mentioning they should begin Phase Two of baroness preparations. Could this become a part of that? If this new look wasn't approved, we could remove the little arms. However, we're not totally sure what all is involved in this next phase of their preparations."

Baron Aldric thought, *You stupid CEOs! We've told you this a dozen times.* "Simple. Their breasts get enlarged a bit. They are presented with their heavy and expensive earrings and their golden veils. More significantly, it's time their waists are further reduced down to the standard for baronesses, twelve inches across, giving their curves a stellar appearance to all. Of course, you can expect they will be a constant source of complaints about that, but that's why they need to have this done now that they are twenty. Give them a year to adapt to the tight constraint before they are blinded and take their positions as baronesses."

Baron Adler added, "With this new modification that removes their voices, why, we won't have to listen to all their complaints about their corsets being too tight. Marvelous really and a blessing. Plus, if this new look is accepted by the Baron's Council, we can show them all off at the Summer Ball, which is in two weeks. After that, I anticipate the hundreds of other barons on Blackwell-C will demand to have their baronesses and daughters redone as soon as possible. Are you two going to be able to meet such a demand?"

"Of course. I'll let my labs know to expect a huge rush to get the new modifications done," Dederick replied.

"Excellent. Then I suggest," Baron Adler took charge, "we notify our wives and daughters about this tonight and begin getting them done tomorrow. Can you deliver the goods this soon?" he asked pointedly, suspecting further delays from the CEOs. Getting them to do what he and the barons wanted had always been challenging.

"We will do what must be done, baron, as always," Dederick replied. *Which is what Gerhardt and I want, not you two.*

"Excellent, then tonight at supper, I'll notify my girls," Adler declared. The other three men agreed to do so as well.

Chapter 2—The Women

No one knew truly what Zelda Berthold thought about her life as a baroness. Any chance of that had ended when she turned twenty-one and became Alder's baroness. In fairly short order, she had four children. The wavy, very blonde Susanne was now twenty. Next came the stronger son and heir to his father's castle, Heinrich, who was nineteen. Their second son came a year later, Herman, but while he too was stronger than most boys were, he was definitely second to Heinrich, something that Heinrich never let him forget. Their youngest daughter was seventeen-year-old Karla, who also had beautiful, very blonde hair.

Susanne finally realized her mother could neither see nor speak when she was around five years old. Her father had helped her learn to walk, which was challenging, for her mutated feet forced her to wear the toe shoes with their seven-inch spiked heel. Her stride was barely four inches, any more and she'd lose her balance and take a fall, something that had happened frequently until she was six and knew better than to try it.

One thing Susanne swore was that no way was she going to become a baroness like her mother. She sensed how terrified her mother was whenever she had to move about the castle on her own, which was far more frequently than one might expect, considering she had a permanent servant girl. All the women had their own servant girl to assist them with their many needs, since none of them was able to do much for themselves. On many occasions, she secretly talked with her mother. That is, she would ask her mother questions she could answer with an appropriate head nod, yes or no.

Thus, she learned just how terrified and lonely her mother actually was. With nothing but darkness, utter blackness, around her at all times, unable to utter a sound, without arms, and wearing her tall heels, Zelda's life was one of true unending misery. Hence, Susanne swore no matter what, she would never become a baroness. In time, her younger sister Karla came to the same conclusion. Always, Susanne looked out for Karla, as they were growing up.

Secretly, Susanne desperately wanted to fly around the galaxy and see the sights, such as the gas clouds. Once, a gypsy band had visited, and she'd listened for hours as they told her about the wonders to be seen in the galaxy. Somehow, someway, Susanne wanted to sail the galaxy. As a helpless UFB girl, she had no idea how she could actually do it, except by marrying the right man.

In contrast, Karla desperately wanted to play music. At every ball and dance held in Thromstead, she always sat close to the musicians listening intently, wishing with all her might that she too could learn to make such wonderful sounds on any instrument. Like Susanne, Karla had no idea how she could do this, but she was determined to find a way. Both girls knew if they were forced to marry a baron and thus become a baroness, their lives would be utterly ruined beyond all hope. Secretly, they made a compact to help each other kill themselves if somehow against their wills they became baronesses. Dying was infinitely better than the horrid life their mother and the other baronesses were living, if living it could even be called.

Vernena Berringer was forty-five and had four children with Aldric, at least she presumed he was their father. Blind, she had no idea if he was the one lying in her bed. As a young teen, she'd been forced by her father to become a UFB woman, in preparation for her becoming a baroness one day. She'd protested, but woke up completely helpless. A week before her marriage to Aldric, total darkness descended upon her, along with no way to make any vocal sounds. After that point, life became an unending nightmare of darkness.

Her eldest was Johan, twenty-one and ready to become a proper baron, Aldric's heir. Renate came a year later with her lovely brown hair, slightly wavy. As a child, Renate loved mathematics and begged her father to hire a tutor to help her learn math. He agreed as long as she didn't protest her situation, which for many years she didn't. Wulf came next and was nineteen. Two years later, Irma arrived, who again had her mother's lovely brown hair. Both Renate and Irma were extremely attractive young women, as were all UFB women. Irma spent hours watching some of the castle servant women as they sewed elaborate quilts. Irma longed to be able to make quilts herself and held on to that as her goal in life, though how she could possibly do it eluded her, but not for lack of trying. Both Renate and Irma had long ago decided no matter what, they would marry corporate executives so they would never be like their mother. In truth, both girls were terrified of becoming baronesses and facing what they believed to be the most horrid life imaginable.

Forty-three year old Athala, Dederick's wife, had a son, Killian, who just turned twenty-one. Like Heinrich, Killian was extremely strong and robust, but more of a bully than a business leader, much to his father's disgust, who gave up trying to teach him how to run a corporation. Their daughter, Nadja, was twenty, and had lovely light blonde hair, slightly darker and wavier than Susanne's was. She dreamed of becoming a secretary for a CEO, but soon realized the difficulty she would have doing so as a UFB woman. Still, she continued to try to learn how to do such things and actually taught herself to read and to write with her toes.

Nadja saw the horrid lives that Zelda and Verena led and swore often she'd never marry a baron, but another executive. "Daddy, I'd rather die than be like Verena!"

Belinda Hagan was forty-seven. She'd given Gerhardt a son Kurt, now twenty-two. Kurt was also exceptionally strong and should have been married before now. However, Gerhardt refused to allow that, biding his time and waiting for Dederick to give his okay. Like Killian, Kurt had little interest in business affairs, let alone electronics. Gerhardt still didn't know just what he was going to do with his son.

Kirsa was twenty with dark brown hair, lush and thick, a gorgeous young woman in her own right. Kirsa dreamed of piloting a deep space transport and growing up, talked of nothing else but that. Although the boys constantly taunted her about it, Kirsa held onto her dream even now, endearing herself to Susanne, who hoped and prayed she could one day fly to the stars with Kirsa.

These twelve children grew up together and played

together every day. By the time the older girls were eight, they knew the boys were bullies and not to be trusted. They often insisted on playing kick ball with the girls, who had to play whatever the boys desired, since the boys were ordered by their fathers to look after and assist the girls. Unable to take more than a four-inch step, the mostly helpless girls weren't able to run or dodge the ball when a boy kicked it their way. Further, their pointed shoes make controlling the ball when they were it and had to kick it towards a boy nearly impossible. The ball shot off in nearly any direction other than the one the girl intended, bring hearty laughs to the boys, who thought this was great fun.

As they grew older, the boys often wanted to play blindman's bluff. Again, the girls found themselves blindfolded. Now in the dark like their mothers and lacking arms and wearing the tall heels, they became nervous and frightened as they tried to move around the room to tag someone. None could ever tag one of the boys and each of the girls felt badly if she had to tag one of them, for that would then make her it and blinded for a time, while the boys constantly teased them.

Things changed for the worse when the girls became young women. After their first period, the powerful sexual drives of the UFB women turned on solidly, confusing the young women even more. Unable to talk about such things with their mothers, who were blind and dumb, they could only learn such things from their servants, who were just girls like themselves. At least, their fathers soon discovered the nature of their situation and solved it, just as all parents of UFB children did.

From that point on, their servants inserted a special vibrator into their privates when they dressed them in the mornings. Five times throughout the day, the electrical devices activated for about a half hour. During these times, it was all the young women could do to stand the intense pleasure-giving devices. Often the boys caught them when the devices were activating and teased them about it, humiliating them even more, but the young women could do nothing about it. Without the devices, by the afternoon, they were nearly insane trying to obtain the pleasure relief that their bodies demanded. At least their fathers explained once they were married, if their husbands bed them in the morning and at night, they could get by the rest of the day.

However, Susanne often caught her mother trying to rub herself against one of her bedposts, usually late in the afternoon. So perhaps her father wasn't correct about it. Hence, the teens eventually began asking Belinda and Athala about such female matters and soon became very close to the executives' wives.

When the older girls were eighteen they began to appreciate the many balls and dances that the barons held and to which they had to attend. For these gala events, they were dressed in billowing ball gowns, which made getting around drastically harder for them, since now they couldn't see their feet and had no way to push their gowns aside. Steps became tremendously treacherous. However, Susanne finally realized this was their golden opportunity to meet other young boys. Surely, not all these boys were brutish like those they'd grown up with.

Before long, romances blossomed. Susanne fell in love with Rudolf Werner, the older son of GD's second in command, Wendel Werner. Rudolf shared her ideas of traveling the galaxy, for a time seeing the wonders of the universe before settling down. Renate fell for Rudolf's nineteen-year-old younger brother, Stefan, who dreamed of becoming an astrophysicist and working on space travel. Naturally, with her keen math skills, Renate and Stefan hit it off very well indeed.

Nadja fell for a twenty-year-old lad, Wotan Detrict, who worked for General Goods. "You would be my ideal secretary, Nadja. Somehow, we must make that happen," he'd told her. Now, the two were hopelessly in love with each other. Kirsa fell for another General Goods young executive, Wenzel Von Trapp, also twenty years old. "I'm going to be a pilot, Kirsa. One day, I'll teach you how to fly a deep space transport ship. It's so simple. You can fly it with your feet." That sold her, and she swore she would only marry him, and he, her.

Lately, Karla found a boyfriend in Dirk Hanover, also

working for General Goods. Dirk played the harpsichord at the dances, and Karla always sat beside him when he played. The two soon became hopelessly in love with each other. Irma found her heartthrob in Ebert Dresden. Like Dirk, he was eighteen. Ebert was a frustrated would be artist. Stuck in a boring accounting job, he, like Irma, dreamed of making beautiful paintings, works of art, if only he could find a way to make that happen. He promised to help Irma find a way to be able to make artistic quilts. Often, they shared artistic design ideas.

For the last six months, over supper each evening, all six young women brought up the fact they wanted to marry their boyfriends. Susanne's idea was that if they told their fathers this often enough, he would finally concede to their demands and arrange or allow the marriage. Cleverly, their fathers merely nodded that they heard them, but never gave their consent nor did they reveal their own intentions for their daughter's marriages.

They couldn't. Because as yet, they didn't have complete agreement between the four men. It was rather a mess. The barons wanted to marry their daughters to each other's sons, thereby keeping the position of baron and baroness within the proper families, strengthening their ties. They presumed that the CEOs would marry their daughter to the other CEO's son. On the other hand, the CEOs had other ideas. They wanted to marry their daughters to each baron's eldest son, while marrying their sons to the eldest daughter of each baron. This would cement the ties between the ruling corporations and the top two barons on Blackwater-C. None of the four men would ever allow their daughters to marry so far beneath their positions, though they wisely never told them that. They heard enough complaining from their daughters already.

Their sons, on the other hand, had their own ideas of whom they wanted to marry, usually out of some conceived wrong that one of the girls had done them. This way, they could get even. Heinrich wanted to marry Nadja to put her in her place. Hermann wanted to marry Renate for similar reasons. Wulf eyed Karla, while Johan wanted to bed Kirsa. Killian wanted to marry Susanne, since she was always making trouble for him. Kurt went after Irma, telling her how many children she must bear for him, a dozen. The boys erroneously believed that their fathers would let them marry whomever they chose.

Finally, unknown to all them, Anne Becker was betrothed to Emil Beifeld, a twenty year old security guard at the spaceport. His father was the mayor of Thromstead, largely a ceremonial position, but he did have law enforcement obligations. Often, he used his son, Emil, to help with his crime-fighting obligations. Thus, when Anne went missing, Emil swore to find her and bring those who kidnaped her to justice. He would soon swear far more than that!

***

That evening at the supper table, for the thousandth time, Adler chastised his sons. "Heinrich, Hermann, stop acting like fools and feed your sisters their supper! After all, one day soon you are going to be married, and it will be your obligation to your baroness to help her eat, so you damn well better become expert at it." Both boys griped, but began assisting their sisters to eat.

"Now then, I've an announcement to make. It is time, past time actually, that we begin Phase Two of Baroness Preparations for Susanne. I'm also going ahead and preparing Karla as well, giving her more time to learn to adapt. Plus, there has been a new genetic modification developed at GD labs, one that makes our UFB women and baronesses far more exotic. So, Zelda, I have arranged for you to have it as well. In fact, Aldric, Dederick, and Gerhardt are also having their wives redone and their daughters prepared with Phase Two as well. So all of you lovely women will look even sexier in a few days. Don't worry. I will see that Susanne and Karla get their incredibly expensive earrings as befitting their high position."

"But father, I have no intention of becoming a baroness. I'm marrying Rudolf and that's that," Susanne complained, fearing the worse. Her stomach knotted, and she nearly upchucked the bite Heinrich had just stuffed in her mouth.

"I'm marrying Dirk, father. I've told you that a thousand times," Karla declared, likewise suddenly becoming afraid of what was about to happen. It was so sudden.

23

"Hey dad, what's Phase Two involve?" Heinrich asked, mostly to further annoy his obviously very worried sister.

"Oh little things. Besides their jewelry, earrings, and such, they have to have the requisite twelve-inch waistline and slightly larger breasts, more like your mother's. As far as the new modification, why, you'll all just have to wait and see, but I know you will just love it, Zelda. So will you, Susanna, Karla. Now enough talk. I'm famished."

As soon as they finished eating, both young women headed off to their bedroom, walking as fast as possible, though that was pathetically slow, always had been, always would be. "Quick," Susanne ordered her servant, "bring my phone and dial Rudolf for me!" Her servant was Elsa Gotte, who appeared to be no more than twenty herself. Elsa complied and listened in on Susanne's conversation.

"Yes, he's made the announcement tonight. They are doing something to us tomorrow. I don't like it. He didn't tell us what it was, but it can't be good. He's doing it to mom too. They all are—all six of us and our moms, if dad's right. Honestly, Rudolf, I'm terribly frightened. No, he's not said anything about who we are to wed, but Rudolf, Phase Two Baroness Preparations can only mean that he's not going to let us get married. You have to do something before it's too late!"

Elsa had heard enough and headed off to draw Susanne's bath. She had some hard thinking to do. Just what were these baron's plans? She'd been looking after Susanne and her sister for years now and had been helping with their four close girlfriends as well. She then sent an electronic message off, asking what action she should take next. Now, Elsa could only wait and see. She hoped and prayed they still had time. *This world is the most sadistic I've ever encountered*, she thought.

The following morning, the four men brought their six daughters to the most expensive jewelers in Thromstead. Long ago, they had arranged for the fancy earrings to be made to their specifications. Each one weighted nearly three pounds and was made from gold and precious stones, rubies and emeralds, chosen to compliment the women's hair color. Each massive earring had many tiers and was about eight inches long. They would rest upon the women's shoulders. One by one, each woman had hers put on her by the jeweler, who soldered them into place. With these costing a half million credits, no baron would ever do otherwise than make them permanently fastened on their ear lobes. That way, they couldn't accidentally fall off. The loss was far too expensive to allow that.

Naturally, all six girls complained that their ears were being torn off, especially when they had to toss their heads about to get their long hair out of the way so they could sit or stand up without sitting or stepping on it. Their protests were ignored. Their mothers wore similar earrings. Then, their nose was pierced on either side, along with another spot on each ear. Their golden veils were then attacked and acted as a thin veil over their lower face and mouth, though one could see through them. Again, the girls protested these veils were annoying, but since their mother always wore hers, they were just protesting in vain.

After that, they paid a visit to the local doctor, who used his medical machine to enhance their already large breasts, making them now nearly the sizes of basket balls, the proper size for a baroness, somewhat larger than a normal UFB woman's breasts. At least the six didn't complain about this alteration. Once they returned home, all were ordered to go change, particularly because their bosoms were busting out of their current day gowns. Now the real torture began.

"I'm sorry, baron's orders," Elsa said as she hooked Susanne up to the corset tightening machine. She'd put the far smaller and very heavily steel boned corset on her, giving her a brief and needed relief from her usual one. "We will tighten it in stages as always, Susanne."

"It's already way too tight! I can't breathe," gasped Susanne. She passed out long before Elsa finally got the corset closed and tied off. She positioned Susanne in a chair and headed off to do the same with Karla, who complained almost as bitterly, though being three years younger and smaller, she didn't faint. Elsa then helped her to walk to his sister's bedroom next door.

Eventually, Susanne recovered. Gasping, she

complained, "Elsa, I can't breathe. It's way, way too tight!"

"And there is too much boning in it," Karla complained. "Now I can't bend at all except at my waist and then just barely!"

"I'm told that in time you will get used to it," Elsa explained. "Now let's get you up and about. Your earrings are incredible."

"But they are ripping my ears off," Susanne complained bitterly, gasping all the while.

"Short, shallow breaths," Elsa replied. "Remember how hard you found your old corset when we first put it on. Give yourselves time to adjust to the pressure. As far as your earrings go, Zelda's ears haven't been torn off, so I don't expect that yours will either."

Just then, Adler entered. "Ah I see you are all dressed now. My, you both look stunning, dears. Such tiny waists. Now then, it's time we go over to GD for the final alteration, the surprise part. Up you go. No, Elsa, you don't need to come with us."

"But dad, I can't breathe in this. I'll faint."

"Susanne, you want to show off your new look to Rudolf don't you?" Oh how Adler played his daughter. Gritting her teeth, Susanne, erect as a board, got to her feet, wobbling more so than normal because of the intense restriction of her new corset. Slowly and patiently, Adler led his two gorgeous daughters out of the room and off to GD headquarters next door by using the tunnels, just as the children always had. He did stop several times to give them a chance to catch their breaths. He knew that if he didn't they would faint, causing more delays.

Once in the lab, Dr. Lanzo helped each to lie down on a cot and then gave each one an injection of his new genetic bio agent. While he preferred to use an injection, he also had the new genetic bio agent in gaseous form, which could be used to handle many patients at one time. With the injection form, little had to be done to protect others from exposure to the agent, unlike the gaseous form. The girls slipped quietly into a coma. "There, they are both under, Adler. In four days, they will revive looking incredibly exotic, and they won't have any

26

vocal cords any longer."

"That last part is only too welcome! I've had about all I can stand listening to their constant chatter and complaints. This is the best thing you've ever come up with, doctor." He then stepped into another room where the other three men were discussing the day's events. Everything had going according to plan. "Now, gentlemen, we can have some peace and quiet around home." All four laughed rather sadistically.

Four days later, right on schedule, the six young women came out of their comas. They tried to say something upon awakening, but found their voices were gone! Now they screamed in terror and panic, before passing out from lack of breath. Again, only silence filled the rooms, though a nurse came by periodically to see if they were awake yet. Finally, after reviving them several times, the women stabilized and noticed their new dainty upper arms. They wiggled them about, but soon discovered that combined with their monster breasts, these new upper arms were practically useless for anything at all, and they might just as well not even have them.

On the other hand, Zelda and Verena awoke and saw daylight for the first time in a quarter century. Unable to speak, they couldn't tell anyone that their eyeballs had been somehow regrown along with their upper arms. Naturally, they didn't bring this to anyone's attention! In fact, no one discovered this detail for quite some time, much to the great relief of both older women!

Susanne's reaction was typical of the six. She bawled and sobbed silently for days. Now she couldn't even talk to Rudolf, couldn't tell him what happened to her, couldn't make her wishes known to anyone. For the six, their new nightmare had just begun. Worse, they no longer could complain about anything or ask for help with anything. They were as silent as their mothers were, though Susanne was the first to realize her mother's eyes had mysteriously regrown and that she could see again.

Rudolf called Susanne several times, even leaving her a frantic voice mail. Thus, later that day, Elsa answered her phone for her and told Rudolf what had happened. After Rudolf ceased cursing, she asked him to let the other five boyfriends know what had happened to their girlfriends. "Look, you can see them at the ball soon. I'm sure they want to see you." She also knew much depended upon how these six boys reacted to what had been irrevocably done to the young women. She couldn't imagine having to live a lifetime as a UFB woman who couldn't even speak a single word. Zelda's cluck-clicks were almost unintelligible, save to handle bare necessities, such as having to go to the bathroom. As Elsa sat in her chair that night having gotten the terrified girls into bed, she knew what she had to do. Minta might not like it, but Elsa had all she could stomach from these barons and CEOs and their plots.

Chapter 3—The Boys

Emil was frantic with worry over the disappearance of his fiancé, Anne Becker. His father, Mayor Beifeld, listened to him and granted him permission to fully investigate this case and bring the guilty to accounts. The mayor doubted Anne would be found alive and unharmed, but he knew his son would proceed with or without his formal permission and so he gave it.

Emil paid a visit to the Becker home, but found nothing in the way of clues there. She had gone to bed at her usual time and simply wasn't there in the morning. However, their front door lock had been jimmied and had to be replaced. So Emil knew she had been kidnaped while she slept.

Knowing that, Emil took a deep breath and thought for a time. At last, he decided to check and see if there were other mysterious disappearances in recent times. He was surprised to discover that same night another two young teenaged girls had vanished along with three boys. His conclusion: the six cases were related. However, he was shocked to discover since that night, other young teens had gone missing under similar circumstances! All told, the tally was now up to twenty of them, about evenly divided between the sexes.

Emil paid a visit to several other homes, searching for anything that might give him a slight clue of who was behind these abductions. Days passed without the slightest hint. At last, he sat back in his chair and began creating a mockup board, giving the name, age, sex, and the address of those who were taken, pinning pins on a map of Thromstead, hoping to see some kind of pattern. They appeared random. Next, he tried using different colors for the dates of the abductions, following the rainbow. That is, the first known abductions, the six, were in deep blue, while the most recent were in red. Again, his efforts yielded nothing but a random pattern.

No wait, Emil thought in a flash of recognition, all the abductions are distant from the baron castles and the corporations. Does that mean anything? He sat back and pondered that datum, though it yielded nothing. Next, he went back and reviewed just who each of these teens was, his or her position in life. Most were still in school. That was again wasted effort. How about their parents? Once more, he began collecting data. This time, he found a correlation. Every teen that was abducted thus far came from a relatively poor and thus inconsequential family.

Bias. Whoever is doing this is heavily biased or damned smart. If they were to take one of the baron's teens or one of the corporation member's teens, why, there would be hell to pay. You can bet they'd stop at nothing to find the guilty party and their missing teens. No, whoever this is, they are picking on poorer families, ones that no one will pay much attention to, well except me that is.

Two entire weeks had passed since her abduction. Emil was no farther along in his investigation. While he wasn't about to give up, he had a sinking feeling after so much time, his Anne could be absolutely anywhere on Blackwell-C. The only thing that kept him going was the fact her dead body had not shown up anywhere. That, he kept checking on every day.

"Son, you are just going to have to accept the fact that Anne Becker is most likely dead by now," Mayor Beifeld consoled his son. "Tonight is the Start of Summer Ball at Castle Berthold. I want you to accompany me son, just as you always have, though I know Anne won't be there. Still, the barons have promised to show everyone a big surprise. As the city's mayor, I have to attend. You know that." He debated whether to add, "You might meet some charming young girl to replace Anne," but wisely decided against that.

"All right, I'll come with you," Emil agreed. Ever since his mother died during childbirth some years ago, he had attended these state functions with his father, though he always took Anne with him. The pain of his loss as he dressed for the ball was acute.

***

Rudolf sat back stunned by the shocking news the servant Elsa had just told him. *The love of my life, Miss Susanne, is being tortured, humiliated—no!* He stopped mid-thought. *She's being turned into a baroness and that means they aren't about to let us get married! My God, now what do we do?* He sat stunned for several minutes before his fear gave way to a vitriolic anger. "They can't do this to her, they can't! I'll stop them, I swear!" He smashed a fist into the arm of the chair, splintering it.

Finally, his anger subsided, and he became a bit more rational. *If she can't even talk now and is wearing the golden veil, she's obviously supposed to marry a baron. Wait. Elsa said all six of them were done this way. Hell, I better let the other fellows know.* Hastily, he called the five other boyfriends and told them the disastrous and shocking news. "Yes, I tell you, they can't speak, and they're wearing the golden veils. Wenzel, you know as well as I do what that means."

Disbelief. That was the first reaction that Wenzel, Wotan, Stefan, and Ebert had when Rudolf called them and told them what had just happened. Shock followed that, as the men realized obviously the barons intended to marry their girlfriends off to some young baron and not themselves. Anger followed. All six men decided to meet and see if they could figure out a way to get their girlfriends back.

That night at Rudolf's small apartment rented from GD, the six young men met in secret. "This is criminal!" Wenzel protested. "Hell, my Kirsa will soon be blind as well as dumb and beyond helpless. That's no life for anyone, let alone a beautiful woman. We have to do something. We have to rescue them, all them."

"Blinded, unable to speak, my God, fellows, our girlfriends are facing a lifetime of utter hell, all at the hands of those sadistic bastards who run our godforsaken world," Wotan barked angrily.

Dirk complained, "It's always been this way. The barons run everything in our lives. No one on Blackwell-C has any real freedom. We're serfs, peasants working all our lives so the barons can live off the fat of our land."

"Hey, these corporations are just as bad," put in Stefan. "I swear they are scheming to take over the barons as well as our world. We're going to soon get an even worse slave master, if what I hear from other worlds of the Federation is true. The hell with traditions, Dirk. Where has that gotten us? What good is a baroness ever been to us? None at all. They are always completely helpless women, sex dolls to be put on display by the barons who show their wealth with all that jewelry and fancy clothes they put on their toys. I don't want my Renate to be another one of those. She doesn't either. We have to do something, fellows, we must."

"Yeh, but what can we do? The barons control everything. They have their own security guards and are locked safely inside their castle fortresses. Even the army is under their control, and now the corporations are here helping them," Rudolf added.

"Simple, fellows, we have to raid them and steal our girls away from these sadistic bastards," Wotan declared.

"And how do you propose we do that? Break into the most secure places in Thromstead? Fight off fifty security guards who are armed to the teeth? And just how do we get into GD and steal Nadja and Kirsa out from under their father's noses?" grumbled Rudolf.

"Hell, I don't know, but somehow we must," Wotan continued to argue.

"Well, you work in GD, Rudolf. Why don't you case the place? Get us a layout. Hell, find out what's going on in there. I've heard strange rumors that really weird stuff is going on in their secret labs," Dirk suggested.

"Right. We have one last chance to see our girls at the coming Start of Summer Ball. We best have a plan by then. After that, it's probably going to be too late. They'll be blinded and married off to barons," Ebert put in what he was thinking about. "You two case your GD headquarters. We four will see what we can do to find a place to keep our girls once we rescue them."

Stefan bit his lip. "Fellows, assuming we can just walk the girls out of there during the ball, which seems to me to be our best chance of rescuing them, have you given any thought about what will happen after that? The barons and those CEOs are going to raise all hell when their six daughters go missing. Guess who they will think took them? Us, fellows. Everyone knows we're their boyfriends. How many times do you suppose Renate has told her folks she wants to marry me? No, if we snatch them from the ball, these most powerful men in Thromstead are going to come after us in a heartbeat." That put a damper on the six, who sat in silence for a time, knowing Stefan was quite right. They would be the first suspects. They'd probably get tortured mercilessly until they divulged where the girls were.

Finally, Dirk whispered, "We're going to have to get rid of the barons and the CEOs as well, all them."

"All the barons in Thromstead?" asked Wotan in disbelief.

"Damned right. Maybe all barons everywhere. Power to the people, that's what we need," Dirk declared. "A people's revolution."

"I'm with you, Dirk," Ebert spoke up. "We'll need lots of d-guns and some PDS and maybe even some bombs if we're going to blast our way into the castles. A people's revolution is just what Blackwell-C needs! Get rid of every baron, every alien CEO. Let our people rule."

"I know several guys who would want in on the revolution," Dirk added. "We aren't alone. Fellows, there are lots of us who want an end to the wicked barons and their hard-handed rule. Probably the whole world will back us. We have to get organized. We have to get the PR rolling."

"PR?" asked Ebert, momentarily confused.

Dirk declared, "People's Revolution. Guys, we're going to start a popular uprising against all barons and corporate CEOs. PR. We're going to overthrow the barons, starting here in Thromstead!"

***

"Barons, today marks a milestone for us all. Thanks to the never ending genetic research by Galactic Dynamics, they have invented a whole new exotic look for our baronesses," Adler announced to the gathering of Thromstead's twenty barons and future barons, many were his own age, but there were several older men and quite a few relatively young men, who had recently become official barons, as well as sons who would be future barons. "Baron Aldric and I are astounded at the incredible new exotic appeal of our wives. At this time, we would like to present our magnificent baronesses who will show off their new look. I'am certain you'll find their exoticness and sexual appeal almost irresistible, but remember, these are *our* wives," he teased the men. "Zelda, Verena, you may enter now and walk around some so my fellow barons can appreciate your new look. Come on in, dears; don't be bashful or shy."

Until now, the two baronesses would have had to find their own way from their quarters down to the second floor meeting room and then enter the room, hoping not to bump into too many chairs and men, all while completely blind and helpless. However, today they could see, thanks to an unknown side effect of the new genetic bio agent. Still, no one had discovered this detail, and they weren't about to let their barons know about it, assuming they even had a way to communicate it to their husbands. Slowly, the pair shuffled carefully into the room, amid gasps of surprise from the many men gathered together for this Baron's Council.

"Now wiggle those little, sexy arms of yours," Adler ordered Zelda, who tried to comply. They were darn near useless for much of anything excepting a little assistance in keeping their balance. Their arms just barely extended out beyond their large bosoms. However, both women had already discovered they could use them to assist going up and down the stone stairs, which alone made them worthwhile in their minds. After several minutes, they were dismissed and they gladly found their bumbling way out of the room and faced going back up the stairs, only now with their new sight, this was easier for them to do.

"But traditionally, a baroness must not have arms," an older baron protested.

"But you have to admit, they looked incredibly exotic," a young, relatively new baron countered. "They are just as helpless as before. They can't use them for anything, and they are incredibly sexy looking with them. Adler, I love the look. Can I have my baroness done?"

"But a baroness must not have arms," another older man declared sternly.

"It is time for a change, don't you think?" Aldric suggested, anticipating what would happen next. He wasn't wrong. At once, the barons took up a very heated discussion over these modifications. As expected, the older men insisted this was very wrong and shouldn't be allowed. The younger men were enamored with the new, sexy look and demanded to have their wives done as soon as possible.

Adler stepped in, "Look, if you don't like the look, those little arms of theirs can be easily removed in just a few minutes with the medical machines. So look, barons, why not try it? GD can perform the changes starting today. I encourage you to have this new procedure done soon. Then, at next month's council meeting, why, we can compare notes. If you truly don't wish baronesses to have these exotic little arms, we can then pass another law removing them." Amid some grumbling from the older men, the motion passed, and Adler sent for Dederick to arrange times for the men to bring their baronesses to GD for the procedure.

Later that day, Adler met with Carsten, who requested an audience with him. "Well, how is that new UFB model working out?" he asked, anticipating this was what Carsten wanted to discuss.

"Well, she's about ready to be activated. Like all new UFB women, they need a couple of weeks to get used to their new limitations. She's stopped gasping all the time and is walking fairly well on her own now, so Monday, she will start earning her keep. I've had her on display this past week, you know, advanced advertising. That's why I'm here, Adler. The advance demand—well, it's just wild! That woman—we're calling her Ada since we've no idea what her name is—already has a list of twenty men who want to take her out for a night! Sir, I need all my UFB women converted to this new form as soon as possible. Besides, Ada's lack of a voice is tremendously beneficial. No complaining, especially with clients. Win-win all around."

Adler smiled. "I figured you would find her extremely erotic. Yes, we can handle your women. How many and when can they be brought to GD?"

"As you know, I have thirty women. I don't want to disrupt my escort service too badly. What say you if I bring half in tomorrow and the other half next week, once these new ones are back in action?" Carsten asked, hoping this would be agreeable. The client demand for the normal UFB women of his had dropped off drastically, bad for business.

"Excellent, excellent, Carsten. I'll have the labs expecting your women. Mind you, I'm obligated to let the other escort services and bordellos know about this new modification, but I'll do it next week after your first batch is returned to you."

"Thank you. That is most generous of you, Adler," Carsten replied. The two chatted a bit before the man departed, anticipating the huge increase in income beginning next week.

Meanwhile, the four young barons-to-be and the two CEO's sons met in private too. Heinrich had undergone another round of chastisement from his father over the breakfast table. He'd had a hard time feeding Susanne this morning. That infernal golden veil of hers made it difficult for him, and his father had chastised him soundly for his bickering and complaining.

Heinrich, Hermann, Wulf, Johan, Killian, and Kurt met in secret this morning, while the barons were holding their council in the meeting room. They met in Heinrich's bedroom. "Well," he began since he called for this meeting, "as you all know, our fathers have gone ahead and put all six girls through Phase Two of Baroness Preparations. We all know what that means—they are going to marry the girls to us barons-to-be. No offense Killian, Kurt, but you both aren't going to be barons, but I know you want to have two of our sisters. Guys, we should work out who wants which girl and then let our fathers know our picks. If we don't, guys, you know them. They'll just tell us who we're to marry, probably as early as next week, though we know they can't marry until they turn twenty-one. Still, once our dads make their decisions, it'll be next to impossible to get them to change their minds. So are we together on this?" he asked.

"Right," Johan replied, "I want Susanne."

Heinrich laughed. "You can have her. She's quite a bitch, though now she can't say a damned thing. I want Renate."

"Hey, I wanted Renate," protested Killian.

"Wait, so do I," put in Kurt.

"Don't I get a choice?" asked Hermann. "I want her too."

"Well, you all can't have her. That's why we are meeting. We have to get this worked out so we can tell our fathers which doll we want," Heinrich pointed out. "So how are we going to work this out?"

"We should go by age," Kurt replied. "I'm the oldest, so I should get first choice."

"Hey, I'm the youngest," Hermann protested. "I won't get a pick, just what's left over. I can't marry my stupid sister."

"He's got a point. So we can't make choices that will end up with that," Heinrich declared strongly.

"Point taken," Killian agreed. "But we should go in age order first and see what we end up with. So you pick first, Kurt. Then, it's Johan and my turn."

"Then I pick Renate," Kurt announced, amid a lot of grumbling, especially from Killian and Heinrich.

"Okay, you pick, Johan," Kurt got the situation defused for the moment.

Johan smiled. "You know my pick, Susanne."

"Well, I'll take Nadja then, if I can't have Renate," Killian declared.

"All right, now it's my pick and then Wulf's," Heinrich stated. "Shit. Well, I guess I'll pick Kirsa then. Wulf?"

"Crap. What's left? Karla and Irma? Hell, well, all right, Karla then," Wulf replied.

"So I get stuck with Irma, is that it fellows?" Hermann grumbled. "Wulf and I will have to wait four more damned years to get married. I don't like this one bit."

"Hey, Hermann, you know dad. He'll probably break it off and find you another one long before that. He's too impatient to wait four more years," Heinrich pointed out. "Aldric will probably do the same thing, Wulf, so there is hope for you two, just play along with us for now, and I'll argue with dad to get you hitched sooner. Exceptions can be made. Remember your history, brother. You too, Wulf."

"Then this is settled. When do we tell our dads about

our picks?" asked Johan.

"Tonight at supper. Let's all do it tonight. That way, there won't be time for the dads to get together and mess this all up," Heinrich declared. The six agreed to do it at supper.

That evening at suppertime, Heinrich and Hermann did just that, announcing that they wanted to have Kirsa and Irma as their baronesses. Adler laughed. He was used to Susanne and Karla announcing whom they wanted to marry every night at supper. Now that they'd been permanently silenced, his boys were taking up where they'd left off! He found that humorous. He paid them lip service, just as he had always done with his daughters. Similar reactions occurred at the Berringer, Koft, and Hagan supper tables. Heinrich got the distinct impression his father wasn't going to listen to his pick and that his father was going to marry him off to a girl of his choosing, not Heinrich's. He left the table slightly annoyed and almost hostile. He knew they were going to have to take another approach with their dads if they had any hope of getting their choices of brides. Just what that may be, Heinrich had no idea. Forcing his father to do something just never had happened before, so why now?

The next morning, the two barons, Adler and Aldric, got together, primarily because of their son's announcements last night. "Now our boys are telling us who they want to marry. I guess we had best put our heads together and make some wedding plans. Surely, we're going to have a battle with Dederick and Gerhardt over this. It's been coming for many years now," Adler stated the obvious.

"Okay," Aldric replied. "What about Heinrich and Renate, Johan and Susanne, Hermann and Irma, Wulf and Karla?"

"That's fine with me. The two CEOs won't be happy with this. We are leaving them totally out," Adler replied. He could care less which boy went with which girl, only that they kept the baron line pure and not mixed with corporate women.

"I know your feelings, Adler, but this isn't going to work, now that I think about it," Aldric pointed out. "Look, if we leave their four kids totally out of this, we're going to have one hell of a battle over it. We want to keep these corporations more under our control. If we go this route, we're alienating them entirely. We're going to have to include them in this somehow. What about giving up our youngest daughters to their boys and having our youngest sons go with their daughters? That would then be: Hermann and Kirsa, Wulf and Nadja, Killian and Karla, Kurt and Irma? This way, our youngest can get married four years ahead of time. We both know they'd have to wait until they turn twenty-one to become baronesses."

"Okay, that makes sense. We're going to have to make a little compromise here or risk alienating them, and we can't do that, not yet anyway. We need them still," Adler agreed.

Around the same time, the two CEOs met to discuss the very same thing. "Look, it's obvious the barons are getting ready to wed off their kids. So we have to act fast," Dederick declared. "I'm all for marrying Nadja to Johan, and your Kirsa to Heinrich. That way, we'll have our girls in with their heirs and one day in positions of power."

"Quite right, but I'm not sure what power the girls will actually have if they are blind and dumb. Still it's a start," Gerhardt replied. "Then marry Kurt to Susanne and Killian to Renate, their eldest daughters. That should cement our ties more firmly, don't you think?"

"Agreed. Now how do we get these barons to agree with our choices?" Dederick asked.

"Yes, that is the problem, since they probably have entirely different choices in mind. I'm sure they don't want to have their top son and eldest daughter in our grasps," Gerhardt answered. "So how are we going to get them to agree with our choices?"

"Damned good question, Gerhardt. We're going to have to promise and give them something they want, but something that doesn't compromise our power base. It can't be weapons; that could well upset the power balance. We can't give him more space ships. It can't be funds; hell they have all they can possibly use."

The two men tossed out ideas for quite some time before they hit upon the right combination. "I agree," Dederick said, "one of the newest model, fully equipped, deep space transports, and a planetary defense shield. Those should do it and not compromise our positions any. Besides we can also make use of the shield, what with all the unrest elsewhere in the Federation."

Later, Dederick mentioned their marital plans to his wife. Unable to speak her mind, all she could do was shake her head no. She tried to get her ideas across to him, but failed completely. Having been turned into a normal UFB woman for him was bad enough, but now this—no voice, no way to communicate anything at all and that he was further proposing to make Nadja into a blind baroness was just too much for her to take. Oh, how she wanted to fight against him and this terrible plan of his. Her daughter, her only daughter was about to become not only helpless but also blind and dumb—this was beyond intolerable. She had to do something to protect her Nadja, but she'd never felt so helpless in her life. Here was something urgent, something she simply had to fight against and she couldn't even tell him "no."

Her Nadja just sat on a chair all day, silently crying mostly, although occasionally gasping for breath. Her new corset kept her quite erect and barely able to breathe. Her earrings were far too heavy, similar to those many baronesses wore. And the golden veil draped across her face—this was all too much. Slowly, she made her way over to visit Belinda, who was sitting with Kirsa. The young woman was silently sobbing to herself, just as Nadja was. None of the women could speak, but Athala pointed a short arm at Kirsa and shook her head trying to indicate "no." Soon, Belinda also shook her head no, but neither woman knew what the other was suggesting, except something wasn't right.

The CEOs' wives, Belinda and Athala, sat silently beside each other. Two weeks ago, they were chatting constantly all day. Now when they both had something absolutely vital to discuss, neither could say a word. Before long, the two older women also began sobbing silently. Each knew this was intolerable, but could do nothing about it. They sunk down into total apathy. Only several days later did the two men finally notice that their wives seemed awfully lethargic and sent them to see Dr. Lanzo, who found nothing wrong with them. The two men knew something was wrong. Neither woman responded in bed any more.

Late one night after a most unsatisfying intercourse with Athala, Dederick asked, "Athala, is something wrong?" She had merely lain in bed not moving the entire time, just as she'd done for the last several days. She didn't even bother to nod yes. What good would it do? She couldn't tell him what was very wrong. Frustrated, he got up and paced their bedroom for a time. He returned to bed once she seemed asleep.

***

The Start of Summer Ball became a pivotal event; some say it was the key that set all subsequent events into play. Wotan, Wenzel, Dirk, Ebert, Stefan, and Rudolf attended along with many others, including Emil and his father, the mayor. Stefan rushed up to his fiancé, Renate. "Dearest, what have they done to you, Renate?" She looked very different. Her waist was far smaller than he remembered. She was having trouble breathing. Her earrings were impressive, but the golden veil she now wore spoke volumes to Stefan, just as it did with the other boyfriends.

Tears streaming down her cheeks, Renate desperately wanted to tell Stefan, but could only silently mouth words, which he didn't understand at all. Just then, Kurt came up to them. "Hey get away from my future baroness, kid," he barked antagonistically, giving Stefan a slight shove.

"Hey, this is a ball. I'm free to dance with anyone I wish, and I choose Renate here," Stefan replied. "Besides, I've not heard the barons announcing any such marriage." He tried to slip an arm around Renate, but Kurt shoved him away and tried to pull Renate away with him. Kurt wasn't paying any attention to Renate though and promptly pulled her off her feet, sending her tumbling onto the floor. Everyone turned to stare, and Kurt's face reddened. He moved away swiftly, leaving Renate in her fancy billowing gown to find her own way back onto her feet. *After all,* he thought, *as my baroness, she's going to have to do it herself, even when she has her glass eyes. I can't be bothered with that.*

Stefan knelt down, "I'm sorry Renate. Let me help you

up. I swear I'll kill him!"

Renate couldn't care less that everyone was staring at her and that she'd fallen. *I can't talk or do anything and I'm sure to be turned into a blind baroness soon. Nothing maters any more.*

Still, Stefan was gentle, and got her upright and stable. Then the musicians began playing, and he put two steadying arms around her, nudging her to dance with him. Renate mechanically followed his lead; her mind, numb.

Normally, Karla would be seated beside Dirk as he played on his harpsichord, but Wulf latched on to her. "You are going to be my baroness soon, I think. So stop looking at that stupid musician over there. Now dance with me." After barely a minute, Karla was gasping for air. She had no way to tell Wulf to stop, that she couldn't breathe, and he basically ignored her discomfort, right up until she fainted, slumping onto the floor, again creating a bit of a scene. Wulf said, "Get up bitch," but she didn't so he left her lying there. Hastily, Baron Aldric strode over to his son, angrier than he dare admit.

He slapped his son hard. "How dare you treat a potential baroness like that? She's fainted. Didn't you see she was gasping for breath? You fool. Go help her up and sit her down somewhere. We'll talk more later." Seeing how angry his father was, Kurt obeyed, picking up Karla who was just coming around. He carried her over to the chair that Dirk always positioned by his harpsichord for Karla to sit on while he played. Without a word, he plopped her down on the chair and headed off to find the booze table. He needed a stiff drink about now.

Elsa had seen both girls fall and managed to get over to Karla without drawing attention to herself. "She's gasping for breath. Give her a minute to recover, Dirk. She'll be all right, but she can no longer speak."

"God, Karla, this is worse than I ever imagined. I swear I'll kill that beast Wulf with my bare hands!" He got a stare from Elsa and then calmed down. He needed to play again, if only to get his and others minds off Wulf's incredible social blunder.

Heinrich, Hermann, Johan, and Killian saw what happened with Wulf and Kurt and their agreed upon baronesses-to-be, and wisely decided to avoid their future baronesses, heading to the bar to join Kurt and Wulf. "What the hell happened, Wulf? Aldric really smacked you a good one," Heinrich asked.

The six young men began talking in whispers. Wulf whispered, "Sometimes, I think I should kill my own father!"

Johan whispered, "You fool. The women can't breathe right yet. They need more time to adapt to their tight corsets. Don't let dad hear you talk like that!" The boys whispered and drank for some time.

At least, Wotan, Wenzel, Dirk, Ebert, Stefan, and Rudolf were able to spend the rest of the evening with their fiancés, at least fiancés in their minds and the girls'. Yet, they were unnerved, appalled, and shocked at the condition of their young women. This made such an indelible impression on the six that before the night ended, they swore to meet in secret tomorrow morning. Something had to be done and soon.

Emil, on the other hand, listened and observed. Everyone was talking about just how erotic, how sexy, how attractive this new modification to the baronesses and their daughters was, how soon all of Thromsteads baronesses and their daughters were going to undergo this new genetic mutation as well. With a few more questions to the right people, Emil learned this new genetic mutation had very recently been developed at the GD labs next door to Castle Berthold.

Suddenly, Emil had a flash of insight. *They must have had to test this new genetic thing of theirs on others before they dared do it to these baronesses and their daughters. Throw away test subjects! My god, I'll bet anything all these mysterious abductions are how GD men got their test subjects. Anne! Dear God, did they do this to Anne? Where is she? Did she die as a result? No, none of them have turned up dead; that much is clear. They must be being held somewhere, GD labs perhaps? How can I get in there to find out?* He had no answer for that one.

However, he did see the six young men, not the future

barons who were off getting drunk, looking after the six young women who were newly modified and having a terrible time at the ball. They seemed very disturbed about what had been done to these young women, and he listened in on some of their chat during the course of the evening. Thus, he began to believe these six wanted to marry the six young women, and yet the young would be barons and executives presumed they would be married to these same women. He did hear two swear to their girlfriends they would kill the barons-to-be. He found this interesting and disturbing at the same time.

Later in the evening, he ran into a friend of his. Eckhard, half-drunk himself, said, "Yep, seen these new exotic beauties before. Carsten has one on display at his escort service or so I've heard. He's going to have many of his women redone to look like these here too. I was going to suggest we go check her out tomorrow night, but hell, we can see what they look like right here." He headed off to refill his glass.

Emil began to wonder. *Look, I know they must have kidnaped these men and women to use them as test subjects. Anne must not be dead because her body hasn't been found. What if she was turned into one of these new kind of UFB women and given to Carsten to be put on display? I'm going to have to pay that house of ill repute a visit tomorrow and check this out. Could Anne be there? My God, if she is. . .*

***

"Then it's agreed," Adler declared. He, Aldric, Dederick, and Gerhardt met midmorning the following day to discuss future wedding plans. After the embarrassments last night at the ball with Kurt and Wulf, combined with the complete and overwhelming acceptance of their new baroness physical forms with the ball attendees, Adler knew it was time to make their play with the corporation CEOs. That Heinrich had once more acted foolishly at breakfast, nearly refusing to assist Susanne with her breakfast convinced him it was time to get these sons married off.

The two barons presented their initial suggestion, the one that left the CEOs' daughters completely out of any baroness positions, knowing the two men would reject that solution out of hand. Somewhat antagonized, Dederick then present his counter proposal, marrying their daughters to the baron's designated heirs, knowing that solution would be rejected at once, but he was ready to counter their protests with his offer of a new deep space transport and the planetary defense shield. Dederick suggested, "Marry Nadja to Johan, Kirsa to Heinrich, Kurt to Susanne, and Killian to Renate. You do this, and we will throw in one of the brand new deep space transports and a planetary defense shield for Blackwell-C."

"Not likely, fellows," Aldric responded. "Our heirs must keep the baroness line pure. This is what might be acceptable to us, along with the ship and shield: marry Hermann to Kirsa, Wulf to Nadja, Killian to Karla, Kurt to Irma. Our heirs will be married this way: Heinrich to Renate and Johan to Susanne."

Both CEOs saw the barons were insistent upon their heirs, that is, their eldest son marrying the eldest daughter of the other baron. In a way, Dederick could see why they so desired this marriage alliance, for it would tie these two powerful barons closer together, just as marrying their sons and daughters with those of the barons would create stronger ties between the corporation leaders and the barons. Dederick agreed, and so did Gerhardt, suspecting this was the best deal they could hammer out at this time.

"Then it is agreed," Adler declared. "Since Karla and Irma aren't going to become baronesses, you have our permission for them to marry when the others do, so you don't have to wait until they turn twenty-one, as traditions demands of baronesses."

"Excellent, excellent. We should hold six simultaneous weddings. It will be cheaper that way," Gerhardt suggested.

"A man who thinks like we do, agreed," Adler replied with a wry smile. "We should notify them tonight at the supper table." All four men agreed to this and set the wedding date to be October 1, Kirsa's birthday. By that date, all four young women would be twenty-one, available to marry, and become a full baroness.

"One thing that bothers me a little," Gerhardt spoke up. "Baronesses have their eyes removed, is that not so?" Adler nodded affirmatively, thinking the man was a fool not to know that. All baronesses were blind and dumb, had been for centuries. Was he that unobservant?

"Then, I presume the women need some time to adjust and still be able to move around on their own?" Gerhardt continued to ask, knowing he was on unfamiliar ground with his daughter becoming a baroness.

Adler decided to answer him, since their daughters were soon to become baronesses. "Yes, it is wise to give them time to adjust, just as they need time to adjust to their final tiny waist corsets. I see what you are thinking. Yes, the new baroness should be most comfortable with her many modifications at the time of her marriage. We should get this final detail taken care of soon. Give the four women time to adjust and learn how to move around on their own, as they must in order to fulfill their duties. I will come by tomorrow morning to brief Nadja on her obligations and duties as a baroness. Aldric, you do the same with Kirsa. We can both do this with our eldest daughters tonight." The men agreed and the meeting broke up.

After the two barons left, Gerhardt commented, "Well, it was wise of us to have gone ahead and prepared our daughters, veils and all. Now only one thing remains, their eyes, but frankly, I'm a bit worried about blinding my Kirsa. How will she possibly be able to move around on her own?"

"I don't know, but frankly old friend, that's my Nadja's problem. She'll be a baroness for one of the two most powerful barons on this world. We all have a price to pay for our positions, Gerhardt, you know that," Dederick replied. Gerhardt nodded and departed for his GE office.

That evening over supper, Adler again had to chastize Heinrich who still didn't actually help Susanne, snickering as the nearly helpless young woman struggled to pull her chair out so she could sit down to the table. Hastily, Elsa did it for her. "All right now, everyone, we've made all the marriage arrangements. We will hold a combined wedding ceremony for all six couples on October 1. Heinrich will marry Renate, Hermann will marry Kirsa, Johan will marry Susanne, Wulf will marry Nadja, Killian will marry Karla, and Kurt will marry Irma. That's that. Heinrich, Hermann, not a single word out of you both. This is final. At least, the women can't complain about it now. I won't listen to a word from either of you boys. This is final, period."

Heinrich started to protest loudly. He didn't want to marry Renate. Hermann felt cheated, he'd have to marry the older Kirsa. Both boys saw the stern, immovable look on Adler's face and wisely kept quiet. Both got up from the table and departed, slamming the door behind them. Quietly, Elsa slipped in and sat between the two young women and began to feed them their supper, though she noticed tears streaming down both women's cheeks and knew they were heartbroken as much as the boys were, but for entirely different reasons.

After supper, Adler removed the golden veil from Karla. "Dear, you won't need this anymore. I'm truly sorry we couldn't arrange for you to become a baroness like your older sister. Still, you will be cementing the bonds between we barons and the alien corporations, so that is something to be proud of. Now go do whatever it is that you women do after supper. Susanne, I must have some words with you, my new baroness-to-be."

Elsa helped Karla up and made sure that she was safely on her very slow way out of the room and that the door was still open. Adler dismissed her. "That will be all for now, Elsa. I will bring Susanne to her room later on." Elsa nodded and headed to the door, slipping a steadying arm around Karla.

Once they were well on their way to the stairs, Elsa whispered, "At least you won't get blinded like Susanne will. That's something." Karla was still crying silently, but she did nod her head, indicating she understood what Elsa was trying to say, to console her a little.

Adler sat across from his gorgeous daughter, who already looked the part of a golden baroness. "The golden veil is your symbol of office. Wear it with great pride. A baroness never speaks, as you well know. A baroness must always display superb posture, never slouching on her throne, because you are the embodiment of beauty for Thromstead. That is why you now wear such a rigid corset and have such a perfect waistline, just like your mother." He recalled hearing someone once say there was more steel in a baroness' corset than the baron's ceremonial sword. He now believed that was a true statement.

"You already have mastered the tall heels a baroness must wear, so I don't need to remind you a baroness is required to walk stately and graceful at all times. Now then, as a new baroness, it is my duty as your father to review with you the responsibilities of a baroness. It is your responsibility to bear the baron as many children as he desires, usually at least four. It is your responsibility to satisfy his sexual needs fully. You're required to always dress formally and to attend all court sessions, sitting stately and beautifully at your baron's side. You must attend all the social occasions as well. You already dance well, so that base is covered. Remember always that falling down in public is a severe disgrace, a horrid blot on you and on your baron."

He went on, "Now as far as your obligations go, you're obligated to wear whatever clothing your baron has purchased for you, whatever earrings, broaches, and other jewelry he gives to you. I believe we already have suitable earrings. You're also obligated to see your daughters are properly prepared for their marriage, though we both know your baron will likely handle this for you. Still, that is as much your obligation as his. Your last obligation is to look as attractive as possible at all times, just as your mother does for me. We never know when an important person might arrive, so a baroness must be ready to be the perfect hostess at such times."

He continued, "You'll always have a servant to assist you, but since you can't speak, I do hope you have already worked out some kind of cluck sound to let her know when you need to go to the bathroom." Susanne nodded. "So remember, in spite of all the restrictions, a baroness' life is one of luxury and great pleasure, as long as you fulfill your responsibilities, obligations, and customs. As you well know, your position is envied by all, especially if you show great poise, grace, and stateliness, when you walk or dance. As you know it is customary for a baroness to mingle with other barons at all social events, charming them, dancing with them—all of which then reflects well on your baron."

He finished up, "So do you understand these? Just nod yes." Susanne did so mechanically. She had no way to tell him no, no, no. "Good. Then tomorrow, you will begin the last phase of your adaption process. I'll go with you, my dear. Now let's get you up and off to whatever you women do of an evening."

Alderic said much the same thing to Renate that night, and in the morning, he escorted the silently crying Renate to the medical center, on the way joining up with Adler, who brought a sobbing Susanne with him. A half hour later, both young women were unconscious, and their family doctor carefully removed their eyeballs, replacing them with charming green glass eyes. Then he roused each woman, thankful that they couldn't make a sound when they awoke. Both Susanne and Renate awoke to an utter, complete blackness, though they could hear their fathers and the doctor talking near them. "Yes, their green eyes look lovely on them. Thank you doctor. We'll take them back to their rooms now."

Susanne thought that must be her father speaking. She wanted to scream, to yell, to do anything to make them undo this horrid thing, but she couldn't. Then, terror struck her harder than ever before, just as it did Renate. Strong arms got her up onto her feet and gave her a push, forcing her to walk! Repeatedly, she nearly fell over, and would have if her father hadn't supported her. Now her never-ending nightmare began in earnest, just as Renate's did, though she could neither see nor hear her.

Once Adler dropped Susanne off into Elsa's care, he headed over to GD to explain to Nadja what the responsibilities and obligations of a baroness were. That done, Dederick took Nadja to his own med lab and watched as Dr. Lanzo removed her eyes, replacing them with beautiful blue glass eyes. By the time he began escorting Nadja back to her bedroom, Gerhardt arrived with Kirsa, who nearly fainted when she saw the blind Nadja being helped out of the med lab. A half hour later, Kirsa's eternal nightmare of total blackness began.

With all the baroness-to-be handled properly, Adler and Aldric met again and decided on their next step. It was harsh, but necessary. Heinrich and Wulf simply had to be handled. Dr. Lanzo already had part of the process underway. It had been—for well over a week now, ever since the young men had been acting up, disobeying their fathers. The new technology offered both men a unique solution to their recalcitrant boys. First, they visited the secret lab, peering in on the developing clones. Satisfied entirely, they summoned Dr. Lanzo, explaining what they intended to do later this very morning.

"Oh, yes. I can have it prepared in a half hour. This will be quite an experiment, won't it? Oh my yes indeed it will," the rather excited doctor exclaimed.

Satisfied, both barons headed to their offices and summoned their respective sons, Heinrich and Wulf. Their conversations were nearly the same. Adler explained, "Heinrich, I simply cannot and will not tolerate such insolent behavior on your part towards future baronesses and your obligations as my heir and baron. You're a total disgrace to all barons. Now, you will pay the price for your disgusting behavior."

"What are you going to do, dad? Disinherit me? You can't do that and you know it. Hermann is an idiot, a poor heir to your throne! We told you who we would be satisfied to marry, but did you listen? Oh no!"

"Shut up Heinrich. I've had all I can take from you." Adler pulled out his concealed gun and pointed it at Heinrich. "No, I'm not going to kill you, but I'm going to make you pay dearly for your total disrespect of all barons." He fired. Heinrich collapsed onto the floor, stunned. Adler summoned two security guards. "Bring him with me. We're going down to sub-level twenty."

A short while later, the two security men dropped the unconscious Heinrich onto a small medical bed and promptly left. Minutes later, Aldric appeared with other men carrying Wulf, depositing the unconscious young man onto the second bed. After the security men left, Dr. Lanzo stepped in with two syringes. "Ah, all ready for this, I see?"

"Yes, do it now," Adler barked. Carefully, the doctor injected both men with his new genetic bio agent. "Four days and it'll be done."

"Excellent, doctor. We'll have the necessary items here by then. Thanks," Aldric replied. Both barons departed, their problem sons solved.

At suppertime, when Heinrich failed to appear, Adler merely said, "Heinrich will not be dining with us for some time." Elsa took over his duties with Susanne, but now wondered what had happened to Heinrich. No one dared question Alder though.

Chapter 4—Adaptions

Heinrich finally woke up. He couldn't breathe properly. His hair seemed to be on his face, and he tried to move it out of the way with his hands, but nothing happened. He cried out, but no sounds came out. He panicked and fainted. Someone waved a foul odor below his nose, reviving him. He tried to yell, to scream, but only silence resulted. "Ah, awake at last, Heinrich," Dr. Lanzo said. "Nurse, sit him up so he can see how he now looks, will you? I've got to revive Wulf who keeps fainting too."

A nurse lifted Heinrich into a sitting position, and he found himself staring into a mirror at some beautiful UFB woman. She looked incredibly attractive, with knee-length, shiny, thick brown hair, monster breasts nicely covered by the red satin, form-fitting gown hemmed at her knees where her black polymer nylons were seductively revealed. She wore matching red toe shoes with their incredible seven-inch spiked heels, oxford style with their laces nicely double knotted so they couldn't come untied. Her waist was perhaps fourteen inches across, which with the tight corset beneath the gown, accented her incredible curves. The image's mouth seemed to be speaking, but Heinrich couldn't hear any words she was saying. Then, he realized he was looking at himself in the mirror! He gasped and fainted again.

Nearby, Wulf had similar reactions, giving the doctor fits trying to keep him conscious. "Oh come on Wulf. You look perfect. So stop fainting on me!" After several more minutes and more revivals, both young men finally ceased fainting, but continued to gasp for breath. Just then, Adler and Aldric entered and stood before the pair.

"Well, well. Yes, doctor, they look perfect. So Heinrich, now you can fully appreciate what Susanne has been dealing with. So can you, Wulf. You both are now perfect UFBMD men. Don't worry. We know you now have intense sexual drives, so we'll make sure you get your chance to be fathers. We expect you to have many super-genius sons in the future.

In a few minutes, Carsten will arrive. From now on, you will be under his care, since we don't have the time to spend, while you learn to adapt to your new restraints. He will send you out as exotic escorts and see you're frequently bred to normal women. Any UFB daughters you have will go to Carsten, while any super-genius sons will come under our care. I hope you both enjoy your new lives and can finally appreciate the many sacrifices your sisters have endured to be the best baronesses they can be. Oh, don't try to speak. Your voice boxes have been removed. I'd say time to get up and start walking, but I don't want even to touch you now, Heinrich. I'll let Carsten's people deal with that."

Aldric added, "Oh don't worry, Wulf, Heinrich. We have clones of you both that are about done and ready to take your places, positions neither of you seemed to desire. Now you have your wishes. You don't have to marry the women of our choices. Goodbye forever, Wulf. Happy life." He rose and left, as did Adler.

Both men began sobbing, but Carsten's men arrived and forced them onto their feet. Wobbling wildly and gasping for breath and since the men gave them a push, they had no choice but to try to walk in the tall heels. It was take a step or fall down, but the men didn't let them fall down or faint. As soon as one started to pass out, a man waved smelling salts under his nose, preventing it, though their silent gasps for breath didn't abate.

Amid this nightmare, Heinrich thought, *My handsome goatee is gone!* Indeed, all traces of facial hair were long gone. Quite why he thought about his goatee eluded him, as he struggled and wiggled to keep from falling down. The nightmare seemed to end when they were finally allowed to sit down on plush chairs in some room inside Carsten's Exotic Escorts. Sitting erect and gasping for breath, they saw Carsten, dressed in an expensive black suit enter and look them over.

"I can see you men will need extensive training. First, you must learn to walk properly. We have just the training tool for that." Carsten snapped his fingers and several servant women entered. "Training corsets please. Then hook them up to the walkers."

The women quickly unzipped their gowns and removed their slips. Then, while the male helpers kept the two UFBMD men standing upright, the women put a second corset on them, one that went from their bosoms down to their knees. Once fully tightened, neither man could bend at all between their bosoms and knees! Now they couldn't sit down. The men pushed them, forcing them to struggle to walk again. The room they entered contained a strange machine. A central steel beam held two arms horizontal to the ground but high over the men's heads. The helpers attached a chain and head harness to the men, while Carsten explained.

"Now this is our walker trainer. You notice you can't sit now, only stand. Once you're hooked up, the machine will not let you fall down. When I start the motor, the arms will force you to begin walking around in circles. You will be attached to this machine all day long for as many days as it takes you to learn to walk without falling down. So it is in your best interests to learn quickly, young men." He then pushed a button, and the machine began pulling on their heads. Still gasping for air, they had no choice but to take tiny steps, either that or be painfully dragged along until they did so. Everyone then left them alone, struggling mightily and sobbing uncontrollably, but quite silently.

A few days later, Adler watched as Dr. Lanzo brought the clone Heinrich out of the growth machine. His *son* looked precisely like Heinrich. The doctor and Adler got him properly dressed and then Adler began.

"You are my son, heir, and future baron. Your name is Heinrich. Soon you'll be married to Renate, who will be your beautiful baroness. You'll meet her later today, son. You have much to learn as well. Your mother is Baroness Zelda, who like all baronesses can't speak and is blind. So is Renate. You're to assist your sister baroness-to-be Susanne with her needs. This will give you all the practice you'll need to be able to assist your new Baroness Renate when the time comes." Adler chatted on, slowly educating his new *son*.

Nearby, Aldric was holding a similar conversation with *Wulf*, preparing him to join his family later this morning. He soon saw the new Wulf had a very different personality, one that was rather kind and understanding. *This is going to work out perfectly.*

Later Adler showed Heinrich around Castle Berthold, which took most of the afternoon. One by one, he introduced Heinrich to his other family members, though the women were silent. "Where have you been?" Hermann asked his brother. He wasn't satisfied with Heinrich's reply that he didn't know. Hermann decided something was funny or wrong with his brother, and began keeping a sharp eye on him, wondering why his father was showing Heinrich around, as though he didn't know anything about this castle or its people.

At supper, the family met as a group. To Hermann's surprise, Heinrich helped the now blind Susanne get to her chair, and he seemed incredibly kind and sensitive to her, as he fed her supper. *What has come over Hermann?* After supper, Hermann took Heinrich aside and began to *interrogate* him. To his dismay, his brother didn't know much at all, not their friends, not growing up with the six girls, or even who the others were. Hermann began to worry and headed over to talk to Johan and see how Wulf was faring.

"It's weird," Johan whispered. The two were meeting in his room where they couldn't be overheard. "Wulf is like a different person. He doesn't remember anything. Dad had to take him all around Castle Berringer showing him what's where, and he still gets lost and confused. Something is terribly wrong with him, that's for sure. We damned well better find out what's happened to Wulf and Heinrich. It could happen to us next!"

"I agree. We best figure this out before we take any action to marry the girls of our choice, not theirs," Hermann whispered back. "So what do we do first? Should we or dare we ask our fathers?"

"I've been nosing around some after Wulf went missing. I got stonewalled, but I did find out Wulf went to see dad in his office, and two security men carried him out, unconscious. Dad must have shot him, but since he isn't dead, probably only stunned him. I did learn the guards dropped him off in sub-level twenty of GD headquarters; that's their top secret research lab."

"Wow. I bet dad did that to Heinrich too. I wonder what they did to them to alter their personalities and memories down there. I'll see if I can find out tomorrow," Hermann suggested.

Unbeknown to the two, Adler and Aldric also met in secret around the same time. "Well, the clones are slowly catching on. There's no problem with the women; they can't speak even if they detect something isn't right or different. Hermann, on the other hand, suspects something," Adler explained.

"Same with Johan. He knows something is very different about his brother. I know he's been making some discrete inquiries, knows I shot Wulf, and had my men take him over to GD's labs. Perhaps, we should tell Johan and Hermann. We can threaten them with the same thing if they tell another soul."

Adler grinned mischievously. "I agree. We tell them and threaten them with it if they tell anyone about it or even let on something is amiss."

When Adler returned home, he waited up for Hermann to get back. "Ah, coming in late I see. Come, we need to have a talk about your brother." Hermann couldn't believe his luck and followed his father into his private study.

"Sit down. This is important, son. Now then, we both know how disrespectful, how hateful, how much disgrace your older brother has caused us. What he's been doing to your sisters—well, I couldn't allow that to continue, and certainly not once he's married to his new baroness. That would bring us all total disgrace and perhaps threaten our position as the leading barons of our world. So I had to act. Thanks to the new alien technology that we now have available to us, a superior solution was available, and I took it."

He rubbed his forehead as though this pained him somehow and continued, "Your brother now gets to experience life as a UFBMD man. Yes, I had him genetically modified. He's doing fine, though he looks like Susanne and Karla used to, before their recent changes. He'll be bred to normal women and give us a number of super-genius sons to help us better run our world. The Heinrich that is now with us is a clone of him, a perfect copy in all ways. However, the clone's personality is quite different. Did you notice how kind and considerate he was with Susanne at supper tonight? This is the way a baron should be treating his baroness, who has given up all for him."

"Mind you, if you ever breathe a word of this to anyone, if you ever let on the new Heinrich isn't your brother, I'll see that you also become a UFBMD man. Anyone can be cloned, you see. Doesn't take all that long either, thanks to the new alien growth machines. Do I make myself clear?"

Hermann swallowed. So much was now clear. For the first time in his life, Hermann feared his own father. He swallowed again, "Yes sir. He was very good with Susanne at supper."

"Good. Then we understand each other. Aldric is telling Johan about this right now, I believe. Now then, Heinrich is still my heir at least for now. If he doesn't work out, then I'll not hesitate to make you my heir, so don't worry about that aspect, son. Now go get some sleep. It's been a rather long day." Meekly, Hermann nodded, rose, and fled his father's study, aghast at what he'd learned.

In the privacy of his own room, he saw why Heinrich was acting so strange; it wasn't Heinrich. Well, he looked like his brother, but he sure wasn't. Rather, what so frightened him was what his father had done to Heinrich, turning him into a helpless, speechless, UFB woman and yet still a man. He couldn't imagine what Heinrich was going through right now. It was unbelievable. He fell into a very, very troubled sleep.

The next morning, the six young men met together as they usually did, only Hermann and Johan now looked at Heinrich and Wulf in a very different way than did Killian and Kurt. Kurt said, "So are we just going to sit back and let them dictate to us who we are supposed to marry or are we going to do something about it?"

Killian said, "We have to do something. I sure as hell don't want to marry Karla. So what can we do?"

"I, I don't think we should do anything," Johan volunteered, shocking the two GD boys.

"What's come over you?" complained Killian.

"Yesterday, you were all for kidnaping the girls, having some priest marry us, and then letting our fathers know what we've done. They'd have to accept it."

"We can't do that," Hermann said nervously.

Heinrich giggled. "I'd sure like to marry you, Johan. You're so handsome. Why do we have to marry those women anyway? Especially if you don't want to do that."

All five lads stared at Heinrich. "What?" said Johan in disbelief.

"We should marry someone we like, and I like you, Johan. You're so strong and handsome. Don't you find me attractive? I certainly do you," Heinrich said. Noticing the five's sudden discomfort, he added, "Aren't we supposed to talk openly about such things?"

"No! Not another word, Heinrich," Johan barked. *What has come over Heinrich? He's never said anything like this to me before. Oh shit, he's a clone too!* "Heinrich, why don't you and Wulf go check on the baroness-to-bes and see if they need anything right now, and let us know."

"Oh sure. We must look after them always," Wulf replied. "Come on, Heinrich. Let's go find them. They are beautiful women. I can't wait to get mine into bed with me." The two left the others.

"What the hell is going on with Heinrich? Has he suddenly gone gay?" asked Killian. "And why are you so opposed to taking action, Johan? Yesterday, you were all for kidnaping the women."

Johan swallowed. There wasn't any choice but to let these two in on the secret. He lowered his voice, "Okay, Killian, Kurt, you must swear to us you'll not tell another soul. If you do, I swear I'll kill you myself!" Both did. "Heinrich and Wulf are clones! Our dads had the real Heinrich and Wulf turned into those UFB woman-man things. Oh, a UFBMD it's called. Dad says they can't speak, are armless, and look just like Susanne did before the recent genetic modification. He and Wulf are supposed to have super-genius sons for dad and Aldric. Plus, our dads told us if we tell anyone about this, they'll turn us into the same things and make clones of us to take our places."

"My God!" exclaimed Killian.

"Double shit!" added Kurt. "I had no idea. So that's why Heinrich is acting so very weird. Wulf too. Guys, we're all in very, very serious trouble." He lowered his voice as though his father might be listening in, "Our dads could well do this to anyone of us, clone us and turn us into one of those helpless UFB woman things!"

"No kidding. I heard they sent Heinrich and Wulf over to Carsten's. I'm going to try and pay him a visit, just to make sure dad's not telling me a lie," Johan declared. "But guys, if this is really true, then we're our dad's pawns. They can force us to do any damned thing they want. We'll be their pawns until our dads die!"

"I can't stomach that," protested Hermann. "Can I go with you, Johan? I'd like to see my brother and see if it's true too."

"Sure. Let's go now while the two are off looking for the girls. Killian, Kurt, you keep them occupied if they come back. For God's sake, don't tell anyone where we are going, not unless you want to find yourselves turned into UFB women who can't speak!"

Killian shuddered. "No, mum's the word. Let us know if it's true."

Johan and Hermann quietly left GD headquarters and walked the mile to Carsten's Exotic Escorts. Once inside, the asked to see Carsten himself, but waited in the plush examination room, where a dozen of the newly modified UFB women were on display, waving their new short arms at the boys, hoping to attract their attention to them. "Goddamn, they are hot women," Johan whispered.

"How may I help you gentlemen?" Carsten's voice took them by surprise. He entered as they were gazing at his merchandise—well half of them. The others were off at GD labs getting their new genetic modifications, which regrew their upper arms and removed their voice boxes.

"We would like to take a peek at Heinrich and Wulf, if we may. Our dads told us they were in your keeping. We just want to make sure they're okay. That's all. We don't trust our dads to have our brothers treated right," Johan took charge.

"But of course. This way, gentlemen. Right now, they are in training and will be so for several weeks. As you know or perhaps don't know, newly created UFB women do need several weeks to get adapted to their new modifications. I assure you soon both men will be doing very well indeed. Ah, there they are."

He had led them to the training room. Both stared long and hard. No mistake. Here were their brothers. Their faces told all, but their bodies told quite a different story. Their light brown hair was now as thick, lush and long as Renate's. Their bosoms were as massive; their figures, nearly identical to all the gorgeous women out in the display area they'd just seen. They wore some kind of full-body corset and had their heads attached to the walking machine. Both were struggling mightily to walk in circles dictated by the relentless movement of the machine.

"See, they are in the process of learning how to walk again. The machine keeps them from falling down and getting hurt. It is always quite a learning experience these incredibly beautiful UFB women undergo," Carsten explained. "And yet, if you come back in a couple of weeks, you will find them doing quite well, just as able as your sisters are." He didn't know they were now blind and facing an almost impossible situation.

Since neither wanted Carsten to have any reason to tell their fathers about their visit, Johan complimented him. "Yes, Carsten, I can see our brothers are in superb hands. They are doing well indeed. Thank you for treating them so very well."

"But of course," he replied. *Stupid boys. It's in my best interests to treat them very well. They're going to make a fortune for me, more than the normal UFB woman does. These UFBMD men are extraordinarily rare.* "Might I interest you in one of my escorts for an evening's entertainment? My women are the finest in all Thromstead and are the very latest models with the erotic short arms. They can't speak so you won't be bothered with their often idle chatter."

When they reached the display area, once more both young men's eyes gazed upon the women. They found the women quite enticing. "Sure why not?" Johan declared. "We will be back this evening."

"In that case, why not pick out your dream woman now. I can reserve her for you until seven tonight. If you come by later, she might have been chosen by another," Carsten suggested.

"Great. How can you choose one, Carsten? They're all magnificent women," Johan declared.

"There is a dance at Wolfgang's Dance Hall tonight," Hermann suggested. "Let's take them there first."

"Excellent choice," Carsten said agreeably. "If dancing it is, might I make some suggestions? Alina and Amala are expert dancers and love to dance." Since all the women looked ravishing, the two accepted his choice of the two raven-haired beauties and promised to be by before seven.

Back at Johan's room, Killian and Kurt had been successful in keeping Heinrich and Wulf occupied helping the blind women learn to walk around their quarters. "Well, what happened?" whispered Kurt, anxious to know if all this was true.

"We saw our brothers. It's just like our dad's said," Johan whispered back, launching into a graphic description of what the two now looked like.

"So what are we going to do about this?" Killian asked. "I don't want to be a puppet. I can't live knowing that at any moment my dad will do that to me and put a clone of me in my place."

"I don't know yet," Johan replied. "Give me some time to think. We must tread very, very carefully or we'll wind up at Carsten's too." Leaving them with that sobering thought, the group disbanded, heading for their homes.

***

Elsa wasn't idle. In fact, ever since the young women's first modifications, she'd been a hive of activity. She'd noticed right away Zelda's eyes had regrown when she underwent the latest genetic modification. Adler still hadn't noticed. That meant, she decided, if they went ahead and removed Susanne's eyes, she could have them regrown by using this same genetic bio agent. Somehow, she needed to get samples of it and the other mutation agents.

However, now that Susanne was blinded, she knew she

had to be Susanne's lifeline and the other three young women as well. She began in Susanne's bedroom. Holding onto the terrified woman, she got her to her feet. "Okay, the first thing you have to learn to do is to stand still and not lose your balance. I know it's so hard to do now, but let's work at it."

Some days later when she felt confident Susanne could at least stand up on her own, she worked with having her sit down and stand up on her own. Here an additional difficulty arose. She couldn't see where her hair was. Thus, she could easily step on it while rising, causing her to fall over, or she could sit on it, causing her sharp pain. "You can feel with it, Susanne, so feel where it is at before you try to stand up. Shake it out of the way by feel. Same thing when you want to sit down. Sense with it and feel where it is. Come on; you can do it, Susanne."

Learning to do this also took several days, during which time, Elsa visited the other three blinded young women and instructed their servants on how to do these two things with their charges. Next, she had to get Susanne walking on her own, at least around her own bedroom.

"Count your steps, Susanne. From now on, you must not think of anything but counting your steps in order to find your way anywhere," Elsa explained. A torturous week later, Susanne was able to navigate around her bedroom, to the women's bathroom, and to her mother's room. She still needed constant assistance with the stairs to go down to the dining area, throne room, and such. The only positive thing was Elsa had several months to get Susanne familiar enough with her castle so she could get around on her own if she had too. She knew these sadistic barons often did that; in this case, it was Adler who made Zelda do just that.

Midweek, their true boyfriends came by to visit the six. They heard four had been blinded and of their promised marriages. Yet, they just had to see their once fiancés one more time. They hadn't given up hope. Elsa led Rudolf to Susanne's bedroom and left them to talk, albeit one-sided. She purposely listened in discretely.

Eventually, she heard what she wanted to hear. "Don't worry, Susanne. Somehow, we're going to rescue you and the other five girls, and take you away from these horrible men," Rudolf whispered. "We're working on a plan now. You just have to be patient with us a while longer. After that, we can get married, and I'll look after you always. I promise, Susanne, I promise."

The next day when Elsa paid a short visit to the servants of the other three blind young women, she discovered their true boyfriends had been by to visit. At least, one servant had heard him suggest that somehow, he would rescue her, but she thought that was mere fantasy on his part.

Elsa now knew she needed to help these six young men get their fiancés out of the baron's and CEO's grasps. The how eluded her just now.

***

As promised, Johan and Hermann took the two UFB escorts to the dance hall. Not only were they superb dancers, they flirted with the men all night long, until at last, when they returned to Carsten's, both men took a small room and indulged themselves and the two women. They found these silent women to be profoundly intoxicating and left the establishment satisfied and the women equally so.

The next day, they related their experience with the escort women to the other four. Heinrich commented, "Ah who wants to dance with UFB women? I'd rather dance with Johan here, if he'll have me."

"You touch me, and you are a dead man, Heinrich!" Johan barked. "That goes for the other four. You get that?"

"Sure handsome. Can't blame a guy for trying, now can you? You five head off and have your fun, and I'll see what fun I can find around the castle. Some of the security men are interesting," Heinrich replied.

Beginning that night, all five men made use of Carsten's magnificent UFB women on a nightly basis. While their fathers knew about it, they approved. After all, they too often went there of an early evening. "Let them sew their oats harmlessly," Aldric suggested. "They will be far better able to satisfy their future wife's needs this way."

"Agreed. But what are you going to do about the new Heinrich? He's a fag!" pointed out Gerhardt. All four men knew this to be a fact.

"Well, for now, nothing. Let him marry and become a baron. At least, he handles Susanne's needs very well, so he'll make a good husband for Renate, treating her properly and well," Adler declared, though he didn't like it. "Besides, if it goes poorly, I'll just redo the process and try for a better clone. Now it's time we showed off our new supermen to the boys, don't you think, Gerhardt?"

"Yes, we have ten of them now, and it'll be hard to keep them a secret much longer. Bring all six by GD tomorrow morning, and we'll show them," Dederick suggested.

"My God, dad, what are they?" exclaimed Killian. He and his five friends, along with the two barons and Gerhardt, were down in sub-level seventeen where the new superman clones were now living and training. The six stared at the strange looking men. Each looked almost identical to the others.

Their necks were so short and thick that they appeared not to have a neck. Their height was around six feet, but their weight was at least three hundred pounds! Their arms were thicker than the boy's legs, and these boys were overly strong for their age, compliments of their father's breeding with their UFB woman mothers, but these men made their bodies look puny! Their legs were enormous and powerful. At the moment, several were lifting weights that none of the six young men would ever dream of attempting to lift! Their overall appearance was shocking and alarming, especially since they were being called the new soldiers for Blackwell-C.

"These men are more than twice as strong as our best men," Aldric explained. "With good training, they'll be the ultimate soldiers and security men. All are identical clones, so we know just how each will perform, no guess work, such as is this one better than that one for this mission. The perfect solution."

To the boys, these soldiers looked more like some kind of human abominations gone very wrong, but they wisely kept their mouths shut, fearing their fathers would clone them and turn them into UFB women as they had Wulf and Heinrich. Johan began to see no way out of this mess. Things had just gotten a whole lot worse. As soon as these men were fully trained and took over security duties, nothing could stop them. Nothing could get by them. The six young men's fears only rose, while any solution eluded their imaginations.

***

How to live eluded Anne Becker. She'd awakened in GD's secret laboratory only to discover that her body had been genetically mutated into that of a UFB woman, but slightly different. She had upper arms for the little good that did her, and she couldn't speak. Terrified, she'd been carried over to Carsten's Erotic Escorts and given to him, as though she were no more than a sack of potatoes. She was powerless to prevent that and unable to communicate anything to anyone, ignoring entirely that she was physically completely helpless now.

Soon her shock, intense grief, and silent sobbing gave way to a deep apathy. True, she was hooked up to their trainer machine. It didn't bother her that she couldn't sit, that couldn't tell them she had to pee, that she couldn't live like this, or that she couldn't even walk. Like a dead weight, the machine simply pulled her round and round in the circle, occasionally leaving a wet trail of urine behind her. Anne didn't resist any longer; pain didn't hurt.

Had days gone by? Anne didn't know. She'd stopped even trying to perceive what was around her. Vaguely, she knew some kind hands took her down, washed her off, fed her, and tucked her into bed, only to get her back into the nearly full-body corset and hook her up to the machine in the morning. Occasionally, her body did start to take the tiny shuffling steps it needed to do to keep from being dragged around like a dead weight, though that didn't last long before she lost her balance and fell only to be prevented from that by the machine, and dragged along without any chance to regain her feet, not until someone came along and stopped the machine for some reason. Was that reason it was time to eat? All was an incoherent blur to Anne.

And yet, each day she did find herself walking for longer periods before falling and being dragged mercilessly. Was it a week? She didn't know, but somehow her body had walked around in circles without falling. Someone was saying this was a good thing, that she was learning, and that she did well. Anne didn't care; praise failed to stir any emotion or thought in her mind, which was numb, thinking of nothing at all, for she was dead to the world around her.

The next day, the servants dressed her in a fine gown instead of the trainer corset. Anne didn't notice. Someone said to rise and practice walking around the room. She sat still until the person forced her to rise, giving her a gently push to start walking. Aimlessly, Anne meandered around, thinking of nothing, aimlessly, forcing the person continually to have to guide her physically, since she didn't respond to any verbal commands at all.

Sit down. Was that someone's voice? Anne neither cared nor paid any attention to it. Someone gave her a downward push, and she fell like a lifeless lump into a plush chair, ignoring the pain coming from her hair as she sat on the now quite sensitive hair strands with their neurons and axons. She didn't notice a dozen other women much like herself sitting in the display room, all dolled up and waiting to be chosen to share an evening with a client.

***

Emil didn't give up his goal of finding Anne. At the Start of Summer Ball, he'd seen an eyeful! While he knew there were a lot of UFB women kept in bordellos and escort services, perhaps ten thousand of women in Thromstead alone, he'd never utilized their services. However, at the ball, he saw the new, improved version, being touted as the new standard, genetically modified UFB woman. He suspected that someone had to test these new agents on humans and that these many missing teens were likely abducted to be their test guinea pigs. His heart sank as he now presumed Anne had been taken and turned into one of these new silent UFB women.

Still, Emil wasn't about to give up. He swore again to find Anne and to dole out justice to those who had abducted her and probably genetically mutated her. Where to start was his next problem. He made some inquires on the side and learned that most all genetic modifications were being done at the laboratories of Galactic Dynamics. A few credits changed hands and a spaceport worker told him that recently GD had received a lot of new equipment from Danforth-C. It had been delivered to GD headquarters in Thromstead.

Emil surmised that these experiments were likely being conducted in the basement labs of GD. However, he had no way to gain access and check it out. Still, knowing this much, he had a good idea who the men were that had been doing the abductions: GD security men. That gave him a new avenue to explore, for he knew where these men frequently hung out, Dorstead's Pub. Most security guards spent off hours drinking and tossing darts in the pub. He'd even been there a number of times.

As far as locating Anne, he had only the vaguest of clues. At that ball, he had overheard them saying that soon Carsten's Exotic Escorts would soon be having a goodly selection of these new erotic UFB women. With locating Anne as his prime objective, he decided for now to focus on her. If he didn't come up with anything concrete on her soon, he would head to the pub and see what he could glean from GD security men when they were there.

Emil dressed up in his best suit. Paying a visit to Carsten's meant he had to look as if he was of the wealthier class of Thromstead. A dockworker couldn't afford even one night with these escort women, but they could afford a half hour with one in one of the many bordello around the city. Quite why any man would do that, he didn't know, but many did. Long ago, his father told him the city received substantial taxes from these many establishments. The mayor always granted anyone who wished to open another one an official charter without even questioning them.

Slowly, Emil paused at the entrance. The ornate sign over the doors read Carsten's Erotic Escorts. He sighed and opened the doors. The odor of fresh flowers filled the air, temporarily drowning out the smoggy air of Thromstead, where factory furnaces and cars polluted the air daily. "May I help you?" a man said, walking up to him.

"Yes, I've heard that you have some of the new type UFB women here. Is that true?"

"Where did you hear that, if I might ask?" the well-dressed man asked politely.

"At the Start of Summer Ball. I was there and saw the baronesses and their daughters. I overheard someone saying your establishment would soon have them. Am I mistaken?" Emil responded with the truth.

"Ah yes. Of course. I have a dozen who are ready to delight you, to satisfy your every need. You're aware they cannot speak?"

"Yes, I saw that at the ball. May I see your selection?" Emil asked. He was led into the display room, his feet sinking deep into the plush red carpet. Sofas were positioned all around the walls and many stunning women sat on them. All but one looked up at him and smiled. Several waggled their new short upper arms about attempting to draw his attention to them, since now they couldn't talk to flirt with potential clients. They were only now working on new ways to do just that. Each woman was simply gorgeous in her own right, not a blemish on their perfectly symmetrical faces, their gowns fitting tightly against their extremely curvaceous bodies.

His eyes lighted on a gorgeous redhead, and she waved her short arms about. His eyes moved on down the line, passing over a blonde, a brunette, and later on, his eyes rested upon an extremely attractive raven haired beauty. Like a sledgehammer, it struck him. This was Anne! He'd found her at last!

Trying to restrain his wild and conflicting emotions, Emil studied her. She didn't look at him, didn't respond at all, not like the other dozen women, who continued to try to attract his attention to them. She didn't appear to be on drugs or doped up. She just sat there like an object someone had positioned there, a life-sized rag doll perhaps.

Trying to control his voice, he said, "Now that one there, the raven haired beauty."

"Oh, I'm sorry sir. Yes, she is all that and more, but at the moment, she is still in training. Having a bit of a tough time with her. I'm sure any of the others will be more than able to satisfy all of your needs," Carsten suggested.

"Ah, but none are like that one. Does she have a name?"

"We are calling her Ada."

"I see. How soon do you suppose Ada will be ready to

work? I'm most interested in her," Emil asked.

"Normally, she should be more than ready right now, but as you can see, she isn't. Perhaps another one of the women?"

"No, it's Ada that I want. I can come back later when she is ready. I'm a patient man," Emil suggested, trying hard to work out just what he could do to rescue Anne. For a moment, he considered explaining to Carsten that Ada was Anne who had been abducted from her home and that he was a city police detective. He could arrest Carsten, perhaps, but more than likely Carsten had nothing to do with Anne's abduction or genetic mutation. His best guess was that GD had simply discarded her when their experiment was finished.

"I couldn't say when she will be ready, sir. Bit of a hard time adjusting, you see," Carsten suggested politely, wishing the man would hire one of his more than willing women.

Subterfuge or the truth? The choices raced through Emil's mind. He was sworn to uphold the law and here was one of the many kidnaped victims. His duty was clear. While he suspected he could hire some men, break in here, and take her away, he would be guilty of breaking the very law he was trying to uphold. He decided that would be a last resort. Perhaps, the man would see reason.

"Mr. Carsten. I'm detective Emil Beifeld. Yes, the mayor's son." He added that last when he saw Carsten recognized the last name. Besides, it might not hurt to throw his father's weight around a bit. "As you may know, recently there has been a rather alarming number of older teens being kidnaped, abducted from their homes while they were asleep. I'm investigating these cases. I'm afraid your Ada is really one of these victims. Her name is Anne Becker. She's eighteen years old."

Emil watched Carsten's reaction carefully. The man definitely was taken by complete surprise. "I'm sorry. I didn't know that. Oh dear. Someone dropped her off here as she physically is, saying she wanted to be an escort."

Whether Carsten was lying or not, Emil couldn't tell. "Don't worry, sir. I'm not here to arrest you. I'm sure you had nothing to do with her abduction or the kidnaping of the other teens."

The man visibly relaxed. "Yes, that is very true, sir. And yet, I've spent a considerable amount on her upkeep and training to date." Emil wasn't a fool. He'd been around and had heard much in his twenty years, especially being the mayor's son. Carsten was feeling him out, looking for a way out of the mess.

"Would a hundred credits suffice? I can take her away with me now and return her to her home. I'm sure you had nothing to do with these abductions, and I'm sure you'll report any other women who get dumped unexpectedly on your doorstep to the police," Emil offered.

"For two hundred, Mr. Beifeld, she's yours, as that will barely cover my costs, and I will keep you *promptly* informed of any others who *mysteriously* appear on my doorstep," Mr. Carsten bargained.

Emil knew he had him, but it wouldn't do to jump at his counter offer. He pretended to think it over a bit. "All right then. You do need to have your costs covered, since you've obviously taken very good care of her, and I'm sure her parents will be most grateful to you for that kindness. And yes, please let the police department know if others are dropped off on your doorstep."

"Excellent, excellent. Please tell the mayor Carsten always does what is honest and right with his women. I run the finest establishment in Thromstead," Carsten hinted. Emil handed over the credits.

The two walked over to Anne. He said, "She is in a very bad way. She doesn't seem to listen or obey your spoken commands. Yet, if you physically nudge her, she will obey. Let me show you." He gently placed an arm around her and nudged her to get up. Anne's body responded to the push. "Put your arm around her, give her a slight push in the direction you wish her to walk, and she will walk. Tell her parents I do hope in time she makes a full recovery," Carsten suggested.

Doing as suggested, Emil's arm gave her a nudge towards the door, and Anne's body began taking her tiny four-inch steps in that direction. Emil said, "I'll tell her parents. Again, thank you for tending to her needs, Carsten. I'm sure her parents will be glad to have her returned alive." Carsten seemed pleased to hear this, but Emil now had to focus on leading Anne out of the building. Soon, he saw what Carsten meant. Anne's body simply followed the pushes and nudges he gave it. Anne seemed beyond distant. What had they done to her, Emil wondered, but kept his attention on her until he reached his car. It took some doing to get her inside, since she didn't respond to spoken commands, though he felt certain she could hear him. Besides, he'd never been around these helpless UFB women before and didn't truly know just what help they did need.

Finally, she was in the car, and he drove off, only then relaxing. Now what, he wondered. Protocol became his answer. He took her to the nearest hospital to be thoroughly checked out, called her parents to report he'd found her, and then filed a report at the station, before heading back to the hospital. One thing was certain. Even if Anne recovered, she had no way to tell him who had done this to her, who had abducted her, if she even knew. On his way back to the hospital, his father called him to congratulate him and to find out how Anne was doing. "Remember, son, her parents are deeply religious."

Emil wasn't sure what he meant by that, but he soon found out. He met her parents at the hospital. They had come at once and recognized their eldest daughter. However, seeing she was now a UFB woman, couldn't even speak, and wasn't even responding to their voices, they ended their relationship with her. "We must thank you Mr. Beifeld for finding out what became of Anne. It may have been best had you just left her at that house of ill repute. We certainly don't want that thing she has become in our home. We know you wanted to marry her. So you can do that if you desire. If not, I'm sure you can find an appropriate bordello will accept her. Good day." Both parents walked out of the room and hospital, sad looks on their faces.

Emil said a silent curse! He now knew what his father meant by deeply religious. Some few on Blackwell-C believed the world had been taken over by the devil. Obviously, her parents did so and believed she was devil's spawn now, whatever that meant. He'd heard it in one of their sermons when he went to a service with Anne and her parents one time.

A doctor came up to him. "Ah here you are detective. I have the complete medical report on Anne Becker for you. As you know, she has been subjected to the alien genetic bio agent that makes women into UFB women. We've recently heard they have a new form, and it is my opinion Anne was subjected to one of those agents. She is perfectly healthy. There is nothing physically wrong with her. However, we have verified she has no voice box and thus can't speak. So any hope you may have had that she can tell you who abducted her is gone permanently, I'm afraid. Her mental state—now that is another matter entirely. She has undoubtedly suffered some major trauma and is still under its effects. The best thing I can recommend is plenty of bed rest. In time, perhaps she will come out of it, as much as can be expected."

He paused and looked around the room for a moment, then said, "Now the hard part. Her parents don't want anything to do with her. So the question we have for you is what should we do with her?"

"I'll take her some place safe and hope she recovers as you said. Thank you, doctor. You've been most helpful," Emil replied. Once more, he had a difficult time getting her up, out of the hospital, and into his car. That done, he sat back pondering his next move. He still wanted to marry her, if only she would come out of this emotional state or whatever she was suffering from. Emil thought about taking her to his tiny apartment, but gave that up. There simply wasn't room enough. He called his father on his cell. "Dad. You're right. Her parents disowned her. I can't, dad. I promised to marry her, and I still will, if only she can recover. I can't take her to my place. It's too small. Ideas?"

"Well, there's the old Beifeld house on Ragor Street. No one has been living there since your grandparents died. You could take her there, but won't you need to hire a servant to look after her?"

"Thanks dad. That's perfect. Yes, I will, unless you know someone who can look after her," Emil replied, finally some hope returning. That home would be perfect, he thought.

"I'll send your sister Amalia over there. She can help for a few days while you make other arrangements for Anne," the mayor suggested.

A half hour later, Emil arrived at the old house. He had a key, since he often visited his grandparents before they passed away some years back. His younger sister, sixteen-year-old Amalia, arrived almost at the same time. "Hi big brother. I see you have finally found Anne. Oh goodness! What did they do to her? Dad said to expect the worst."

"I'll explain once I get her inside. Go get the lights on." Once more, he had a difficult time getting the inert body out of the car and into the house. Getting her to sit was the easy part. Emil then outlined all he knew about what had happened to her.

"Well, she should be bathed. Come on. Let's get her out of all this and into the tub. Tomorrow, we can visit the UFB women's store, find her some clothes, and whatever else she's going to need. Gosh, just look at her raven hair! It's so thick, shiny, and long. I don't remember it being this long." Amalia chatted away, and soon the two had her undressed and into the bathtub, where Amalia took over, shooing him out and insisting he get them some takeout food.

By the time Emil returned with sacks of carryout, Amalia had her out of the tub, sitting at the dining room table, and wearing her grandmother's robe. Anne sat there expressionless, staring off into space. Quickly, Amalia set the table, and Emil dished out some for himself and Anne. He did find if he brought a bit up to her mouth and touched her lips with it, she responded by opening her mouth. All the while, Amalia chatted about just what they would need to get in the morning, including laying in groceries.

When they finished, it was getting late. "I'll take her into my bed tonight, in case she needs something during the night, sis."

"Fine, but don't you dare take advantage of her. Besides, she can't walk or stand very well without those super tall heels on. Honestly, I don't see how anyone could walk in them, but her feet are so weird and nothing else will fit her. Night Emil. Yell if you need something," Amalia said cheerily, adding, "I do hope she recovers."

A bit later, Emil had her sitting on the bed, her robe removed. Now he had a good look at her new physical form. Carefully, he draped her hair out of the way and sat down beside her, putting a loving arm around her. "Anne, it's me, Emil. Remember? We were going to get married before this happened to you. I will always look after you now. As soon as you recover, we can get married. I love you so, and I never gave up looking for you. Now let's lie down and get some sleep. I'm exhausted, Anne." Gently, he laid her down, being careful with her hair. After crawling in beside her, he moved her onto his shoulder, cradling her lovingly.

As Anne drifted into sleep, she felt warm and safe, and finally remembered who Emil was. In the dark, a smile appeared on her face, and she slept. In the morning, Emil was quite happy. Anne was beginning to respond! At least, she wasn't the apathetic vegetable she had been the night before. After getting her up, the bathroom needs done, and out to the dining room for warmed up leftovers, she began silently sobbing, but both Amalia and Emil noticed a distinct change in her; she was responding to their words now.

Seeing her responding and sobbing, Amalia took charge. "I'm going to take her measurements, pay a visit to the store, and get her some things. Plus, I'll get some groceries too. You take care of her. Wipe her face too, big brother. I think she's coming out of it, whatever it was."

"Thanks, sis. I owe you big time." Amalia left, and Emil helped Anne over to a sofa and sat down beside her, still cradling her in his arms. "It will be all right now. You are safe. We're at my grandparent's home. No one can harm you here. As soon as you recover, we'll get married too. I'm not going to lose you again. Once was entirely enough, Anne. I know. You can't speak. The doctor said you no longer have a voice box, but Anne dear, we'll manage anyway. At least, you still have some arms left and can sort of hug me. That's something I think." He chatted on, occasionally dabbing her face.

A while later, her tears stopped, and she seemed agitated. Emil made a wild guess. "You're quite angry, aren't you?" He was surprised to see her nod yes vigorously. "Well, you have every right to be angry. I promise you one day I'll find who did this to you and get justice." She nodded vigorously.

It dawned on him right then. "Hey, you can answer yes-no questions, Anne. That's great. We can communicate that way! I just have to keep on asking questions until we get it sorted out. Cool. I do love you so." She nodded, and he hinted, "You love me too?" She nodded vigorously, bringing a smile to both their faces.

Amalia returned close to noon with a car loaded with groceries, apparel, and even an electrostatic hair machine. She bubbled, "Oh, it's so good to see Anne looking so much better. School doesn't start for weeks yet, and dad said I could stay here and help look after Anne. I got her all sorts of clothes, and they insisted she had to have that hair machine too. Dad's paying for everything, by the way. Anne, you look so very much better today. Anne nodded yes vigorously, while smiling.

"We've worked out a way to communicate, sis. You ask yes-no questions and Anne nods. It's working well. You just have to guess the right question to ask," Emil explained. "You fix lunch, and I'll unload the car."

Later, the two began to dress Anne. Amalia explained, "We're going to try to leave that horrid corset off her. She and I rather decided that last night when I gave her a bath. I don't think she can breathe in it. I asked the UFB clerk about that, and she says the UFB women wear that rigid corset to reduce their back pains from their extra heavy breasts. So Anne, when you need a back massage to ease the pain, you just wiggle a bit, and we'll do it for you," Amalia chatted. While she had a wide selection of new outfits for Anne, wisely, Amalia asked her about what she wanted to wear.

Anne pointed an arm to the one simple cotton day dress. Amalia understood and asked, "Panties?" Anne shook her head no. "Oh, so you can use the bathroom easier. Got it." Anne nodded yes. And so it went. She still had no choice but to wear the tall heels though, and Amalia tied their laces securely so they didn't accidentally come loose and trip her. "There you go, one gorgeously hot young lady," Amalia exclaimed. Anne smiled.

Emil said, "Ladies, I really do need to do some work yet today. I'll be back by suppertime. Call me if you need me though." He leaned over and gave Anne a loving, passionate kiss, and she responded in kind. Emil left the home elated. He had his Anne back! Now for some payback.

Chapter 5—Plans and Counter-plans

Emil didn't quite know what his next move should be, but he felt he needed to alert the six young men he'd met at the Start of Summer Ball. Their fiancés were in trouble, especially since they appeared to be baronesses in the making. These men were not likely to be allowed to marry their sweethearts, that much was clear. Still, he'd been able to rescue Anne, and she was able to survive, so the six young women might be able to manage too, if only they could be removed from the clutches of the barons and CEOs.

One thing was uppermost in Emil's mind: these leaders were ultimately responsible for Anne's mutilation, as well as the awful mess their own daughters were in. Emil felt a responsibility to inform these young men what the situation was, that these barons and CEOs had probably been behind the mutilations of their supposed fiancés. He placed a number of calls, arranging a meeting around two that afternoon at a local pub, one that neither security guards nor the barons attended.

Right on time, Wotan, Wenzel, Dirk, Ebert, Stefan, and Rudolf arrived together. Emil waved to them and the six joined him. "Fellows, I met you and your fiancés at the ball, if you remember me. I've just found and rescued my Anne," Emil explained, and then outlined in detail all that had happened, including his theory that the CEOs had been behind the abductions and certainly the genetic mutations. "So fellows, if you truly love your women, you're going to have to act and soon," he ended.

"We know. We've just visited them. My God, Emil, they've blinded four of them. Now they can't talk or see. They're more helpless than helpless," Stefan declared angrily.

Rudolf added, "Plus, we now have someone on the inside feeding us information. We have until October 1 to get them out of there. That's when they are supposed to marry those beasts of men who call themselves barons!"

"Right!" barked Dirk. "These barons—all them are fat

cats, never doing an hour's work in a year, living off the sweat of the common man's labors. The barons are totally wicked, evil men!"

"Correction. Sadistic bastards," put in Wotan.

"Right. So we aim to bring down all the barons. Turn Blackwell-C into a free society, where the average man has a say in the running of our world," added Ebert.

"Don't forget the alien CEOs. We're getting rid of them too," Wotan pointed out. "They all have to go. We're starting a PR, a People's Revolution, here on Blackwell-C."

"Well, the barons have a long history of abuse of power," Emil agreed. "I can't believe they've made or allowed over ten thousand UFB women in the escort services and bordellos. That's just not right, and yet it's the norm. What they're doing to their own daughters—it's unbelievable. I know baronesses were always like that; I took history in high school. Long ago, the baronesses weren't blinded. Still, no one should treat women as though they were mere object, mere things."

"Right! You see our point," Dirk agreed with him. "Precisely the point. Plus, look at our world's economics. One way or another, everyone ends up working for their baron or now the corporations, who don't do a damned thing to better our world. They just suck up the life blood of others, giving back nothing except perversions and sadistic actions."

"About the only valuable corporation is General Goods, where some of us work now," put in Wotan, "but they don't have any real power. That's in the hands of GD and GE. Look what they give us: more, weirder, and worse genetic mutations. It was one thing centuries ago for them to amputate the baroness's arms and cut out her tongue, but now they are genetically mutating them. That's vastly worse, don't you think?"

The lads nodded their complete agreement. "Well, back then, it was only the few baronesses who suffered. Now, we have over ten thousand ordinary women who have been turned into helpless UFB women and ply the prostitution trade, sex dolls," Emil pointed out.

"We agree," Stefan broke in. "What's worse, those women you talk about—they're supposed to be earning a very good living, but we've yet to find any trace of those women who have gotten old, retired, and collected their small fortunes. Not one. I've looked everywhere. They retire all right, but then they vanish completely."

That didn't sit right with Emil. *Could they be being murdered?* "Fellows, let me look into that aspect. You say they just vanish without a trace?"

"Right. And no trace of their small fortune either," Stefan added.

"Okay. I did want to tell you fellows if you can rescue your women, they will respond well to yes and no questions. There's hope for them at least. Have you any idea how you are going to get them out of their castles and corporation headquarters yet?"

"Well, no not yet, but we have time," Stefan answered. "Right now, we're organizing the PR. When we strike, we want the whole world behind us."

Emil thought these fellows were being a bit unrealistic, a bit naive, but they were youthful, just as he was. They discussed several more things and then dispersed. Emil headed off to put in a few hours at work. He had much to ponder.

When he returned home, he was very pleased and surprised to see Anne standing inside the door waiting for him. She moved slowly up to him and gave him a passionate kiss. "Missed me, eh?" he teased, and she nodded yes. Together, with his steadying arm around her, they headed to the dining room for supper.

***

That night, four of the six barons and future executives met in secret again. All were shocked at what they'd seen. Superman soldiers. Even their physical appearance seemed an abomination to their eyes. "What the hell are we going to do now?" asked Hermann. Purposely, they had left the two clones out of their meeting.

"I sure don't know, but we have to be damned secret about it or we will end up as Wulf and Heinrich," Kurt pointed out the obvious. Seeing their brothers looking as they did filled the brothers with real terror of their fathers and the CEOs.

None of the four doubted for an instant their fathers wouldn't do the same to them if their fathers discovered they were plotting against them.

"We could use our guns and just kill them," Hermann suggested.

"Not if you want to live afterwards. Their security guards will shoot us in return without batting an eye," Johan pointed out.

"So what are we going to do?" asked Killian, growing frustrated. There seemed no answer, and he was terrified of ending up like Wulf.

"Whatever we do, we have to also take out those genetic freaks they are calling supermen," Johan declared.

"And those insane doctors who are doing all this," added Hermann.

"So how do we do it?" Killian asked.

"We need some bright ideas. Let's all think about this some. We have time. It's quite a few weeks until October comes. We must strike before the wedding day so we can all marry whom we want and take over for our hopefully deceased fathers," Johan said decisively. They all agreed to this.

***

Elsa wasn't idle either. Her heart figuratively went out to Susanne, Renate, Nadja, and Kirsa, who were now blinded on top of everything else. Irma and Karla could still see and no longer had to wear the golden veils. She continued sending along helpful hints to the other women's servants, but she knew she had to come up with some real help for these six women. What also bothered her was the fact that within the last fifty years, tens of thousands of poorer women of this world opted voluntarily to undergo the UFB woman mutation and then enter the prostitution trade, where they supposedly made a fortune. She'd not seen one of these women who had retired, though over a thousand had officially retired. Where had they gone? Had they really received their one lump sum payment, a small fortune? Knowing these men as she did, she highly doubted they were ever given their promised funds.

However, she had checked up on these UFB women, several times during the last fifty years. She found them all being very well treated, quite healthy, and in good spirits. None was allowed to become pregnant, unless they retired first. Several had done that, but were never seen again. At least, these women lived well, ate well, and were very healthy, something nearly unheard of on other worlds. This trade usually turned quite nasty for the women and usually within a few years of taking up this line of work. This was the only redeeming quality Elsa could see about the situation. Worse, according to world statistics, more women were volunteering to become UFB women and joining the trade each year. In Thromstead alone, nearly a thousand new women joined up the past year. Planet-wide, the numbers were far higher.

In fact, as far as Elsa was concerned the only tangible thing the corporations brought to this world was the creation of UFB women. Well, General Goods was the exception, she checked her blanket thought.

After tucking Susanne into bed one night, Elsa sat beside her thinking the situation over carefully. There was the UFB woman genetic bio agent. This was in use throughout the Federation of Planets. Besides turning the woman or man into a stellar beauty, it removed their arms, gave them enormous bosoms, malformed their feet, and created very long hair filled with neurons and axons, allowing each strand to have a powerful sense of touch. This much was common knowledge.

Here, in the GD labs, they have made a modification, most likely created by Dr. Lanzo, I suspect, but I have no proof yet. This modification allows the women to retain or regrow their upper arms only, but it also removes their voice boxes. However, Elsa also noted it restored or regrew the person's eyeballs. So here was the start of a cure for Susanne and the three others who were blinded.

Elsa also knew on a distant rim world, someone had come up with a cure that regrew arms and partially restored their feet. She suspected no one on this world knew about that discovery and could care less about it, but she definitely did.

Only today, she had finally received an off-world reply to her frantic message she sent weeks ago when the girls had undergone their genetic mutation and lost their voices. The reply was simple. "Only if there is no other way." Now, Elsa pondered that reply, placing it in context with what she knew about these genetic bio agents. Elsa sighed. There was another way, perhaps several. The boys that the six young women wanted to marry might be able to rescue them somehow. If that happened, they would need a way to undo some of these horrific modifications. She knew the six were second-generation UFB women and had been quite happy with their bodies and limitations, at least up until this latest genetic modification.

Besides, their boyfriends only knew them as UFB women and had fallen in love with them as they were, so if she could just get them back to that state, their boyfriends would be quite satisfied, as would the six young women, who knew nothing else. How to do that? The answer was simple. She had to get samples of these different bio agents. She could then get them duplicated in quantity and given to the six young women. Simple enough, except they were kept in the most secure location deep inside GD headquarters, most likely in sub-level twenty, deep underground.

Mid-August came. The young women only had six weeks remaining before they would be married off, and the game would be over. Finally, Elsa decided she simply had to act on her own. She had to have those samples. Around two in the morning, Elsa acted.

Carefully, she opened a cavity in her chest and removed a small device. She strapped it around her waist and activated it. It was a personal invisibility shield. Donning soft-soled shoes and double-checking that she gave off no scent, she headed out of Castle Berthold and down into the long tunnel that everyone used daily. She slipped past a dozing guard and headed on down the tunnel, arriving shortly at the entrance to GD headquarters. The door was shut, but she could see a guard on duty just inside. While she could just open it and enter, her invisibility would certainly spook the guard. She stood there for a few minutes before acting.

She opened the door and stepped inside. As she calculated, the guard looked up and saw no one. "What's going on? Anyone there?" he called out. Hearing nothing, he got up and looked at the illuminated empty tunnel, before mumbling,

"Crazy door. Another stupid malfunction. They should get the damned thing fixed one of these days." He sat down and continued reading his book. Elsa silently headed on into GD.

Dim lights provided the nighttime illumination, just enough to see by, though Elsa was prepared to use other means. Reaching the central elevators, she entered, when the doors opened in response to the usual button press, only this time nothing would be visible on their security recordings. She had pressed a number of the above ground floor buttons before, but never those marked with the SB designation, the sub-levels, of which there were twenty. She pressed the bottom button and waited. A security card reader lit up, waiting for a card to be swiped. Clearly, the elevator wasn't going down without a proper ID card scan.

Security, Elsa thought, *is a double-edged blade.* After quickly looking over the inside, she spotted the single recording camera and disabled it. Then, she jumped up, shoving the false roof cover aside. On her next jump, she latched on to the framework at the top of the elevator and pulled herself up. Very dim safety lights illuminated the otherwise black shaft, but she saw what she anticipate would be here, a metal ladder attached to one side of the shaft, the emergency access line. Hand over hand, Elsa headed downwards.

Approximately every dozen feet, she passed by an exit door. Each had a number on them with SB1 being the first she reached. *Nineteen to go,* she thought and continued her long downward climb. Elsa continued down moving at a brisk, uniform speed, pausing but a split second as she passed a set of doors. Finally, she reached the bottom set, though the shaft continued down slightly further. She used the emergency handles to force the doors open and stepped onto the floor of Sub-level Twenty, the secret genetics research laboratory of GD.

Again, dim night lights provided safety illumination, and Elsa began the much more difficult part. She was in an unfamiliar place with unfamiliar equipment, while looking for unfamiliar bio agents. These points were driven home to her after only a few footsteps into the main lobby area of the level.

The only clue she had was the dimensions of the level should be the same as any one of the above ground levels, compliments of corporate standard constructions, a fact she proved shortly.

She found coma recovery rooms. In fact, she saw two women undergoing the latest UFB woman genetic mutations, but moved on. Then, she came across six chambers that she'd never seen. Further, they were not in her data banks. Inside, she saw six very weird, human-like men. *Are they being grown somehow? All are identical to each other. Clones?* Suddenly, the strange behavior of Heinrich began to make sense. Baron Adler had cloned his own son. It was the clone who seemed to be attracted to men, but was being extremely kind to Susanne and Karla. If so, where was the real Heinrich? Dead perhaps? She didn't know, but moved on.

Eventually, she came across another locked room. A placard read: Bio Agent Supplies, but the usual yellow and black bio hazard warning stickers were plastered all over the door. Once more, the door could only be opened with the right ID card. Elsa made a decision. What she needed was likely inside. Carefully, she observed the area, spotted another security camera, and disabled it. Returning to the door, she shorted out the card reader, rewired it. The door opened.

Inside, lights turned on, activated by motion sensors near the door. Finally, Elsa got a break. Dr. Lanzo was meticulous with his bio genetic agents, labeling each very carefully. His larder was well stocked, she thought, and for both broad airborne coverage and single-person syringe injections of each genetic bio agent. She took one aerosol cylinder of each of the two types and a single-person syringe of each, stuffing them into a bag she found inside the room. Satisfied, she ignored the rest of the agents and headed back out of the room.

"I hear you. Show yourself," a deep male voice called out. "I saw the door opening so I know you are there." Like a cat, Elsa slipped away from the voice, but managed to get a view of him. She stopped in her tracks. There was the adult-size version of the weird human-like things being grown in the strange cloning chambers. Its neck was so thick that at first

Elsa thought it had no neck at all. Its arms were thicker than a man's legs, while its legs were probably twice as thick. The man was wearing a security guard's uniform, ill-fitting his most unusual form, and he must weigh in at over three hundred pounds, probably all muscle she concluded.

So they are manufacturing their own security superman guards. Ah, strong but slow. The guard moved rather slowly, though he was intent upon getting to the elevator doors as quickly as possible. He stood before the opened doors, just as they began to close. Not seeing anyone inside, he pushed the elevator call button, forcing the doors to reopen. He poked his head inside, looked around, and stepped back out. Though the doors tried to close again, they hit his body and quickly reopened once more. Baffled, the guard then moved away from the elevator, returning to his post.

Elsa took this opportunity and made a swift, silent dash for the doors, ducking into the elevator as the doors closed. She pressed the button for the main level and waited as the elevator began to rise. A red message flashed on the panel just above the array of floor buttons: Security Check In Progress. I wonder what that means. Elsa didn't have long to wait to find out. The elevator stopped at the next floor, Sub-level Nineteen. She pressed back against one side as the doors opened to reveal another one of the no-neck security guards, who poked his head inside, saw nothing, and spoke into a comm device, "All clear."

The doors closed and the elevator rose up to the next floor and stopped. Once more, the doors opened and a similar guard glanced inside, reporting, "All clear on eighteen." So it went all the way up. Evidently, Elsa figured she'd triggered some kind of alarm, and this was the security men's response, checking the elevator on each floor. Well, she thought, they aren't seeing a thing.

When she reached the main floor, the doors opened to reveal that same security man she'd encountered when she first entered the building. He still carried book in one hand, but had a d-gun at the ready in his other. He glanced inside, holstered his gun, and retrieved his comm device. "All clear on the ground level. Probably another glitch in the system." He turned to return to his post at the tunnel entrance doors. Elsa made a dash through the doors as they were shutting. The guard turned, probably hearing a bit of noise behind him, but again saw nothing as Elsa froze. If he moved back to the elevators, he would run right into her invisible form!

He shook his head and turned back, continuing to walk back to his post and chair. He had a small desk with several small monitors on it and many switches. He sat back down, plopped his feet up on the desk, and continued reading from his book. Elsa now had a problem. While she could just walk out through the door, its opening would again rouse suspicions. Already she'd raised more suspicions than she desired. She could wait until morning, when many people came and went through the doors here, and she could easily slip out undetected then, but that would mean she would be late getting to Susanne and assisting her. Again, that would draw suspicions to her. What to do?

She studied his switchboard carefully. An idea formed. Silently, she flipped a switch that opened the doors. The guard looked up, put down his book, drew his d-gun, and stepped towards the open doors. Unlike the rather dumb superman-guards below, he said nothing, but his eyes glanced in all directions, as he moved quietly to the opened doors, holding them apart with his free hand. Elsa positioned herself. He shook his head and turned to head back to his seat. At the last instant, Elsa ducked through the closing doors back into the dimly lit tunnel, undetected.

Minutes later, Elsa entered her own servant's quarters and turned off her PIS, her personal invisibility shield. She carefully stowed it back in her chest cavity and examined the four items in the bag. Each cylinder was labeled, complete with deploying instructions that a child could follow, compliments of the meticulous work of Dr. Lanzo, who carefully left nothing to chance or to a misunderstanding. Even boxes with the syringes contained single usage instructions: Inject into a vein. She then hid the four in her room and lay down on her bed to think.

She now had the means to cure the women, but she'd have to get these duplicated. That should be easy enough, she concluded. The baron had a duplication machine in the dungeon level. With this clever machine, she could make as many copies of these items as desired, assuming the machine didn't run out of basic ingredients. No, the question now facing Elsa was: did she tell the six boyfriends of the girls about these cures or not. She decided to see if they could actually mount a rescue effort. Time enough for cures after the girls were safely out of the baron's clutches.

***

"I have an idea," Stefan announced to his five close friends. "I've just heard that due to the incredible popularity of these new style UFB women, GD is going to ship a large number of cylinders of the new genetic bio agent to several other cities around Blackwell-C. Guys, this is it. We get our hands on this stuff, and we can use it to give the sadistic barons a taste of their own medicine. I've got their route plans!"

"Dynamite, Stefan. Love it," declared Dirk.

"Ych, but," broke in Wotan.

"But what?" Stefan nagged him, annoyed that he wasn't completely enthusiastic about his revelation.

"But if we attack them and steal the lot, won't the barons set a hue and cry for us? Certainly, they will increase their security arrangements, and we won't have any chance to use the stuff on them," Wotan pointed out his real concern.

That he was spot on sobered the six, until Stefan changed his plan. "Hey, what if we can somehow manage to steal just one sample? We can then duplicate it as many times as we want. GD has a fabrication machine, as do all the other corporation headquarters. If we do it right, they'll just mark the loss of one as a clerical error."

"Now you're thinking, Stefan," Wotan changed his mind. "Brilliant."

"Even better, I think I can get myself assigned to the delivery team," Rudolf suggested. "I've some connections. I should be able to filch one somehow. Come on; let's see this itinerary of yours, Stefan." The six looked it over for several minutes, comparing the locations to a world map.

"We need to make the loss either not noticed or look

like an accident," suggested Wotan. "Look, one delivery is to Leeds Medical Center. It's right by the Dorfmund River. What if you accidentally dropped one into the river? We could then retrieve it, and they'd think it was just an accidental loss."

"True, but we don't know if the water might ruin the stuff. Nice idea, but too risky," Stefan decided. "What if we have someone on the receiving end slip one out of the shipment for us? Do we know anyone who works at Leeds Medical Center?"

"Hey guys, leave the whole thing up to me," broke in Wenzel. "The deliveries will be the responsibility of General Goods, and I can get myself onto the delivery team, perhaps as their pilot." The six discussed other ideas, but ended up with Wenzel's plan as their best chance to rip off at least one of the bio agents undetected.

Three days later, Wenzel reported to the transport. "Your pilot reporting as ordered, sir," he saluted to the lieutenant in charge of this special delivery run. While he already knew their itinerary, he asked, "Flight plans, sir?"

"Here. Top secret. Top security. We're making a dozen drop offs today. Follow that list exactly. No deviations. Two guards and one supply clerk. We'll be making the deliveries. Got it?"

"Aye sir." So much for top secrets, he thought. He observed the three men loading racks of yellow cylinders, clearly marked as bio hazards with their distinctive yellow and black stripes. Each pallet contained a number of these cylinders nicely strapped down, easy to count. The clerk checked off the pallets as they were being loaded onto the ship, while Wenzel watched them, working out how to steal just one cylinder out of all these.

When they climbed onboard, playing dumb, he asked the clerk, "An epidemic or something going around?"

The clerk looked up. "Er, no. These are just the annual deliveries to the medical centers around Blackwell-C. Bio hazards require top security."

"Oh. I feel better already. Kind of worried there was an epidemic going around or something," Wenzel replied. He headed to the pilot's seat and got them airborne. In a half hour, he sat the transport down in the landing bay of a medical center. Now he watched the activities of the three men, looking for a way to snatch one.

With a watch's precision, the clerk re-counted the cylinders on a pallet, consulted his chart, and removed six, laying them aside. "Okay, delivery time," he announced. The three carried the heavy pallet down the bay ramp and over to a waiting clerk who counted the cylinders, making a checkmark on his clipboard. The center had three guards with him, and they took over for the lieutenant, clerk, and guard, who walked back to the transport. Once there, the clerk made another checkmark on his list and signaled Wenzel to take off again.

Each pallet contained sixteen cylinders, but any given medical center didn't receive that many. The counts varied. As the hours progressed, the pile of loose cylinders grew and shrank. As they approached the Leeds Medical Center, Wenzel decided to act. When the three left the ship carrying another nearly full pallet of cylinders, he snatched one from the extra's pile and headed back to the galley. There, he wrapped it in a waterproof container and dumped it into the disposal, returning quickly to his post at the bay doors. He was just in time. The lieutenant turned towards the ship and headed back along with the other two.

At the next stop, Wenzel fired off a text message and then erased it from his sent folder on his cell phone. Trash. Leeds. That was the entirety of the message. Two hours later, the clerk finally found the slight discrepancy. "We are short one cylinder, lieutenant!"

"What? How can that be? Come on; let's search the ship. Wenzel, you search too. Missing one cylinder," the lieutenant barked. Wenzel searched diligently along with the three men.

"It's one of those yellow things, right?" he said, looking into the same place as the clerk had just searched.

"Right. It has to be here somewhere. No one has come onboard while we were off, have they?" the worried clerk asked.

"Of course not. Who would want to come onto a delivery transport? Especially one carrying this hazard stuff.

Say, I'm not in any danger from it, am I?" Wenzel played dumb.

"Not unless the cylinder has ruptured. No, it has to be here," he insisted.

An hour later and after they'd torn the ship apart looking for it, Wenzel said, "Come on guys. Maybe you just miscounted or something. It's not here. It must be at one of the other stops we made, don't you think?"

The lieutenant said, "He's right. It has to be at one of the other centers. So just mark this one as complete with one less cylinder and let's be done with it. You certainly don't want them to conduct a full scale investigation of you, now do you?" he asked the clerk, whose face grimaced.

"Er, no. But. Well, that must be it. Someone will have an extra one. Can't hurt. Okay, I marked it done too. Let's get out of here." The lieutenant signaled Wenzel, who eagerly complied. Two hours later, they landed back at the spaceport outside Thromstead and took separate shuttles back to GD headquarters, while Wenzel headed over to General Goods.

That evening, Wenzel received a simple text: Got it. He smiled. Now they potentially had the means to end the barons' rule of their world and the CEOs' as well. Next, they faced the how question.

***

"What are you saying dad?" Killian asked. "That someone had stolen bio agents? Why would they do that? Are we providing them all they ask for?"

"I don't know son. I guess I may be an alarmist. Look, Dr. Lanzo is certain a cylinder or two are missing from his safe, but honestly, Sub-level Twenty is locked up tighter than a drum. Of course, the medical center's claim of being short one cylinder is probably just some stupid clerical goof. You're right. Why would anyone want to steal these? Heck, we almost give the stuff away at cost, dirt cheap really. Got to keep the locals content with their ever-growing demand for more UFB women."

"Security tapes show anything?" Killian asked. An idea jelled, something he'd not thought of before.

"No, I reviewed them myself. Nothing. Must just be

clerical errors."

"Hey, mind if I go down there and check it all out, review our security and all that, dad?"

"Heck, why not. Just don't antagonize Dr. Lanzo. He's very busy."

With a valid excuse to explore the security arrangements of Sub-level Twenty, Killian headed down with several purposes in mind. Were clones of himself and his other three friends being grown? Was it possible to snatch some of the bio agent? He could care less if some had potentially gone missing. That was his dad's problem. Stay alive and marry who he wanted—those were his goals right now. Ever since their last secret meeting, he had been paranoid that his father was about to turn him into a UFB woman and substitute a clone for him. The shocking images of Wulf and Heinrich were etched into his mind. Yes, the four had paid another visit to see for themselves what had truly happened to the two, not taking Johan and Hermann's word for it. Now those images burned in Killian's mind.

After reaching the bottom level, Killian began nosing around, checking on security arrangements. One of these new weird guards was on duty, a rather dim fellow, but powerful, Killian thought. "Doc says someone stole things from the safe," he said to Killian.

"But how? There's nothing on the security video for the last two weeks," Killian pointed out.

"But Seth-22 swears he saw doors opening."

"But did he see anyone there? Nothing on any camera feeds," Killian countered.

"Well, no, but," the man stopped mid-sentence, unable to determine what to say next.

"So you are saying an invisible man came in here and stole stuff?" Killian taunted the rather dopey fellow.

"Well, suppose not. Never seen an invisible man. Wonder how I could see one of them?" the oaf mumbled.

"Right. I'll check out the safe next." Killian left the man pondering the un-ponderable and walked passed all the growth clone chambers, glancing into each one, terrified that he would see himself!

"Oh, come to investigate my theft?" Dr. Lanzo startled him. Killian jumped nervously.

"Er, yes doctor. I'm under orders not to bother you. Dad says you're very busy."

"Of course I'm busy. But someone has broken into my safe and stolen bio agents, son. Come. I'll show you. Maybe you will listen to me," the doctor griped. Killian sensed he wasn't pleased with Dederick's response.

"So this is where all the dangerous stuff is stored?" Killian asked.

"Precisely. Kept under lock and key. See, this card reader only allows access by those with proper security, Dr. Marko, our nurses, and me. Not even your dad has access. Now here, you try to open it with your card," Dr. Lanzo insisted.

Killian swiped his card and the door opened. "See. I'm certain you don't have access to this bio hazard safe. Something isn't right here," Dr. Lanzo declared, convinced he'd shown this lad just what was what.

"Stay here for a minute. Back shortly. I want another test," Killian ordered, his mind racing. *Could this be a real security breach?* He found the oaf security man and had him follow him back to the bio hazard safe. "Swipe your card here, please." The man did so and the safe opened.

"So much for your secure safe, doctor."

"That's what I have been saying. Something is clearly wrong here," Dr Lanzo declared, vindicated.

"Okay, I'll look into it, doctor, and get to the bottom of it." The doctor nodded and left Killian to do whatever he did. Killian stepped inside and began reading the various labels. *So simple a child could use these*, he thought. Stacks of cylinders were stored on two separate racks. One set contained the original UFB bio agent, while the other contained the new modified one. These, Killian ignored. He wasn't interested in turning a whole bunch of women into UFB women. Then, he spied the single dose versions, stored in disposable syringes. Once more, they were stored on two separate shelves, each clearly marked.

Absolutely no one was watching him and he pocketed

four of the new modified version syringes. That done, he headed back to examine the card reader. He noticed it was a bit loose on the wall and sent for some tools. A half hour later, he had the unit disassembled and saw two wires had been crossed. He redid the wiring, reassembled the unit, and tested his ID card. This time, the safe didn't open. He smiled. Clearly, someone had tampered with this lock, but as far as he could tell, the place was packed with bio agent cylinders and syringes. Perhaps the thief had yet to plunder the safe. That made sense to him. He left a note for the doctor, saying he'd repaired the card reader and left.

Once in his private bedroom, he stashed the four syringes where no one would likely find them and then sent a secure text to his three friends, asking to meet secretly here tomorrow evening after supper. He also suggested they dress up and later visit one of the many erotic escort services to help assuage suspicions.

When they subsequently met, Killian whispered, "Guys, I have a solution for us." Gingerly, he picked up one of the syringes and showed the three. "Got four of them, one for each of us. Simple to use, just inject into any vein. This is the new modified UFB bio agent, like what was used on our sisters.

"Terrific, Killian! Now we have a way to dispose of them before they dispose of us," Johan declared. "But how are we going to inject them? We can't just give them a shot. Even if they are sleeping, they will feel it and wake up."

"Haven't worked that out yet, only when we can make best use of it," Killian responded. "Look, our best chance to pull this off is at the Autumn Ball, when all the other barons are here to celebrate. We inject them say two days before that, and at the ball, announce that our fathers have resigned and given us their positions. Plus, we can say they wanted to be like their wives. If anyone doubts it, we can show them their comatose bodies."

"Brilliant Killian, positively brilliant indeed!" Johan declared. "Now all we have to do is figure out how we can safely inject them."

"How about a bit of ether? Toss a vial in their bedroom around two in the morning. Wait a while, and then enter and inject them," suggested Hermann.

"Coolest. But where will we get the ether?" asked Kurt.

"I know a guy over in General Goods who can get us the stuff," suggested Killian. "I'll see about it tomorrow." He carefully stowed the syringe. "Now we best head off to the erotic escort service. Keep up appearances. I know my dad has been keeping tabs on my activities."

"Same here," Hermann added. "He thinks it's a good idea I frequent these places—says it's good for me." All four laughed and headed out to have some harmless fun.

"I know we have had our differences, Wotan," Killian began. Mid-morning the following day, he paid a visit on one of the rivals for the six young women. "But I need a favor. I need four bottles of ether on the quiet. I have a hundred credits extra for you if you can keep this between us. What say you?"

Wotan was rather surprised to find Killian paying him a visit. *Why does he want so much ether? Who is he planning to knock out?* "Well, I don't know. What are you planning to use it for? That much could cause some real harm."

Killian wasn't about to tell him what he wanted it for, but it was obvious to him Wotan was concerned. "Look, it's not going to be used against you or your friends. True, we've had our differences, especially with the six women. Let me put it this way, Wotan, you and your friends stand to benefit greatly from this, perhaps as early as fall."

Fall? Obviously, he was planning something. Wotan decided to play along. "Okay. No questions asked. No one to know. Four bottles. Have them for you tomorrow night. Meet me at Johan's Pub, say around nine."

"Great! Trust me, you won't regret this. Changes are coming," Killian replied. His mission was about done now.

"I know they are planning something," Wotan whispered to his five friends. He'd texted them and arranged this meeting that same night. He outlined what Killian had said during his surprise visit.

"What do they want four bottles of ether for?" asked Stefan. "That's enough to knock out a room full of people."

"Don't know, but he alluded to it happening this fall.

My guess is that they are planning something around the time we are, the Autumn Ball. All the barons of Thromstead will be there," Wotan answered.

"Well, I can't imagine anything those sadistic fellows can do that will in anyway help us or our world," declared Stefan.

"Still, it won't hurt to go along with them," Rudolf advised. The six agreed and Wotan delivered the ether the next night. He also sent word to their inside person in Castle Berthold that perhaps the barons-to-be were planning something around the time of the Fall Ball and that they now had a lot of ether.

Chapter 6—People's Revolution

Stefan's new organization began taking root. Slogans started appearing plastered on walls around Thromstead and other cities.

No work, no pay. PR.

Fat Cats, enough is enough. PR.

The only good baron is a dead baron. PR.

What have barons done for you in the last month, last year, last century, ever? PR.

Throw off your yoke of suppression. PR.

Tired of sadism? Get rid of your barons. PR.

Why should 99% slave for the other 1%? PR.

Work for yourselves and families, not the barons. PR.

Get rid of perversion and sadism. Oust the barons, PR.

"Well, it's starting have an impact," Stefan announced to his five close friends. Emil joined them to find out more about the People's Revolution. He'd seen signs around the city and wondered if there really was any hope.

"No kidding. But the barons send out goon squads to take them down or paint over them almost as soon as they go up," Rudolf pointed out.

"Critical mass," Stefan ignored his comments. "Once we reach a critical mass of supporters, of people, then the tidal wave will sweep across the sands, unstoppable by human hands."

"So why are we here tonight?" asked Wotan. They had been exceedingly careful in their organization of the People's Revolution. Organized in cells of six, only one knew the identity of one person in the cell above theirs. These six young men formed the topmost PR cell. As of early September, the numbers of cells had mushroomed to well over two hundred, giving an estimated number of supporters at around twelve hundred active supporters worldwide. They were gaining some press attention now as well.

"We're here because I've been contacted by two other

groups with similar objectives as ours, the Righteous of God and the Worker's Federation," Stefan answered. "The religious group will be here shortly, so don your face masks. We don't want our identities known just yet. Give Emil one too, will you Wotan?"

Before long, a man wearing a priest's robe entered the secure meeting room in the back of a disused warehouse. "Ah let us welcome the representative of the Righteous of God," Stefan announced the visitor. "Please come and sit. Share your worries and concerns with the PR high council."

The middle-aged man bowed respectively and took the only other seat. "I've come because we believe your cause may be similar to our own eternal struggle against the filth, corruption, sadism, perversion, and greed that has for untold centuries kept our world in abject poverty and barbarism. If your goals and objectives meet with ours, the Righteous of God is prepared to back the People's Revolution, to bring positive, holy change to Blackwell-C."

Stefan acted as the spokesman. "Our objectives are straightforward. The barons and their ruling system have long, long outlived any useful reason for existence. The barons and their rule must be terminated forever. In its place, we propose free and open elections to form a democratic system of rule. That also means we must overthrow the yoke of these new alien corporations, who have brought their sadistic gifts to our world, these supposed UFB women genetic mutations."

"This is what we, the few religious faithful of Blackwell-C, have wished for, prayed for, and worked for since ancient times. I'm afraid our numbers have been shrinking, due in part to the widespread adoption of the many houses and forms of prostitution. The aliens have brought the Devil and his minions to Blackwell-C, corrupting tens of thousands of our young women, turning them into devil's spawns, while corrupting our young men leading them to sin with these awful creatures that look like grotesque women."

He chanted on about the evils, sins, and sadistic men for quite some time. Finally, he gave the PR the full support of his Righteous of God. After he left, Stefan said, "Well, that's some support. As we all know, religion is pretty well dead on our world. His group has about ten thousand supporters across the entire world, not large, but quite outspoken. Next up is the Worker's Federation. These are big-time players."

Their representative entered also wearing a mask that was a comical caricature of Baron Adler. "Call me Mr. X. As you know or should know, the Worker's Federation is gigantic. We represent millions of workers across our world. For two centuries, we have been fighting for better working conditions, better housing, better medical care, better food, better supplies, better safety, and better darn near everything."

"Well," Stefan replied, "that's what we intend to do. Wipe out the barons and their sadistic rule forever and to stop the alien corporations from consuming our world in their greedy hands."

"I doubt you can do that, son, but power to you if you can. Of course, what with all the alien new inventions and gifts, our members now are demanding additional compensations for their labors, and the barons are only slowly giving what our workers desire. Dragging their feet, some insist. Right now, our people are demanding a UFB woman in each worker's household. Not these new abominations that can't speak and have useless upper arms, mind you, but the real beauties, what the aliens call the perfect woman, the UFB woman."

"Huh? Are you telling us that the average worker on Blackwell-C wants a UFB woman in his house?" asked Stefan, very much surprised to hear this detail.

"You bet. They are stunning, gorgeous, beautiful women. What man in his right mind wouldn't want such a woman in his house to come home to after a long, tough day at work. Besides, they are supposed to deliver incredible sex. Workers need the encouragement, the support, and the gift these women can provide to them. So how does your PR stand on this issue? Mind you, right now this is the hottest issue our members have. Why should only the filthy, corrupt barons and wealthy class have sole rights to these incredible women? Hell, it's the backs of our workers that keep our world running. It's they who should have this luxury, not the lazy rich bastards."

"Well, we don't see why your workers can't have UFB

women in their homes. Look, we six here wanted to marry six of them, but the barons are trying to make that impossible for us," Stefan admitted. That was all the man wanted to hear, and he fully threw the support of the Worker's Federation behind the PR movement.

In less than a week, the results of this support were widely visible across Blackwell-C! So much so that finally the barons could no longer ignore the PR. Here in Thromstead, Baron Adler called a special meeting of the nearly two dozen local barons.

"This PR movement has now gotten the support of the Worker's Federation," Adler explained. "While we've been slowly giving more UFB women to the city, it's obviously not enough. We are going to have to take these people seriously."

"Well, let's just raid their meetings and wipe them out," one baron suggested.

"Let's make assembling in groups of five or more illegal. Arrest any who disobey," another suggested.

"Hell, just gas them, turn then into the UFB women they desire," another barked.

"Hey, they would still be men," Adler cautioned.

"What about making that assembly law and then sending in our new super-soldiers to break up larger assemblages?" Aldric suggested. And so the ideas came and went. By the end of the meeting, the barons finally agreed on how they were going to handle the situation.

Baron Adler summed up, "Okay. We will announce our new policy. No assemblage of people can exceed five. Illegal demonstrations against the rightful government of Thromstead and Blackwell-C will be terminated. Those arrested will be subjected to the genetic bio agent and turned into UFB women and UFBMD men. The women will then be given to the various establishments where they will be put to more profitable work. The men will be sent to our new breeding complex in the Blackwoods. There, they will be bred to volunteer women, who will give birth to more beautiful UFB women and super-genius sons. Their sons will be raised by us barons, who will put their revolutionary discoveries to good use." Everyone agreed he had all the points made.

Later that day, he held a special press conference and outlined these new changes, adding, "Mind you, there will very likely be collateral damage when we gas those illegally assembling. Those accidental victims, those men and women who get genetically mutated, will be the responsibility of those who chose to violate the law and defy your ruling barons." He also refused to take any questions from reporters. Baron Adler never answered any reporter's question. Never had, never would. They were beneath him, second-guessing a baron's decisions.

"There, that should put a mountain of ice on this stupid People's Revolution thing," he explained to Hermann when he returned. "Tomorrow, son, I want you to pay a visit to the Blackwood complex. I'm told Wulf and Heinrich have been moved there, and two women have volunteered to breed with them in hopes of having super-genius sons."

Hermann didn't wish to go, but he knew he dared not refuse. He just might find himself there the next day! The Blackwoods complex was about ten miles south of Thromstead, located of course in the Blackwoods, a dense forest of dark trees. The complex was a sprawling one, having once been an assisted living center for the aged. Rising costs had put them out of business, especially since the barons stopped financially supporting the center. Now the barons owned the complex, but until now, it had remained vacant.

Hermann found a dozen staff had been hired. One was a medical doctor and four were nurses and assistants. The rest managed the facility's needs. He found his brother and Wulf now had their own private room. Heinrich was still dressed quite elegantly, and if Hermann didn't know better, he'd swear she was one of the perfect UFB women, the new style of course. Heinrich tried to get his brother's attention, to tell him something, but of course had no way. Hermann quietly departed when his brother began sobbing. He couldn't face that. Besides, there wasn't any cure for Heinrich.

Now more than ever, Hermann swore they would take care of the barons and the two CEO leaders, before they turned them into such pathetic, helpless abominations. A very sober Hermann returned to the castle. *Perhaps, that's why dad sent me there, to warn me.* At their next secret meeting, Hermann related what he'd seen to the other three.

Kurt suggested, "Well, now we know where we can send them, the new UFBMD men that we make." The four agreed on that.

Two days later, the barons put their new law and procedures into operation. Unknown to them though, the Worker's Federation had an entirely different motive behind their challenge. First, as they later explained to Stefan, they wanted to create just such an incident that would raise anger against the barons and more support for the PR movement. Second, they saw this as a sneaky way to obtain more UFB women from the barons, who simply weren't creating them fast enough or giving them to the Federation of Workers.

Twenty women volunteers, wives of key members of the federation, along with two men, assembled in City Park, holding a now illegal assemblage. Standing on a box, the men chanted all the usual slogans, as though this was an actual rally. Meanwhile, the volunteer women, wearing men's clothing, stood before them. Some carried placards with the usual slogans. Others waved pennants in support of the PR movement.

As expected, Baron Adler soon received notice from the mayor an illegal assemblage was in progress at City Park. Later when Emil questioned his father about his involvement, Mayor Beifeld replied, "Son, I had no choice but to notify the barons. They pay my salary. If it didn't report it, they could arrest me." Now, Emil was convinced the barons had to go.

After consulting with Dr. Lanzo, Adler ordered one cylinder of the older genetic bio agent be dropped on the crowd. It took his engineers an hour to rig up a release mechanism to the cylinder that would release the gas rapidly. Twenty minutes later, a GD shuttle pilot flew over City Park and released the *bomb*. When the falling yellow cylinder was fifty feet above the small group, this new release mechanism triggered, releasing the cylinder's contents in one big flash. The toxic agent spread out like falling rain over the entire area, though as it spread, it became diluted. According to Dr. Lanzo's estimates, those outside the park shouldn't be effected.

Unfortunately, there was collateral damage. Six women with their seven children playing on the nearby swing sets were infected, as well as the small group of protestors. Naturally, the incident received wide press coverage, but what was unexpected was the sudden disappearance of the protesters. The husbands of the women wore gas masks and dashed in to pick up the comatose bodies of their wives, carrying them off to an unknown location. When the baron's crew finally believed it was safe to enter City Park, they found only the comatose bodies of the collateral victims. Later, the husbands of these innocent women and fathers of the children insisted on having them returned to them once they recovered from their comas. Baron Adler acceded to those demands.

The Worker's Federation used this incident to gain even more support. The day after, groups of three volunteer workers marched through the streets of Thromstead, carrying signs, photographs of the victims lying comatose on the grass, and shouting. "This is what your barons do to you. Barons attack innocent women and children. How long before the barons get you?" They also chanted more unspeakable things as well. Yet, they were within the law, as only three were present on any given street. Nearly three hundred volunteers spent the day marching the streets.

The Righteous of God did the same but for entirely different reasons. Their message was one of sinners, devil's spawn, greed, and corruption. They too were careful to have only three members in the marching, protecting group. Unlike the Worker's Federation, only a dozen were on the streets, but the four groups spent the entire day protesting.

Terrible Tuesday became a rallying cry for days. Cleverly, some twenty-two working families received precisely what they most desired, a UFB woman in their midst.

Next, the Armed Forces of Blackwell-C decided to weigh in on the events. General Ernst Von Dorfsted of the North Group and General Franz Himmel of the South Group with several members of their staff, including Colonel Achima Nacht and Colonel Hilda Angst representing the women in the military, paid an unexpected visit to the two top barons here in

Thromstead. Sitting stiffly in their bright red uniforms with black trim, the group waited patiently in the throne room for the two barons, baronesses, and sons to receive them. Shortly, Baron Adler and Baron Aldric entered, escorting their wives, while their four very curious sons followed along behind them.

Johan received word of this unexpected visit and whispered to Hermann, "What's this all about?" Hermann shrugged, suggesting maybe it was because of their retribution on yesterday's protesters. The barons took their seats, while their wives struggled to get into theirs. The four young men moved around behind the thrones, more curious than threatened.

"Welcome, generals, colonels. What can we do for you today?" Baron Adler opened the meeting cordially. He too was curious, not worried. Normally, the generals responded to a summons by the barons, not the other way around.

General Ernst stood and spoke first. "Barons, baronesses, this business now being called Terrible Tuesday in the press."

"Ah yes. Well, we simply can't have illegal protests disrupting our city," Adler cut him off. "After all, either we take action or we have to call in your services. In this case, the number of rioters, protestors, criminals were small. We saw no need to involve you and your fine men and women, generals."

"Yes, we definitely appreciate you not involving the military in this most unfortunate situation," General Franz replied. "And yet, the Worker's Federation does have some valid points, particularly with respect to the UFB women, baron."

"Please, do go on," Baron Adler hinted, suspecting what the man may well desire. "It is our fondest wishes that the brave, loyal men and women who join our armed forces are well-fed, well-trained, well-armed, and their needs met."

"Yes, that is as it should be," General Ernst suggested.

General Franz continued, "I believe you have said it, their needs met. While our soldiers are indeed well fed, trained, and armed, there is one need that is, shall we say, rather incomplete, always has been, but perhaps now, not always will be."

"Some needs of our soldiers aren't being met?" Baron Aldric broke in, feigning shock. "Please, do tell us about those needs. As your commander-in-chief, it is our responsibility and duty to see that those brave men and women who protect us and our entire world have everything they need. You have only to ask."

General Franz explained, "Our soldiers have needs just as you men do, the wealthier of Thromstead, and even the workers. What man wouldn't want to have his own incredibly beautiful UFB woman around, eh? While there are many more now than they were even a couple years ago, our soldiers can't afford such women as can be found at Carstens' for example. As you have seen, even the lowly workers greatly desire these beauties and are demanding access to them. We've come here today to request that you barons provide UFB women for the Armed Forces."

"Yes," broke in General Ernst, "we've drawn up a plan that calls for one UFB hostess per squad. North Group needs four thousand UFB hostesses, as does South Group. With each squad having their own UFB woman hostess, think of the morale boost that will give them."

Baron Adler laughed, "General, you don't have to sell me on that point. I believe we all agree it's high time our soldiers have such a perk, don't you think, Aldric?"

"Oh very much so. The security of our world depends upon our brave men and women of the North and South Groups. We should see to this at once, Adler," Baron Aldric replied.

General Ernst cleared his throat and motioned to Colonel Achima. She stepped forward a foot. Her hair nicely tied in a bun beneath her red cap, she spoke forcefully, "And also a few of the special UFBMD men for us brave women soldiers, barons."

Adler laughed, slightly embarrassing the two colonels. "Excuse me. I wasn't making fun of your request. Rather, I'm amazed it has taken this long to surface. Of course, you women have similar needs to men. Yes, you should have your own hosts as well. How many are we going to need?"

"Oh, well in that case, twenty would be ample, barons.

Thank you for considering your female soldiers' needs as well as your men's," Colonel Achima responded. From the looks on the two women's faces, his response was what they had hoped for.

"All right then, I will make a new proclamation today, calling for eight thousand female volunteers to become your new hostesses and twenty men to be your new hosts. Of course, they will need comparable salaries to yours, perhaps a bit more, which we will cover," Baron Adler stated. "However, their upkeep and clothing allowances must come out of the Armed Forces' budget. Can you handle that much?"

"Yes. We can make allowances for their care and clothing needs, barons. How soon may we anticipate their arrival? The boost to your soldiers' morale will be enormous," General Ernst asked what he truly wanted to know.

"If we could have them all together today and the conversion process started, it will be at least two weeks before they have adjusted to their new physical conditions and be ready to undertake their new roles as hostesses and hosts. We'll get on the acquisition process today and keep you fully informed. Thank you for bringing this vitally needed situation to our attention," Baron Adler responded and giving them a subtle hint the meeting was over. The generals and colonels bowed and departed with very pleased looks on their faces.

Once they were gone, Adler commented, "Well, that was certainly unexpected. We have to go along with their requests, naturally. We can't alienate our soldiers, that's certain. Come on, Aldric. We have to figure out where the devil we're going to get eight thousand women."

"The hard part will be the twenty men," Aldric added.

"Oh I'll volunteer," Heinrich pipped up. "I could be a fine host or hostess, either way, dad." Adler grimaced and didn't deign to give him a reply.

The two barons paid Dr. Lanzo a hasty visit. "Yes, yes, no problem. I can have the genetic bio agent ready for you yet today."

"Good. And start a new Heinrich clone while you are at it. I'm going to give Heinrich his wish," Adler added. Aldric smiled, he knew that was coming.

That afternoon, Baron Adler made another worldwide announcement on all news channels. "Greetings. I have just met with our top generals. Together, we have worked out a new set of extremely vital positions in our Armed Forces. Each squad of our brave soldiers must have a UFB woman hostess. Additionally, we will need a few men to become hosts for the female soldiers as well. We can't omit their needs either. We need eight thousand young women between the ages of eighteen and twenty-five who want to volunteer to become a Blackwell-C Armed Forces Squad Hostess, and twenty men to volunteer to become Squad Hosts for our female soldiers. The pay for these new positions will be fifty thousand credits per year, payable upon retirement from service. Yes, these brave hostesses and hosts will be very well paid for their service to help defend our world from attacks. Those who wish to undertake this new and valuable career path are to notify your local baron as soon as possible. Once the slots are filled, waiting lists for the future will be created. So if you wish to get in on this golden opportunity, I suggest you act quickly. The slots will fill up extremely rapidly. Thank you."

Considering the average worker's pay was barely thirty thousand per year and a solider's pay ten thousand more, Baron Adler hoped women would jump at this opportunity. "But dad, how can we possibly afford this?" Hermann asked his father after the broadcast was finished and they headed back to the castle. "That's four hundred million credits per year!"

Adler laughed loudly, embarrassing his son. "Kid, you have an awful lot to learn before you are ready to step into my shoes. Look, hardly any of that will ever be paid out. The UFB escort women work at their jobs until they get quite old, since they retain their youth and beauty at least until they are sixty. They accumulate their wages. When they retire, the women simply vanish. No funds are ever lost. As far as the army is concerned, the basic hitch will be for four years. But as we both know, the women volunteers will likely want to stay on indefinitely, and when they do retire, they will disappear too. We're never going to be out any substantial funds, just the occasional ones here and there to keep up appearances."

Shocked to hear this, Hermann wisely didn't respond. *So all these women we've been visiting at the escort service are never going to be paid? Good God. That's not right! We have to change that! I wonder what else we don't know about.* Later that night, he relayed this shocking news to his three compatriots, who were just as shocked about this as he was.

The six leaders of the People's Revolution also heard the baron's public address and met to discuss this strange twist. "Well, this way, the barons keep an even tighter leash on the army," Stefan pointed out. "Still, it doesn't impact us. The generals obey whoever is their commander-in-chief and will continue to do so as long as they get their money and now their UFB women hostesses."

"This is getting confusing," Rudolf commented. "We have to guarantee the Worker's Federation they'll get all the UFB women they want and now the army too. At the same time, we have to convince the Righteous of God we're eliminating the UFB women. How are we going to do both? We wanted to make Blackwell-C a better world."

Stefan laughed, "Hell if I know, but first we have to defeat and eliminate the barons worldwide. Focus on that, guys. This new situation with the army will certainly keep the barons occupied, giving us a better chance to get them. Come on. We have planning to do. It's already September. Time's running out."

An hour after his announcement, the phones began ringing at the barons' castles, but their staff took the calls, naturally, taking down the names of the volunteers. A mass conversion was planned for Friday and the volunteers were told to report to a special warehouse by ten that morning. Meanwhile, under Dr. Lanzo's guidance, the warehouse was prepared for the women and possibly few men. He also advised twenty other cities on how to handle the sudden influx of volunteers. The barons also had to assist the UFB Women's Apparel stores around the world gear up for this enormous influx of new women to clothe. This meant the fabrication machines controlled by the barons were cranked up to generate thousands of women's garments, shoes, and their needed electrostatic hair machines. General Goods was responsible for delivering mountains of the items to the warehouses and UFB Women's Apparel stores around the world. So yes, it was a hectic few days for all.

As Adler anticipated, they had their eight thousand volunteers in just over one day. Considering the incredible pay these women would earn, who couldn't turn such an offer down? As one new volunteer exclaimed when she learned she was accepted into the hostess program, "Wow! I'll be rich in just four years!" Of course, none of the volunteers knew the UFB women would have such intense sexual drives that they would find it terribly difficult actually to retire after just four years. Adler also knew this but didn't mention it to Hermann either. That son was too dumb to become his heir.

Heinrich was elated to learn Adler agreed he could become an army host! Gaily, he headed to the warehouse, cheerful as a lark. He had no idea another clone was being grown to replace him later on. The generals were quite specific about what they wanted in hostesses. They had to be the original form, since hostesses were required to be able to speak. However, the colonels wanted their hosts to be the new version with the short upper arms and no voices. Wisely, the barons complied with the army's wishes.

Friday night, across the world, twenty-one warehouses held eight thousand women and twenty men who were now in their mutation comas. All were expected to come out of them sometime late Tuesday night. Then would come the extensive adaption period. At this point, the generals sent along volunteers to assist the new hostesses and hosts as they learned to adapt to their new situations. By the beginning of fall, these women and men finally joined their squads and began their new jobs as hostesses and hosts. For quite some time, the entire North Group and South Group paid little attention to the defense of the world, but then there wasn't any attack going on or uprising to put down.

Chapter 7—First Strike

September 21 was the official beginning of fall on Blackwell-C. Quite why this day of the month was chosen to represent the occasion was lost in history. Astronomically, fall began on Blackwell-C on September 15. The Autumn Ball was scheduled to take place on that date, beginning officially at seven that night, though the many guests would be arriving at Castle Berthold around six. Each year, Adler and Aldric took turns hosting the event, and this year it was Adler's turn. Thus, for several days before the event, much of the baron's staff was involved in preparing the huge ballroom for dance. Many preparations had to be made, since over five hundred were invited, though many more party crashers were also allowed in. The barons showed *generosity* at these events.

"Are we ready?" asked Johan. He and his three companions met around seven on the nineteenth in his room to discuss last minute details. Tonight, they would strike a blow for their own survival and desires.

"You bet. I saw a new Heinrich clone being grown down in the secret lab yesterday. So dad's gotten rid of the current gay Heinrich clone," Hermann said with distaste. "That clone is getting what he wants." All four laughed cynically. *Still, probably that clone would have his heart's desires fulfilled,* Johan thought.

"Good. So we wait," Johan explained for the sixth time, "until two in the morning. Set our watches. Drop the ether bomb. Wait an hour before going in there and make damned sure you are wearing your mask. Remember, inject it onto a vein, and disintegrate the syringe with your d-guns once you are finished. We don't want any traces to come back to us."

Johan continued his last minute orders. "Remember, we want to delay discovery of just what's going on for as long as possible. So we tell our mother's servant that our dad is sleeping in, that he has been overworked these past few days and is catching up on sleep. Delay discovery of their comas for as long as we reasonably can without drawing undo attention to us. Then, when it can't be avoided, send for the doctors and act shocked and surprised. Probably, we will need to conduct searches for intruders who attacked our fathers and all that. Put on a good show. Then, one by one, we will each announce, as our father's heir, we are taking over. You all know what to do after that. We can make announcements to the world at the Autumn Ball, including our desired fiancés."

"We have it down, Johan," Hermann grumbled. "We are ready. Just a few more hours and we'll be free from the constant threat of being turned into UFBMD men, like Heinrich and Wulf. We'll have avenged them too. I'll see the new Heinrich clone is terminated. Let's do this, guys!"

"One for all and all for one," Kurt declared, and they shook hands and left Johan's room.

***

"All for one and one for all," declared Stefan. At the same time over at General Goods, Emil, Stefan, Rudolf, Wotan, Wenzel, Dirk, and Ebert were holding their own meeting. "We have the gas release mechanism installed on all the cylinders. How goes the fake ID cards, Emil?"

"I got them ready, one perk of being the mayor's son. I'll have my revenge on the men who kidnaped my Anne. Let's hope they don't change their codes." He handed out the various cards to the others.

"Let's go over the plans and layouts again to be doubly sure we've not forgotten anything," Stefan suggested. "We all go to the ball as planned, let our fiancés know not to worry, and that we will be rescuing them soon. Then, we will all leave except Wotan and Wenzel. After we leave, they set off the two bombs, one in the ballroom, and one in at the entrance to the dungeon where all the security men are quartered. Emil and I will go back to our headquarters, GD, and unleash four bombs there—top floor, ground floor, Sub-level One, and Sub-level Twenty. Dirk and Ebert will sneak into GE headquarters and unleash four bombs there. Same pattern. Rudolf will head over to Castle Berringer and unleash two bombs. We meet at the entrance of Castle Berthold wearing our bio containment suits around midnight. We go in and rescue our fiancés. Then, we make a public announcement."

110

"Are others equally prepared to attack the other barons at their celebrations?" asked Emil. He knew that only taking out these barons wouldn't solve the problem. Other barons in other cities would just take over later on, though they'd probably fight among themselves for such power.

"Precisely," responded Stefan. "They will be launching their attacks at precisely eight o'clock. By nine, gang, there won't be a single baron or baron's heir left on all Blackwell-C. The PR will succeed. In the morning, we'll go on national news and announce total freedom for all Blackwell-C, and we'll have free elections within a month. Two more days, gang, and we'll be free of the barons' yoke and free from the alien corporations."

"And I and Anne can finally rest in peace. Those who did this to her will be punished," Emil declared.

"Right, Emil. Nothing can go wrong now. We'll be victorious in just two more days!" Stefan declared.

"But what are we going to do about the Worker's Federation's demand for vastly more UFB women for their members?" asked Rudolf. "How do we sell that to the religious nuts?"

"We will worry about that later on, after we have taken control of Blackwell-C," Stefan declared. "First things first. Are we all clear? Okay then. We will meet again tomorrow night to double-check our preparations. Stay alert and don't attract undo attention to yourselves." They agreed and the meeting broke up.

Emil arrived home to the waiting arms of Anne, who stood just inside the front door wobbling to keep her balance. She and Amalia heard his car drive up, and Amalia had helped her up and into position. "Miss me, my love?" Emil said, his arms opening before her. Together, they met and hugged. She gave him a passionate kiss, her best way of telling him she missed him.

After helping her get to the sofa, the three sat down. "Well, it's still on. Two more days and we'll have our revenge on those who abducted you and did this to you. Then we can finally have closure, Anne."

Amalia spoke up, "Emil, so many young women are

now getting themselves modified into beautiful UFB women. Eight thousand became army hostesses. I know four of them. They were ecstatic about the opportunity. Fifty thousand credits per year is incredible pay. They'll be gorgeous super-models and fabulously wealthy in no time."

"Yes, but they will also be helpless too. Sex dolls. Surely, you don't want to be that do you?" Emil asked.

Amalia flushed beet red. "But Emil, you aren't a woman. We have to be beautiful to attract just the right man. Beauty is one of our prime weapons, so to speak, but you probably don't know anything about that."

"Amalia, you don't want to spend your life helpless like Anne," Emil replied. Anne shook her head no, trying to add what little she could.

"Big brother, you forget I've been to many baron's balls too, with you and dad. Susanne, Karla, and Renate—they are full of life and doing very well—okay, that was before they got modified as Anne is and now blinded. That's beyond awful! But before, they were happy and full of life. Plus, they were just incredibly beautiful, if you hadn't noticed. What girl wouldn't want to look like a super-model? Besides, dad's told us they don't even age, not until they get positively ancient. So you two are lucky. Anne's going to look positively gorgeous almost forever, not like normal women. I don't want to look all baggy and ugly by the time that I'm forty." She had no real idea of just what she'd look like at forty, but it seemed ancient from her sixteen years.

"But Amalia, you are only sixteen and still growing up. Already, you are beautiful," Emil countered. Anne nodded yes vigorously.

"Ha. My nose is slightly crooked. My teeth are a bit angled. I have an ugly blemish on my right cheek. My hair looks bedraggled and thin. My left cheek is slightly higher than my right cheek. Don't tell me I look pretty. I don't, Emil, and a girl has to look beautiful to find the right guy," Amalia insisted and declared. She was too embarrassed also to say that her breasts were too small.

Emil realized he wasn't getting anywhere with Amalia, so he tried a different approach. "Look sis, we're not religious nuts, but I can tell you that the right man will come along and love you as you are, for what you are. Anne and I found each other and fell in love. We were going to be married before she was abducted and so terribly changed. True, she's beautiful now by many standards, but she can't talk and is almost helpless. Sis, that is a horrible price to pay just to look pretty. You shouldn't be worrying about boyfriends for several more years yet. Trust me. The right man will come along, sis. He will."

Seeing she was hitting an immovable object, Amalia cleverly changed the topic, asking how the PR plans were coming. *I have to find a way for me to become as beautiful as Anne is, whether Emil likes it or not. There must be a way, but I don't want to join the army to do it. I don't like all that fighting and stuff. Maybe the way to do it is to join the Worker's Federation protests.*

Worker's Federation hadn't remained idle. After Terrible Tuesday played totally into their hands, they continued to hold similar *protest* assemblages, but spaced five days apart, giving them time to get their current *crop* of newly made UFB women recovered and back with their husbands. Already they had carried out five more of these *protests*, each with the same, predictable results. The barons unleashed the older bio agent on the illegal protesters, ignoring the inevitable collateral damage. However, after Terrible Tuesday, whenever anyone saw these large groups beginning their protest marches, they fled in fear. Thus, indirectly, subsequent collateral damages were now almost nil.

Typically, the Worker's Federation kept the number of women in the assemblage to twenty, a manageable number at one time, though at least one male had to volunteer, acting as the spokesman for the group as they marched. The women wore men's clothing and hats, helping to maintain their cover as workmen protesting.

Amalia had kept close watch on these events, since she was staying with Anne all the time and there was little else to do except watch the TV. She carefully noted when each *protest* occurred and discovered they were spaced five days apart. If they kept to the same schedule, the next one would be tomorrow afternoon. That night while she waited for sleep to come, Amalia decided to take matters into her own hands. There was no reasoning with Emil. She believed he just didn't understand women.

The next morning after breakfast and Emil headed off to work, she got Anne handled and announced, "I've got to run some errands. I'll be back later. I'm going to have one of my friends drop by and check on you." Anne nodded and she left, heading straight for a local Worker's Federation office. There were dozens of these around the city.

She entered and went to the receptionist. "I'd like to volunteer to be one of today's protestors and become a UFB woman," she said politely.

"Oh wonderful! So many have volunteered. We need you to fill out this form. You must list the person we contact to come and get you after you enter your coma. The contact person will be notified when your new initial clothing, shoes, and hair machine are ready to be picked up," the receptionist explained. Amalia filled out the form, listing Emil as her contact and her father as the secondary contact. That done, a man told her where to report, and Amalia happily headed off to join the small group of women.

At a stonemason's warehouse, she found other women were already there, chatting excitedly about their coming genetic modification, while changing into work pants, shirts, and boots. Each helped the other to tie up their hair and position a hat to help disguise them. Around one, a man entered and handed out signs, placards, and banners for the women to carry. "Are you all ready, ladies? On behalf of all workers of Blackwell-C, we thank you for your gifts." With that, they lined up and headed out onto the streets of Thromstead, chanting the various slogans.

As they marched along, many locals showed their support by tossing a fist into the air, but then they just as quickly moved away from the small group! They marched along many blocks, and Amalia began to believe this wasn't going to work, that the barons had given up trying to stop them. Just when she was about to give up the whole idea, a small shuttle appeared overhead. She saw a yellowish gas cloud appear just over the group's heads. It smelled sort of sickly sweet. The man leading them ordered them to stop and inhale deeply. Amalia did so. Her body felt strange, rather weak. Slowly, her legs began to give out, and she slumped to the ground, slipping into a coma.

"Yes, Amalia Beifeld. That is the woman's name. She's listed you as her sponsor. You're to come pick her up at this location. We'll be in touch in three days asking for her measurements so we can provide her with the initial clothing, shoes, and hair machine," a man said. He called Emil around two that afternoon, telling him Amalia had volunteered to become another UFB woman.

Emil gasped! Carefully, he jotted down the address. Swallowing hard, he found his voice, "Anne, it's Amalia. She's gone and done it! She's in a coma. I have to go pick her up. Will you be all right for a short while?" Anne nodded and began crying for Amalia. Oh how she wanted to be able to speak and convince Amalia this wasn't the thing to do, but she couldn't.

An hour later, Emil carried the comatose Amalia into their home, laying her on a couch. Anne's face was wet, but she watched Emil, as he undressed Amalia. "I've got a card here telling me what must be done, not much really now. In three days, someone will come by here and take her measurement for clothes and shoes. I have to call dad now. Why did she do this?" Emil lost it. Tears grew and seeped down his cheeks. Wiping them, he placed the dreaded call to his father, the mayor.

Mayor Beifeld took the alarming news with more grace and poise than Emil had. "Okay son. Amalia must have wanted this. I'll send someone over to look after Anne and her while you are out. Hedda has always been a faithful housekeeper. She'll be there in a hour son."

She was a bit late, but the forty-year-old housekeeper arrived, talkative as ever. "Golly me. So little Amalia went and got herself changed too. Rash of that going on these days, but for the life of me, I can't see why. Well, it's done, so there's no going back, mind you. Still, I'm here now, and I'll take good care of your misses for you while you are at work, Emil. If I understand this whole thing, little Amalia here will be in a coma for four days. So there's not much we can do for her until she wakes up. Of course, then we all will be busy with her. Golly me." She would have rattled on, but just now Emil needed to get back to work, though he needed a stiff drink first.

***

At two a.m. and right on schedule very early that same morning while Amalia was asleep and before she headed off to the Worker's Federation office, Hermann quietly rose and carried his small jar of ether into his father's bedroom. He paused and listened. He father was sleeping soundly. Next to him, Zelda was too. He pulled his mask up, covering his nose and poured the ether onto the floor. Hastily, he slipped back and closed the door. Quietly, he returned to his room, sat on his bed, and stared at his watch. This was the longest hour Hermann ever had. Three o'clock seemed to refuse to arrive!

At last, it did and he took out the syringe and donned the mask once more. A minute later, he opened Adler's bedroom door. The faint odor of ether still hung in the air, but both were knocked out, alive, and breathing. He walked up to the bed, standing beside his father. He pulled back the covers, expecting a hand to grab his, restraining him from injecting the syringe. Nothing happened. Carefully, Hermann inserted the needle and pushed the contents into the man's vein. He pulled it out and covered his father back up.

A minute later, back in his own bedroom, he fired his d-gun at the syringe on the floor. Energies flashed and the syringe vanished. *That's that*, he thought, climbing into bed himself. For the first time in weeks, Hermann felt safe and secure. No longer did he worry his father would be genetically mutating him and installing a clone in his place. Besides, he was about to take his place as Baron Berthold!

He rose in the morning and made sure he was at the breakfast table when Elsa helped the blind Susanne get to the table, with Karla following along behind them. Zelda's servant woman brought her to the table as well, commenting that the baron wasn't awake yet.

Hermann volunteered, "That's all right. We'll let dad

116

sleep in today. He's been terribly overworked these past days, what with all the protests going on and the planning for the Autumn Ball in two days. Let him sleep in today." Everyone agreed and after breakfast went about their normal duties.

As Hermann walked around the castle checking on various details for the ball, he received three texts. Each simply said: Done. He smiled. This had all worked to perfection.

However, around one, a security captain found him. "Sir, there's another one of those worker's protests going on. The baron's still sleeping in. Your orders, sir? Same as before?"

"Yes. Let dad sleep. Same orders. You'll take care of it?"

"Yes. It's become routine now." He saluted and left to order the air strike.

Late afternoon, Hermann decided to act. He called up Dr. Lanzo. "Doctor, could you come over and check on my father? He's been sleeping in, but maybe something isn't right. He's still not awake, and it's almost suppertime. I'm a bit worried."

"Sure, I'll be by in a few minutes." The doctor didn't tell him that he'd already discovered that Dederick and Gerhardt were both in a coma, now resting on beds down in Sub-level Twenty. He arrived carrying his black bag, and Hermann, looking terribly worried, led him to his father's bedroom. Suspecting something was wrong, Elsa quietly trailed along behind them, keeping well back from the bedroom door, but close enough to hear them.

"Oh my! Another one!" exclaimed Dr. Lanzo. "Hermann, I'm afraid your dad is in a coma, a genetic bio agent induced coma!" He looked the man's body over and pointed to a spot on his arm. "Look here, he's been injected with the bio agent. We need to get him to my basement lab where I can look after him."

"What?" exclaimed Hermann, feigning shock and surprise. "Guards! Guards!" Two security men came running. "Dad's been assassinated. There is an assassin running around the castle! Search everywhere and find the assassin," he ordered.

"Hermann, your dad's not been assassinated. He's been injected with the bio agent. He's not dead nor is he likely to die," the doctor corrected him.

"Well, what do I tell them to look for if it isn't an assassin?" Hermann asked.

"We know what you mean," one guard volunteered. "We are on this!" He dashed off to sound the alarm.

"I've sent for a cart. Hermann, your father isn't the only one who has been attacked today. Gerhardt and Dederick are also in comas. Probably the same person got to all three of them," the doctor explained.

"What about Baron Aldric?" Hermann asked.

"Son, you are right. I best go check on him now. This is a disaster!" Hastily, the doctor left to do just that, while several of his assistants and one nurse arrived to transport Adler down to the research lab. Hermann went with them as a dutiful son should, keeping up appearances for now.

"So they got to your father too," Killian greeted Hermann as he arrived in Sub-level Twenty with his comatose father.

"Yes. Just awful. My security guards are looking into it now. They got to Dederick too?" Hermann asked, continuing the masquerade.

"Yes, just terrible. I've had my people change all our security codes. Here, let me adjust your ID card with the new codes so you can get down here to visit your father. They got to Kurt's dad too. He's over at GE now looking into how this break in security could possibly have happened. Shit, another one?" he broke off as Johan joined them, helping Dr. Lanzo push a cart bearing the comatose Baron Aldric.

Shortly, Kurt arrived and all four had their ID cards updated with the latest security codes. The four *discussed* the security breech that had resulted in the genetic mutations of their fathers.

"Well, I'm now head of GD," Killian announced. "I'm seeing to an orderly transition now."

"Same here," Kurt added. "I'm the new head of GE. Will the Autumn Ball go on as planned?"

"Absolutely. I'm now Baron Hermann and will host the

ball as planned. Baron Johan and I will announce to the world what has happened to our fathers at that time. By then, our combined security guards will have apprehended the beastly criminal who did this to our fathers."

The rest of the day, the four continued to keep up their *appearance* as shocked men, issuing all the right orders. After supper, the captain of the guards at Castle Berthold nervously reported to Baron Hermann. "Sire, we've gone over all the video, checked all the locks. I'm sorry to have to report we've found no trace of the would-be assassin, though that's not the right word for the criminal. We believe someone slipped into your father's room last night. We've checked with Dr. Lanzo, but none of his bio agent supplies is missing. Frankly, baron, I'm stumped on this one. So I've no choice but to submit my resignation and accept whatever punishment you feel I deserve."

"No trace? Incredible. Captain, this isn't your fault. Now if this criminal fellow had broken in, knocked out your guards, slipped past you, and gotten to my father, then yes, it would be your responsibility. In this case, captain, we don't even know how the man got in here. Maybe clues will come from GD, GE, or from Castle Berringer. Let's hope so. Meanwhile, keep extra vigilant. They might come after me next."

The captain couldn't believe his luck. If this had been Adler speaking, he knew he'd probably be shot and by the baron's own hand. Hermann was being very kind, but then, he reasoned, he wasn't his father. *Perhaps, things might be better around here with Hermann in charge and not Adler.*

The next morning, the day before the ball, the four new leaders met, standing over their comatose fathers. Dr. Lanzo joined them, explaining, "They're as comfortable as we can make them. In two more days, we'll be able to measure their bodies. Based upon standard developments of these mutations, we'll be able to order appropriate apparel and shoes in the right sizes for them in time to have them nicely dressed when they wake up. Have you fellows made any decision on where they'll live and who will take care of them when they awake?"

"We haven't the facilities here to care for them as men," Baron Hermann answered. "The best thing and most humane thing will be to send them to Blackwoods. There, they'll be able to satisfy their powerful sexual drives and not take that out on our mothers."

"Perhaps, that is for the best," the doctor admitted. "UFBMD men certainly do have most powerful sex drives. I don't think it would be healthy for your mothers to have to try to satisfy them. I'll make the arrangements for you."

***

"Guys, we have to make some new arrangements!" Stefan exclaimed. It was late that night. Emil was also present, though he hated to leave Amalia who was still in her coma and would be for another two days. "Rudolf and I just learned that Baron Adler, Baron Aldric, our CEO Dederic, and GE's CEO Gerhardt have all been subjected to the genetic bio agent. Apparently, someone snuck into their bedrooms last night and infected them, likely with the syringe version of the agent. In three more days, they'll awake to be UFBMD men, the new version, unable to speak but with short upper arms. I've heard they'll then be taken to Blackwoods and allowed to breed as often as they desire."

"Good God!" Emil exclaimed. "Someone is doing our dirty work for us."

"No kidding. Hermann has taken over for Adler and Johan is now Baron Berringer," Rudolf added.

"Who's running GD?" Emil asked what he wanted and needed to know. His vengeance was directed only against the men who had kidnaped and harmed his fiancé.

"Killian is stepping in as CEO there, while Kurt is running GE," Stefan explained. "Worse, all of our security ID codes got changed tonight, even GE's. While Rudolf's card and mine will get you access to the headquarters, they won't get you to the more critical areas in the sub-levels."

"Shit. I need to get all the way down," Emil declared, but the six already knew just how badly Emil wanted to execute his revenge.

"Don't worry yet. We still have a day and a half to get those codes," Stefan countered. "I'm going to try to clone some

120

ID cards tomorrow. If nothing else, we can manually go down the elevator shaft. I brought you all the plans for GD. Standard corporation construction means GE will be laid out identically to GD." He handed out the new ID cards with their new basic security clearance codes in them.

Stefan continued, "So none of this is going to affect Wotan and Wenzel, who will take out everyone at the ball and in Castle Berthold. Rudolf will not be impacted, since he's taking out the security at Castle Berringer. Dirk and Ebert, these new codes will get you into GE headquarters. I don't think you'll have any other difficulties there. No, the real problem will be with Emil and me trying to take out all of GD. With so much top secret stuff and things going on in their lower sub-levels, we might have a hard time getting down there. Somehow, Emil and I just have to succeed, since it's these GD maniacs who are the primary driving force, with GE's help, of course."

"Fine, Stefan," Dirk spoke up. "But any ideas who got to those four men? Where did they get the bio agent? Obviously, those four evil men had an awful lot of enemies."

Rudolf answered, "We don't know. Security men have been all over GD headquarters today, but we were informed they found nothing. My bet is it was an inside job. But all four? That's what bothers me. One person getting such intimate access to their private bedrooms? How could that be? We're having enough trouble just getting basic access codes."

Emil spoke up. "Hey, as your local detective, it sounds to me more like four inside jobs. You're right. It is highly unlikely one person obtained such intimate access to all four men's private chambers. Besides, why didn't the men wake up when someone injected the syringe into them? I sure would wake up. I hate needles."

"What are you suggesting, Emil?" asked Stefan, getting suddenly curious.

"That they were first somehow rendered unconscious before they were injected. No, if I were investigating these crimes, I would begin by looking for four different suspects, ones who stood to gain by the men's becoming totally disabled and who would have total access to the men's bedrooms and late at night," Emil explained his thinking.

Stefan rubbed his chin. "Emil. You know what you are suggesting? That Hermann did this to his dad? Johan did it to Aldric; Killian, his dad Dederick; Kurt to his dad, Gerhardt."

"Yes, that is where I would look first."

"What kind of a man would do this to his own father?" asked Wotan.

"A ruthless, unethical, sadistic baron or CEO," Emil answered, rather biased.

"Well, just as good since we're going to get rid of them all," Stefan declared. "Thirty-six hours from now, the barons and CEOs will be history."

***

Mid-morning, a day before the ball, Stefan carried a package from GD over to Castle Berthold. At the main entrance, he announced, "A package for Miss Susanne Berthold. I'm to deliver it to her personally. Killian's request." The guard let him in and told him she was on the third floor, most likely practicing getting around the ballroom. Dutifully, he headed up there hoping that his contact would be with her.

He entered the ballroom, now filled with a flurry of last minute action. Servants were putting up gold, brown, and black ribbons. The sweet odor of fresh flowers filled his nose. Looking around at the hustle and bustle, he spotted the blind Susanne trying to navigate on her own around the room. Elsa was at her side, constantly giving her guidance. Stefan moved over to them. "Ah, the beautiful Susanne. I'm Stefan from GD. Killian sent over his bouquet of flowers for you to wear to the ball." He handed it to Elsa, since Susanne could neither see it nor hold it. Stefan felt truly sorry for the poor woman, so abused by her father.

Elsa said, "Thank you. Susanne, you stick around. I'll go with Stefan here and get them in some water so they don't wilt. You'll be all right. Remember, count your steps." All Susanne was able to do was nod her head.

A few minutes later in Susanne's bedroom, Stefan whispered, "We desperately need the new security codes for GD's Sub-level Twenty, where they are keeping the four infected men. I can't get it from Killian, but maybe you can get

122

it from Hermann. No matter what, it is going to happen at the ball."

"I will try my best. Good luck," Elsa whispered back. Stefan departed. So much depended upon those codes.

Chapter 8—Strike Two

The day of the ball arrived, September 21. Stefan began to worry. Elsa had sent him only general access codes. Meanwhile, Emil and Hedda looked after Anne and Amalia, though there was still nothing they could really do for Amalia, whose arms were nearly gone, dried out husks. Already, Emil could see all of Amalia's believed imperfections were gone. *She will be pleased with that, if nothing else.* He was quite certain she'd been exposed to the original bio agent and would be able to speak, unlike Anne.

Emil explained, "Don't worry dear. Tonight, we'll have closure. The men who did this to you will be permanently handled. I so swear. Now, I have to put in an appearance at work. Catch you later. Call me, Hedda if there is any change in Amalia." He left, but didn't go directly to work. Instead, he called his dad from his car.

"Hi dad. No, no change in Amalia. It is the older UFB agent, so she will be able to speak. That's positive, not like poor Anne. No, what I'm calling about dad is to tell you that no matter what, don't go to any of the baron's balls tonight. Not if you value your life."

"What? As mayor, I'm obligated to go to these formal balls son. What's going on?" Mayor Beifeld asked. This wasn't like Emil at all. Did he know something?

"Dad, I can't say more. You have to trust me on this one. Amalia is going to need you and me. Pretend you've come down with the flu. That makes an acceptable excuse. Whatever you do, don't go to any baron's ball tonight, I beg you," Emil insisted. He dared not tell his father the truth, for he might spill the beans, ruining everything. Still, he had to make sure his dad wasn't going to the balls.

"Emil, I know you mean well, but I simply must put in an appearance at the Baron Berthold's Autumn Ball," the mayor insisted.

Emil sighed. "Okay dad. How about us sharing a drink later this afternoon? I've got some interesting news I picked up, though you'll probably be hearing about it tonight at the ball."

"Now that's being more reasonable, son. Sure, come by around three. I'll be free after that."

Emil started his car and made another stop on his way to work. One thing was certain, he wasn't about to let his dad go to that ball! At the spaceport, he was sent out to check on the new deep space transport that had just arrived. The Shining Star was brand new and fully equipped. Emil's job was to see that the ship was secure and that the new private access codes were installed, replacing those from the factory. This was a present to the barons from the CEOs. Others were given the task of unloading the rather complex planetary defense shield that was also promised to the barons.

Emil had worked at the spaceport for a number of years and had seen quite a few fancy transports, but this one was suitable for the barons. As he checked out the ship, he discovered that it came loaded with every available option, including its own invisibility shield. All it lacked, as did all transports, was its own offensive weaponry. After looking over the Shining Star, he then headed back down the bay ramp and closed the doors. Emil then did his job, entering the factory access code, and when the menu appeared, entering the new, private code the barons chose.

Around three, Emil arrived at the mayor's office in downtown Thromstead. "Hi dad. Got time for that drink now? Just saw the baron's new deep space transport. Man, it's loaded with every damn option in the book." Emil made light talk and slipped a strong mickey into his father's glass. He hated knocking his own father out, but he knew he couldn't live with himself if his dad went to the ball and was genetically modified along with the barons and their supporters. A few minutes later, he laid his dad down on his father's bed and made him as comfortable as he could, placing his shoes on the floor nearby. Then, he headed home.

After supper and feeding Anne, Emil changed into his finest suit, one that just barely allowed him access into the formal ball. "How do I look, dear?" he asked Anne. She grinned broadly and nodded yes. He gave her a long, loving kiss. "Okay, I'm off to the ball and our revenge. If anything bad happens to me, Hedda will look after you until dad gets here. I've given him a mickey so he will miss the ball and probably wake up with a headache. Still he will be alive and that's what matters. I'll be back as soon as I can. Remember always, Anne, I love you, and will always love you no matter what." Anne leaned towards him, and he responded by sharing another farewell kiss. Then, he rose and left.

Castle Berthold was packed with guests, so many that the courtyard lot was filled with shuttles and cars. Wisely, Emil parked his on the street, knowing he wouldn't be staying long. Faint sounds of music drifted out into the chilly nighttime air, as he walked briskly up to and through the castle gates, flashing his invitation to a guard. The ballroom was on the third floor, and, as he entered, he found the place already quite packed with people.

After glancing around, he spotted the many local barons with their wives in tow, along with their heirs and children. Plus, most all the important people of Thromstead were here as well, all avid supporters of the ruling barons and quite wealthy. He spotted his fellow conspirators moving about the dance floor and accepted a glass of wine from one servant as he entered, feeling somewhat out of place among all these people, people who fully supported all the corruption, unethical treatment, and sadistic practices of the barons, the least of which had been the experimental genetic testing on his Anne.

Stefan spotted him and moved discretely over to him, whispering, "No sub-level access code yet. Still on though."

"May I have your attention," the loud voice of Hermann rose over the light chatter and soft music. "Johan and I have something to tell all of you. Some of you may have already heard this sad news. Two days ago, some fiend broke into this castle and Castle Berringer and injected Baron Adler and Baron Aldric with the new genetic bio agent." Audible gasps echoed around the room. He paused diplomatically and then continued, "Yes, our fathers will wake up two days from now, unable to speak, and find themselves UFBMD men. We'll have them nicely looked after for the rest of their lives. At this time,

I'm now Baron Berthold and Johan here is Baron Berringer, our father's heirs. My older brother Heinrich has already become one of our armed forces' new hosts, a UFBMD himself. That's what he wanted. So please enjoy the festivities this evening. In the days to come, we two new barons will be meeting with all of you. Let the dance begin."

The four conspirators had fully intended to find their special young women their fathers had been preventing them from marrying and dancing with them. Unfortunately, even though the dance music began in earnest, many others insisted on chatting with them, particularly their fellow barons. Most wanted to know how the attacker gained access to the castle.

Stefan quietly whispered to Emil, "Now." As they headed across the room, Stefan also came up to Elsa, who was still looking after Susanne, who looked simply terrified. Emil heard him whisper, "Get out now." Elsa nodded. He and Stefan slipped out of the ballroom and left the castle. Once clear of the gates, each man got into his own car and headed the short distance over to GD headquarters. Emil got out and slipped into Stefan's car.

"So was her servant woman your inside contact?" Emil asked.

Stefan nodded. "She couldn't get the code for Sub-level Twenty from Hermann. Apparently, Killian has been changing that one code every night. So we go to Plan B. Let's get these bags inside and get changed." The two men each carried two large duffel bags inside the main entrance of GD headquarters. Stefan worked here, was well known, and was allowed in without any questions asked or even an ID card check. The two went into his office and locked the doors.

Hastily, they changed from their suits into black jeans and shirts, with sneakers. They got out their safety masks, which would prevent exposure to the bio agent, but only for a minute at most. If they were exposed to it any longer, they too would be infected. But a minute was all they thought they would need. "Okay, I'll take a bag up to the top floor and activate the release valve. Then, I'll come down here to the main floor and unleash the second one at precisely 8:10. Your stolen ID card should allow you to take the elevator to Sub-level Four. When the doors open, activate the release valve, and toss the bag out of the opened door. Press all the remaining floor buttons. Take it down as far as it will allow you with this security code. I have no idea how far that will be. Once it stops, you exit through the ceiling panel and use the side ladder to climb down to Sub-level Twenty. Release the second bag there and then get your ass back up to the elevator. Press the main floor button. If you're not back up by 8:10, my second bomb will go off. Even so, the mask should keep you safe as you make a mad dash out of the doors. They're only twenty feet away. If you run into any trouble, use the comm device in the bag to reach me. Maybe I can help. Just know the men who are running the kidnaping are stationed on the bottommost three floors. Good hunting, Emil."

Back at Castle Berthold, Wotan and Wenzel ambled back to the extensive bar. A quick check and they spotted their four bags carefully hidden beneath the tables loaded with drinks. Their agent had placed them right where they were paid to place them. No one was looking, and together, they ducked down, hiding beneath the tables. The opposite sides were covered with paper sheets in autumn colors. Quickly, they switched on the short timer in each of two bags, picked up the second ones, and ambled along the side of the room, exiting the main doors. A second later, the timer ended. Automatically, the gas valves opened, spewing the genetic bio agent out into the room.

Just outside the doors, Wotan closed them, while Wenzel attached the magnetic door locking mechanism to the doors. This temporary lock would keep everyone inside for a time, though with enough brute force, it could be broken. Now they donned their masks and headed down the steps, while releasing the gas from one of the two remaining bags. When they reached the main floor, they tossed the last bag with its release triggered down the stairs, turned, and headed towards the main exit of the manor house. Discarding their masks, they spotted the few guards who were outside. "Hey, something is going on inside. Your baron needs you inside right away!" Wotan yelled and watched the guards respond, dashing into the building, likely to their own doom.

Minutes later, they reached their shuttle, climbed in, and headed to General Goods headquarters and Wotan's room, where they waited on word from the others. If all went as planned, the seven wearing bio containment suits would next meet at the entrance of Castle Berthold around midnight to go inside and rescue their young women, their fiancés. Once in their room, Wotan sent a single word text to the others, Done. Fingers crossed, the pair waited, but watched each other, worried they might have been sufficiently exposed to the bio agent themselves. Nervously, they waited, but didn't fall unconscious.

A half hour later they received another text that said, Done. Five minutes after that, a third Done came. The pair began to relax. Their plan was actually working!

Stefan had no trouble unleashing the first bomb on the almost vacant top floor. His timing was precise; that was his nature. At exactly 8:10, he stepped out of the elevator and tossed his second bag bomb off to his right, slipped a mask over his face, and raced out of the main entrance, knowing he had a very serious problem to solve and virtually no time in which to solve it.

Emil swiped the ID card in the elevator's reader and pressed Sub-level Four. The elevator began descending. As it did so, he got his first bomb ready to go. As the doors opened, he pressed the release button, and just as they were about to close, tossed it through the doors. He donned the mask, pressed all the remaining lower buttons. They all lit up except for the bottom four sub-levels, the very ones he had to reach if this attack was to be successful, if he were to get justice for those who had kidnaped Anne.

As the doors opened and closed, he slipped the loops of the bag over his back, and pushed the ceiling tiles out of the way. Fortunately, no one appeared when the doors opened on these other levels. He was standing on top of the elevator looking at the crude ladder rungs that ran up one side of the dimly illuminated shaft, when the elevator stopped on the lowest level the ID card allowed. To his utter dismay, the strangest looking security man, if man he was, stepped inside and looked up at him through the ceiling.

The man was huge and had the appearance of no neck, so great were his muscles. The man's arms were bigger around than Emil's legs, and the man's legs were incredibly thick. Emil guessed he must weigh well over three hundred pounds if not more. "Come down here now or I'll break you in half," the bass voice called out.

Emil didn't hesitate. He jumped and caught the ladder rungs and headed downwards as fast as he could climb. No way was that freakish man going to prevent him from obtaining justice for Anne. Emil was thin and moved swiftly down. Glancing up, he saw the giant of a man now standing on top of the elevator. "Get back up here before I break every bone in your body!" Emil had no doubt that this man could do just that. Well, it didn't matter if he could reach the bottom, open the doors, and release the bio agent bomb. *I just have too.*

It was a long way down. He was passed Sub-level nineteen and was almost there when the huge man lunged for the ladder rungs, just as he had. Then, it happened. The rungs were not built for these new supermen. Worse, he'd jumped, just as Emil had, and that added gravity to the mix. When his ultra-powerful hands gripped the first rung, the combined force of his weight and his downward momentum literally ripped the steel bar from the side of the elevator tunnel.

Emil looked up in time to see the steel rung cascading off the wall coming down at him. At the last second, he avoided it, but above him the falling giant grabbed the next rung and the next and the next, ripping each one off of the shaft's wall. After tearing off ten of them in a row, the man was falling too fast to react to grab another one. Emil pressed his body up to the wall as tightly as he could. The falling giant swept past him, very nearly latching on to him, pulling Emil down with him. As it was, he only ripped Emil's shirt nearly off his back! A second later, a loud thud echoed up the shaft.

Panting for breath, Emil continued his way down. Reaching the doors, he activated the safety opening mechanism, turned on the release valve, and tossed the bomb back through the quickly closing doors. Mission accomplished. He didn't stick around but began climbing upwards. The sickly sweet odor seeped through the gas mask at this point, and Emil began to worry. He had what? A minute, Stefan said. He reached the ripped out section of the ladder and all hope left him. No way could he cross this long stretch, not if he had hours instead of seconds. Hastily, he dug out his cell phone and sent Stefan a brief text.

Stefan looked at the incoming message from Emil. Done. Rungs gone. Can't get up. At bottom. Help. After staring at it, he forwarded it to everyone, accidentally also sending it to Elsa. He followed that with another text, Get bio's ready, meaning their bio containment suits.

He met the others at Wotan's place. Together, the six men headed to a small warehouse where they stored a small bus and the bio containment suits. They were somber; the loss of Emil rather destroyed their elation at actually pulling this attack off successfully.

"What are we going to do about Emil? He's at the bottom and likely in a coma. Is it possible to reach him in these suits? If the rungs are gone, how do we even get down there?" asked Wotan.

"Damned if I know. Maybe we could take the elevator down to the bottom floor and somehow get down the rest of the way using the ladder," suggested Rudolf. "But how do we get him up? Ropes? Plus, we have to get our six women out of there first."

"Right. Keep on track. Emil knew the dangers. We'll get our fiancés out of the castle first and to safety at the warehouse. Then, we'll have to find a way to get to Emil, assuming he's still alive and didn't fall down to the bottom after sending the message," Stefan suggested.

At midnight, wearing their strange looking bio containment suits, which were much like space suits, the six climbed out of their small bus as close as they could get to the entrance of Castle Berthold, which was only at the main outer gates, since the courtyard was jam packed with vehicles. An eerie silence filled the midnight sky, though all the lights were still on.

In single file, the six men headed into the castle, though they could still see yellow fumes drifting past them. "Watch it, the stuff is still here. Don't get a tear in your suit or you've had it," Wotan pointed out the obvious.

They barely reached the second floor when they suddenly saw all six young women! Irma and Karla were awake and staring wide-eyed at the six strange "things" coming up the steps towards them. Lying beside them were Susanne, Renate, Nadja, and Kirsa, all were unconscious! "It's us, Karla," Stefan called out, though his voice was somewhat muffled. "Stefan, Rudolf, Wotan, Wenzel, Dirk, and Ebert. We're here to rescue you six. What's happened to those four? Bad fall? Crap, they can't answer."

When he reached them on the second floor, Karla waved her short arm towards a small paper on the floor. "A message, Karla?" he asked. She nodded vigorously. Stefan picked it up, read it and passed it on to Rudolf. It read: Gone to rescue E. Text where you are at. E. "Did Elsa write this?" Stefan asked. Karla nodded yes again.

"How's she going to do that? Why wasn't she knocked out like all the others?" Rudolf asked. Since no one had any answers, the men began carrying the women out of the castle and into the waiting bus. That done, the six headed back inside and up to the ballroom. They just had to have visual verification they'd gotten all the barons and their heirs. Someone had indeed busted the magnetic door lock, but only one man had made it out and then only three feet. One by one, they spotted the men. Finally satisfied, the six headed back down and out to the bus.

An hour later, they had their fiancés safely inside the warehouse and had discarded the bio containment suits. A cursory examination of the four suggested they were in comas. "How come they are in a coma? We used the same new genetic bio agent that was used to modify them in the first place," asked a worried Stefan. No one had any answer, though Elsa had, but she was elsewhere.

After sending Stefan the text, Emil headed back down the ladder, but somewhere near the bottom, his strength failed. The last thing he remembered was falling. He had no idea he fell only three feet and landed on the flattened superman guard.

Elsa realized at once this was precisely the correct genetic bio agent the four baronesses-to-be needed to be exposed to. While it was the same agent they had been exposed to, it should now regrow their missing eyes. At least, she hoped so. It certainly had with Zelda and Verena, whom after the attack she'd carefully helped to their bedrooms to await help. After that, she carried each of the four young women out of the ballroom and placed them where the six lads would easily find them. She helped Karla and Irma down the stairs and to sit down beside the four. She wrote Stefan a short note and told Karla she had to go rescue someone else, and that their boyfriends would come and pick them up if they just waited here.

As she headed down the tunnel to GD headquarters, a route she often used, she knew now she had another purpose to get to the Sub-level Twenty. She wanted to obtain many more samples of these bio agents, particularly the older one. If these young women were to have any chance at a real life, they had to have their voices back. Her plan was simple, if it worked. Inject the six with the older agent. With luck, their upper arms would dry up and fall off, but in the process, their voice boxes would regenerate. The six second-generation UFB women, who had grown up as UFB women and were quite content with their bodies, would be back to where they began life. This was the least that she could do for them.

Also, Elsa suspected Emil might also need these cures, since she presumed Stefan used the same new genetic bio agent in all the attacks. Hence, she wanted to raid the mad doctor's safe and steal a number of cures, as well as seeing if anything could be done for Emil. The bio agent didn't affect her in the slightest. To facilitate her rescue, she'd stolen Killian's ID card off his comatose body. Surely, he would have access to Sub-level Twenty, where she wanted to go.

The tunnel entered at Sub-level One. The guard station was empty. No, there was one guard there, lying on the ground comatose. She moved swiftly to the elevators and waited for it to arrive. Once inside, she swiped the stolen ID card and pressed the bottom button. She allowed a human smile to crease her lips when the button lit up. Down she went, but couldn't help noticing the ceiling tile above her was gone.

When the elevator reached the bottom floor and the doors opened, she could still see the yellowish bio agent in the air, though the circulation fans had already spread it out throughout the entire complex. She saw comatose men, strange men, the supermen, lying about. This time, she knew precisely where she wanted to go. As she approached the bio agent safe, she saw Dr. Lanzo lying on the floor, his hands reaching for the safe's door. She guessed he was trying to get inside and be sealed off from the gas. He'd been too slow. She retrieved the doctor's ID card and swiped it, saving her from having to rewire the lock mechanism.

Stepping inside, she discovered the doctor had been correct. Had he gotten inside in time, he'd be just fine. Elsa found a large bag and headed to the racks of agents. She took a dozen of each type of single-use syringe and then added one cylinder of the two types of gas agents. While she didn't have any use for the cylinders, she had other contacts that did. That done, she closed the safe and headed back to the elevator.

She placed her precious bag against a far wall and jumped up through the hole in the ceiling tile. On top, she stepped over to the ladder and began descending. She only had a few feet to descend. The bottom of the shaft was barely three feet from the bottom of the elevator. Poor Emil lay on top of one of these weird supermen, his chest touching the bottom of the elevator. Carefully, Elsa pulled him free and checked his vitals. He appeared unharmed but definitely in a coma.

Tucking him under one arm as though he weighted nothing, Elsa began the short climb back up above the elevator. A few minutes later, she had his body lying on top of the elevator, hands and head drooping down through the hole. She carefully jumped down and then pulled Emil's body down inside the elevator. Finally, she jumped back up, found the ceiling tiles and pulled them back into place. No sense leaving clues, she thought. She pressed the main floor button, changed her mind, and pressed the tunnel level, Sub-level One. Up it went.

When the doors opened, she slung Emil over one shoulder, picked up her precious bag, and headed back down the tunnel to the castle. Why? She couldn't risk someone seeing her carrying a grown man over her shoulder, and she needed transportation. Back at the castle, its courtyard was filled with vehicles. She took the first car she came to, sitting Emil down gently on the backseat and her bag on to the passenger's seat. It took her all of thirty seconds to hot wire the car. She drove off slowly, heading into the city proper. She parked on a side street and waited for Stefan's text telling her were they'd taken the six young women.

That came hours later, and she pulled up beside an old warehouse not too far from the spaceport. Following the text directions, she got out and knocked on the sliding doors twice, then once, then thrice. The doors slid open, revealing Stefan's tired face. "Wow. It's you, Elsa. We didn't think you made it. Drive the car inside before anyone sees it."

After doing that, she said demurely, "Could you strong men get Emil out of the back seat? He's rather heavy."

"How on earth did you ever get him out of the elevator shaft? Why aren't you in a coma, twice over?" Stefan asked the obvious questions.

"I ducked out and came back when the gas was diluted enough. I found Emil at the bottom, managed to get a rope on him, and got him up. More importantly, fellows, I've got some good news for you concerning your young women."

"Incredible, Elsa. Thank you, thank you for rescuing Emil. What news?" Stefan replied, suddenly duplicating what she'd last said.

"The reason four are in a coma now is their eyes are regenerating. I noticed Zelda's eyes regrew when they subjected her to this new bio agent. So has Verena's. However, the barons never did realize their wives could see again. Anyway, when they wake up, they should have their sight back. I have no idea how long that will take. Once that is done, I want to inject all them with the older genetic bio agent. If my theory is right, it'll remove their upper arms, but also regrow their voice boxes. If so, they'll be back where they were when you first met them."

"Elsa, I could kiss you! Thank you, thank you!" exclaimed Stefan and the other five added their praise to his.

"Save your kisses for the women. They'll need your love. If Emil ends up like the six now are, then I'll do the same with him, giving him back his voice."

"Hey, they did this to his wife. That's why he wanted to get revenge on the men who kidnaped Anne and did this to her. Can you do it for her as well?" Rudolf asked.

"Certainly. Where is she now?" Elsa asked.

"Er, we don't know. But he is the mayor's son. So the mayor probably would know. I didn't see him at the ball," Wotan answered. "I'll call him in the morning and find out."

"Guys, we best get some sleep. Karla is already out," Wenzel whispered. The group did just that, lying on blankets near their girlfriends. Elsa lay down beside Emil and pretended to sleep. Her mind raced. Just what did these boys intend to do next? They had certainly removed the barons here and the two powerful corporation CEOs. But what about the rest of the world? She doubted very much this was all going to work out as these young boys had planned. Her loyalty right now was safeguarding these women, Emil, and this unseen Anne. *Once they are safe and recovered as much as possible, I'll send for new orders. This Blackwell-C situation has gotten completely out of hand.*

Chapter 9—Now What

The next morning, Elsa discovered the six conspirators had not made any preparations for this day. While they'd fully planned their attack, they hadn't given any thought to what came next. No food, no water, no plans. Worse, chaos had erupted, that much Elsa knew, though the lads didn't yet. She was monitoring the news channels, at least the audio portion.

"Look boys, Karla and Irma are hungry and need to use the bathroom. We're thirsty as well," Elsa pointed out to the boys.

Stefan flushed. "Er sorry. We never thought this far ahead. Sorry. We'll go get some supplies right away."

"Hold it right there. Have you any idea what the situation is like out there today?" Elsa asked. All six stopped and flushed. They hadn't. "Look, probably by now the whole world knows almost every baron and heir is gone, as are all the people in GD and GE headquarters. Stefan and Rudolf, you can't show your faces. If you do, everyone will want to know why you weren't victims as well. How do you propose to explain that away, eh?"

"We hadn't thought of that," he admitted sheepishly. "She's right. Rudolf and I don't dare show our faces right now. Too many questions. Okay, you four, it is in your hands. We need food, water, and stuff."

"What stuff?" Wotan asked. Elsa groaned. These boys had no idea of their fiancé's needs!

"Electrostatic hair machine, for starters. Clothes, shoes," Elsa added.

"Okay, we can get those at work," Wotan said, relieved. "We'll make a food and water run first and then see if we can locate Anne and get back to you." The four headed out of the warehouse, returning later with breakfast sandwiches and several bottles of water. Then, they left to go to work, to try to obtain what the women needed, and to find out where Anne was staying.

"Mayor Beifeld?" Wotan asked.

137

"Yes. Speak softly. I've a splitting headache. Worse, the world is a goddamned mess this morning. All the barons are in comas, as are hundreds of others. I'm trying to handle this disaster."

"It's about Emil, sir. He too was a victim, but we've rescued him. He is in a coma now, but we know he has a wife, Anne, and she's a UFB woman and must have help. So we want to take him to her and help her manage for now."

"What? Emil too? God, can it get any worse? Hell, he warned me not to go to the ball last night. I think he spiked my drink. If he hadn't, I'd not be here today. Okay, here's the address. My daughter, Amalia, is there too, in a coma. Foolish girl went and got herself infected too. I will try to come by later today, if I can. Thank you for taking care of my son. I'll make it up to you later."

After hanging up, Wotan had a new bright idea and headed back to the warehouse. "Elsa, we know that Anne is staying at a nice home, but Emil's sister is also there and in a coma too. Got herself infected. Why don't we take everyone there? That should be a very safe place for us all."

"Finally a bright idea. Make it happen, Wotan," Elsa declared.

An hour later, Elsa relaxed. This was exactly what was needed, a nice home, no hassles, and no stress such as was always present around the castle. The housekeeper Hedda was a bonus, and Elsa felt confident that between her and Hedda, they could keep things on a even keel. At once, Hedda sent the "boys" out for many more groceries, while she and Elsa made up additional beds for the incoming six women and their six boyfriends. Anne, however, hovered over the comatose Emil crying silently to herself.

Once the organized chaos died down, Elsa asked Anne if she would like to have her voice back, but at the expense of her short upper arms. She nodded yes vigorously, and Elsa explained what she was going to do—inject her with the original genetic bio agent, and she's probably be in another coma, but awaken from it with her voice restored. Anne nodded yes vigorously. She then injected Anne, Karla, and Irma with the original version of the genetic bio agent.

An hour later, Elsa examined all of her new patients, as she called Amalia, Emil, Anne, Karla, Irma, Susanne, Renate, Nadja, and Kirsa. She had the nine arranged in a long row, covered with blankets to keep them warm. Now, all she could really do was be there to help them as they came out of their comas. She anticipated Amalia would awaken in two more days, and that she would be the most difficult to handle. Unknown to everyone, Elsa had been around the UFB women of Blackwell-C for nearly a half century, watching over several of them, though changing *positions* with different barons from time to time to hide her *age*.

She knew from experience just how terrifying it was for a woman to awaken to find she had no arms and with such a deformed body that was otherwise in many ways the epitome of beauty. Now if they still had their arms, reasonable size breasts, and normal feet, they would actually be what these sadistic men called the ultimate beauties. Hence, she had a good deal of experience dealing with new UFB women when they first awakened, and she was determined to make this be as easy for Amalia as possible, especially since the foolish girl was only sixteen.

Of course, Emil would also be trouble, perhaps even more so since he would then look like one of these women. She'd never been around UFBMD men, but suspected their reactions would be far worse. Elsa hoped and prayed when Irma and Karla awoke in four days, they would quickly bounce back to their wonderful selves that she had known nearly all their young lives. She also believed once the other four regained their sight and were then given the second round of her *cures*, returning their bodies back to their original second-generation UFB women's state, then they too would quickly bounce back. Now all she could do was wait and get the men in their lives to get their women the apparel, shoes, and hair machines they needed to survive well. Much would have to be handled after that, but this came first.

The next day, she was pleasantly surprised when a representative from the Federation of Workers called to have her take Amalia's new body measurements. She assured Elsa that she could precisely estimate the young teen's final measurements and would be sending over two initial outfits and a hair machine for Amalia, compliments of their federation.

Elsa also knew everyone else would need new clothes and shoes, along with more electrostatic hair machines, what with nine who would be in desperate need of easy hair care. Hence, she took time to get them all re-measured, except Emil. Since she had no idea of exactly what he would look like, she made an estimate. One thing struck her as she carried out the measurement on the eight women, and that was just how similar some of their measurements actually were. Bust sizes varied very little between them, except for the younger Amalia. Waists varied not at all, being precisely fourteen inches across. Shoe sizes were likewise almost the same, eight or nine. Thus, she made a good guess at what Emil's measurements would wind up being when he awoke. Being off an inch or two on hemlines wouldn't matter much at all.

Amid the massive confusion of September 22, she sent the boys off to several of the UFB Women's Apparel stores to purchase four complete outfits for the nine, along with eight more of the hair machines. Combined with also fetching enough groceries to feed the rather large group, the six men were kept busy throughout the day.

After supper, they gathered around the TV to catch up on the news. While Stefan and Rudolf had expected to be making worldwide announcements about what had been done, they knew they dared not. Much suspicion would be leveled their way, since everyone else who worked at Galactic Dynamics headquarters in Thromstead had been infected. However, several other People's Revolution members stepped forward and claimed the PR had been behind the destruction of all the barons and the evil alien corporation men of GD and GE. "Now Blackwell-C is free at last. Soon, we'll be announcing free and open elections for new leaders," the spokesman declared.

"See, it's all working out, even if you aren't right there running the show, Stefan," Wotan pointed out. Stefan growled, but had to concede the point. It appeared all was working out as planned.

The news did give exact counts of the number who were infected at the four locations in Thromstead, and by the evening news, added tallies from the other barons' castles around the world. The PR had been entirely efficient, infecting all the current barons, their heirs, and most all their other sons. The news also reported the exact breakdown by sex: two thousand five hundred six women and three thousand six hundred ten men. These figures included three dozen children under the age of thirteen, mostly the young of some of the barons and baronesses.

More importantly, the news explained due to the enormous scope of this terrorist attack on the ruling elite of Blackwell-C that Generals Ernst Von Dorfsted and Franz Himmel had assumed control of Blackwell-C. The sheer number of victims pulled out of the castles and buildings had to be identified, next of kin notified, and later cared for when they awoke from their comas. As of September 22, the generals invoked martial law. Thousands of soldiers fanned out and began the recovery operation, putting the comatose bodies in available warehouses. An appeal went out to anyone who knew someone who had gone to any of the barons' balls to come by the appropriate warehouse and identify those they knew. Thus, the figures, which were presented in the news that evening, represented the Armed Forces counts and were quite accurate.

Stefan's comment told Elsa all she needed to know. "Well, I didn't anticipate the army would get involved! This isn't good. We best stay put here a bit longer. Besides, I want to be here when Renate wakes up." His companions felt the same way, that their fiancés took priority now.

Thus, during September 23, the men helped get everything ready for the revival of the women and watched the news unfolding. By the end of this, the second day after the attacks, the army had brought a bit more order to the mess, as well as a startling announcement. In fact, General Ernst asked Mayor Beifeld to make the key announcement. Looking very tired and depressed, the mayor faced the cameras to give his short speech.

"The army has now confirmed all current barons and

their heirs and of age sons have been victims of these terrorist attacks. Our ruling elite have been disabled in one strike. The generals are asking all retired barons, who are still able, to contact them at once. The phone numbers are being shown at the bottom of your screen. However, at this time, the whereabouts of six baronesses-to-be is unknown. These women, who were most likely at Baron Adler's ball, are: Susanne and Karla Berthold, Renate and Irma Berringer, Nadja Koft, and Kirsa Hagan. If you have any knowledge where these young women are, please also contact the generals. The numbers are at the bottom of your screen. Finally, a number of others, some of which who worked for corporations here in Thromstead, are also missing. A listing of all unaccounted for people in your city will be shown on your screen now. Again, if you know the whereabouts of any of these people, contact the generals at the indicated numbers. Thank you."

Next, the screen displayed four columns of names, very nearly filling the screen. The six lads gasped. Their names were among the missing. "We could say that we left the ball and got drunk and were sleeping it off," Stefan suggested.

"No good. We were seen at the ball," Dirk countered.

"Plus, everyone knows these were our girlfriends, and we wanted to marry them. Guess who will be at the top of the list of suspects?" Rudolf added. "If we turn the girls over, lord knows what will happen to them. The whole point was to rescue them and get them away from those sadistic barons forever."

"Well, we didn't think about the retired barons. Maybe there won't be enough of them to do much," Ebert added, "but if they know about our fiancés, they could well try to force them to marry someone else and make them the new barons. After all, they are rather the barons' heirs, kind of."

"The longer we wait, the harder it is going to explain away our absence," put in Dirk. "Besides, we have already been seen around town on all these errands. We've even used our bank accounts. What the hell are we going to do?"

"We're doomed either way. If we step back into the world, they are likely to quiz us about our fiancés. If we don't, they could decide we're prime suspects and start hunting us down," Stefan concluded. "Damned either way."

Elsa decided to offer the confused lads some advice. "Look, you four should return to your jobs and lives in Thromstead. Stefan and Rudolf's reappearance would likely raise too much suspicion. I'd recommend they stay here and help take care of the nine, since Hedda and I can't handle all nine at once, fellows. If asked, you four can say you've been helping some other victims recover, such as Amalia and Emil. Pretend you found Emil outside the castle and rescued him, but were terrified of going inside the castle and being infected yourselves. There's enough truth in that to assuage suspicions. Besides, I don't expect everyone here to be out of their comas until around the last days of September."

The six decided to follow her advice. She added, "Say, while you are out and about, check and see if the fancy new deep space transport the barons were promised has arrived at the spaceport, but do it discretely. It may be your only ticket out of here."

Just then, Amalia began stirring, and Elsa went to her side on the makeshift bed. "Oh, what's happening? I feel groggy, thirsty, have to pee. Oh, I'm awake! Oh, it's happened hasn't it." Amalia came too and recognized where she was. "Oh, this is hard. How do I sit up? I want to see how I look. Who are you?" She struggled to sit up, and Elsa helped her, but Amalia had never seen the woman who was helping her.

"I'm Elsa, Susanne's servant. There you go."

"Mirror. There's a mirror in the bathroom. I just have to see how I look."

"Of course. Easy does it." Elsa helped her stand up, wobbling on her toes, as her now very long, thick hair slipped down to her knees.

"I can't stand up and keep my balance very well. Oh, they are really big. Oh, I can't see my feet over them. To the bathroom," Amalia gushed. "Oh, I didn't think walking would be so hard. Don't let go of me, please. This is really scary. I didn't think it would be quite like this."

Elsa helped the young teen to the bathroom, but insisted she sit down and use the toilet first. That done, Amalia just had to see her new look. "Good. My ears are right now. Look, my nose is straight, perfect. Oh, my teeth are also perfect now too, great! That ugly blemish on my right cheek isn't there. Wonderful. And my hair—gosh it's better than I ever imagined it could ever look. Now, I truly am very pretty. Everyone knows a girl has to look beautiful to find the right fellow, and now I do. Only, this is so very much harder than I imagined it would be. I keep trying to use my arms and hands, and they aren't there anymore." Amalia chatted away, excited about her now super-model looks, more or less ignoring her obvious difficulties.

"Come. Let's get you dressed and your hair done," Elsa hinted, trying to pull her away from the mirror. *Foolish young girl*, she thought.

Amalia insisted on wearing the tight-fitting, black nylons, but Elsa insisted she not wear the corset. "Remember all the trouble Anne had wearing it." She agreed and accepted the garter belt instead. Finally dressed in a simple day dress and the new tall heels, Elsa got her over to the electrostatic hair machine and told her how to activate it.

"Wow, this is utterly incredible! What a feeling! Oh, I'm feeling with my hair, as if they are a thousand really long fingers or something. This is the coolest," Amalia gushed. She ran the machine through its short cycle ten times before Elsa could get her out of it.

"Now you need to practice walking on your own. Remember to toss your head to get your hair out of the way before you sit or stand. It's very painful if you sit or stand on it," she cautioned the teen.

"Oh, this is so hard, Elsa. I can't even see my feet. How do I keep my balance?"

"Tiny steps, tiny steps," she replied, keeping one arm around her.

"By the time she got back into the living room where the other eight were lying in their comas, she sighed, "Well, this is much harder than I ever imagined. Maybe this wasn't such a good idea after all."

Elsa laughed. "Dear, it certainly wasn't, but it can't be undone. You are going to have to make the best of it now."

"Oh no! Emil! What happened to him? Is he going to be all right?" Amalia nearly fell over in panic when she spotted him lying beside the others.

"He got infected as well during the big terrorist attack. Much has happened since you were infected," Elsa hinted.

"This is terrible. He's not going to be able to help Anne and me. Whatever will I do now? I'm hungry." A confused Amalia began to realize just how bad her silly notion really was. Her youthful enthusiasm vanished.

While Elsa fed her, they watched the news. Slowly, the magnitude of what had happened while she was in her coma became clear to Amalia, and she wished with all her might she'd not been so foolish, that she wasn't so helpless now, not when her brother so needed her. "I'm just a stupid little girl, aren't I?" Amalia finally broke down, sobbing.

Much of the next day was spent on helping Amalia learn to get about on her own. Stefan and Rudolf took over from Elsa and acted as her support, allowing Hedda and Elsa to cook up a large batch of stew. Elsa anticipated five would likely be coming out of their comas sometime the next day, and she wanted to get them well fed before she injected them with the next part of her theoretical cures. If they all woke up around the same time, the able-bodied would have their hands full with the five.

In fact, Susanne, Renate, Nadja, and Kirsa all woke up within minutes of each other. All four blinked and realized they could see again. Giant smiles instantly appeared on their faces. Elsa explained, "My first cure worked on you four. Your eyes are back. After we get you to the bathroom and fed some healthy stew, I'm going to inject you with my next possible cure. With luck, your voices will be back too, though it will cost you your upper arms. Is that acceptable to you?" she explained and asked each. Huge smiles and head nods told her all she needed to know.

Hedda, Stefan, Rudolf, and Elsa helped them to the bathroom and stuffed them full with the stew, before getting them back to their makeshift beds. Elsa then injected each with the original UFB woman's genetic bio agent. Within a minute, the four were back into comas once more. Just in time too, for Emil finally woke up, shocked, terrified, and unable even to speak.

"It's okay, Emil. You and the others are all safe, Amalia too," Elsa quietly explained to the terrified man who now looked like the other women. "We're going to get you up and to the bathroom first. After that, we'll get some much needed food in you. Then, I'll inject you with the next cure, and when you wake up, your voice should be restored. Is that all right with you? Just nod." Emil nodded, but as they got him up and he saw the condition of his body, he lost control of his wild emotions and sobbed silently throughout the entire ordeal. Even Amalia's soothing words didn't help, and he cried until he went into a coma once more.

"He'll be fine, Amalia. Just remember, men take these awful physical changes far worse than you women, since he'll always look like a UFB woman and not a man now."

"I think I understand. I'll be here for him," Amalia replied, but knew darn well she really couldn't do anything truly useful for him, not any more. She again cried herself to sleep. Both Stefan and Rudolf got a rude awakening, seeing these first reactions of Amalia and then Emil. Both seriously began to doubt what they'd done to nearly five thousand men, women, and few children had been the right thing.

The next day, Karla and Irma revived from their comas, while that night Anne did so as well. "Fantastic! Elsa, this is so fantastic that I don't even have words for it. I can talk again! You don't know how absolutely horrid it was to be unable to communicate anything at all!" exclaimed Karla.

"I feel fantastic, like I'm whole again," Irma gushed. "Thank you, thank you all for this priceless gift."

Later when Dirk and Ebert came by around suppertime, the two young women were waiting and pushed their bodies into the men as soon as they got inside the front doors. "So you did miss me," Dirk teased Karla. She just continued to kiss him passionately, shutting him up.

Over supper, the two women were brought up to date on the latest martial law edicts and the casualties. Then, Anne woke up, just as happy as the others to be able to speak again. "Oh Amalia, why did you do it?" she exclaimed when she saw her husband's sister.

"Now I'm very beautiful too, only I wish I had listened to you and Emil. It's so very much harder than I ever imagined it would be," Amalia admitted. "And I can't help Emil when he most needs me."

"We can give him our support and love, Amalia. I don't know what else we can do. We are so helpless," Anne replied.

"Well, not as helpless as you might think," Karla spoke up. "We were born like this. So give yourselves time, and you'll be perfectly comfortable being as we are. Besides, we can do a lot with our feet, if they don't tie our shoes on so we can't take them off. Elsa knows, because she often took mine off so I could use my feet. Of course, that was when dad and my brothers weren't around." She continued to chat, offering the two a wee bit of hope.

During the next three days, Karla and Irma did just that, showing Amalia and Anne just what they could do with their feet and toes, including more or less feeding themselves. After that, all four insisted they be allowed to do that, much to the relief of the young men.

The second day, Karla saw Amalia frantically rubbing herself against the backside of a chair. When Amalia saw Karla watching her, her face turned beet red. Karla smiled, "Come into the side room where we can talk in private. I know what you're doing, and it's normal." The very embarrassed Amalia followed Karla.

Once they were alone, Karla explained, "All UFB women have incredibly powerful sexual drives. I'm not sure why we do, but we do. It is almost impossible to keep from pleasuring yourself. I used to have to do it four times a day until Susanne saw me and helped me, rather she got Elsa to help. We were supposed to be wearing special panties with a vibrator thing that goes inside us. It is programmed to do its thing to relieve us at least four times a day. But there is another type that we can turn on and do it for us when we want it to. You just have to squeeze it with your vaginal muscles and it turns on. Once I started wearing that, I stopped going nuts all the time. When you get married, if you have sex in the morning and at night, you are supposed to be able to get by the rest of the time without needing it. That's what we have all been told. Once I get married, I can tell you for sure if that's right or not. I'll see that Elsa gets all of us one, since we are all going to need it."

"You mean I'm not going nuts or something?" Amalia asked.

"Hardly. We just have a very powerful sex drive. I think whoever invented this genetic bio agent wanted the UFB women to desire sex all the time. Stupid men, most likely. Come on; let's find Elsa and see if she can get us fixed up."

Later that day, Elsa inserted the device into Amalia and slipped the special panties up so it kept the device from slipping out. "I've set it for four times a day, Amalia. Let me know if you need it more than that or less."

"And I'll tell you how to make it do it when you want," Karla whispered.

"Oh God! Yes, oh my, yes, this is what I've been desperately needing. Thanks. Oh, oh." Amalia's eyes rolled, and Elsa and Karla left her to enjoy it in privacy.

Finally, the night of September 29, the other five woke from their comas again. Susanne, Renate, Nadja, Kirsa, and Emil awoke to discover their short upper arms were gone, but their voices were back. All four women cheered and began chatting furiously with their boyfriends or anyone who would listen!

Amalia and Anne sat with Emil, as Elsa got him dressed in a simple day dress, much like all the others. "Our hair is simply out of this world, big brother," Amalia did her best to find something positive for Emil to focus on. Both had thick, lush, shiny raven hair that fell in gentle, silky waves to their knees. In contrast, Anne's hair was light blonde, but otherwise identical in all ways to the other's hair. All UFB women and men's hair had the same physical characteristics, except color.

"But we are helpless. We can't walk or do anything for ourselves. And just look at me. My voice sounds like yours, a woman's voice, and I look like all of you," Emil complained bitterly.

"But you have what I want and need," Anne teased him, causing him to flush, far more so than he normally would

148

have.

"But Anne, I can't possibly take care of you now. I can't work and support us. I'm as helpless as you and Amalia are. We're doomed. You should forget about me, try to find a normal man to love, and take care of you," Emil pleaded.

"I want you, silly. We're married and that's that. I don't know what we will do, but I love you, and I won't be separated from you, Emil, not ever," Anne insisted.

"But what are we going to do?" Emil pleaded.

"First, you have to learn to walk well and to do as much as possible for yourselves," Susanne broke in on their conversation. "Look you three, we six were born like this and haven't known anything else. We'll help you and show you all the tricks we know. That has to help, especially since we don't have to wear those awful corsets. Give yourselves time and you will be getting around as well as we six always have."

"But how will I support Anne and Amalia?" Emil wailed, I can't possibly work at the spaceport now."

"Hey, that reminds me," Wenzel interrupted them. "Elsa asked me to check on that new deep space transport the corporations gave to the barons. It is still parked at the spaceport. Ownership papers list it as belonging to the Berthold family, but those papers have not yet been delivered to the baron and probably won't be now."

"Oh," Emil said, "I know the new access codes to open its doors. Elsa, write these numbers down." He rattled off the new codes. "Anyway, what are we going to do now?" he asked again.

"Well, our plan to be holding free elections has gone by the boards, at least for now. The generals are controlling things at the moment," Stefan admitted his failure.

"Marry us," Susanne spoke up. "Before anything else bad happens, marry us!"

The six young men laughed, kissed their respective fiancés, and promised to get a priest here tomorrow to do just that. That settled, Rudolf wrote out an official request to have the ownership papers delivered to Susanne Berthold. He asked that Dirk send these along the official channels when he went out to find a priest and obtain the six marriage licenses in the morning.

For her part, Elsa had taken a wait and see approach during these past four days. She was very much relieved to hear the six were actually serious about marrying the women. Plus, if Susanne could actually get those ownership papers, then perhaps there was hope for this bunch. She knew Emil's question was the single most important one, but was more or less being ignored by the six young men, obviously in the dark about the new situation they'd created on Blackwell-C. What to do was the key question these men and women should be addressing, but she did not intend to push them in any given direction. These were their own lives to live, not hers, as much as she wanted to protect and help the women.

Chapter 10—Seizing the Day

The first that General Ernst heard of the terrorist attack was on the late morning of September 22. His aide, Colonel Achima Nacht knocked, entered, saluted, and said, "Sir, you might want to turn on the news." He nodded, and she moved over to the opposite wall, activating his big screen system. The newscaster was reporting on the chaos that was found at Castle Berthold.

"My god, a bio agent attack on the castle? Get me Castle Berringer on the phone. Also get anyone from Galactic Dynamics on the phone too," he ordered.

Achima did as asked. Minutes later, countering his impatient stare, she said, "Sir, no answer from either one."

"Okay, sound general quarters. Order a platoon to go check out Castle Berthold. Another platoon to check out Castle Berringer and another to check on GD headquarters. Find me someone who's in charge," he barked.

"Aye sir." Achima saluted, pivoted, and left to issue the orders. She returned to his office to wait on the field reports. An hour later, the platoons began reporting in. Yes, there had been a massive bio agent attack at the ball. Unexpectedly, another bio agent attack had been carried out on those in Castle Berringer and then at GD headquarters.

"What the hell's going on? All right, colonel, order a sortie into these locations. Mandatory bio containment suits. Streaming video. We need to see the extent of the damage at these places. Send out patrols to all the other major buildings in Thromstead and have them checked out too."

"Aye sir. A call's coming in from General Franz," she replied.

"Put him on and get those orders obeyed, colonel. Ernst here. We've a bit of a situation here, Franz."

"We are getting reports from six cities. Barons' castles have been attacked with a bio weapon. I'm sending in teams to analyze the bio agent involved. What's the situation up north?" Franz asked.

"You too? Damn. We're under a terrorist attack for sure. Three key installations here in Thromstead, two castles, and GD headquarters that we know of have been struck. Estimates suggest the attacks came last night. If too many barons are eliminated, we must declare martial law. Agreed?" General Ernst asked.

"Agreed. Keep this line open," General Franz replied.

By late afternoon, the two generals had a grip on the situation. All the ruling barons and most of the wealthier class were victims of the new genetic bio agent, confirmed by field tests. However, they wisely decided to wait until the next day to go in and start removing victims. No one wanted to risk exposing themselves to this horrific agent. Horrific was the adjective used when a man was impacted, but a wonderful, marvelous thing when a woman was impacted. The men had a double standard on the genetic bio agent issue.

They had no alternative but to declare martial law. The following day, word spread that the People's Revolution may have played a role, but they were calling for free and open elections for new rulers of Blackwell-C. Both generals passed this whole notion off as mere crackpots trying to gain control of the government of the world. Martial law ruled.

Considering the sheer number of victims, both generals decided the most effective approach was to transport the victims to warehouses and make them as comfortable as possible. That done, the lengthy process of identifying the victims began, ending with a plea from Mayor Beifeld for those who might know someone who was infected to visit these warehouses. One by one, the victims were identified.

The third day, military officials began contacting known relatives of the victims. After confirming the identity of the victim, the relatives were given an opportunity to take the victim home with them, once they revived and were given an initial set of apparel to wear. After that, the support and care of the victim fell to those relatives.

However, more than half of the victims went unclaimed. Either their relatives didn't have the facilities to handle them or they didn't want that responsibility. Hardly any of the male victims were *claimed* by their relatives, though all children were taken in, along with a goodly number of the women.

Virtually no one took in the barons, their baronesses, or their children. By day six, the generals faced the decision on what to do with nearly three thousand victims, primarily men. The Blackwoods complex agreed to take on five hundred younger men, which the generals quickly accepted, sorting, and sending them off to that assisted living complex. Then fortune stepped in. Many local bordellos and escort services began calling, suggesting they could take some as well, primarily women, but a few men. Once more, the generals accepted the offers, sending all the remaining women off to these establishments, along with two dozen younger men.

They still had well over fifteen hundred men on their hands, if these mutations could still be rightly called men, though certainly not in the minds of the generals. At last, with no place to send them, the generals ordered them to be terminated and their bodies cremated. This was the fate that befell the many barons and their sons, along with many wealthy men.

In Thromstead, by the end of September, General Ernst's soldiers occupied all the many barons' castles, along with GD and GE headquarters. Following his orders, all these locations were thoroughly searched, valuables confiscated, and a complete inventory done. Wisely, the generals ordered all the genetic bio agents confiscated and put under tight military control.

On September 28, the two generals with their two colonel aides met in Thromstead to discuss what was to be done next. "Look," General Ernst began, "all the rightful rulers of Blackwell-C are gone. Only a handful of retired barons exist, and they are hardly capable of restoring order here. Plus, with them has gone all the wealth of our world. Those funds are now in our hands. The question before us is what is to be done now?"

General Franz replied, "Well, the Worker's Federation is calling for a new world order, one in which they have a strong say in the running of Blackwell-C. Also the People's Revolution is calling for free and open elections. Yet, what does that mean? You and I are the only ones who know what's going on worldwide. Do we dare turn the running of our world over to a bunch of factory workers and farmers? What do they know about off-world commerce, trade, and even the running of affairs? Nothing. Just who is to be elected to what? Are they intending to elect new barons? And then we have those religious nuts calling for a drastic change and the elimination of all UFB women, for God's sake."

"Well, we certainly aren't going to eliminate the UFB women!" General Ernst declared. "Do you realize our soldiers' morale has never been so high as it is now? Some are demanding we provide two UFB women hostesses per squad. Plus, all our support staff who are not in specific squads are demanding their own UFB women hostesses. With all the confiscated funds in our possession, we can afford to pay these women a thousand times over."

General Franz laughed. "Quite true. I've had the same requests from my men and women," he added that last after a frown from his Colonel Hilda. I say let's expand our UFB women hostesses program. Plus, this is also the major argument being forwarded by the Federation of Workers. They seem to want a UFB woman in every worker's family."

"Well, one thing is certain, Franz, we can't turn control of Blackwell-C over to this Federation of Workers or to the People's Revolution. It's up to us. Martial Law isn't going to cut it for very long. What about you becoming the Director of Southern Blackwell, while I become the Director of Northern Blackwell? Achima here can become the Director of Women's Affairs of North Blackwell, while your Hilda becomes the Director of Women's Affairs of South Blackwell. We can use our soldiers to enforce our rule. We can set up military posts in the old castles to help run things. The cities can keep their mayors and all else they now have. We four would merely replace all the constantly bickering barons?"

"I like that idea, Director Ernst," Franz grinned. "I like that a lot. It would still be a military dictatorship, but disguised and made more palatable. If we make sure to satisfy the Federation of Workers' demands and perhaps some of the People's Revolution's demands, things should run smoothly."

"Excellent. That's settled. We'll divide the confiscated funds equally. Wait a minute. The Armed Forces already gets its funding from the annual taxes. If we also get the portion that is going to the many barons, we'll be swamped in excess funds," General Ernst pointed out.

"Quite true, general," Colonel Achima said. "The barons get fifteen percent of a person's annual income, while the Armed Forces get five percent. We could up the Armed Forces percentage to six percent to help defray the expenses of all the UFB women and then cut the barons percentage down to five percent. This would allow the taxpayer to keep the other nine percent."

"You've a bright woman there," General Franz commented. "Give the average taxpayer a substantial tax cut, and we will have the full support of the population of workers. But I'd up the Armed Forces cut to seven percent and the Director's cut to five percent, allowing the taxpayer to keep the other eight percent. Positively brilliant, colonel. In later years, if we find this is insufficient, we can always increase the tax percentages."

"I agree, brilliant, Colonel Achma. Seven and five percent it shall be. Now, why don't I get a representative from the Federation of Workers here to discuss their supposed needs?" General Ernst suggested.

Several hours later, the same man who had discussed terms with Stefan and his group entered, again wearing his comical mask. "It is for both of our protections. If you saw my face, then either I would have to kill you or you would have to kill me. Now then, I presume that you have something concrete to propose to the millions of Blackwell-C workers?"

The man doesn't beat around the bush, thought General Ernst. "Well, yes, that is why we asked to meet with a representative of the Federation of Workers. I will be the new Director of Northern Blackwell, while Colonel Achima Nacht here will be our new Director of Women's Affairs of Northern Blackwell."

The man laughed. "Why am I not surprised the military is taking over from the barons? We have had our suspicions all along it was the military that was behind the attack on the barons. Who else could have timed it so well and across the entire world, eh? So why am I here? Do I need to point out you need the support of the millions of workers on Blackwell-C?"

Now we hadn't thought of that. So people believe that we, the army, carried out this terrorist attack? Damn. We'll have to correct that misconception. General Ernst said, "In no uncertain terms, the military forces of Blackwell-C had no hand in these terrorist attacks. We were taken by surprise, just as has everyone else. Now then, I've asked you here for two reasons. First, we are about to propose a change in the tax structure. The Armed Forces will receive seven percent of a person's income and the director will receive five percent. In other words, we are proposing cutting everyone's taxes. They can keep the other eight percent they were paying to the barons. How will that set with your workers?"

"What? That drastic a cut in taxes? Well, I can tell you that will be cause for rejoicing everywhere and not just within the worker's ranks. Excellent plan. And the second reason?" the man replied.

A bright one here. "The second is to ask if there isn't something else the Federation of Workers desires? I must apologize for not knowing precisely what worker's demands are these days. Until now, my sole focus has been the military and keeping our world safe. We have heard something about your desires to have one UFB woman in every worker's home."

"Now you have hit the festering wound with many of our workers," the man said leaning forward. "You see, until now, only the wealthy could enjoy the many benefits that these, the most beautiful women on Blackwell-C, can provide. We have been lobbying the barons to make UFB women available or affordable to the average worker. Yes, our platform has been to grant one UFB woman per household. As you probably know from the newscasts, we have begun implementing just that with volunteer women protestors, who the barons then attacked with their bio agent weapons, providing us with what we greatly desired, UFB women in worker's homes."

Colonel Achima spoke up. "Am I safe in assuming these new UFB women in the worker's homes are their wives? Are they being treated well? Their needs looked after? Not being physically abused?"

She couldn't tell if he was smiling or not. He responded, "Until now, it has been wives of workers who have stepped forth and volunteered to become UFB women. We desire the older version, the ones who can speak. The new ones like our late baronesses-to-be here in Thromstead are useless if they can't speak, for these are wives and mothers and must be able to speak to help run the family home. Of course, obtaining the fancy clothes and hair machines are far too expensive, but the Federation of Workers has been helping out on that front. So yes. Our ideal goal is to provide for one per home."

"Excellent, excellent. As the new Director of Northen Blackwell, I'm willing to make it the law. Every worker's home must have a UFB woman in it, and she must be well cared for, never mistreated, and all that sort of thing. We now control all those genetic bio agents and can use fabrication machines to help supply the necessary apparel. If we did this and lowered the taxes, what would be the Federation of Workers' position towards this new form of government?"

He answered shrewdly, "You're asking if the Federation of Workers would fully back this new government?"

"Yes."

"Then, I can speak for the Federation and give you an unqualified yes. Full support. Might I ask you what your intentions towards the People's Revolution will be?"

"Hell, man, we don't even know how to contact those radicals, let alone know what they actually want. All this talk about free elections? Elections to what? Mayor? Barons? Until we can meet with one of their representatives, I can't possibly say what our position with them will be."

"Then in light of what you're promising the Federation of Workers, allow us to search out them and send one of their representatives to meet with you," he suggested.

"You can do that? Excellent. Make it happen," the general replied. The two shook hands and the man left.

Around four in the afternoon, Stefan received a phone call from his contact in the Federation of Workers. The man outlined what took place at the meeting with General Ernst

Von Dorfsted. "Now he wants to meet with a People's Revolution representative. My advice, if you do, take pains to hide your face. These are the military for heaven's sake."

Stefan gathered his six friends around him, though Elsa had to help Emil handle getting seated, for he was barely able to walk at this point. He outlined what he'd heard from the Federation of Workers representative. "Look, whether we like it or not, the generals have taken over. At least, they are lowering the taxes substantially, and they are giving the Federation of Workers what they most wanted. I don't dare show up in person, so I figured I'd call him. But what do I ask for? He's not going to buy free and open elections of our rulers."

"Well, you could ask for a blanket amnesty for any crimes the PR people may have done in the past," Dirk suggested. "That might get us off the hook."

"What about Susanne and Karla inheriting their father's estate or funds?" suggested Rudolf.

They chatted for a while longer and decided they really weren't going to be able to get any other concessions from the military. Using a burner phone, Stefan placed the call to the general. However, he called from inside a car that Dirk drove around the streets of central Thromstead. If the military tried to track him, they'd find a moving target. Meanwhile, Ebert followed along in a second car in case they needed to ditch the first car.

"This is the founder of the People's Revolution speaking. The representative from the Federation of Workers told me you wanted to discuss the situation with me," Stefan said. He recorded the call to play back later to everyone else.

"Yes, this is General Ernst Von Dorfsted. Shame we can't meet in person. Nevertheless, this is what is going to be happening shortly." He proceeded to outline the new governmental organization, the new taxation rates and tax cuts, and his concession to the Federation of Workers. "I'll be quite blunt. What will it take for you to throw the complete backing of your People's Revolution behind us?"

"You have already done much that our people desired. Three additional things, all small, and I'll bring the People's

Revolution behind you. First, a general amnesty for any crimes those in the PR may have done in the past to forward our cause. Second, allow the surviving UFB daughters of the late barons to inherit their fair share of their father's wealth. Third, we have always desired free and open elections of our rulers. In this case, when you are ready to retire, we want free and open elections for the next Director of Northern Blackwell-C and for the southern director. Of course, you may pick one of the candidates who will run, but the elections should be open for anyone to run for the director."

The general had his phone on speaker, and everyone listened in, though Colonel Achima was also tracing the call. She pointed to the big screen, which showed the caller's location. The general grimaced. He was moving rapidly and rightly concluded he was in a shuttle or car. "This is all that you desire for your people to fully back the new government?"

"Yes sir. That is sufficient."

"Okay then we have a deal. If you will listen to the news this evening, all these changes will be announced for the world to hear. Goodbye." He hung up. "Too bad we couldn't get a fixed location. I was half a mind to send a patrol to apprehend him. Well, his demands are almost trivial. What crimes? We've not heard of any."

"Not true, sir," Colonel Achima pointed out. "Some are saying that these PR people were behind the terrorist attacks."

"Now that *is* foolish talk. Mere rabble rousers couldn't possibly have executed such a set of well-coordinated attacks across our world," the general dismissed her idea. "Order a news crew in here. We must make our announcements tonight and get this whole matter settled."

At the supper hour when many people turned on the evening news, General Ernst Von Dorfsted, General Franz Himmel, Colonel Achima Nacht, and Colonel Hilda Angst appeared on the screen, though Ernst did all the talking. In front of each was a new placard displaying their new positions, such as Director of Women's Affairs, Northern Blackwell-C in front of Achima. All wore their dress uniforms.

With the whole world watching, he carefully outlined the form the new government was taking, pointing out that nothing was changed with local city government, and that their mayors would retain their current positions and powers. Then, he carefully explained the new taxation rules, pointing out each taxpayer was going to keep eight percent over what he'd been paying in previous years. He then outlined the new laws to be enforce beginning the following Monday.

They included the blanket amnesty for the PR group, the ability for UFB daughters of the barons to inherit their share of their father's wealth, the holding of free and open elections for new directors when he and Franz chose to retire, and finally the new law that demanded a UFB woman in every household, not just the workers. Plus, he announced another ten thousand women would be hired to become UFB women hostesses in the Armed Forces, receiving a yearly salary of the same fifty thousand credits. He stated that the bordellos and the escort services could have as many UFB women of the two types as they desired. His address lasted for close to an hour as he carefully explained each point in some detail. What he didn't say was neither he nor Franz actually intended to hold free and open elections when they chose to retire. How could some farmer possibly be a general? Foolishness beyond all foolishness, but this got the PR people satisfied, which was his objective for now.

"Well, it's not what I had in mind when I began all this," Stefan stated after the broadcast finished and they turned off the TV. "Perhaps it is the best that we can hope for."

"Duh, we forgot the military in our plans," Dirk added. "Dumb us. Still he gave us amnesty and the girls a chance to get their inheritance. I say we did well."

"It remains to be seen if they'll actually get any money," Rudolf grumbled, not trusting the generals at all. "Still, tomorrow, we should file their six requests and see what happens."

Emil had an entirely different point of view, exacerbated by his own genetic mutation. "Look at what we have done to Blackwell-C. Soon, the helpless UFB women will not be few in number—baronesses and escorts—but now tens of thousands in the army and many millions in normal homes. We have brought about a horrible fate for the women of our world, none of whom ever should have been so horribly mutated. Worse, fellows, it is a genetic mutation. That means if they go through with this plan of having every working man's wife be a UFB women, while they will have normal sons, they are only going to have UFB daughters. In just a few generations, every woman on Blackwell-C will be a helpless UFB woman. Who will be left to care for their needs? No one but men. I tell you, we have done the worst thing imaginable for our women. Anne and women are not objects or things. Too many men on this world sure do think they are."

"But we didn't do this; the generals have and the Federation of Workers," Stefan protested, suddenly seeing the truth of Emil's nightmare scenario.

"No, but we made it possible for them to do this," Emil countered, "and now I'm completely helpless to do anything about it. I can't even walk on my own yet."

"But I would love my daughters, even if they are like me and you," Anne protested. "We're people too. Oh, I see what you mean, Emil, about us being treated as objects not people."

Susanne added, "And baronesses are totally just *things*. We weren't even allowed to be a people even. I want to travel, and see the galaxy and the gas clouds the gypsies told me about when they were here years ago."

Rudolf added, "She's right. Once we're married and get things sorted out, I've promised to do just that, only right now, we're not sure how we can do it, but we will."

"I'm going to learn to fly space ships," put in Kirsa. "Wenzel promised to teach me, but after we get married and, like Rudolf says, get things sorted out. Hey, we six were people while we were children, well mostly, more so than once we turned sixteen. After that, dad treated us as just another one of his things.

Nadja added, "I think we all were happy as children, except for all the harassment from the boys. Oh I see what you mean. Killian and the others did treat us as things even when we were little. Well, we aren't things; we're people, but have to have more help than other people. I still want to be a secretary, but I have no idea how I can be, not yet anyway."

"Kirsa is right. We were doing very well, until we turned

sixteen and they started making us wear all those impossible corsets and gowns. That's when dad really began treating me as a thing," Renate added her observation. "I love math and was learning all I could, until I turned sixteen and dad began turning me into his baroness-to-be thing."

Nadja spoke up. "Hey, Emil has a very scary point. If they make everyone's wife into a UFB woman, she can only have UFB daughters. I know that much about the genetic mutations from dad. Probably thirty years from now, there won't be a normal female left on our world. Who is going to look after all the women then? I bet those generals haven't thought this through. I can't see him wiping my butt and dressing me." Everyone laughed at that image.

"It's my fault, really. It was my idea to get rid of all the barons," Stefan said sadly. "I should have just figured out a way to get you six out of their clutches without harming them. I'm to blame, and it's my fault our whole world is going to be wiped out."

Rudolf said, "Snap out of the guilt trip. We all played our parts. Besides, it will never get that bad. If I know those men, once they see our world heading that way, they will import other normal women and make changes to this stupid policy. Right now, we have to first get married and get our wives their proper inheritance. Then, we can figure out what to do next. Susanne and I are going to go see the galaxy somehow."

The next morning, Dirk's priest arrived, bringing with him the six marriage licences. After a simple set of weddings, the forms were signed, and the priest was paid his fee. Dirk then headed off to file the papers, making their marriages legal. While he was gone, the others found the newly made website for the daughters of the barons to submit their claims of inheritance. One by one, the men helped the six fill out their claims and submit them.

In the middle of this activity, a courier came by to drop off the official owner's papers of the new deep space transport, the Shining Star. Officially, Susanne and Karla were now the proud owners of the ship. Once they finished submitting the six claims, Emil insisted everyone memorize the access code that opened the bay doors of the ship. Plus, he had Wenzel make a trip to the spaceport and pay the docking fee. "Look, they won't let the ship take off unless the one time docking fee has been paid. This way, you can leave anytime you want to leave. That is the spaceport control tower's regulations." Wenzel left to do just that. The fee was a hundred credits, which he covered.

That evening, Hedda made a special wedding cake for the new brides, and they celebrated together. At this point, Elsa decided she should speak up for the six brides and possibly for Anne as well. "New husbands, listen up. There's another detail about your UFB wives you must know tonight. All UFB women have extremely powerful sex drives that simply must be satiated. That's what those vaginal stimulator devices have been doing for them. Until now, they need orgasmic relief at least four times a day. Experience has demonstrated if you husbands will satisfy your wife in the morning when you wake and then at night, she will be able to avoid having to have these devices in her during the day, which is the optimal way to go. So you men have another detail to make sure gets handled." She saw mostly reddish faces around the room and knew she'd touched on an embarrassing topic, but one she knew had to be brought out in the open for the well-being of the women.

She ended, "Okay, it's time the new couples head to bed. I'll help Emil and Anne, while Hedda helps Amalia. See you all in the morning."

Once in the privacy of their small section of the house, Emil whispered, "I'm sorry Anne. I didn't know this. I'm sorry if you've been, well uncomfortable all this time. Now, I don't even know how we can do it, but we have to try. Besides, we both want a family."

Anne giggled. "I know. It's been murder trying to suppress it. I'm so glad Elsa explained it all. I love you and that's all that matters to me." Elsa had them ready for bed, but had no idea how they could get the job done. This was beyond her experiences, so she just let nature take its course. Later she checked with Anne and learned they'd figured out a way to do it, and Anne was fully satisfied, much to Elsa's relief. One less detail to have to be straightened out, if ever she was to be able to leave this group of UFB women.

***

Much of October came and went. Emil, Amalia, and Anne were kept busy practicing their walking skills and many other tricks the six UFB women knew. Finally, Emil was somewhat comfortable moving around on his own. Some confidence returned. The four men continued working at their General Goods jobs, but Stefan and Rudolf continued to stay at the house, helping Elsa and Hedda cope with the nine who needed assistance with so many mundane things of life. After these three intense weeks, both men had learned much. Destroyed forever were any notions there was anything super valuable about UFB women, rather they saw the women as victims of sadistic men and sadistic minds.

Towards the end of October, the six women finally received their promised inheritance. Kirsa and Nadja each received around four hundred thousand credits. Susanne and Karla each received around five hundred thousand credits, while Renate and Irma each received four hundred thousand credits. Of course, no one had any idea if these amounts were fair or not. Still, as far as they were concerned, they'd received small fortunes. In late October, they finally were able to meet and decide what to do next.

***

Soldiers arrived at the Dortmund farm, some ten miles south of Thromstead. Implementation of the new law of one UFB woman per family was well underway across Blackwell-C, giving the tens of thousands of soldiers some real action instead of their routine, boring preparation drills. The soldiers put their backs to this new, challenging assignment put before them by their new Director of Northern Blackwell-C, General Ernst.

After opening the door for the soldiers, four marched in and their corporal explained, "We are here to take your choice of one UFB woman per family off to become your UFB woman. Who is your choice?" He glanced around and saw a rather typical farmer's family, farmer, wife, four young children.

"But we can't afford one of those helpless women here,"

164

the farmer protested. "Can't you see she has four young children to care for?"

"Irrelevant, sir. One per family, your choice. I must remind you that if you protest too much, then we are obligated to take you, sir, and make you into one, only those are called UFBMD men. So who will it be?"

"But if you take me, who will run our farm? If you take my wife, I won't be able to farm as much, since I'll have to take care of her and my children," he continued to try to make these soldiers see reason. This was a stupid law, a criminal one.

"That is irrelevant. One per home. Which one? This little one here?" he pointed to their three-year-old girl.

"No! You can't do this to her. She's only three years old," the mother wailed, putting her protective arms around her older daughter.

"You or her," the corporal barked. The poor woman refused to allow them to harm her daughter and allowed herself to be carted off, all the while begging her husband not to interfere for fear he would be taken and all would be lost. Outside, they pinned a badge on her dress giving her name and location along with GPS coordinates of this farm.

The results of this new program were not entirely clear for some time, but only half of the fall's harvest was completed because of the severe workforce shortage. The farmers had little choice but to spend many hours of their days now looking after their gorgeous but mostly helpless wives. By spring, severe food shortages were felt planet-wide.

Soldiers entered a baker's home. He and his wife pleaded she was needed to help run the large bakery store, and without her, they couldn't produce all the loaves their customers wanted to buy, let alone take care of their growing family. When that argument failed, she pleaded she was pregnant and the process would harm her unborn child. Again, the soldiers ignored their protests and took her anyway, affixing a badge to her dress giving her name and address. At least they allowed her to give her three children a goodbye kiss before whisking her away.

Production of bread was cut in half that day and on all subsequent days after that. Further, when she was returned as a gorgeous but helpless UFB woman, production dropped even further, since he had to spend far more time at home helping his wife, though the children, the oldest of which was now six, tried to help their mother as much as possible. Three months later, she gave birth to a daughter. She shrieked when she saw her new daughter was armless and would grow up to be just like her. Her husband did manage to make a carrying sack for her to be able to carry her daughter. A few days later, she and her daughter *fell* from an upper story window, breaking her neck and crushing her daughter. After that, bread production returned to half of the original amount once more.

The soldiers entered the home of one of the devoutly religious family. Holding his Holy Book before him, he swore angrily, "Get out of this holy house. Take your Devil's Spawn elsewhere. Only the Holy Ones are allowed to cross our threshold. The Power of Our Lord resides in this home. We are under his Holy Protection. If you dare harm us, Lord God shall striketh thee down in Holy Flames!" He continually pressed his Holy Book out before him as his shield against these heathens, these Devil's Disciples, these unholy men in their fancy uniforms.

True, the soldiers soon learned to hate going to the homes of those who were deeply religion and likely members of the Righteous of God. These people simply couldn't be reasoned with. Quite why these men didn't want the incredible sex that UFB women offered, the soldiers couldn't fathom. Their two hostesses were simply incredible, satisfying their needs each day. They soon discovered if they took these men's wives, when the wives were returned as UFB women, the men simply killed them, tossing their bodies into the street gutters as the filth they believed they'd been turned into. Likewise, since these holy men protested beyond tolerable limits, the soldiers often took these men to be converted. Once returned to their homes, these crazed individuals quickly found ways to kill themselves. The generals simply ignored all this, seeing an easy way to get rid of those who were opposing their new rule.

***

General Ernst decided to make the headquarters of the Director of Northern Blackwell-C be the former Castle Berthold. In the old throne room, he began running his affairs from the baron's throne, while Colonel Achima Nacht sat in the former baroness's throne, where she began to figure out just what the Director of Women's Affairs was actually to do. General Ernst didn't give her much to go on, but he did assign her an all-female squad, led by Captain Hedda Von Dorfsted. They brought with them their own host who they called Fedde, since he had no voice box and no one knew his actual name. Fedde serviced four members of the squad each day, much to their pleasure, making a complete circuit of the squad every three days.

The first week of October, Director Achima and Captain Hedda began to formulate some ideas to help support women's needs. At the end of the week, she presented her first major proposal to General Ernst. "Sir or Director rather, in some families, the woman is the more highly educated and skilled worker. In such families, I propose her husband should be the one to be made into the UFB woman." She explained her reasoning to the general who listened at least politely, she thought.

"Allow me to give this some serious thought, Colonel or rather Director of Women's Affairs," he responded. Achima was pleased he both listened to her major proposal and was giving it serious consideration.

Back in his new private office, General Ernst grimaced. *She has a good idea, I suppose, though I intensely dislike it. Women should know their place in our society and not take positions away from qualified men. Achima is supposed to be looking after women's affairs now. Wait, the women who need looking after are these fabulous UFB women. She should be focusing on them. She needs proper perspective.* He laughed. *No, she doesn't have a proper perspective, that's what is wrong.* An idea formed, and he cleverly got it executed on the sly.

In the middle of the night, a medic slipped into Colonel Achima's private bedroom, which had once been that of

Susanne's. Their squad's UFBMD Fedde was lying in bed with her, his thick long hair draped over her body and somewhat intertwined with her own blonde hair that she'd let down at night. First, he held an ether soaked rag over the sleeping woman's face. Brief resistance ended. Then, he carefully injected the genetic bio agent into a vein in her arm and quietly departed.

When Captain Hedda came by to pick up Fedde and join her director for the day's work, General Ernst stopped her. "Yes, take Fedde off to his next appointment. Director Achima is currently in her coma. I've decided she needs proper perspective as the Director of Women's Affairs, so she is becoming a proper UFB woman herself. When she recovers, you'll be her assistant as always, and Achima will then have the proper perspective her new position demands. I'll see proper apparel and one of those hair machines are installed here later today. That will be all, captain."

Down south, the next day General Franz followed the lead of General Ernst and secretly had his Director of Women's Affairs properly converted as well. However, Captain Hedda quickly spread the word throughout the northern Armed Forces of what happened to Colonel Achima, the highest-ranking woman in the services. From this point on, all service women lived in fear that they too would be genetically modified. As soon as their terms of service expired, they wisely did not re-enlist.

Four days later, Achima woke to her own living nightmare, though she was now incredibly attractive and her thickened, shiny, wavy blonde hair looked magnificent. She couldn't breathe easily, stand on her own, or walk for some days. However, Captain Hedda saw to her needs and made sure Fedde serviced her once each day.

The start of the New Year saw the new law in the process of being fully implemented across Blackwell-C. In time, every home would have one UFB woman or man in it. However, the sharp drop in production and services was just then beginning to be felt everywhere, though the severe food shortages would not become acute until late spring. The first sign the new directors saw was the significantly lower than expected annual taxes that were collected. The average worker's income was lower than it had been last year, but only by perhaps a tenth. That would change drastically in the coming year, though the directors had not yet realized it.

Chapter 11—Decisions

November came. Emil was now almost competent at getting around on his own, as were Anne and Amalia. All nine were somewhat able to feed themselves using their feet and toes, totally unlike the millions of other new UFB women across the world. However, Stefan and his five friends noticed finding groceries had become much more difficult. They had to visit several stores in order to pick up all Hedda had on her list for them to purchase.

Mayor Beifeld did finally pay a visit to his son and daughter, but spent most of the visit trying to keep from crying too badly. He did explain shortages were appearing here and there around Thromstead and suggested the cause was the sudden loss of able-bodied women, due to this new law of one UFB woman per home. He left them all rather depressed with the future prospects for the world.

"It is just as I predicted," Emil pointed out. "I wouldn't be surprised if nearly half of the production of this world is now gone."

"You think women help that much?" asked Wotan.

"How can that be?" asked Stefan, baffled. "I've not seen many factory workers who are women. Women are a part of GD's workforce, but they don't hold critical positions."

"Perhaps this wouldn't have happened if they did," Emil stung them. All he had now was words and his mind. Everything else had been taken from him or so he believed at this time.

"But how?" Stefan pressed him, respecting his opinion, even if he looked like his wife, Anne.

"Look, while women might not have been working on factory floors in large numbers, they now require vast amounts of care, like we nine do. Someone has to take care of them. I bet anything their husbands are now spending much of their usual working hours not at work, but at home dealing with their new UFB wives and doing the household chores they used to do, such as grocery shopping and washing. Between the female workers no longer working and the husbands who can't work as many hours, production will be down in all sectors, most critically that of food production," Emil guessed correctly.

"He might be right, fellows," Wenzel suggested. "Just look how hard it is for us to get the weekly groceries now. Last time, we had to go to six stores just to get Hedda's list filled. Oh, I see what Emil means. Men have to do the grocery shopping now. If our wives were not UFB women, they would likely be getting the groceries, not us."

"Division of labor. I follow you," Rudolf spoke up. "I wonder who is handling the secretary duties now. Probably they have to pull men off their old jobs just to handle what the women workers used to do. Emil's right. Things are going to get really bad around here and soon."

Susanne interjected, "So isn't this a good time for us all to leave and go see the wonders of the galaxy? We are owed a honeymoon, fellows."

"She's got my vote," Rudolf replied.

"You would, she's your wife, and you've wanted to travel as well," Stefan teased him.

Dirk decided now was the time to share a rumor that had been circulating around General Goods this past week. "Gang, there's something else. I know this is just a rumor, but word has it the alien corporations are not taking this situation here lightly. Some are suggesting GD and GE are coming back to Blackwell-C to retake what they lost and punish the world for the attacks on their two headquarters here in Thromstead."

"Can they do that? Won't the generals put a stop to their meddling in our affairs?" asked Stefan. Several shrugged their shoulders.

Emil said, "As corrupt as GD and GE CEOs were, I would certainly expect them to retaliate in force." That sobered them all.

Elsa who had been quietly listening to this discussion decided now was the time for her to speak up. "If I might add to what Dirk has hinted at. . ."

"Please do," Emil acknowledged her, having come to depend upon her wisdom, to say nothing of her having saved his life in the elevator shaft.

Elsa said calmly, though carefully, "I've been around a long time and have had some contact with other Federation worlds. Don't ask how. Anyway, these corporations are fanatical when it comes to meeting resistance to their take-over plans. With the annihilation of their two main headquarters here in Thromstead, it's a complete certainty they'll be returning carrying a very heavy hammer with them. They see this as a direct threat to their survival, especially in these times where many of their corporation-controlled worlds are rebelling against their totalitarian rule. I'm actually surprised they haven't reacted before now."

"Won't our Armed Forces be able to hold them off?" asked Dirk. While he didn't like what the army was doing, still, they should be able to defend their world from the aliens.

Elsa answered truthfully, "Your army will be as effective against the corporation forces as UFB women are against your soldiers, Dirk. Pitiful at best. You have some idea of just how ruthless Dederick and Gerhardt were, but those who controlled those leaders are much worse and will likely stop at nothing to regain control over Blackwell-C, likely total, absolute control at that. Why they haven't done so yet, I can't say. But he's right. They are coming, and I sure don't want to be here when they come."

"Why? What can they do?" asked Dirk. Everyone was now listening intently to Elsa's every word.

"They could simply nuke every major city on this world, killing everyone."

"But that's genocide isn't it? They can't do that, could they?" asked Stefan, shocked.

"They can and have done so. They then bring in new people from other overpopulated Federation worlds," Elsa explained, wondering if everyone on Blackwell-C had no knowledge of Federation history or was it just these adolescent lads that were so ignorant?

"But we have a planetary defense shield," Stefan protested.

Dirk spoke up, "Hey, I heard the soldiers won't be getting around to its installation until next year. They have their hands full going door to door enforcing the one UFB woman law."

"That settles it," Emil declared. "I'm helpless to defend my wife and sister. I vote we use the Shining Star and go somewhere soon, while we still can."

Susanne looked at Rudolf and added, "We're with Emil." Rudolf grinned, blowing her a kiss.

"We all should go," Renate spoke up. "All of us, unless Hedda doesn't want to leave, since she's got a family here."

"All in favor raise your hand," Ebert called out.

"Sexist pig," Irma teased him, "most of us don't have a hand to raise." He flushed red, but everyone was in total agreement to leave Blackwell-C soon.

"So where do we go?" asked Emil. "I know nothing of other worlds."

Elsa smiled. *They've played into my hands.* She broke the silence, "We should go to a rim world called Scorpi-C for two reasons. One, they have rebelled against corporation rule and are now a free world. Their whole sector is free as well. Two, they may have more cures for you. They are able to regrow arms on their own UFB women victims. I don't know if this cure will work on you or not, but it's worth a try."

"What? There is a way I could get my arms back? And Anne's and Amalia's?" Emil exclaimed, a surge of long lost hope swelling inside his overly emotional body.

"I can't promise you their cure will work on you, but it is worth a try," Elsa answered. "It depends upon your DNA, I think, but I'm not a doctor or a geneticist."

"Let's go tomorrow!" Emil pipped up, unable to contain his racing emotions. He'd always been calm and unemotional, but after his genetic modification into almost a woman, his emotions frequently swamped his reasoning powers, something he simply didn't understand.

"One second," Stefan said quietly. "Who is going to fly the ship? Who is capable of galactic navigation?" Silence.

"Damn it! I used to be able to fly one, mostly," Emil answered, fighting to keep from breaking down again. "I mean I might have been able to fly it. I used to fly local shuttles. It can't be much harder I suppose."

Elsa remained silent. Already, she'd told them too much. Fortunately, they'd not bothered to ask her how she knew all this about distant rim worlds. She wasn't ready to blow her long-standing cover here on Blackwell-C. Instead, she fired off an electronic data burst, outlining the situation as it now was, though she knew she wouldn't be receiving a reply for at least a couple of days. Much was going on in this mid-arm region, not just on Blackwell-C. Resources were extremely thin. Secrecy was paramount.

***

In Achima's private bedroom at the castle, she sat erect on the edge of her bed, her long blonde tresses draped over her right shoulder. Her long-time and dearest friend, Captain Hedda Von Dorfstad, sat on her left, having just let her own black hair down for the night and was brushing it out for the night. Hers fell to the small of her back. Both women loved long hair, but now Achima's was radically different and even longer. "All is lost, Hedda, gone, stripped away from me and my son," Achima said sadly.

"I know dearest, I know. We both wanted to have a super-genius son. I checked with the medic this afternoon, you know, about your continuing to wear that awful corset. He said your internal organs were moved around, lowered or something. Guess that's why your pelvis region is larger now. He said the corset wouldn't be interfering at all. Still, I don't know whether to believe him or not."

Achima sadly said, "I was going to call him Fritz, the peaceful ruler. But now, he's just going to be another one of those freaky men and not a super-genius."

"I know dear, I know. I'm still going to call my son Jan. For days after the madman got to you, I was terrified he was going to convert me too. I rather thought he found out we were pregnant with sons from the freak Fedde and that he was going after me too. But it's been nearly a month, and he's not done it, so maybe we are safe."

"But I'm not safe. How can I even have a baby, like this? I can't hold him or anything," Achima finally broke down again, though at least she was in her own room and with her dearest friend.

"I'm here, and I always will be. God, I hope so. Anyway, I heard some scary news today. Some of the squad was over at General Goods and heard talk that the corporations were going to respond to the destruction of their GD and GE headquarters and personnel," Hedda explained.

"What kind of response?" Achima stopped sniffling and tried to act more responsible. It's just her emotions were running wild, probably due to the pregnancy.

"According to Hedy, it could be really bad, maybe even so far as a nuclear attack on us. They say there are overpopulated worlds out there in the Federation, and they could just bring in millions of new people once we're all gone."

"Might not be a bad idea," Achima commented, a sour taste in her mouth. She wanted the general dead, but now could barely walk, let alone fight.

"I know dear, I know. What we need is to get off this world. Go somewhere where we can be safe and raise our sons."

Achima looked up, "But we would need a transport ship to do that. We can't take a commercial one. The general would be on us in a blink. Desertion and all that."

"I know that. That's why I think we should just steal one. We both can fly it—sorry, well you used to be able to fly a transport. Still, it's our only chance to flee before all hell breaks out. Do you know food is running low? I heard the quartermaster talking yesterday. He's having a hard time finding potatoes and apples."

"Okay, I'm convinced, Hedda. We have to leave. But how can I steal a ship? I can barely walk. I'll just slow you down. You go and leave me to my fate, dear. Save your son," Achima sighed.

"Don't be heroic. I'm not leaving you. You'd not leave me if the tables were turned. So don't ever say that again. Now, the question is just where is the best place to steal a deep space transport? I used to know a fellow who worked at the spaceport. Tomorrow, I'm going to look him up, see if he can get me the layout of the spaceport, and where they keep the transports. Then, you and I will make our getaway plans."

"Really? Thank you, Hedda. Thank you. Are you ready

to lie down? I could use it now," Achima whispered.

"I know dear. Your drive is incredible, but I do love to share with you. You know that," Hedda whispered back and gently pressed her lips onto Achima's, knowing just how fast that would trigger Achima's sexual drives. She wasn't disappointed.

The next morning, Captain Hedda found her contact's address from Mayor Beifeld and drove her jeep over to his address, a small, modest home. Wearing her army uniform and her hair tied in a tight bun, she walked briskly up the steps and knocked on the door. Either he was here or he was at work. She knew he was married. That much was on record when she looked him up, but his address wasn't, which was why she went through the mayor, having remembered he had once said that his father was Thromstead's mayor. A strange young man, probably in his late teens, opened the door.

"Excuse me. I was told that Emil Beifeld lived here. I wish to speak to him on an urgent matter. Is he here or at work?"

"Hello. Yes, he's here. Just who are you? What does the army want with him?" Stefan nearly panicked when he saw the colorful uniform of the soldier of some rank at the door. That she wanted Emil startled him further. Had the army finally figured out he and Emil had attacked GD headquarters?

"Captain Hedda Von Dorfstad. I'm an old friend of Emil's. I'm here unofficially. Please, I must see him," she explained, her alto voice rising slightly. *Should I just push my way inside? No, play it cool.*

"Well you wait here. I'll see if Emil will see you. Okay?" Stefan insisted, not daring to take a chance. He closed the door and ran into the living room where the others were gathered. "Emil, some Captain Hedda Von Dorfstad is here to see you. Says you are an old friend of hers. Says it's unofficial, but I don't believe her. Should I just send her away?"

Emil thought for a second, "Oh, yeh, I remember her. She joined the army. I'll see what she wants. Let her in, we'll talk in the hallway." He tossed his head about getting his long black hair off to one side and carefully rose to his feet, avoiding stepping on it. He began his slow, shuffling walk towards the hallway, knowing the captain would be there long before he was. He was right about that. Stefan let her in, telling her Emil would see her in the hallway shortly. He left, though he kept watch from the living room doorway. Captain Hedda's eyes opened wide, as she saw a gorgeous woman with knee-length black hair taking her tiny four-inch steps towards her. She blinked several times.

"My God! Emil? Is this really you? What happened?" Captain Hedda gushed, forgetting any pretense of formality.

Still moving slowly towards her, in his new soprano voice, the embarrassed Emil said, "Yes, it's me, Hedda. I was genetically modified, but that's pretty damned obvious. Give me a couple of minutes to get to you."

"Oh it won't take you that long. At least, you are walking well. My Achima isn't walking half as well as you are." A handshake was out. She decided against giving him a hug. Hugging Fedde always got him sexually aroused, and she certainly didn't want that to happen to Emil.

"Hi. You look well. So what brings you to see me? I'm pretty darn useless now. I can't even help my wife or sister who also got genetically modified," Emil said, finally drawing close to her.

"Can we talk frankly and privately, Emil?"

"Of course. What's up?"

"Well, I don't know what all you've heard, but my dearest friend, Colonel Achima Nacht—well she got modified too, against her will, by General Ernst. You see, we both wanted to have super-genius sons and managed to get our host, the UFBMD Fedde to get us pregnant with sons. Now her hopes are dashed—well you know that better than I do. Anyway, we desperately want to leave this world, and we need a deep space transport. Mind you, we both can fly one—well that's not true now. Achima can't. So we want to swipe one from the spaceport to make our getaway. I remembered you worked there—sorry, used to work there, and I thought maybe you could tell me the layout and where they keep transports that we could possibly swipe," she finished up with a sigh. *He probably can't help us now. I should have just left when I saw her, er him. Should I offer to take him with us? What if he knows, but insists taking him with us is his price?*

"Captain Hedda, they have the transports locked down. The only way you would have any chance of stealing one is to know the access code to its bay doors. Without that, you would partially have to destroy the ship to get the doors opened," Emil explained.

"Sorry to have wasted your time," she cut him off.

"Wait, captain. My group owns a deep space transport, and we want to leave here too, but we don't have anyone who is qualified to fly it. Well, I might have before—well, you know what I mean. If you are willing to fly us to where we want to go, I'm certain the others will be very happy to have you and Achima come with us. Only we want to leave as soon as possible. We are scared the corporations are going to launch a counterattack any day now. What say you?"

Hedda's downcast look vanished, replaced with an exuberant one. "We accept! You are saving us. I could kiss you!" Hedda's relief was dramatic.

"Better not. Anne might get jealous," he teased her. Seeing her questioning look, "My wife, another UFB woman. They kidnaped her and did it to her, but I found her and rescued her. We can be ready to leave, as soon as you and Achima get here. Just tell us when, and we'll be ready to go."

"You are serious, aren't you?" Emil nodded. "Okay then, we'll come by around ten in the morning. I need time to get her ready—guess you know that very well. Ten tomorrow. We'll be on your doorstep. Thank you, thank all of you. You are saving us and our babies." She forgot and gave him a hug.

Having overheard the conversation from the doorway, Stefan called out, "Way to go, Emil! We've a way to leave. I'll go tell the others!" He dashed off. As Emil began his slow, careful walk back to the living room and the others, he fought back tears. He wanted to rush and tell Anne and Amalia, but had no way to move any faster than this pitiful pace. When he got back, the others were chatting excitedly about this wholly unexpected opportunity.

"So you know this captain?" asked Anne.

"Yes, I met her a few times at the spaceport. Couple of years back before she joined the army. She's all right and taking a big risk. They could be shot for desertion or worse. We better get packing. How are we going to take all this stuff with us?"

"I can't live without the hair machine," Anne half-teased, but the nine knew she was dead serious about it. None of them could do without it.

"I'll go rent a truck, and we can ferry stuff out to the ship today," Wotan offered.

Packing became the game for the day. The women did have quite a lot of apparel to bring along with them, and the nine hair machines, though they decided to leave one for everyone to use tomorrow morning. Emil remembered food. "Hey Wotan, when you guys unload the stuff on the Shining Star, be sure to check on the state of provisions. There might not be any food supplies, since the ship was dropped off and has been basically in storage since then."

"You got it boss," he hollered back. When the four men returned from their first trip, Wotan reported there was water but nothing else except some emergency rations. Making a wild guess on travel time, Emil suggested they lay in enough supplies to last the eighteen of them for a week. Better safe than sorry, he thought, trying to think ahead. Then, he remembered to have them check on the fuel situation, hoping normal refueling policies had been used. That is, when any space ship landed at the spaceport, the control tower automatically fully refueled the ship, naturally collecting the expensive refueling cost. It ensured the spaceport had ample operating funds at all times. Much to Emil's relief, that was the case. The Shining Star was fully fueled. He knew that was enough fuel to travel halfway across the entire galaxy, and they only needed to go perhaps half that distance. Now he relaxed, but felt horrible that he could do nothing at all to help Elsa and the six men pack. *If I could just get my arms back,* he thought, but immediately felt his eyes watering and tried hard to prevent the tears, failing miserably.

"Oh! Ten of us," exclaimed Achima, when Captain Hedda helped her walk carefully into the living room where everyone was excitedly awaiting their arrival.

"Wow, Achima, you look gorgeous. What a change from

what we saw of you on the TV," Amalia declared.

Emil rose carefully and said, "I best do the introductions. Most of us are married. This is Stefan and Renate."

"My God! You, you are the baroness's daughters. I recognize you six!" Achima interrupted him.

Renate flushed. "Yes, we are, but not any longer. We are free of those sadistic fathers."

Emil continued, "Rudolf and Susanne. Wotan and Nadja. Wenzel and Kirsa. Dirk and Karla. Ebert and Irma. I'm Emil, Achima, and my beautiful wife, Anne, and my young sister, Amalia. This is Elsa, who has been Susanne's assistant since she was a little girl. Gang, Hedda and Achima, but you know that. We're ready to go. We can't tell you how much we appreciate having you with us. None of us can fly the transport. Well I used to be able to, and Kirsa and Wenzel really do want to learn how to do it. We best get going since we're pathetically slow moving."

The six ex-baronesses-to-be headed towards the door and Renate called out, "Just prop the doors open for us, Stefan. We can manage."

"How can you walk without someone holding on to you?" asked a surprised Achima.

"Oh, we were born this way. Nothing to it, except we've had nearly eighteen years of practice. We do very well on our own. We've been teaching the others how to feed themselves using their feet and toes. Kind of hard, but beats having to have someone do it for us. We can show you too once we're on the ship," Susanne happily explained.

"I'll feel better if someone can support Anne, Amalia, and me," Emil broke in, hating to have to say this, but knowing that the three of them did need the steadying support, especially with the short stairs out front. A half hour later, everyone was crammed into the rented car of Hedda's, Wotan's car, and the rented truck. The trip to the spaceport took just a few minutes compared to the half hour getting out and into the car. At least, the gate man allowed them to drive the vehicles up to the waiting transport, especially when he saw the ten helpless women in the group.

Another half hour passed before the ten were safely onboard and strapped into their passenger seats. Wenzel insisted on sitting in the navigator's seat so he could watch what Hedda did, as she began the lengthy pre-flight checks. Meanwhile three others drove the two rented vehicles back, dropping them off, and returning in Wotan's car. By the time they returned, having walked from the car park to the ship, Hedda was ready to lift off, complete with tower clearance.

Captain Hedda didn't dare voice her fears and those of Colonel Achima's. They were going AWOL from the army, deserters. If anyone got wind of their flight, they would face severe punishments. Plus, it would dash these people's hopes of leaving Blackwell-C. Silently, she kept her fingers crossed, knowing Achima was doing the same thing, even though she didn't have fingers. Only when the lights on her panel showed the bay doors had closed and locked did she breathe a sigh of relief. She fired up the engines, acknowledged the tower's permission to take off, and applied the power. Up they went, slowly gaining altitude, while the passengers watched their world below slowly shrinking. Only then did Achima breathe a huge sigh of relief, very nearly fainting.

"Why are you still wearing that awful corset?" Susanne asked. "We really don't need them if the fellows will massage our backs often enough to keep the pain from building up. Breathing is so hard."

"Didn't know we could," she answered gasping slightly. "Guess someone can get me out of it later on. Where are we going?"

Before anyone could answer her, Hedda's voice came over the intercom, "Okay, we're in orbit and free and clear of our miserable world. Destination anyone?"

Wenzel answered, "We're supposed to go to Scorpi-C somewhere out in the rim. Elsa knows where it is."

"Coming," Elsa yelled, rapidly headed on up to the front. She gave Wenzel a quick introduction in the use of the hyperspace navigation system's menus. "There, that's it. Select it. Press Enter. Good. See it has put those coordinates into the system."

"Great. You know something about this," Hedda

replied, a bit surprised. "Now Wenzel, press the Fuel Needed item. Tell me what it says."

"Two days at half fuel at half speed. Does that mean we have enough fuel?" he asked.

"Yes, it means that if we go at half our top speed, we would only use up half of our fuel and take two days to get there," Hedda replied. "Of course, as you see, there are other options. But that's fine with me. I don't want to run out of fuel. So press Accept." He did so. "Now press Execute. Everyone, we're about to jump into hyperspace. Be there in two days." He hit the button, and the ship giggled slightly, but the world outside the ship turned entirely black, the void of hyperspace.

"So why Scorpi-C? Where is it? Is it safe for us?" asked Hedda, unfastening her seat belts and motioning for Wenzel to do the same.

"I'll explain when we join the others," Elsa answered.

A minute later, the three joined the others in the passenger bay. Elsa said, "Achima, Hedda, Scorpi-C is way out on the rim, Abelard Sector. Why there? They have had a rebellion and have thrown off corporation rule, though the corporations still conduct normal business there. It is a free world and a free sector. More importantly, some of their geneticists have invented some cures for the UFB women. One cure does regrow their arms. I want to take our people there and see if that can be done for all ten. Mind you, it might not be possible. It depends on your DNA somehow. I know nothing about that though. So Achima, there may be some hope for you and the rest yet. We'll see in a couple of days. Now as your mother hen, we should get everyone assigned cabins and some of you fellows can get started on the cooking. I'm not a cook."

***

Four days later, at the GE Medical Research Laboratories on Scorpi-C, the ten finally received the greatest news ever. They'd arrived safely, made inquiries at the spaceport, and were sent here. The doctors took DNA samples from all ten before making any suggestions. Now the doctors presented them with their choices of cures. "Yes, your DNA will allow you to have your arms regrown. In addition, your breasts can be reduced by about half to an H-cup size. Your feet can be partially repaired, but you will need to wear six-inch heels, a marked improvement everyone says. We need to know which of these cures you each want."

"All them," came the ten replies. Achima then asked, "What about my baby? I'm a month pregnant."

The doctor smiled. "You son will have the same cures that you elect to have and will be just fine." Achima sighed with relief. "Of course, you will be in a coma for about four days while the bio agent works its genetic mutations on your bodies. When would you like to begin?"

"Now!" came ten responses almost in unison. He smiled, anticipating that, for he'd seen these reactions hundreds of times now.

He then said, "Based on many, many similar cases, we will know your new sizes once the cures are done. While you are in your comas, your companions can acquire proper fitting apparel and shoes for you. The cost is ten thousand credits, but only if you can afford it."

Susanne piped up, "I'll pay for everyone's cures." That brought a smile to the doctor's face. He wouldn't be doing this group non grata.

Right on time, four days later the ten woke up to entirely new lives. While they were celebrating, Elsa announced, "Susanne, you and the others are now able to care for your own needs. At this time, I will take my leave from you and head off to find others who need my help." She gave the young woman a hug and shook hands with the others.

"But where will you go? Do you need money? How can we ever thank you?" Susanne asked, shocked to see Elsa leaving her. She'd been her assistant all her life.

"I don't need money, dear. I'll go where I'm needed. We may meet again one day. Bye all." Elsa hated this part of her job the most. She'd formed real bonds with these six women, Susanne in particular. However, she had fulfilled the bargain she had made with Zelda over twenty-one years ago. She'd seen Zelda's daughters to safety. Now she had to decide what path to take next. Blackwell-C was becoming a total disaster world.

Chapter 12—Corporations' Ire

Blackwell-C was located at the edge of the Zellar Sector, Mid-arm, and its corporations were theoretically under the control of the regional offices on Zeta Minor-C. In late September, via the General Goods CEO on Zeta Minor-C, the GD and GE CEOs learned of the terrorist attack and total loss of all personnel at their main headquarters in Thromstead, Blackwell-C. Now they fully understood their mistake in hiring local men to be their CEOs there. On the positive side, they did know that the Blackwell-C GD CEO had acquired the new growth cloning machines and were conducting experiments with them.

Thus, they appointed two new bright young and rising men to be their new CEOs of Galactic Dynamics and Galactic Electronics on Blackwell-C. Both men were highly intelligent and had just married appropriate UFB women, second-generation ones at that. Perfect corporate executives read their bios. Felix Gott and his new wife Lisa were twenty-two. Lisa had stunning blonde hair, which she allowed to reach nearly ankle length, preferring it to grow some beyond knee-length that her genetically modified body demanded. The new GE CEO was George Gebberly who had just married Beth, a gorgeous and vibrant brunette. They too were both just twenty-two.

At a private meeting with the two regional CEOs, both men received identical marching orders. Study the situation on Blackwell-C and take appropriate actions to secure this world permanently under corporation control. Haste was not important, total control was. When they asked further, their bosses indicated they could use any means necessary including a complete repopulation of the world. Both Felix and George understood why.

Already, the corporations' iron hand control over many of their subordinate worlds in this sector was being severely challenged. Two such worlds had already broken away, declaring their independence of the corporation rule, but not without having lost nearly all their space fleets in the battles that led to their independence. GD and GE could not afford to lose yet another world, even if this one wasn't truly worth all that much to the corporations' pocketbooks. This world produced very little that was exportable to other worlds.

As the pair of new executives looked over what was known of the history of this backwater world, they wondered even why the corporations were interested in salvaging the world. Still, they had their orders and their opportunity to show top management just what they could do. During October, of necessity, they received daily reports via the CEO of General Goods there in Thromstead. That the generals of their armed forces had taken over control of the world, they found most interesting. Apparently, the ancient tradition of feudal rule by local barons had been ended.

As the figures came in, they began to realize why this had happened. With over five thousand exposed to this new version of the genetic bio agent, the barons would be unable to speak besides being stunning looking *women* and helpless. Thus, the two men could not salvage even one of those who used to work for GD and GE there in Thromstead. Nor was there any chance that control by barons could be re-established. The generals had tried that, bringing in the retired barons, who were now only a handful of old men, hardly capable of rebuilding that system.

Felix and George studied the new *laws* created by the generals with their new titles of Directors. They saw tax law changes as being beneficial to the workers, believing this was a very positive change. "From what we are seeing," Felix commented to George, "it seems these generals know precisely how to solidify their control over this world. Give the average person a significant tax break, more take-home pay. Apparently, the men on this world greatly prize you UFB women," he added, bringing a smile to both Lisa and Beth's faces. "Their workers are demanding a UFB woman in every household. How very interesting indeed. I wonder if these generals can actually make that happen. They must have access to the genetic bio agent from GD headquarters and are duplicating it in quantity in order to create this many UFB women."

"We should see how this plays out, Felix," George pointed out. "On most worlds, only we top executives have and can afford the incredible luxury of you fabulous UFB women." Beth again smiled lovingly at her new husband.

By November, from the reports coming back from General Goods, apparently this new law of the generals or directors rather was being widely implemented and accepted. They had even appointed a UFB woman to head up a Director of Women's Affairs. However, neither Felix nor George had any idea what these two women actually did or even if they had any real authority. "We must have more data before we take action," Felix pronounced and George agreed. Besides, winter was coming to the world, not a great time to launch attacks.

Meanwhile, Felix and George created a population progression program, based upon the population of the world and the number of UFB women in households, figuring most would be workers' wives. Both men sat back staring at the projection results. In thirty years, the only women then bearing children would be UFB women. All those normal women and children not currently modified would be modified when they married, presuming this law remained in effect. Within thirty years, only stunningly beautiful UFB women would be born to the many mothers. Statistically, the numbers from the UFBMD men would remain minuscule.

Beth and Lisa moved up behind the men and looked over their shoulders. Lisa asked, "If all the women are like us, UFB women, then who will become their personal assistants? Obviously, we have to have our assistants."

"My goodness, Lisa, you've hit it precisely. Who'll be their assistants? The only possibility will be men, who'll have to be pulled off their jobs to care for the women. What are those two generals thinking?" Felix barked, annoyed and shocked.

George and Beth started laughing. He answered, "Too much of a good thing can make you sick." All four laughed, though the situation was dire. The path this planet was on was one of implosion, perhaps starvation because of a lack of food production and distribution capabilities.

"We're going to also have to save these idiots from themselves," Felix declared.

"Our job just got a whole lot more difficult," George added, grimly.

"But how can you save them?" Lisa asked. "If all their women end up like us, they can only have more baby girls like us. I suppose you could import a whole lot of servant girls or something to help their women. After all, we love to have children as much as any woman does."

"We need to do two things," Felix proposed. First, we have to get that idiotic law canceled. Second, we're going to have to maintain a goodly supply of normal women somehow. Importation must be a last resort. After all, how could we expect to import only women and into such a dangerous situation? No, we need to study those new growth clone machines. That may be our answer, cloning many normal local women to make up the losses. We need a complete population breakdown."

"I'll get on that. Come on Beth. You can lend me a hand," George volunteered.

"Yes, I'd love to dear, if only I can remember where I misplaced them," Beth teased him. Between these two, this was their favorite amusement, never failing to bring a big smile to their faces. *This is why I married her,* George thought, *an amazing sense of humor. That and her brilliant mind.* He made contact with the CEO of General Goods in Thromstead, asking for a complete population breakdown, knowing that would take some time to obtain, especially under their current situation.

Mid-November, George and Beth finally had the solid numbers they were after. Blackwell-C had somewhat of a population explosion during the last century. It boasted one billion inhabitants. Discounting older generations, the current children, those who were not married, and their average number of children per family, fifty million married women of childbearing age became the target pool. Per the two generals' own figures, they had already reached some ten million women, primarily those in and around the major cities, with another ten million likely to be done fairly soon. The remaining thirty million women were going to be vastly harder to reach, living in very rural areas and smaller towns. With only around forty thousand soldiers to fan out and reach these women, completion of the general's grand plan was going to take them far more than all next year.

George and Beth rightly concluded that they had time to save the world, though it was plain that many normal women must be cloned and inserted into the population pools of the large cities where the conversion of the wives to UFB women was nearly complete. Doing the nasty calculations in her head, Beth concluded with a steady flow of cloned normal women being input into the mix, it was possible to arrest the decline and obtain equilibrium within about twenty years. As long as there wasn't another huge influx of women being turned into UFB women, the world would be stable.

"Just don't clone ugly women," Beth jested, "or no man will marry them."

Lisa asked an entirely different question, "Just what actual benefits will GD and GE get from controlling this backwater world? It doesn't export foods. It doesn't export rare earths. Honey, can you scroll the screen for me? I'm trying to see just what actual value this world is to your corporations."

"One second, dear," Felix said, moving over and scrolling the listing down another page for her. "I've got some additional ways we can take over. I could expose the world to the Tincture Plague. It is guaranteed to wipe out half their population in six months before the virus reaches the end of its life cycle. Now if there was one that only sickened soldiers, we could land and take over the world easily."

Lisa continued scanning the lengthy list. She sighed, "Honey, I just don't see any real commercial value in this Blackwell-C world. Apparently, they export engine assemblies, but all the parts to make them are first imported. Well, GE does export copper wire and some small quantities of silicates destined for circuit boards. Even the exported gold, silver, and precious stones are minuscule compared to other worlds. Honestly, honey, I don't see any financial value in this

Blackwell-C world. What am I missing?"

"Oh surely, you must be missing something. Move over. Let me look. George, have a look too. This world must have some value to our corporations or why else would we be sent there?" Felix asked, slightly annoyed.

Both men stopped and looked over the import-export documents for the past years. "Well, this doesn't make much sense. Unless all the data isn't here, this is truly a marginal world. So why are we being given carte blanche to regain corporation control over it?" Felix asked.

George commented, "Well, if we decide to land with say two hundred thousand soldiers and launch a big battle to retake the world, the sheer cost of that operation exceeds this world's net exports. It would take a hundred years to cover the corporation's costs to bring in the soldiers. We must not be seeing something of critical importance with this world."

"Hum, maybe this is a career making test," Felix began developing other reasons why they were given this special assignment. "If we retake this world using two hundred thousand soldiers and the cost of that action will, as you say, consume the net exports of the world for the next century, then that would reflect horribly on our management skills. Hell, I would even fire myself for squandering corporation resources. Yes, George, Lisa has stumbled upon the truth of our new assignments. It simply must be a test of our management skills."

"I do believe you are right, Felix, and we almost blundered in major ways, in all likelihood ending our new careers! So we have to play it smart and regain control of the world at little or no corporation expense," George declared, "but how?"

"Well, we were given one fact: time wasn't a critical factor. If it had been, we would have been assigned some infantry divisions. Hell, this world has never even had a Federation Infantry Division stationed there, only their own world's Armed Forces, a pretty pathetic bunch by all accounts," Felix pointed out.

George mused a moment. Beth spoke up, "I just calculated the cost of putting and then keeping a Federation

Infantry Division on Blackwell-C exceeds their net exports by five to one and ten to one, respectively."

"Huh? Beth, simple terms please," Felix complained. Sometimes her brilliant math skills and manner of speaking zinged over his head.

"Silly man, it would take five years of exports to cover the cost of landing an infantry division there, but if it was permanently stationed there, it would take ten years of exports to cover one year of its occupation. In simple terms, Felix, using an infantry division on Blackwell-C is prohibitively expensive. Only an idiot is going to spend five to ten times what something is worth."

"Oh, I get it. So why didn't you just say that in the first place?" Felix grumbled. He hated being shown up by anyone, especially by a UFB woman, who was just supposed to be the ultimate sex doll. Looking for a way temporarily to have the women elsewhere, he recalled, "Say, Lisa, don't you have that interview for your new personal assistant today?" He knew it was today, in an hour to be precise.

Lisa's longtime assistant was retiring and didn't want to move from this world to the *primitive* Blackwell-C and had given her notice two days ago, taking Lisa by complete surprise. However, she had recommended another woman, one who had lived on this backwater world and who had been the personal assistant for one of their strange baroness's daughters. Her assistant had said, "Child, those daughters used to be very much like you, only as I understand it, they couldn't speak or see. So I'm sure this young personal assistant is quite good at her job." Given that recommendation, Lisa had agreed to meet this new woman and give her an interview before Lisa posted a help-wanted ad. The meeting was in an hour.

"Yes, it is. Don't worry, honey. I'm watching the time. Come on, Beth; you can interview her too, since we're nearly always together. I value your opinion. I certainly must have a good assistant," Lisa suggested. Carefully, the two women tossed their heads, getting their long hair to slip over to one side out of the way of their feet, rose, and began their slow walk out of this large study and planning room. Approaching the doors, they smiled as the automatic doors opened for them.

"Bet they don't have these on this backwater world," Beth commented.

Some fifteen minutes later, they reached the spacious apartment's living room, where Beth's servant joined them, bringing a tray of teacups, a fresh pot, and straws. She knew these two beautiful new brides valued their semi-independence and allowed them to stand and toss their hair about until it slipped over one shoulder out of their way, and sat down on the sofa. She then poured their tea. Inserting the straws, she slid them expertly over the end table to where both could easily reach the straws. Since their heavily steel boned corsets prevented much bending, this end table was quite tall, perfect for the two young women. "I will answer the door, madams," she said politely and left the room.

"Oh, I do so hope this assistant will work out. I just hate trying to break a new one in," Lisa complained. "I had to do that twice now, such a bother. They never seem to know what we truly need or when."

Beth giggled. "I know. Royal pain. We aren't completely helpless or stupid." Both giggled and sipped their tea. The doorbell sounded, and shortly, Beth's servant woman entered leading another young woman. "Madam Lisa Gott, this is Miss Elsa Gotte. Elsa, this beautiful young blonde is your potential employer. Her constant companion is Madam Beth Gebberly. I will retire now."

"Pleased to meet you, Elsa. Help yourself to some tea and sit," Lisa said politely. *The woman is perhaps in her early twenties, probably my own age. Not overly attractive though. Rather plain dress.*

Elsa did as asked. After sitting down, she said, "I do speak English rather well, but I may have a strange accent. I do hope you'll find me suitable to be your assistant," Elsa said, equally politely.

"Well, yes a bit strange sounding, but I can understand you perfectly. So you come from this Blackwell-C world? She mentioned you once were the personal assistant for some baroness's daughters? What were they like?"

"Oh beautiful, charming, intelligent young women, much like yourselves when they were younger. Second-generation UFB women. However, the barons on this world had strange customs and traditions. Their wives were called baronesses, you see, and as far back in history as anyone knows, no baroness was able to speak. In ancient times, I understand they cut off their tongues. Barbaric. The beautiful young Susanne, a baroness-to-be, had her voice box removed in preparation for her marriage to a baron and becoming his baroness. I was her servant since she learned to walk. Of course, when that awful terrorist attack came and genetically mutated all the barons and the generals took over our world, she fled for her life. She discharged me, and here I am looking for another similar position as a UFB woman's assistant. I assure you I'm quite capable of handling your needs, though I'm not familiar with your tastes and routines."

Lisa inhaled slightly. "Oh how barbaric! I can't imagine not being able to speak. These barons, why, they must be true barbarians indeed to so mistreat us UFB women."

"Sadistic is more appropriate, madam," Elsa suggested.

"Yes, that too. It would be advisable to have a servant who speaks the local language well. What's it derived from? Oh, some German dialect. We've not yet used the language machines. Such a bore. We'll have to learn it once our husbands finally decide when we are going there. Now then, you don't mind working for highly intelligent women do you? Beth and I are quite bright, you see."

Beth added, "And quite independent. We both are second-generation UFB women ourselves, and we prefer to be allowed to do many things on our own."

"That is most wise of you young women. Susanne was also rather independent, so I'm familiar with this aspect. She preferred to nod slightly to me when she needed assistance, rather than having to ask aloud. Later on after she lost her voice, that proved invaluable for her." Elsa leaned forward slightly, as though about to reveal some secret, and said softly, "When we were alone, I even taught her to write using her feet and toes. Susanne was quite proud of that achievement." She sat back and said, "Now I know only too well most *normal* people believe a UFB woman is completely helpless in all things, but from a long experience, I know this is a complete fallacy. One of Susanne's close girlfriends, a UFB woman herself, is positively brilliant with math and does incredible calculations in her head. Impressive indeed."

Lisa smiled and had an idea. She nodded slightly towards her teacup. Elsa picked up her signal and refilled her cup without batting an eye or drawing the slightest attention to it, though her eyes glanced at Beth, who didn't nod, and Elsa sat the pot down. "Oh, I do so think you'll be splendid, Elsa," Lisa declared. Catching Beth's nod, she said, "You're hired. Now then, Beth and I should show you to your room next to mine and where all our things are located. I trust you won't mind assisting Beth when she is here with me. It's so awkward having her assistant just sit around doing nothing while Beth is here, so we usually send her assistant home when Beth is over here. She is over here most of the daytime of late. Our husbands are working closely together just now. You must meet Felix at lunch and also George. Follow us," Lisa ordered, tossing her hair again so she could rise without stepping on it.

The tour took the rest of the morning, since the two women moved so slowly. Elsa quickly saw these two were extremely fashion conscious, living up to their status as the ultimate in female beauty. Nothing but the finest gowns and leather heels were in the woman's closet. Even the sheets on her bed were blue satin, impractical, but sensuous. As they approached the dining room table, Lisa explained, Felix likes to feed me, though today, he may wish to discuss things with you instead."

After being introduced to the two men and shaking their hands, Elsa saw Felix was more interested in talking with her about Blackwell-C than helping Lisa with her lunch. Without a word, Elsa began assisting Lisa, entirely seamlessly, while answering Felix's questions.

"Yes, I have spent many, many years on Blackwell-C, always as the personal assistant of some of their women, who began life as UFB women but were further modified to become baronesses when they married."

"I see. Yes, rather barbaric barons," Felix replied.

"No, sadistic."

"Well, yes that too. So tell me, were you there when all this trouble began?" Felix probed.

"Yes, I was the assistant for Baron Adler's daughter, Susanne, and her sister too, though I often helped all six of those charming UFB young women. It was an accident I wasn't also genetically modified. I believe something like five thousand were. All the barons and wealthier class were victims, as were some aliens who worked for the corporations," Elsa said.

"Some new form of genetic mutation was it?" Felix asked, though Elsa knew he must already know about it.

"Yes, I believe Baron Adler said it was developed in Galactic Dynamics' research laboratories. This mutation grew upper arms on the UFB women, but removed their voice boxes. On normal people, it changed them into UFB women, but again with upper arms and no voices. Honestly, it just ruined the perfect images of the UFB women. Those short upper arms were useless, though Susanne was able to wiggle them a bit to help keep her balance, especially after she was blinded, preparatory to getting married and becoming a baroness."

"Oh, how utterly ugly those poor women must have been with those upper arms interfering with their beautiful forms," declared Lisa. "Positively barbaric—no, sadistic, right Elsa?" She recalled Elsa's word and used it. Elsa nodded politely.

"And then these generals took over?" Felix asked.

"Yes, someone had to step in and deal with the loss of the entire ruling class. You see, in many ways, Blackwell-C is or was a feudal society, with the barons and wealthiest controlling the world. I believe there was some form of rebellion also going on at the time of the terrorist attacks, Federation of Workers and the People's Revolution, I believe."

"Yes, that's what we've been hearing from our contacts on Blackwell-C," George stated.

Felix said, "I'm beginning to understand the picture better. So with this particular genetic mutation, the barons would be helpless and unable to speak. That would remove them from power instantly, leaving a vacuum. Nature abhors a vacuum, as Beth often reminds us." Beth smiled politely, and he continued, "What we can't fathom is why would these generals make a law that demanded one UFB woman in every household? How could the average working man be able to afford them?"

"I surely don't know, but I believe the average man greatly admired the beauty of the UFB women and desired having one as his wife, just as you both have. No other woman can possibly compete with these UFB women," Elsa said, knowing she was striking all four's vanity. She hit the mark squarely.

"Of course, we're the ultimate women," Lisa declared. "All men drool over us, though we often find that rather annoying—you know, we can't even walk down the street without having men fawning over us." Beth giggled.

Felix regained control of the conversation. "I see. Still was that enough excuse for these generals to make that law?"

"Mind you, I'm not privy to everything that went on, but I did hear rumors this was one of the demands the Federation of Workers was making of the barons, who were hogging all these incredibly beautiful women for themselves and their wealthy supporters. You can't blame those working men for wanting gorgeous women too," Elsa answered, wondering if these men had any idea what this new law was doing to production and for the long term future of the world.

Beth spoke up, "Well, those generals are idiots. Do you realize, Elsa, in just thirty years, there won't be any normal women left on this world, not unless something drastic is done soon? I calculated the breaking point is thirty years. When that happens and there are no normal women around, who will be the personal assistants of the millions of UFB women? It would have to be some of the men, who then won't be able to work much. The whole world is doomed. I predict worldwide starvation coming, unless something drastic is done to prevent it."

"Incredible, Beth. I can see what you mean. When we left, already finding a week's groceries was difficult. We had to visit a half dozen stores just to lay in the week's supply. Oh dear. May be we shouldn't be returning to Blackwell-C," Elsa hinted.

Felix responded, "Well, that's what we corporation executives are working out now, the best way to rectify this mess. Tell me, did they ever catch those terrorists?"

"Not that I've heard. To be honest, I don't think the generals care about that," Elsa answered.

Felix commented, "Well, honey, I do believe you've chosen a superb new personal assistant. Please have her join us in this afternoon's planning session. Her local knowledge may prove valuable to us." Looking at Elsa, he added, "You see, we value our highly intelligent wives and are involving them in our discussions over what and how to remedy this awful mess on Blackwell-C. Please, join us after lunch."

"Of course, any way I can be of assistance to Madam Lisa is my objective," Elsa replied politely. They had no idea this was precisely what Elsa's new assignment was and that others had arranged for Lisa's longtime assistant to *retire*.

Lisa advised Elsa, "You see, their bosses have just given them this new assignment. They have carte blanche to do what they believe necessary to regain corporation control over this backwater world. Beth and I are helping them, but we've already figured this must be some kind of executive test of our husbands, since she and I can't find much of anything that makes this world worth spending any substantial amount of funds on retaking it. How very strange."

As the four rose from the table, Elsa softly asked, "Should I clear the table?"

Lisa giggled, "No, the kitchen staff handles that. You come with us."

Elsa spent the afternoon with the four, listening to their plans as they developed and answering questions, precisely her current assignment. Her main question remained unanswered though, just why did the regional corporations so greatly desire total control over this backwater world, which from her own experience provided little in the way of valuable exports?

She quickly saw Lisa and Beth were the true *brains* behind these men. Both women had already determined the real reason for the corporations' desired takeover wasn't visible. Lisa showed her the annual net exports list, and Beth summarized the resulting conclusions. Using the army to regain control was not cost effective, for example.

Late in the afternoon, Felix ran his hands through his head. "Damn, this is frustrating. I can't find a single reason why Blackwell-C is so important that our regional bosses what us to spare no cost to retake control of this world! It's not even in any strategic location in space. Beth just ruled that idea out too. Elsa, is there something on this world that's incredibly valuable but outsiders don't know about?"

Elsa laughed. "Hardly. By the standards I've seen on this world and here in your home, Blackwell-C is just a primitive, backwater world with nothing of any real value to offer anyone, let alone corporations. Unless," her voice trailed off purposely.

"Unless what?" Felix probed. She'd definitely attracted his full attention.

"Well, I heard the barons talking about some kind of special clone growth machines GD had in their research labs. What they are, I surely don't know," she lied. "But if those were so vital, why not just land a salvage ship and recover them?"

"Yes, so you know about the clone growth machines. I considered that, and I agree with you, just send in a salvage ship. True, my boss wants them and any related research recovered, but that didn't seem to be a critical action, just something I should do once we have regained corporate control over the world. So, George, why is this so vital? I swear I'm going grey over this one."

"Vanity, thy sullied reputation speaketh volumes," Beth declared.

"Huh?" exclaimed a confused Felix. "Beth, would you please speak plain English for once?"

"I hath spoken plain English, but thou does not understand the obvious," Beth teased him. "My hand doth slapeth thy face." She and Lisa giggled, while Elsa stared at the two women. What was going on?

Ceasing her giggles, Beth said, "Okay, plain English for

you, Felix. Unless there is some deep, dark secret on this Blackwell-C world, the only thing that remains for a reason is that your bosses have lost face by having completely lost control over this backwater world. Vanity dictates they have to find some way to save face, to cleanse their presumed sullied reputations in the eyes of other corporation executives here and on other worlds in this sector they oversee. Their actions or inactions allowed primitives on a backwater world to overthrow corporations' rule completely. Somehow, they have to save face and regain that control. Plain enough, Felix?"

"You think that this is all about regaining control so others don't see them as foolish and as losing control? I can see how this might be so, Beth, what with so many uprisings going on all across the Federation," Felix replied, his ire evaporating, seeing clearly Beth's point, now that she spoke plainly.

Lisa added, "Why else make such a top priority out of this mess, when financially, there is nothing much to be gained?"

"So this is nothing more than saving face?" Felix asked rather shocked.

"Yes, unless there is something absolutely vital we're not being told, something that isn't in all these records," Beth answered.

George responded with, "Let's say this is the case. Then, it's in our own interests to regain control by a means that does not cost much at all. If we use an infantry division, for example, it would take over twenty years of exports to pay for that, wholly financially unsound."

"Excellent point, George. Whatever we do, it can't cost the corporations much at all," Felix declared.

"Then cut off the heads of the two snakes," Beth spoke up.

Elsa knew immediately what she meant, but Felix once again said, "Huh? Beth, please," he pleaded.

"Two generals are running the world, calling themselves directors or some such thing," Beth explained. "So you cut off their heads and the rest of the army is leaderless and directionless. You simply take over."

"Ah brilliant as always," Felix complimented Beth. "And how do we do that?"

Elsa volunteered, "Well, when I left, they were staying in the former baron's castle. General Ernst Von Dorfsted made his headquarters at Castle Berthold in Thromstead. I don't know where General Franz Himmel is staying, somewhere in the south in a baron's castle there. Perhaps, your contacts on Blackwell-C could find out. Look, if these local terrorists could so easily attack the castle and wipe out the barons and wealthy, it should be easy for your vastly more able men to do the same. Cut off their heads, figuratively I suppose."

"Hey, why not just use that same new genetic bio agent on these generals and everyone else who is there?" George suggested. "After all, it is their use of it that is dooming their world to destruction."

"Brilliant! Plus the cost would be trivial. We land and resume control," Felix declared, greatly relieved at last a workable solution was starting to gel. "Elsa, can you draw an accurate layout of this baron's castle?"

"Of course, since I was there nearly twenty years while Susanne was growing up." Elsa then suggested, "You know, the local groups were demanding free and open elections for their leaders before all this happened. Perhaps, you could solidify your control by giving them just that. After all, they'll need local leaders, since I doubt very much you want to be bothered with the myriad details of running this primitive backwater planet."

"Point very well taken. Lisa, you certainly hired the right assistant, honey," Felix replied enthusiastically, bringing a smile to her face. "I wonder what kind of leaders they should have? Not more sadistic barons, I hope."

"So what will we have them elect?" George asked. "President, dictator, legislators, council members—the list of local leader types goes on and on."

Again, Elsa offered a suggestion, "Our people are used to having a baron lead them. I think we've had enough of their sadistic ways. So why not have them elect a president? But make a rule that only UFB women can run for this highest office? After all, UFB women are the ultimate in beauty and command the respect of all men," she subtly hinted, hoping the men would read far more into this than she was saying. She dare not add to it, not with Lisa and Beth here.

"A UFB woman president, leader? But they had many barons who controlled each major city. They met as a group and made the laws of the world," George pointed out. "So each city would elect their own UFB woman for their local president and then these presidents would meet as a group to rule the world. I get it."

Slowly a devilish grin grew on Felix's face. "And these helpless women would easily be controlled by our corporations. No offense honey, but you are helpless, compared to normal men."

"We women nurture life, honey. We bring new life into this world. It is about time we have a say in the running of our worlds, though I see what you mean. Of course, you executives would be able to influence directly these presidents. More importantly, honey, on this world, there are now millions of UFB women. This would be seen as a powerful incentive by them and everyone else if they, representing the ultimate in womanhood, were to be their rulers. Let the average man drool over their leaders." She and Beth laughed loudly.

"Do I really drool over you, honey?" Felix asked seriously.

She winked at him and he flushed. No other answer was needed.

"Okay then," Felix declared, "we have our solution. It won't cost the corporations much at all, if anything. Now all we have to do is get it implemented. Like I always said, George, we marred the two best UFB women in the galaxy!"

"In that case, honey," Lisa teased him, "you best prove that to me in bed tonight."

"You too, dear," Beth added coyly. Both men flushed and promised to do so.

Chapter 13—The Return of the Corporations

Late December, the deep space transport carrying the two new CEOs of Galactic Dynamics and Galactic Electronics, their wives, Elsa, and all their possessions landed at the spaceport on the outskirts of Thromstead. "Sure is rough terrain around here," Felix commented, getting his first view of this world to which he was now assigned.

"Most of the inhabitable portions are similar," Elsa commented. "Farming is difficult, or so I am told."

"Well, I can see why there isn't much of value for the corporations here," George commented.

Upon landing, they were met by the CEO of General Goods, Mr. Wolfgang Schmidt, who, after the terrorist attack, had more or less taken charge of corporation interests on Blackwell-C. An hour later, the group got a tour of the GD and GE headquarters where they would be living and working. "Since the attack, I have keep the place locked up," Wolfgang explained, "except."

"Except what?" Felix interrupted him.

"Well, except for the bio agent storage safe down on Sub-level Twenty. The generals and we believed containment safe was the safest place to store these bio agents. When the generals need more, I take their personnel down there and run it through the fabrication machine for them. I assure you that I lock the place up securely after that. They usually make a visit per week now, since the one UFB woman per home law is still being implemented. The generals have told me that it will probably take them all next year to fully implement it in the more remote areas of Blackwell-C. They've nearly gotten to all the major cities now."

"Excellent. In the future, the generals will have to contact me personally to get access," Felix declared.

"Of course, sir," Wolfgang replied, acknowledging Felix had corporate rank over him and General Goods—that GD and

GE were in control of the corporations on this world as they were on most Federation worlds. "Might I ask, are you planning to end this ridiculous law of the generals?"

"Of course. As you have reported, obtaining enough food is now challenging. We don't need to make it far worse," Felix stated the obvious. "As I told you on the comm channel, I will need four men who are willing to undertake a risky venture for me. Five grand each for an hour's work. They must be trustworthy and not squeamish. I need them as soon as possible."

While the two leaders toured their respective facilities, Elsa and Lisa began unpacking their many bags and shipping crates in the CEO's private quarters section of the top floor of the GD building. Elsa pointed out to Lisa, "Look, there and there are the old baron's castles. That one is where General Ernst now runs the northern part of the world. Amazing views from here. As was told to me, the barons wouldn't allow the alien corporations to have buildings that were higher than their manor houses."

"Oh how utterly primitive. So that is why everything is underground, well not everything. I just couldn't live underground. How ghastly," Lisa declared.

Via a geo-sync satellite, Felix and George studied the reddish forms that were the soldiers inside the baron's castle close to GD headquarters. Typical military —they easily spotted the two dozen sentries on duty patrolling the outer perimeter just inside the fifteen-foot tall walls and along the roof of the manor house. Several dozen more were inside, though some appeared to be congregated in the basement rooms, which according to Elsa used to be where the baron's guards were quartered. The two men divided this immediate task. George took the southern baron, while Felix took the one at hand. Their attacks had to be synchronized so one general couldn't send advanced warnings to the other.

Their plan of attack was the essence of simplicity. Wearing bio containment suits, a personal defense shield, and a personal invisibility shield, two men would enter the castle, one taking up an initial position in the lowest level, while the other went to the top floor, signaling the other when ready.

When their cell phones vibrated, they would open the valves on the cylinders in their backpacks, allowing the genetic bio agent to flow out freely and rapidly. At this point, they would move slowly down or up, depending on their location. Once they met, they'd return to the main exit, close it, affixing a simple magnetic lock on the doors. Attached to the lock was the common bio hazard warning labels, which even these locals knew what it meant.

The plan was the essence of simplicity, with little actual risk to the two men carrying it out, unless they foolishly engaged the soldiers in and around the castle. From the top floor office of GD, the two CEOs coordinated the attack the following afternoon. Each of their pairs of men was traceable via their cell phones. Thus, as the men watched the IR images from the satellites on their monitor, they could coordinate the attacks simply by monitoring the cell phones' GPS coordinates.

On December 30, the short-lived reigns of the two generals ended. When the outer perimeter guards suddenly saw the yellow and black bio hazard warning labels on the locked doors, without fail, they all retreated and headed back to their barracks across town to report and await orders. The highest ranking surviving soldier in Thromstead, a major, called a brigade commander, was stationed two hundred miles away with the bulk of the northern army, trying to coordinate the new law's implementation in the lesser populated zones of Blackwell-C, just as his southern counterpart was doing. Upon receiving the terrible news, he halted all further implementation of the new law. Taking a regiment with him, he headed back to Thromstead to survey the situation.

Based on the intelligence from General Goods executives, Felix learned of this and sent word for the brigade commander to visit him first. Again, utilizing the data and some doctors from General Goods, Felix requested that corporation's aide in retrieving the bodies and getting them to the appropriate staging areas that had been used in the past. Yes, Felix and George made excellent use of the existing corporations' CEOs, who knew better than to resist these two new CEOs, since the Galactic Dynamics and Galactic

Electronics corporations were the undisputed corporation leaders throughout the Federation. "Follow the protocols that were used before," Felix ordered.

That meant that the comatose bodies were lined up on cots and stripped. Then, each was labeled with their name and sex. After that, via the brigadier, army records were consulted and their next of kin notified. They were given two choices: come and get the person and prepare to care for them or let the corporations take care of them. By the time the brigadier arrived, sixty-three soldiers were accounted for, laid out for inspection and identification, including six female soldiers. The brigadier asked which form their genetic mutations would be taking and sighed when Felix told him the newer version was used so that the general could never issue another order.

Most in Thromstead now knew the results of the new version and virtually no one claimed their relatives, but the brigadier took the six women to be used as future squad hostesses. The men were taken to Blackwoods, joining quite a few other men being cared for at that assisted living facility. The initial meeting with the brigadier commander was short and to the point. Felix said, "The corporations have returned and put an end to these madmen generals and their laws. We are in control now for the moment. After you help take care of the identification and notices for the victims, return to GD and we'll discuss future arrangements. That is all brigade commander, that is unless you wish to join your general." The brigadier saluted and left.

When he returned, he found a friendlier Felix awaiting him. "Now then, I will be making a planet-wide announcement shortly, but I wanted you to be the first to be informed. As of now, that foolish law demanding a UFB woman per home is abolished. If we don't take swift action, your whole world is doomed in an estimated thirty years."

"Why?" asked the brigade commander.

"The changes are genetically inherited. These UFB women will have daughters who are themselves UFB women. If this law was continued, around thirty years from now, nearly every woman on Blackwell-C will have become a UFB woman, who of course must have a personal assistant to help them with their many needs. Their helpers could then only come from the men of this world, who won't then be able to work at their jobs. World starvation and worse will result. We will be taking steps to rectify this so your world won't be facing extinction."

Felix then continued, "Now then, as I understand the resistance movement on this world, they want free and open elections for their leaders. I'm granting that. These elections will be held the last day of March, giving the candidates time to prepare and all that. As I understand the former ruling situation, each baron ruled over part of the city and the surrounding lands. I will keep that same organizational pattern, far less confusion for everyone. Your new leaders will be called local queens, but these leaders can only be UFB women. No men, no normal women, just UFB women will be allowed to be your new local rulers. Of course, the corporations reserve the right to overrule the local queens when their decisions affect us. Further, you, brigade commander, will now be in charge of the northern armed forces, replacing your general. I will be entrusting the new planetary defense shields to you and your southern brigade commander, who George of GE is now briefing about all this as well. This is a vital mission, sir, providing protection of the entire world from space attacks. This is what your stupid generals should have done instead of trying to wipe out your entire civilization."

"So your first official orders are to locate where the parts of the shield are stored and work out an installation plan. If you need assistance with the details, contact General Goods, since they have installed them before. That will be all, brigade commander." The tall man saluted and left. With the exception of the proposed rulers, everything Felix had said made perfect sense. Besides, he was now recognized as being in charge of the entire northern army with no one above himself. Maybe, he thought, he could get one of the new queens to promote him to general.

That evening, Felix and George held their first newscast interview, with their wives sitting beside them. "Hello. I'm the new Galactic Dynamics CEO here on Blackwell-C. My name is

Felix Gott. My beautiful wife, Lisa. This is the new Galactic Electronics CEO, George Gebberly, and his brilliant wife, Beth. We have called this news conference to relay vital news for all of Blackwell-C."

"First, as of today, the generals' insane law of one UFB woman per home is discarded and terminated forever. Let me explain why. Obviously, these women are the ultimate in feminine beauty, obviously. But there can be too much of a good thing." He then explained what would ultimately result if this law were continued to be enforced, that in thirty years, all women would be UFB women. Felix made perfectly and graphically clear, beyond the slightest doubt, the catastrophe that would subsequently result. Since food shortages were pronounced, this ultimate result was more than clear to the city dwellers.

"Now there could well be families out there who no longer want their current UFB woman in their family, while there could be other families who want a UFB woman in theirs. So if you fit into either category, call up General Goods and let them know. We will do our best to resettle those who are desirous of a change. Further, if your work has been seriously impacted by the conversion of your family member, also contact General Goods. Soon, we will find some relief for you. We need to get food production back to where it should be."

Felix then outlined what the armed forces would be doing and that the generals had been removed from all power. That done, he launched into a description of what the new local government would now be. "All right. In the past, local rule was handled by your barons. As I understand the system, a baron controlled a portion of the city and surrounding lands. That area or zone remains as your local government. However, I'm told that the revolutionaries have been demanding free and open elections of their rulers. I stand here tonight to tell you that we have heard your demands and will be implementing them. Yes, free and open elections for all of your local leaders."

"Now we aren't going to just elect new barons. I'm afraid the sadistic barons are a thing of the past. No, I've given the situation here on Blackwell-C considerable thought. Your new elected local leaders will be called queens. No men. Further, the only candidates for your queens must be UFB women." He paused for dramatic effect and to allow the unseen viewers a chance to react.

"Why UFB women? Several reasons. First, this world has more of these beautiful women than probably all the other worlds in the galaxy combined. That alone makes this world and these women unique. Second, as you well know, a UFB woman is unable to work at most all usual jobs a normal woman can perform. Yet, she is perfectly capable of being a local queen and ruler, as long as she has her assistant with her. So this is a small way of providing a way for these UFB women to contribute to the overall survival of Blackwell-C, beyond just being a wife and mother. Third, with millions of these women, and many having been forced to become one against their will, we owe it to these stellar beauties to have some of their own in positions of power to help guarantee that all UFB women are properly cared for and such."

"The first election of your new leaders, your UFB queens, will be the last day of March. That gives you and them three months to decide to run and to campaign for votes. The only rules are she must be a UFB woman, residing within the section the former baron ruled and whose castle she will then occupy and rule from. Other than those two rules, she can be anyone of your choice. She who has the most votes will become your local queen. One of their first actions will be to meet as a group and decide how long their terms of office will be and when additional elections will be held. I will provide election guidelines the week before the elections in late March. Yes, free and open elections have arrived. That is all. Good night."

"Dear, I wonder if I qualify to run for queen?" Beth teased Felix.

Felix scratched his head. "Damn, I didn't think of that. I suppose that there isn't any reason you couldn't, but I wouldn't advise it just now. We are seen as the aliens here."

"I was just teasing you. Some of the General Goods and other corporation UFB wives might want to run. That's what I was actually thinking about," Beth replied.

"Well, why not? Most votes wins," Felix concluded.

"Tomorrow will be a busy day," George interrupted. "All of our junior executives and their families are due to arrive at the spaceport. Once they're settled in, we will have to hire hundreds of local men and women to fill the more mundane posts. Busy days ahead. Felix, we should make our report to the regional CEOs tonight."

Late that night, the two men did just that. The response was just what the two hoped for, "What? You've already regained total control? Only expense is twenty thousand credits? No Infantry Division costs? No space fleets? Incredible, Felix, George, just unbelievable. We've certainly picked the right young men! I must say that you two are our most outstanding up and coming new CEOs! Well done, both of you, very well done!" After more accolades, the call ended with two very pleased executives.

During the organized chaos of the next week, Elsa managed to slip away long enough to place a secure off-world call to Susanne on Scorpi-C. Elsa quickly outlined what had just happened, knowing that the group would greatly appreciate news from home and that the generals were gone. "Yes, the situation is stable. If you wished to return home, it is safe to do so," Elsa hinted.

"Wow! What a change!" declared Renate. "I would never ever have thought UFB women would become our leaders!"

"Makes sense," Stefan declared. "Look, the corporations want total control of our world. With the generals and barons both history, they've got what they wanted. What better way to keep us in line by having UFB women as our local leaders. I bet these women will be fairly easy for the corporations to manipulate."

"But we can go home, that's the important thing," Nadja pointed out. "Besides, we could bring these cures back to our people. I bet there are thousands of them who would give anything for these cures."

Rudolf spoke up, "She's got a good point. In fact, we probably can get the full support for these cures from these new CEOs. They seem to realize the sheer number of helpless

UFB women has really crushed the work force, particularly in the food production system. I bet they would welcome us with open arms."

"Except that Rudolf and I and Kirsa and Wenzel want to take a long trip around the galaxy and see the sights, like the gas clouds the gypsies told us about," Susanne added.

"But if it's safe, I want to go home and keep on learning how to play music and the harpsichord," Karla hinted. "Dirk's a good teacher."

Emil added, "And Amalia should get back to school. An education is important. I think Anne and I should accompany those four while they travel around the galaxy, just in case of trouble. Six is better than just four, as long as we are back before the babies arrive."

Amalia broke in, "But I want to see the galaxy too. Okay, I was foolish once. I won't be foolish again. I can see how important education is now. Once I graduate, you have to take me on a sightseeing trip too."

Susanne giggled. "I promise, Amalia, just as soon as you graduate."

Achima looked at Hedda, and then said, "Make that eight. We are coming with you. Neither of us wants to go back just yet. After all, we are still deserters from the army."

"That's settled then," Stefan took charge again. "We'll see about purchasing a bunch of the cures to take back with us and leave as soon as we get them. How many cures do you suppose we should buy?"

"How about a hundred?" suggested Susanne. "I would think that they could be duplicated in the fabrication machines, just like the nasty bio agents were."

***

On January 7, the Shining Star arrived back at the spaceport at the edge of Thromstead. As they walked across the tarmac to the customs section of the control tower, many eyes stared at them, but for different reasons this time. Their knee-length hair gave them away as UFB women, but their bosoms were half the usual size, and they had arms and were walking well. After their ID cards were checked, they were welcomed back. Emil took Amalia and Anne off to pay a call on their father, the mayor, while the six young couples headed directly to GD headquarters, carrying one of the bags of the new cures. Hedda and Achima wisely remained on the ship, presumably guarding it.

The mayor had aged considerably from the stress of the past months. However, tears of joy streamed down his face, as he hugged his son and daughter, who now were whole, more or less. "It is a miracle, Amalia. Arms, you have arms again. And you too, Emil. It is truly miracle! Come, sit, and tell me all about it. How is this possible?" Amalia was very eager to tell her dad all that had happened. He was even more pleased to hear that he would soon be a grandfather as well. Later, the young couple paid visit on Anne's parents, and they were just as shocked and yet pleased to see them, even more so when they learned they were about to become grandparents too. That Anne looked nearly normal went a long way with her parents who had previously disowned her.

***

"Welcome. Sorry, I don't know you or your history, but please, come in. Have a seat. My lovely wife, Lisa," Felix said, ushering his unexpected visitors into his top floor office. He stared hard at the women who were UFB women, but not UFB women. Even Lisa stared at them.

Susanne spoke for the group, introducing them. "We six were at one time baronesses-to-be." She outlined roughly what happened and that they ended up as usual UFB women. "We paid a visit to Scorpi-C in the Abelard Sector out on the rim. There, their doctors have invented partial cures. You see, none of us wanted to remain a UFB woman, though we were born as UFB women, second-generation I believe is your term for us. As you can see, the cures have regrown our arms, which are slowly regaining strength. It also reduced our breast sizes to something more reasonable so now we don't have to wear those restrictive corsets. Our feet are partially repaired, but we still have to wear these taller heels, but let me tell you, it is a thousand times easier to walk in these. Anyway, we have brought back samples of the cures."

Lisa spoke up, "But why would you ever want such nasty cures? You were perfect UFB women, the ultimates. I

210

don't understand. Don't your husbands want perfect wives? I would never want to get such cures."

Karla answered, "Not everyone wants to be a beautiful sex doll. I want to play music. I've always wanted to make music, since I was six years old and attended my first ball. Irma here wants to make beautiful quilts and Nadja wants to be a real secretary. Kirsa has already achieved what she's always wanted to be—a transport pilot and a competent one at that. You see, Lisa, some of us want to do other things in life than be as limited as we were as UFB women." She attempted to be as polite about this as possible.

Susanne hastily added, "We know probably thousands of women have been forced to become UFB women and would dearly love to have these cures so they could once more continue doing the work they used to be doing, especially those connected to the food production industries." She purposely mentioned this, knowing just what the situation was like. Even before they left, finding a week's groceries was tough and by now, she thought rationing might well be in effect.

"Fascinating that you mention this and have brought back samples. You see, drastic measures must soon be taken. With so many UFB women, this world is doomed unless we find some ways around so many helpless women. I was making plans to import women from some of our overpopulated worlds to supplant those who can no longer work. Honestly, we are having a devil of a time finding food just now. Too many women were effectively removed from the food production and distribution system, and as a result, everyone suffers," Felix explained.

"Now you come back offering a miracle, which is just what Blackwell-C needs right now. With your permission, I would like to begin a new program, offering these cures to all UFB women here who desire it. Wait, I suppose she should also have her husband's permission as well. I don't want to be the cause of strife in a man's marriage. If we could just get half of them back to work, we can save this world from extinction. Of course, you six women would be given full credit for your lifesaving miracle cures."

211

He added, "You've heard about our new local leaders, the freely elected queens who must be UFB women?" The twelve nodded, and he cautioned, "While your people here will likely call you heroines, realize you can't be elected to be their queens. I'm purposely limiting that top post to only true UFB women, giving them an opportunity to help their world."

"I think that is a splendid plan," Stefan spoke up.

Susanne giggled. "If we were still stuck as UFB women, then we might have jumped at the chance to be local queens. Now that we are able, we all want to do all sorts of other things, as Karla has said. We just felt it was our obligation and responsibility to bring back the cures for those on our world who desire them."

"Amazing, simply amazing," Felix continued to exclaim.

Lisa frowned. "I surely hope *most* of these new UFB women will turn *down* these cures," she said decisively, but then backed off a bit, "well, except for those who are needed in food production work. Honestly, we *are* the ultimate in beauty. I suppose if you decide you made an awful mistake getting the cures, you could ask Felix to redo you as UFB women again."

"Thank you for the offer. We will keep that in mind," Susanne said diplomatically. "One other thing, the cures work on men too. One of the men in our group was turned into a UFBMD man, but he's had the same cures and looks pretty much as we do now."

"How interesting. We do have quite a few men who have been victims as well. While every man would dearly love to have a UFB woman as his wife, there are few women who would accept a UFBMD man as her husband. I will give this considerable thought, though I'm sure I won't be giving it to the barons or the generals. They've caused far too much damage to this world. Again, I will get a program implemented tomorrow and your names will become famous across Blackwell-C."

They took that as a signal the meeting was over, and they rose, shook his hand, and left. Once outside, Stefan commented, "Well, that went better than I thought it would."

"He's not stupid. He knows damned well he has to get

the lost production situation rectified in short order," Susanne replied. "We've just given him an easy way to do it."

"I think we should keep some samples back as our private stock," Nadja declared. Several gave her a questioning look, so she explained, "For two reasons. First, Lisa suggested we could be re-genetically modified. I don't trust aliens. We could find ourselves back where we started. Second, Felix said even if the woman wanted the cure, if her husband didn't want her to get it, she wouldn't receive it. She may well try to contact us to get the cure anyway. I know I certainly would if Wotan wouldn't let me get it."

"Men!" barked Renate, and the women laughed, but the six men looked rather sober.

***

During the ensuing week, the seven couples found new homes. Emil and Anne decided that they would stay with Emil's father, whose health had definitely taken a turn for the worst. Once they returned from Susanne's galaxy tour, they would stay with him, particularly since his house was rather large. The other six scoured the city, found six apartments close together, and got many of their things moved in, though they soon purchased much more. Intending to depart on their trip within a week, Susanne and Kirsa and their spouses fixed up their new apartments, but left the bulk of their possessions back on the Shining Star for now, as did Emil and Anne.

On the other hand, from the moment the women first set foot on the streets, many men and women too closely watched them. They were *different*. Further, Felix made his grand announcement of the cures the next day. Everyone in the group was actually quite surprised to hear Felix giving them full credit for bringing the cures back with them from some distant world. He even went so far as to display a group image of them, taken while they met with him in his office. He did, however, point out that these *cured* UFB women were ineligible to become local queens. All this brought them quickly to the attention of many, and several reporters wanted to interview the women, but wisely, they turned them down. Shortly after this, the reporters figured out just who these six women were and again begged them for interviews to no avail.

Here in January, the women were learning to deal with walking in the winter snow in their six-inch heels without taking nasty falls. They had never actually been allowed outside in the wintertime, though they had often watched the boys playing in the snow. In their tiny toe shoes, they had no chance of being able to stay on their feet. Now they could, but only just barely. Besides, they were all excited about buying the furnishings for their new apartments.

Dirk, Ebert, Wotan, and Stefan soon found new jobs. Both GD and GE were hiring, and their prior experience working for the corporations was a large plus. At least, the four felt that they could easily support their families without dipping further into their wives' inheritances, which they had to rely on until now.

Since everything seemed to be working out well, Emil, Anne, Rudolf, Susanne, Wenzel, and Kirsa said their farewells and headed to the spaceport, ready to *explore* the galaxy, as Susanne often suggested. Armed with a number of *must see's*, they were very excited to be departing on this sightseeing trip, Susanne's lifelong dream come true. Achima and Hedda were very glad to get started, having done nothing but sit around the ship all week. With great pride, Kirsa lifted the Shining Star off Blackwell-C, while Hedda entered the coordinates of their first stop into the hyperdrive unit. A minute later, they stepped into hyperspace beginning their long tour.

Chapter 14—The Election Results

By the third week of January, only a handful of UFB women stepped up to be candidates for their local queens. Elsa suggested, "Lisa, Beth, why don't you go on the news and encourage more young UFB women to sign up to be candidates? Show them this is possible, that it's something they could do." Elsa knew if there was to be free elections, each queen post had to have at least one candidate. As it now stood, only three women had volunteered and signed up to be a candidate. While she didn't know the reasons for the seeming lack of interest, she wanted to get several women for each position so the people could see a democracy of sorts in operation, a step forward in her estimation.

Lisa and Beth decided to do just that. On camera, Lisa said, "Look, fellow UFB women out there in our city, this is something that we can do and we must do. We must show everyone we are more than pretty sex dolls, that we have brilliant minds and can lead just as well as men can. If no one else signs up for the old Adler and Aldric sector queens, then Beth and I will, and you can elect us to be your queens and local leaders, even if we don't know much about this city yet, having only arrived a few weeks ago." Felix came on after that and gave his official okay to allow Lisa and Beth to run for the office of queens here in Thromstead, adding a bit more nudging to the mix.

That strategy proved effective. Within two days of Lisa and Beth's announcement that they had entered the race, sufficient other local women volunteered. Beth had two competitors, Carla and Belinda, while Lisa faced Alina in the elections. The press now had something of substance to report on and did so, arranging a series of local debates between the candidates. The debates gave the newscasters some of their highest ratings ever. Nearly everyone tuned in to watch the women debate and to ogle over these incredibly beautiful, if mostly helpless, women, dressed in very fancy gowns.

One debate was rather noteworthy, that between Carla

and Beth. Beth talked first, wearing her finest strapless, satin gown, a cherry red one, designed to attract everyone's attention to her exquisite form, which it certainly did. However, Beth's speech and debate style came across as highly intellectual, though her points were precisely made, accurate, and of importance to the local inhabitants.

On the other hand, Carla's speech was plain and simple, down to earth, as one commentator described it afterwards. She wore a rather plain brown gown with two shoulder straps. Even though her massive bosom would certainly hold a strapless gown up nicely, she didn't feel like a sex doll. While she had little choice but to wear the expected UFB women's apparel, she chose to present an earthy look. Her speech was directed at the people she had known all her life.

"Hello. I'm Carla Osterbrok and a candidate for your queen. Many of you may recognize me as a baker. Yes, I and my husband ran the Osterbrok Bakery. Those of you who patronized our shop know the quality of our breads. Some months ago, that was taken from me and from you, when the insane generals enforced their evil new law. Either I became a helpless sex doll or my husband did or one of our two daughters. As any mother out there will testify to, I wasn't about to let this terrible thing happen to one of my daughters, let alone to my husband. So here I stand today, a helpless sex doll, unable to bake the breads many of you loved."

"I have two choices now, which is far more than the general gave me. I can take advantage of this miraculous cure our heroines brought back for us and regain my arms and go back to baking bread or with your support become your queen. As your queen, I promise you I will do everything I can in my power to provide all the assistance to other UFB women, to all women, and to all you men as well. We can work together to bring about a better world from this incredible mess that it is in today."

"So yes, right now, I feel it is my duty to try to help. That is why I joined the running for your queen. With your vote, I can be your queen. If you prefer Beth, that is also fine with me. In that case, I will go ahead, get my cures, and get back to baking bread for you. Thank you."

The brigade commanders were put in charge of conducting the free and open elections. Soldiers prepared the ballots, verified that the voters did live in the appropriate sector of town for the candidates they wished to vote for, and marked the ballots for the many UFB women who made the huge effort to leave their homes and go to the polling centers to cast their votes.

Carla Osterbrok won handily over Beth, becoming queen at Castle Berringer, while Lisa unexpectedly won, becoming queen at Castle Berthold. "Oh dear, I actually won, Beth! You simply *must* come with me to the castle and *help* me be the queen. You are so *much* more knowledgeable about such things. You simply *must*. And Elsa must come with me at all times to be my hands."

Beth giggled. "All right, but Lisa, just what are we actually to *do* as the queen? If we're to do anything, we *must* have a staff. I'll speak to George tonight and see if he can get staff for each of the new queens."

This was precisely what Elsa wanted and needed to know. While it sounded like *good news* to be making these UFB women local leaders, just what would they actually be able to accomplish? Just how much power would the corporations give them? Elsa's current assignment was to find out. With Lisa's surprise election, her task became much easier. Besides, she was intimately familiar with Castle Berthold.

By the end of April, each of the new queens had their own local staff of ten men and women. On May Day, all the queens met at Castle Berthold to discuss just what they should and could do as queens. What were the most pressing issues that needed resolving? Taxation and women's issues were at the top of the list. The taxation issue was quickly agreed to by all. They decided to lower the rate for the Armed Forces to just six percent of a person's income. The queens agreed to take only two percent for their wild guess at operating expenses. That meant everyone got yet another significant tax cut, sure to please everyone. The corporations wisely went along with this, but quietly raised the prices on their goods to compensate for their loss of tax revenue they had under the barons' rule.

Several queens reported they had been requested to intervene on behalf of a number of UFB women who wanted the cures, but their husbands were refusing to allow them to get it. Per the initial declaration by Felix, the women were not allowed to get the cures. The women wanted the queens to allow them to get it. This became their second topic.

Lisa argued, "But there isn't anything finer than being one of us, a UFB woman. Honestly, those with the cures look awful compared to us. Since the husband is supporting his wife, she should go along with his wishes."

Clara argued against Lisa. "Look, the woman may not be being well-treated at all. Her husband might not be providing for her many needs. Also, she may have once had a good job before she got turned into one of us helpless sex dolls. As short as we are on skilled manpower, she should be allowed to get the cures and get back into our workforce."

The queens went along with Clara, passing a ruling that called for an investigation by the respective queen's staff. If the women was being mistreated, not properly cared for, her needs not being met, or if she had been a skilled worker, then the queen could grant her the right to get the cures immediately. Once more, Elsa was surprised at the corporations' response. They accepted it with one slight reservation. Assuming she wasn't being mistreated, if she had been a skilled worker before becoming a UFB woman and if that skilled position was no longer in dire need of filling, then the cure wouldn't be granted on that basis alone.

By summer, the queens once more began the traditional hosting of the local holidays, beginning with the Beginning of Summer Ball, made possible by the alleviation of food rationing. Slowly, life was getting back to some semblance of normalcy. Karla proudly joined Dirk and the other musicians playing for Lisa's ball. While she was just a beginning musician, for her, this was an important event. She was making music, something she'd longed to do since she was six.

Attendance at this first concert was somewhat lower than expected. Far too many recalled the last ball at which so many of the wealthy men and women, along with the barons, were attacked and genetically modified. At the mid-summer ball, attendance began to pick up and by the Autumn Ball, the ballrooms at the various castles were as packed as they had been under the barons.

Elsa continued sending off positive reports on Blackwell-C, a total turnaround from all her many previous years of reports. *I just cannot believe that these changes are really happening, on this world of all places. Still, I haven't found anything amiss yet. I certainly would never have predicted this world could so change for the better. Is it possible that the corporations are turning over a new leaf? That would be a first. Still, vigilance pays off. Keep alert, keep watch. Why do I keep on thinking this is all too good to be true?*

Chapter 15—Encroaching Darkness

The corporations put their major thrust and emphasis into the restoration of the food production industry. Many unskilled workers were reassigned to helping on farms, processing plants, or distribution centers, even local grocery stores. Manufacturing of heavy equipment and space ships had the least priority, and by autumn, those industries had lost over half of their personnel. Besides, demand for those products was way down, particularly since the corporations continued to supply new cargo ships and transports to Blackwell-C.

The only manufacturing industries that continued at their usual pace or expanded were those that somehow related to food production, distribution, household appliances, and of course cars. The shifting of workers from one local company and industry into another was slow, but quite steady, driven by market forces, which were quietly being monitored by the corporations. They simply didn't want another winter filled with food shortages like last year's near disaster.

The one industry outside food production that gained substantial workers was the Element Resupply Companies, which provided refills for the fabrication machines that the corporations brought to this world in quantity. These machines could duplicate any non-living item that was small enough to fit in its 3-d scanning hopper. Of course, the duplication process pulled in the appropriate elements from their various internal supply compartments. As items were duplicated, elements needed to be replaced, the sole purpose of the many Element Resupply Companies on most all worlds. During the current year, the number of workers in these companies nearly doubled. This would shortly play an important role.

For example, one needed a new computer. It was vastly cheaper to stick one into the scanning hopper and allow the fabrication machine to duplicate it than it was to make a large plant to manufacture them from scratch—that is, as long as one had access to the amounts of silicon, germanium, and rare earths such duplication required. During the year, what was being duplicated at such high rates? Apparel, shoes, and the electrostatic hair machines that were needed by the ever-increasing number of UFB women being made late last year. These millions needed more than the one or two initial dresses they were given when they underwent the mutation process. At least, this manufacturing process kept the cost of these in the affordable range even for the least well-paid workers. It had to be in order to implement the generals' orders.

The trouble began slowly with a barely detectible ultra-high frequency in the kilo-yatta-hertz range, a signal only Elsa was able to detect, though she thought nothing of it when she first began hearing it, presuming it to be general background radiation. Certainly, the people around her didn't audibly detect it.

Behavior, change of. Much later on, Elsa categorized the first symptoms, though they were so subtle everyone missed this as it began. At the local queens' meeting in early October, Queen Clara Osterbrok suggested, "Fellow queens, I do believe Thromstead does need more of us magnificent UFB women, don't you all think so?"

"What's that?" asked Lisa.

"Oh, shouldn't we have more UFB women here in our city? Thromstead is the capital city of our world. We set the standards our sister cities follow, don't we?"

"But I thought you were against having more UFB women," a confused queen stated the obvious. Clara had even based her election platform on giving women the power of choice, particularly on getting the cures.

"I tend to agree with her," another queen piped up. "Thromstead simply should have more of us beautiful women around."

"Yes, they are both quite right. After all we are the ultimate in the female form," another said.

One of Lisa's aides, a normal woman who conducted women's surveys for her, said, "Oh, I would like to be like all of you breathtaking women. Why can't we have them allow more of us to be modified into the ultimate of beautiful women? I volunteer."

"But I need you to handle my surveys, Bertha," Lisa explained. "I need your hands, though I suppose I could get another, once you become a gorgeous UFB woman. Funny, I never knew you wanted to be like us."

"Oh, I think many of us greatly admire you beautiful women," another queen's aide declared.

Beth, ever the observant one, said, "Excuse me, queens. What exactly is going on here? What are you suggesting? That we allow more women to become UFB women? Don't you realize the dire consequences of creating more at this time? Already, we have only barely managed to avoid a disaster with having too great a number of UFB women for this world's population."

"Oh, I'm just suggesting we have a few more," Clara admitted.

"Yes, some of us would truly like to become ultimates in beauty as well. After all, you queens are special, and we'd like to be special too," one of the aides stated roughly what she'd said earlier.

"But you've been against this—until today that is," Lisa added, growing more confused, not less. "It is out of character for some of you, isn't it?"

Beth defended the women, "Well, people do change their minds, Lisa. That is an established scientific fact. In this case, it's clear us UFB women are vastly superior women, so it's quite reasonable and justified that other women would also like the opportunity to be so very much more than they are. It's only natural, right Clara?"

"Huh? I'm not quite sure what you're saying, Beth. I just think we should allow more women to become as we are, to achieve the pinnacle of beauty and perfection," Clara replied.

"Yes, that's right, the pinnacle of beauty," another aide piped up. "Some of us would like that very much."

Beth protested, "But you know already we have far too many of us on this world. My calculations show unless we keep a tight control on our numbers, ignoring the obvious fact we are the pinnacle, the ultimate in female beauty, in less than two generations, this world will have only UFB women, and men will be forced to have to care for our needs, since there'll not be any normal women around to be our assistants, and that will cut the available workforce by nearly seventy percent, leading to the inability of the world to sustain its population."

Clara chuckled. "I've no idea what you've just said, Beth, but you're already one of us, so you needn't worry."

"Well," Lisa said strongly, "I think we should move on to other, more pressing issues." She got the other queens back on track, discussing whether they should hold a Mid-winter Ball. Everyone soon forgot about that strange exchange.

A few days later when the queens met again, the same topic arose once again, only this time, Elsa swore some of the normal women and queens were somewhat more insistent about allowing more UFB women to be created. Again, Beth spent most of her time trying to get them to grasp why that shouldn't be allowed. In the end, they decided to hold a Mid-winter Ball on the last day of the year.

The third week of October, three female secretaries petitioned to meet with the queens at their meeting. Quite surprisingly, all three begged the queens to be allowed to become UFB women. Considering the ban that had been in place for months, Elsa was surprised when the queens voted in favor of allowing the three their requests. Only Lisa voted against it, though Beth argued for some minutes against it. As soon as they granted their permission to the three, several aides, who had been suggesting they too wanted to become UFB women, once more pleaded to be allowed to do so as well, arguing that since the queens had just allowed the three secretaries to do so, then they should be allowed to do it as well. Over Lisa's protests, the queens agreed and sent their requests for the seven to be converted as soon as GD could arrange it.

Elsa knew Felix fully understood the magnitude of the workforce problem on Blackwell-C and that he'd veto the queens' requests. In a shocking reversal of her expectations, he Okayed the requests and arranged for the seven women to undergo the conversion the following day. When Beth heard this, she complained he was making a mistake and again outlined the dangers the world faced with so many UFB women around. He shook his head, apparently baffled by what she was saying versus what the queens said, and allowed his decision to stand.

Several days later, Queen Lisa had ten more women paying her a visit. Two had already had the cures. Each begged her to allow them to become beautiful, perfect UFB women. Lisa twisted her mouth, baffled by these unexpected requests. Looking at the two had received their cures, she asked, "But you were UFB women and chose to get the cures and not be perfect. I don't understand."

Glassy-eyed, one spoke up, "My queen, I must have made a mistake. I must be a UFB woman, beautiful and perfect like yourself and Beth. You're so beautiful."

If Lisa had a soft spot, it was her vanity. "Well, of course all women should be perfect and beautiful. That is nature's way. Of course, you all may have the conversion process. See my assistants to get your names and addresses logged. I'm sure the process can be started yet today. Oh, Alina, as soon as you have their information, please send word to Felix to get them in today. We mustn't make them wait."

"But Lisa, what are you doing?" Beth protested. "We can't have more UFB women, not until the balance is restored. You know that, don't you?"

"Oh don't be a whiner, Beth. A few more won't hurt," Lisa said rolling her eyes in disgust.

Beth looked at Elsa, who only shrugged, saying, "It isn't my place to interfere in the queen's business." *That noise in my head is more pronounced today. I wonder where it is coming from? Oh well, here comes more petitioners.*

Unknown to Lisa, Beth, and Elsa, each of the other nine queens in Thromstead also had around ten women petitioning to have the conversion process done on them this same day. Six of the nearly ninety women had already had the cures. The other queens readily granted them permission.

Early afternoon, Felix darted through the tunnel system to visit his wife in the throne room of the castle. "Lisa honey, do you realize you queens have just sent nearly a hundred more women to me to get the UFB woman procedure done? Nine had already had the cures. Why?"

"Oh, they must have made a mistake, honey," Lisa replied. Elsa noticed that her eyes had a rather vacant stare in them, quite the opposite of Beth. How curious, she thought.

"Well, in that case, it's all right," Felix replied, completely out of character Elsa thought, but couldn't see his eyes as he turned and left the room.

"I just don't understand what's going on here," Beth complained to Elsa. "His reaction is nuts, pardon my use of such slang. I'm rather distraught. Why is it that no one is listening to reason anymore? I'm going to have to have a long talk with George and Felix tonight," she declared. Elsa would have sworn Beth would have placed both hands on her hips in defiance had she had them. *Maybe she can do some good*, Elsa thought.

If Beth had any luck with the two CEOs, Elsa didn't know. She missed their meeting. because she had to instruct several new assistants who had just been hired to replace three who had recently become UFB women themselves. Now their cook was requesting she be allowed to become beautiful and perfect as well. Elsa did her best to convince the cook to change her mind, but the glassy-eyed woman paid her no mind, frustrating Elsa.

Daily, the queens allowed more women to undergo the procedure, averaging a hundred more each day during the early weeks of November. Worse, from Elsa and Beth's point of view, the queens were allowing girls as young as twelve-years-old to be converted. Queen Lisa and Queen Carla were now adamant. "Look," Queen Carla declared, "any woman who wishes to become perfect and beautiful as we are simply must be allowed to do so. It would be criminal of us not to allow them to be as gorgeous as we are."

Mid-November, Beth and Elsa sat on either side of Lisa as she again held court. Elsa was frustrated as usual. She'd had to train another three servants and a cook, not once but three times now. It seems these newly hired assistants lasted only four or five days before they begged to be allowed to become beautiful and perfect too. As Elsa and Beth expected, more women came to request they be allowed to undergo the process. Elsa looked on shocked to see Renate, Nadja, and

Irma among the petitioners. She rose and walked over to her friends.

"Renate, Nadja, Irma, what are you doing here?" Elsa asked. She noticed their eyes. All had that same glassy, not there look in them.

Renate said, "We've made a mistake. We must be perfect and beautiful for our wonderful husbands." Elsa protested some and Renate added, "I do my math in my head. I don't need arms."

When Elsa questioned Nadja, who was now a secretary for one of the lower executives in GD headquarters, she replied, "I don't really need hands, Elsa, not if I am beautiful and perfect." Elsa gave up. There was no talking sense to any of them! Worse, Elsa was very irritable this morning, something totally foreign to her.

Beth cussed, "Damned it. Why doesn't anyone listen to me? I'm a genius you know. And this is wrong, totally wrong!" Elsa had never heard Beth swear before, let alone be so antagonistic. It wasn't her way, but Beth's eyes did not have a vacant stare in them. However, that low-level background *noise* in the kilo-yatta-hertz range was much louder today.

After allowing these women to have the procedure done and sending them over to have their information jotted down by her new assistant, Lisa looked up to see Felix wandering in. He seemed lost and confused as he approached Lisa, who said, "Hi honey. Got even more women who want to be perfect and beautiful."

"Oh very good, very good. I need to be perfect for you too, honey. George agrees with me. He wants to be perfect for Beth. What am I doing here?" Felix whispered, apparently realizing he'd walked into the queen's throne room. He turn, muttering something to himself and left.

Beth and Elsa had a frustrating day with Beth complaining about a nagging headache and Elsa feeling irritated, something new and foreign to her. The Gott and Gebberly families always met at the Gott's for supper, sharing the news of the day. However, Lisa and Beth finally gave up. "I don't know where Felix has gotten to nor George," Lisa complained, "so it will serve them right if we just go ahead and eat. Elsa, please." Elsa began feeding her, while Beth's new servant watched Elsa's moves, trying to emulate them as she fed Beth.

As they finished up, their doctor dropped by, "Ah good. You both are here. I came by to tell you that your husbands are doing fine. They will be out of their comas in four days, and we'll have appropriate apparel and shoes ready for them at that time."

"Huh?" exclaimed Lisa.

"What are you saying?" asked Beth, wishing she could rub her head. Elsa looked up annoyed.

"They are in their comas now. They wanted to be perfect for the both of you, beautiful UFBMD men. Didn't they tell you?" the doctor asked, growing worried a mistake had been made and that it would be his head.

"No they didn't. Well maybe he tried," Lisa said, recalling Felix's weird visit to the throne room.

Visibly relieved, the doctor said. "Excellent. You should see about acquiring servants for your husbands. There are now ten other men undergoing the procedure, all from GD and GE headquarters. Rather strange, but mine is only to follow orders. You may check on them if you wish. Sub-level One. Good evening."

"Come on. Let's check on them now," Lisa declared. Elsa helped both women up and put a steadying arm around each. Together, they headed out of their suite, taking the elevator. All three were surprised to find their husbands lying naked beneath blankets. The group of men undergoing the procedure were kept separate from the many women. Elsa was shocked to see Wotan, Ebert, and Stefan lying there beside Felix and George. While the two wives sat a moment beside their husbands, Elsa slipped into the adjoining room and gazed at the comatose women. She spotted Renate, Irma, and Nadja there as well. *What is going on,* she wondered, rubbing her own head?

Once she had the women tucked in for the night, she went to her room and placed a call to Dirk and Karla. "Do you know that Renate, Irma, and Nadja are in comas again, going back to being UFB women? And that Wotan, Ebert, and Stefan are too? The men are in comas as well."

Dirk put the phone on speakers and said, "We know. They've been talking about it for several days now," Dirk answered.

Karla added, "We tried talking them out of it, but we couldn't. Both Dirk and I really want to make music and we can't do that if we lose our arms and hands. Elsa, it's so strange. We both have these strong urges to get it done, but we're fighting it because of our love for music. What is going on?"

"I don't know," Elsa replied more irritated than ever, though she kept her voice steady. "It's wild. An epidemic. Even Felix and George have just voluntarily undergone the procedure. They are in comas too. Something is not right here, and I aim to find out. This isn't like any of these men."

"But what could it be?" Dirk asked.

"Don't know. But you two keep on resisting those urges," Elsa suggested. After the call, she sat back and began analyzing the known data, beginning with the men who were undergoing the mutation process. All of them, she noted, worked for either GD or GE and their offices were on the second and third floors. What began to bother her was what else wasn't there, what was missing.

No men from lower floors were undergoing the process. Further, no other men from around Thromstead were either. The outbreak of *insanity*, as she began to call this phenomenon, was limited to those two buildings and then only to the top two floors. How very strange. This can't be an accident.

The next day, she discussed what she'd learned that evening with Beth, while Lisa continued to carry out her queen duties, mostly allowing more women to undergo the process. "So Beth, what are the odds this phenomenon is simply chance?" Elsa asked. She already knew the odds, having computed it last night. However, as always, she needed to work with the locals, get them to see what was going on, and to take appropriate action.

"Well, how very unusual, Elsa. Roughly one chance in a million, though it could be much lower. We should keep an eye on this," Beth answered.

"Perhaps, you should suggest the men working on the upper two floors temporarily move to lower floors," Elsa suggested.

"Ah, yes, that is very observant of you, Elsa. I will take care of that right now. You stay here with Lisa. I can manage this." Beth tossed her hair to one side, carefully rose to her toes, and began her slow shuffling walk out of the throne room. Elsa knew she was being very brave to do this on her own, since there were several flights of stairs she'd have to negotiate on her own. Beth's new servant hadn't shown up for work this morning and both guessed she was down in the infirmary undergoing the UFB woman conversion too.

"Queen Lisa, may I have your permission to contact some other queens? On your behalf, of course," Elsa asked.

"Sure go ahead. I've got my hands full with these women all wanting to become beautiful and perfect, as they simply must, you know," Lisa pronounced, just as glassy-eyed as always.

Elsa placed many long distance calls to the many other queens. When she finished, she excused herself and headed off to find Beth, who was making her slow, careful way back up the stairs to the throne room. As Elsa slipped a steadying arm around her tiny waist, Beth said between slight gasps for breath, "Well, that's done. I have convinced them to move to lower floors. I told them that if they didn't do that, they might find themselves down in the infirmary with Felix and George. What's weird, Elsa, is that several said perhaps they should do just that! I think I talked them out of it. This is getting weirder and weirder!"

"It certainly is, Beth. I just got off the phone with many queens in other cities. Guess what?" Elsa asked. Beth just gasped slightly. All this exertion was more than she was used to doing at one time. "None of them have had more than one or two requests from women wanting to become UFB women. And those few had relatively high ranking corporate executives as husbands, which makes their requests understandable, more or less. Beth," she continued but was interrupted.

Beth gasped and said, "Something is going on here,

229

sinister even! Probability is now one in a billion or more!" She gasped again and had to pause on the stairs to catch her breath. Her extreme corset wasn't designed to allow her such mobility and action as she'd just done.

"Beth, we have to find out what's going on in Thromstead before it's too late, if it isn't already!" Elsa declared.

"We must. Find out. Today. My headache. Is back," Beth said between gasps.

"Relax, Beth. Catch your breath. I'm sure you and I can figure this out," Elsa replied. She noticed she too was even more irritable than yesterday, but that kilo-yatta-hertz range background noise was louder than ever. "Say, can you hear a high frequency noise?"

"No. I sort of feel. Something though. Whitish, I think. I'm recovering. Bit more time," Beth answered.

"I wonder if this noise can be detected by some electronic sensors?" Elsa asked.

"Well, it should be, but that's such a high frequency that I doubt that any of our sensors could detect it. Ah, but it should be also emitting lower harmonics, and those we might be able to sense. I know a fellow over in George's building who is a genius at signal detection. We should pay him a visit now."

"Okay. I'll go with you. Lisa has enough helpers around her so she should be able to manage without me for a time. Shame you had to come up all these stairs only to go back down them."

Beth laughed. "Going down is far harder. Thanks for the support. Honestly, I don't know what George was thinking when he decided to become a UFBMD man. I guess we'll need lots more servants now. I mean I'm totally used to all this, being a second-generation UFB woman, that is, I've always been as I am, but from all I've seen in the past, Elsa, I'm really frightened of how the women and especially the men will react when they come out of their comas."

She went on, "I've seen two men who underwent it. From the way that they carried on, you would think someone was killing them. Screams, panic, stark terror, I think is the proper designation with which to gauge their reactions. Of course, those two men were, well being polite, they were gay and wanted to be women, which is why they got themselves converted. And yet when they came out of their comas, they were in stark terror, just like so many women I've seen who under went the process, though honestly, I can't imagine why they all feel such terror, can you? I mean I feel perfectly fine, normal in all ways, well, except of course I need assistance with many things." Beth continued to chat all the way to the electronics engineering research department on Sub-level Ten of the GE building. The tunnel did lead onwards to Castle Berringer, but the two stopped here and took the elevators downward.

"Ah, Mrs. Gebberly, you're looking stunning this fine morning. What brings you way down here?" the middle-aged man with a small black moustache said, looking up from his worktable. Circuits and parts lay strewn in what Elsa thought was a grand mess. The smell of solder was in the air.

"Engineer Ivan, this is Lisa's servant, Elsa. We have a problem, a very, very serious problem and are hoping you may be able to help us. Elsa, you explain it better than I can."

"Ivan," Elsa acknowledged his bow. "For many weeks now, I have been sort of sensing a low background noise I suspect might be in the kilo-yatta-hertz range. Recently, it has been getting steadily louder. Beth senses it as a sort of white noise. It's giving Beth bad headaches, and makes me rather irritable. Plus, as you know, thousands of women here in Thromstead have insisted on becoming UFB women, including many who already had the cures and now want the cures undone."

Beth broke in, "Of course, we should not and must not allow them to become UFB women. The future survival of the world is at stake, just as George and Felix told everyone when we first arrived here. That was my calculation, by the way, which, using his computer, George later proved was correct. What's weird, Ivan, is Thromstead's queens are behind this completely, even Lisa, who darn well should know better. Even Felix and George are backing all these new requests, totally out of character for them."

She continued rapid fire, "And now both George and

Felix have gone and gotten themselves converted too. In three more days, they will be UFBMD men. What's even stranger, many men on the top two floors of GD and GE here have insisted on becoming UFBMD men too and are up in the infirmary. And yet, Ivan, not one man who works on any other floor has had such notions, nor has any other man anywhere in Thromstead! This simply doesn't make any sense. The chance of this happening by pure chance is only one in well over a billion, not remotely likely, if at all. Plus, there's more. Elsa here has talked with all the other queens outside Thromstead. Only a couple of GD executive's wives had requested they be allowed to become UFB women. So something, Ivan, is really going on here. We think it might have something to do with this background noise."

Elsa finally was able to speak again. "Precisely. The men weren't impacted until this noise became really loud. Plus, as the volume rose, so did the number of women demanding they become UFB women. There is a precise correlation between the strength of this white noise and this insane desire to become UFB women and now men."

"How utterly fascinating," Ivan replied. "White noise couldn't possibly be causing this insanity, but still if it is causing headaches, we should locate its source. Probably some piece of machinery is acting up. We don't have any electronic devices that operate in the kilo-yatta-hertz range. That's way, way beyond anything useful, and GE is practical if anything," Ivan declared.

Beth said, "I told Elsa we didn't have sensors that could detect such a high frequency noise, but then I remembered harmonics. Perhaps you could work up a circuit we could use to detect some of the lower harmonics and then somehow triangulate where it is coming from. Like you said, probably a piece of equipment long overdue for oiling or something."

"Of course. This is so intriguing that I'll get on to it today. Not much else to do really, just been tinkering here. I'll keep you posted, Beth, Elsa," Ivan promised. The two women headed back to Lisa's throne room, arriving in time to help with lunch.

That afternoon, the GE and GD doctors paid a visit to

Lisa, complaining that their infirmaries were filled to capacity. Lisa had already allowed another hundred women to get their modifications, so she ordered the doctors to open up a warehouse to house the new requests, much to the chagrin of the two men, who grumbled all the way out of the throne room.

Late afternoon, Lisa, Beth, and Elsa visited the infirmary in GD headquarters, checking on their husbands. However, they witnessed some fifty women as they woke up from their four-day comas, to find their bodies genetically modified and turned into proper UFB women. All three, and especially Elsa, anticipated hearing screams of terror echoing through the sub-level infirmary. The three were shocked to hear no such cries of panic and terror!

Elsa moved close to one woman who was being helped up after she revived. The staff had her fully dressed in her first UFB woman's outfit, complete with mandatory tight corset. "Oh, breathing is hard. Do I look beautiful now? Am I perfect? I have to see." The woman gasped slightly but didn't seem to be at all alarmed by her shortness of breath or her extreme difficulty trying to sit up on the edge of the cot. "Mirror. Please," she gasped. When the nurse complied, between gasps, she exclaimed, "Oh. I am. Perfect. Beautiful. Wonderful."

The nurse then helped her to her feet. As expected, the woman wobbled wildly trying to keep her balance on her toes. "Oh so silly of me," she said as she struggled mightily. "I must walk gracefully. I'm not graceful yet."

"Give yourself a couple of weeks to get used to it, Belinda," the nurse explained. "Come on. I'll support you. We need to get you to your home where your husband is anxiously waiting for you."

"Oh yes, I must. I must. I'm so beautiful and so perfect now. He'll be so happy, if only I can walk. It's hard, isn't it? Well, I do look so perfect now," Belinda said between gasps and wild wobbling, vanishing into the hallway on her way to the elevators and home.

"Well, obviously, we UFB women are the ultimate in beauty, but these women are acting really weird, Elsa," Beth whispered as they watched woman after woman respond in much the same ways as Belinda had. "It's like they are stuck on perfect and beautiful, which of course we are. Why keep saying it, since that is obvious to everyone?"

"Beth, notice their eyes," Elsa whispered.

"Kind of glassy, not all there? Is that what you mean? Fogged over like," Beth answered, searching for words to describe something she had no real description of.

"Exactly, almost as if they were brainwashed or something," Elsa whispered a hint to Beth.

"Oh! Not brainwashed, Elsa, but hypnotized! I do think these women are somehow hypnotized! Honestly, every woman I have ever seen waking up from her coma acts frightened and terrified at first, usually screaming some too. None of that here. So they must be hypnotized. Hey, and that could explain why all these women are wanting and demanding to become UFB women! And the men too. Someone is hypnotizing everyone."

"Everyone in Thromstead, Beth?" Elsa countered with logic.

"Oh, I see what you mean. Well, someone could hypnotize one woman, perhaps, but you are right. How could they hypnotize thousands of women and some men? Still, that's the best description yet. Come on. Let's check on George and Felix. I wonder how badly they'll scream when they wake up? After all, they won't look at all like a man any more. No one can even tell they are men unless someone removes their panties," Beth explained, though Elsa certainly didn't need to be told this.

The next day, Elsa got a frantic call from Mayor Beifeld. "Elsa, can you talk some sense into Amalia? She's determined to get all her cures undone. She insists she wants to become a UFB woman again. I can't seem to talk any sense into her. Please, Elsa. She will listen to you," the mayor pleaded.

"Sure. Put her on," Elsa replied and shortly heard Amalia's young voice. "What's all this about? You want to become a helpless UFB woman again? I thought you wanted to get your education?"

"Oh yes, yes I do. Very much. I have a new boyfriend now. Jan. He's promised to take notes while I'm in my coma.

Then, when I'm back at school, he promises to help me with everything I might need. I so want to be perfect for him. I must be beautiful and perfect. You can understand that, can't you? Make dad listen to me. If not, I'll just sneak off and have it done anyway. I will be perfect for Jan. He loves me, and I love him. He will help me with everything at school."

Finally, Elsa got in a word, "But who will help you at home?"

"Oh dad can or we can hire an assistant part-time, since I won't need one when I am at school."

When the mayor came back on the phone, Elsa said, "I'm afraid Amalia isn't listening to me either. She'll just get it done anyway. Best let her do it for now. Something weird is happening to us here in Thromstead. Beth is working on finding out what, since George and Felix both have gone and turned themselves into UFBMD men and are still in their comas. I'll keep an eye out for her here, mayor."

That evening when the three paid another visit to see the two husbands, Elsa spotted Amalia and sat beside her cot for a brief spell. Later that night after helping the two women into bed, she again called up Dirk and Karla to make sure they were still holding out. "Yes, we fight it by practicing the harpsichord for hours. It is working, though I have a headache," Karla explained.

In her own bedroom, Elsa sat back and began to review every detail, convinced some people were able to withstand this new form of hypnotism or brainwashing, whatever it actually was. Her conclusion was someone was purposely doing this to Thromstead alone, and it was likely some kind of test. But would they soon do this to the other major cities and all of Blackwell-C? If so, the world would be doomed long before Beth's original prediction of thirty years.

The next day, the two men were scheduled to wake up, as were Wotan, Ebert, and Stefan. Their wives had already awakened and were sitting beside their husbands, waiting for them to revive. Elsa visited the three women but got little more than the fact that they were now beautiful and perfect women for their husbands. That their husbands now looked like they did and would be just as helpless didn't seem to register with them.

Elsa sat beside Lisa and Beth, ignoring Lisa's chatter about just how perfect and beautiful her Felix now looked. Finally, the men came out of their comas within minutes of each other. The nursing staff had already gotten them fully dressed in their first new outfits, complete with the usual heavily steel-boned corsets that shrunk their waists to barely a foot across. Their distinctive moustaches were gone, as well as their arms. In fact, looking at them, Elsa couldn't tell they were men; rather they looked like ordinary UFB women in all respects, though from her experience with Emil, she knew that one part of the men's anatomy was intact. Still, Emil had reacted very badly to his modification and perhaps rightly so, since his male appearance was gone forever.

"Oh," Felix groaned. Lisa heard his new soprano voice for the first time. "I feel groggy. Oh. I'm awake. I'm now perfect and beautiful. Lisa. You're here. Help me up. I need to see what I look like. Can't breathe," he gasped, struggling in vain to get up from the cot. Elsa slipped an arm around his waist and gently helped him into a sitting position. His rich, thick, shiny black hair fell down to the floor. It too was knee-length. He sat there gasping for breath, as George woke up and Elsa got him into a sitting position. A nurse moved a full-length mirror over to their cots, and both men finally got to see their new appearances.

"Oh I look. Very much like you. Lisa, honey. My hair, so black. I was hoping. It would be blonde. Like yours. Can't breathe right. I'm now perfect. Beautiful for you, honey. My voice. It's so high. I feel funny. Have to pee. Lisa, honey, can you. Help me pee?"

Lisa giggled. "You look beautiful and perfect, honey. Sorry, I can't help you much. Nurse, he needs to pee. We're going to need more servants, but Elsa can help some until we get them, can't you?" Elsa nodded and watched how Felix managed standing and walking in the super high toe heels.

"Not graceful. Really hard," he said between gasps and wiggling about rather wildly, just as Emil had. "Catch on soon. Hope so. Didn't know. Was so hard. To walk. Don't let go. Of me." The nurse led him off to use the bathroom, while Elsa turned her attention onto George and Beth.

"Well, you've certainly gone and done it this time, George," Beth chided him.

He ignored that. "I look. Perfect. Beth, I'm beautiful. For you. Now we are. Both perfect. Oh, I need a drink. Gotta pee. This is hard. Can't breathe. Ouch. Stepped on my hair. Silly." Just then, another aide appeared, helped him onto his wildly unsteady feet, and made him walk to the restroom as well.

"I think he's lost his mind or something," Beth whispered. "I'll tag along. Be back soon. Will need your help too, Elsa." She tossed her hair about, getting it out of her way, carefully rose, caught her balance, and took her tiny four inch steps following after George. Elsa took this opportunity to see how Wotan, Ebert, and Stefan were faring.

She found them also awake and chatting with their wives. Their reactions were nearly the same as those of Felix and George. No terror. No fright. No alarm over the loss of their masculine forms. Just silly comments about being perfect and beautiful for their wives. Elsa observed, but could formulate no conclusions. The men's reactions were completely wrong! She noticed the three men's eyes. They were glazed over. Elsa filed the observation and reminded herself to check on the eyes of Felix and George.

While she wanted to help Stefan, Wotan, and Ebert, she couldn't. Her current responsibilities lay with Felix and Lisa, and to a lesser extent George and Beth. When the aides brought the two gasping and wobbling men back with their wives following behind them, the doctor arrived and told her, "You may take them to their suites now. They are perfectly healthy."

Elsa slipped an arm around each man, relieving the aides who had many others to help. "Okay, let's get you up to your suite, Felix. Tiny steps. Lisa, Beth, why don't you walk in front of us so your husbands can see how you manage." The two women did so.

"Kind of hard," Felix said, still gasping periodically. "Won't faint. Can't faint. Have to be perfect. For Lisa."

"Right. Can't faint. Be perfect. For Beth," George added

between his own gasps. She felt both men were struggling mightily to breathe beneath the unyielding corsets, which kept them from slouching and provided the back support for their now basketball sized bosoms. "Be perfect. For Beth," he repeated several times.

It took her a half hour to get them into Felix and Lisa's bedroom, though she left Beth and George sitting on the couch. Carefully, she got both undressed and ready for bed, though they both still wore their corsets, which were only removed when necessary. It was obvious both Lisa and Felix were highly aroused, but Felix had no idea how to do anything but sit erect on the edge of their bed. "Like this silly, remember?" Lisa whispered. She'd gotten to her knees and could now move about the bed. "Get his hair between his legs so he can move around on his knees too, like me, Elsa. Right. Like this," Lisa continued moving a little. Eagerly Felix followed suit, and Elsa quickly left them work out the rest for themselves.

A half hour later, she had Beth and George ready for bed, and helped them get onto their knees on their bed and with their hair draped between their legs so they didn't step on it. Again, she saw that both were aroused and quietly left them, returning to her own room over at GD headquarters. Long Elsa sat and reflected on what she'd observed. She was convinced something diabolical was going on here in Thromstead, and she knew she simply had to get to the bottom of it before it was too late, if it wasn't already past the point of no return.

Several new servants arrived in the morning, all rather young girls, none over twelve Elsa estimated. She gave them directions on what to do and turned their training over to Lisa, while she dashed down to the tunnels and over to GE headquarters to do the same with George and Beth's new servants. Again, she was surprise to see young girls here as well. *Are they running out of potential servant women?*

All George could talk about was how perfect he now was, how great sex was, and that he needed to do it with Beth often during the day, completely embarrassing Beth and the young servants. Elsa whispered, "Get him practicing walking today." Beth nodded, and Elsa left, running back over to check on Felix and Lisa. She wasn't surprised to hear him telling the new servants who were feeding them just how perfect he now was and how perfect Lisa was. At least, he stopped talking about how great sex was.

Elsa suggested, "Lisa, I know you have your duties in the castle throne room. Felix needs to practice walking, so have him come with you. While you are carrying out your queen duties, have him continue practicing his walking."

"Right. His voice is so strange. He's an alto now, not a bass. Kind of strange, but nice," Lisa replied with a more or less vacant stare.

"Hey, I'm perfect. Never shave again," he said between gasps. "Must walk. Perfectly."

Elsa left them and headed down to check how Ivan was doing with the noise detector. "Another couple of days and I'll have it. Don't worry. It should work," Ivan stated, a bit annoyed with the interruption. Elsa left him and found a quiet place to reflect on the events.

During the ensuing days, hundreds more women came by GD to undergo their greatly desired conversions into UFB women. Elsa began digging into population records of Thromstead, leaving her charges alone, since there wasn't anything she could do for them, except see they practiced walking, handling stairs, sitting down, and rising, which required the men to learn to toss their hair out of the way. She correctly assumed the young servant girls could manage this.

December arrived. Elsa had contacted the Shining Star, informing them of the events in Thromstead and asking them to come back to help unravel this mystery, but to return well-armed. Why? At this point, Elsa's population studies yielded an alarming fact. Nearly all the adult women in Thromstead had become a UFB woman, if they hadn't been before! Well over ninety percent.

There were a few holdouts, such as Karla, but they were few. Younger girls were pressed into service as assistants for the many women and now younger boys were too. Worse, some of the older girls began asking to become UFB women as well. While the queens gave their permission, as did Felix and George, at last the doctors stood up to them.

"Look," the GD doctor declared harshly, "we don't dare do this to children this young. I must insist they're at least thirteen. It is a terrible health risk to genetically modify children when they are too young!"

The queens bought his argument, reluctantly, telling the young girls to return when they turned thirteen. Elsa and the doctors knew this was a fabrication on the doctors' part. Anyone could be genetically modified. The doctors didn't want to see young children undergoing this life-altering modification until they truly understood what they were doing.

With hardly any new women turning up to undergo the process, the doctors estimated the infirmaries would be emptied in another three days. Meanwhile, Ivan finally contacted Elsa. "It is ready to go."

"Coming immediately!" she replied, and dashed down to the tunnels, sprinting over to GE headquarters.

Chapter 16—Conspiracy Uncovered

Ivan looked like something out of a freakish science fiction movie. He held his device in his hands. A revolving torus slowly moved in circles around the base. A giant amplification circuit and power pack was strapped to his back, many wires going over his shoulders to the device in his hands. "It's harmonics. It doesn't reach into the kilo-yatta-hertz range, but it does pick up lower frequency harmonics. And yes, there are some very strong ones hitting Thromstead. Now we must triangulate and locate this malfunctioning piece of machinery."

Clearly, Elsa thought, *Ivan still believes it is an errant machine causing this, but there must be a whole lot more going on than that.*

Elsa carried a map of the area, while Ivan moved from location to location around the city. Three hours later, they had determined six lines of sight, and they all crossed at the same point some ten miles due east of the outskirts of the city, high on the side of Mount Hoft. Together, the pair hiked outside the city, following several roads, taking more bearings that further solidified the location as being somewhere on the slope of the mountain.

"Still convinced this is a malfunctioning machine, Ivan?" Elsa asked.

"Can't be. There's nothing there but the picturesque mountain, but that's what the reading are saying. Come on. Let's get a car and do more checking."

"And some binoculars," she added.

An hour later, the pair followed the road that went the closest to their marked location on the map. The terrain forced the road to bend around to the south. The pair stopped at the turn and took another directional sighting. It pointed nearly due north and a little more east of their location. "Yes, somewhere up there on the mountain side," Ivan declared, wrapping up this observation. This is getting stranger by the minute. Let's backtrack and take the north road."

An hour later, they again had stopped as the mountain forced this road to veer northward around Mount Hoft. The mountain wasn't that tall, its peak a little over five thousand feet, though that was some three thousand above the average elevation of hilly Thromstead. Ivan took another observation, adding it to the map, which only continued to prove the signals were coming from high upon the side of Mount Hoft.

Using the binoculars, Elsa scanned the snow-covered side of the mountain. She wasn't certain what she was looking for, just something out of place. After a time, she spotted a small antenna array. "What do you make of that?" she asked, handing him the binoculars, while temporarily holding onto his contraption.

"By golly. That does look like a signal array. On the small side, but it's directional, that much I can tell from this distance," Ivan said.

"Pointing down to Thromstead?" she asked.

"Yes, pointing down to our city. I wonder what that is?"

"Well, let's not take any chances. If someone is purposely trying to harm everyone in Thromstead, we best come back with forces of our own," Elsa advised. The two returned to the city. As they parked the car, she added, "Ivan, don't say anything about this to anyone. It could get you into big trouble if those behind this find out. They could kill you or worse, turn you into a UFBMD man."

"Shit! Won't say a thing!" Ivan agreed. She saw the expected reaction from a man threatened with being genetically modified into a UFBMD man.

The next morning, Elsa got the phone call she had been waiting for. "Hi Elsa. We're back," Susanne said happily. "Got two more with us than when we left. Achima and Hedda each have a son now. Plus Kirsa and I are both pregnant. We're starting our families too. So what's all this mystery thing about? Oh, Rudolf says that we're at the spaceport now. Wenzel's off renting a car. Where do you want us?"

"Slow down, Susanne. Don't come into the city. Stay at the spaceport. I'll come join you on the Shining Star. Explain shortly," Elsa said and quickly hung up. She called up Ivan and he promised to bring his contraption and meet her at GE's garage on the main floor. That done, Elsa headed up to the top floor to find Beth.

"Glad you are here. All George wants to do is make out. I know we have powerful sex drives, but this is even too much for me. What's up?" Beth said, glad to get away for a moment. George still wasn't able to get himself up from sitting positions without falling over or nearly so, and he wisely didn't get up and follow her.

"You're now the highest ranking executive of GE that isn't under the hypnotic effect. Come with Ivan and me. I'll explain in the car where no one can overhear us," Elsa said softly so George couldn't hear.

"Okay. Glad to get away for a while. George, you're to practice standing up, sitting down, and your walking. Back later. You two, make sure he does," she ordered the two twelve-year-old girls, now their only assistants. Elsa put a steadying arm around Beth, and they headed down to the car park area on the ground floor of the GE headquarters. "Oh, hi Ivan. What's that thing you've got on?"

"We'll explain in the car," Elsa cautioned her. Once she had Beth in and buckled up, she told Ivan, "Head to the spaceport. We're meeting up with some others who aren't hypnotized. I'll explain everything in a couple minutes, so I don't have to do it twice, Beth."

A half hour later, they pulled up beside the Shining Star, and the group was standing by the bay doors, breathing in the chilly air of winter here on Blackwell-C. Elsa helped Beth out and up the bay ramp. Once inside, she introduced everyone. "This is Achima and Hedda Von Dorfsted." Rudolf had alerted her to the fact those two had gotten married on the trip, hoping would help them get by when they finally returned. "This is Rudolf and Susanne Werner. Wenzel and Kirsa Von Trapp. Emil and Anne Beifeld. Yes, he's the mayor's son," she picked up Beth's questioning look.

"This is GE's CEO's wife, Beth Gebberly, and GE engineer Ivan. I've told you all about the crazy things that have been going on here in Thromstead. Ivan and I now have proof of what's been happening. Someone is deliberately using some kind of electronics to hypnotize women and a few men in

Thromstead, forcing them to become UFB women and UFBMD men. Both her husband, George, who heads GE, and Felix, the CEO of GD have become UFBMD men, along with many others who used to work on the top two floors of GE and GD headquarters. Also, his wife, Queen Lisa is hypnotized as well. Beth here has fought it off, and Ivan works in a sub-level and wasn't impacted."

"I've done a population study and as of now, nearly every adult female in Thromstead has become a UFB woman, along with two dozen men. Children are now taking over as assistants! But thanks to Ivan here, we have located where this signal is coming from. Ivan, show them the map we made yesterday." He dug it out and unfolded it.

"But that's up on the mountain side," Rudolf pointed out.

"Exactly. Looks inaccessible, but there must be a way to get there," Elsa insisted.

Beth spoke up, "Well then, we need to raid this place, find out who is behind this, and put a stop to it. I'm deputizing all of you to help me do this."

Rudolf said, "Okay. We will. But we need to see if there is some way in there. Come on. Let's put the Shining Star to good use. Kirsa, take us up, and let's see if we can find a way in by air."

Thirty minutes later, the transport hovered above the mountainside. Using the IR scanner in the comm center, Hedda called out. "Bingo. Big heat signature down there. Large underground complex. I see two forms moving about so far."

Rudolf spoke into the intercom from the navigator's seat. "Hey, I see what looks like a small access road winding up there from the South Road. That must be the way in." After further conferring, they headed back to the spaceport. Susanne, Kirsa, and Anne remained onboard, looking after the two babies. Besides, all three were well along with their pregnancies. Walking around in the deep snow in their six-inch heels was too risky for them.

The others piled into Rudolf's rented car and Ivan's car. They brought along several large duffle bags, but were all bundled up against the cold. Elsa noted that they'd acquired some very nice, fleece lined boots, though Achima's had the six-inch heels her feet demanded, as did Emil's and the other three women back on the ship. Too bad their feet couldn't be fully repaired, Elsa thought as they piled into the cars and headed back through Thromstead. Eventually, they left the eastern side of the city, taking the southern road that Ivan and Elsa had used yesterday. When they got to the bend where the road finally turned south, from which it derived its name, they halted and got out.

Sure enough, they saw a narrow gravel road, snow covered, winding off in the distance. It had not been used for some time, certainly not since the last snowfall. Considering how winding it was, they decided to hike to the underground facility. For Emil and Achima, this proved treacherous in their spiked heel boots, but nearly impossible for Beth with her toe shoes. Hence, Rudolf simply carried her, swapping off with Wenzel every so often. Elsa put an arm around Emil and Achima, as did Hedda. Between them, despite slipping and sliding, Emil and Achima managed to hike along fairly well.

An hour later, they approached the spot. An array of directional antennas was quite visible, pointing towards Thromstead down below. Also, Ivan spotted another dish pointed towards GD and GE headquarters. He pointed out, "This location was chosen so one dish covers both buildings. They line up nicely from this spot."

"My god! That's a Grade Ten blast door!" exclaimed Achima, pointing to the sole entrance to the bunker below. "It's going to take some serious charges to get that opened."

"Look around some," Emil suggested.

"Definitely this is the spot," Ivan said, operating his detection device. "Hot signal."

"Hey, look over there. Smoke? Steam?" Rudolf pointed to a faint waving area of snow. Everyone could see heat waves and a trace of smoke.

Used to giving orders, Colonel Achima said, "Okay. Break out the smoke bombs. Drop them down the shaft. That should force those inside to open the doors for us. Keep your PDS on, and gear up, everyone. Could be a battle." Duffle bags opened, and Beth and Elsa saw all kinds of weapons, which were quickly handed out. Elsa strapped a PDS onto Beth's waist beneath her heavy coat and then one on herself. Then the two watched as the others grabbed various weapons and took up covering fire positions before the blast door, positioned carefully by Colonel Achima. When she gave the hand signal, Rudolf pulled the pins on two smoke grenades, dropped them down the metal chimney, and ducked back.

"I think that was an explosion," Emil said a bit later. The heavy underground bunker absorbed most of the sound from the grenade detonations.

"Everyone, stay alert," Colonel Achima ordered. "Patience. Patience."

Three minutes later, the blast door opened, and a rush of acrid smoke rushed out, followed by two coughing men. One was armed and began firing his d-gun wildly. Achima, Hedda, Rudolf, Emil, and Wenzel returned fire, killing the guard four times over! The other man continued coughing and yelling, "Don't shoot! Don't shoot!" Quickly, Hedda moved in and secured him, making sure he didn't have a concealed weapon on him. She then tied his hands behind his back.

"What is going on here?" Beth demanded. "Look, I'm the wife of the GE CEO, who is indisposed at the moment, so I'm in charge here. Answer me. What is going on? You are wearing a GE uniform. Speak up before I lose my temper."

The man looked at Beth, radiating distaste. "You aren't my boss! I ain't saying nothing. You don't know what you are messing with! If you want your precious husband to remain a CEO, you best all just leave here right now."

"I assure you, I'm not about to leave here, not without knowing precisely what is going on. We know somehow this facility has been hypnotizing half of Thromstead, forcing them to become UFB women and UFBMD men. So speak up or I will let these good people pound it out of you." Beth attempted to talk *tough*, but the man didn't give in to her demands.

"Looks like the smoke is clearing out, Beth. Give it a few more minutes, and we can go inside and see for ourselves," Emil pointed out.

"If you value your lives, you won't go inside," the man

barked back, but he sounded more nervous than before.

"Look, whatever your mission here was, it is now compromised. We'll soon learn the truth. It will go easier on you if you cooperate now, rather than later," Beth continued to demand answers from this GE engineer or technician. She wasn't quite sure of his status.

The observant Beth saw his hesitation and continued, "Come on. You know what we do with traitors on this world? We make then into UFBMD men, but with the new version that removes their voice boxes and gives them short upper arms. That's what you are facing once we go inside and see what's going on for ourselves. Last chance."

Elsa saw that same shock and fright on his face that she'd seen on Ivan's and other men. "Okay, okay. Promise me you won't do that to me and I'll tell you."

"I promise I won't have your voice box removed and all that," Beth said, though she didn't specifically mention the normal UFBMD mutation.

"This whole thing is a regional GD-GE experimental test to see if the technology they got from Ragnar-B some time ago actually works. I can now say concretely that it certainly does. I've been monitoring GE and GD's communications and based on your own counts, I have all adult women of Thromstead to get themselves turned into UFB women. I've been able to do as the regional bosses asked and got the heads of GD and GE here converted into UFBMD men, along with most all others who spent much of the day on the top two floors of those two buildings. Pinpoint accuracy, you see. All this was planned long before you and your CEOs arrived on this world. This secret installation went up over two years ago now, but when the terrorist struck, the field test had to be delayed until you and your new CEOs arrived. The corporations now have the ultimate weapon in this new Mind Controller. That's what we are calling it. It's so simple, a child could use it."

Beth gasped, "So George and Felix were setup! We knew something wasn't right about this assignment, but we couldn't figure out what."

The man laughed. "Yes, your two executives were setup

all right. Expendable, that's what the regional GE CEO told me. Expendable men."

Beth fumed, but did her best to remain in charge. "Smoke has cleared. We best go inside and see what this is," she declared.

The bunker was setup for long-term habitation by the two men, with sleeping quarters, a gaming room, a well-stocked kitchen, and comfortable bedrooms. However, the front portion held the exotic electronic equipment, along with recording devices. On a desk was a very detailed log listing dates, power levels, and the number of known men and women who responded at that power level. The data went back to just shortly after Beth and her husband arrived on Blackwell-C, though the power levels were quite low at first. The scientist was patient and very thorough, documenting every test he made, as he gradually increased the power levels.

"Elsa, please call the brigade commander for me. Tell him where we are at and to send a platoon of soldiers here. I want this place dismantled and brought back to GE headquarters. It must not be allowed to fall into the regional CEO's hands, not ever, not after what they've done to so many on this world!" Beth barked.

Colonel Achima cringed. Would she and Hedda be arrested as deserters? Then, she got a bright idea, based on her leading the assault on this bunker. She gave a secret hand signal to Hedda, who had the same thoughts but now relaxed.

"Okay, how do we turn it off?" Beth demanded of the man.

He indicated the main power switch, but Ivan interrupted him. "Hey, that is likely to blow the circuits. There is usually a correct power down sequence," Ivan cautioned them. Grimacing, the man outlined the sequence of five switches. Ivan barked, "Okay. But if this damages the machine, I swear I'll inject you with the bio agent myself!" The prisoner visibly began shaking, but swore it was the correct one. Ivan followed the instructions and the Mind Controller powered down. Elsa felt the low level noise vanish entirely.

Ivan then began gathering up the equipment, searching the cabinets, and declared, "This is more like it. A manual of operation."

"It isn't finished yet. I'm still working on it. You need me," the man said.

"What is your name?" Beth asked once more.

"Electronics Technician Bert Cluster," he replied.

"Okay Bert. You keep on cooperating, and I'll take that into consideration," Beth hinted. He grumbled.

A half hour later, shuttles and armored vehicles swarmed around the bunker and the brigade commander marched in, joining the group. "What is going on here? Who are these people? Oh, is that you Colonel Achima? Captain Hedda?"

"Yes sir. Colonel Achima reporting, sir. The captain and I have been on a lengthy secret mission for the late General Ernst, resulting in the capture of this vile enemy base of operations, sir. Beth is acting CEO of GE and GD right now, as Felix and George are temporarily indisposed. This man has been using this new electronic Mind Control device to force all the women of Thromstead to become UFB women along with all the top executives of both GD and GE headquarters. Ivan here has got the machine turned off now, so hopefully no one else will be demanding to be genetically modified sir."

"At ease, colonel, captain. Officially, you were both listed as missing in action. Good cover for your secret mission. However, your hitches were up last June, but you certainly can resign up for another tour. Beth, what do you want done with this bunker? Do you realize it has a Grade Ten blast door?" the brigade commander took charge.

Beth said, "Dismantle the Mind Control machine. Ivan can assist you. I want it brought undamaged to GE headquarters. It must never be allowed to fall into enemy hands. With it, they could make your entire army surrender without firing a shot! Then, search this large complex. Confiscate anything you think useful or valuable. After that, blow this place up so it can never again be used to attack Thromstead."

"A woman after my heart! It will be done, CEO Beth," the brigade commander replied, and began issuing orders.

"Let's get back to my place," Beth suggested. Readily,

her group departed, though Ivan stayed behind. Two other soldiers carted Bert Cluster off. Beth was fuming all the way back. All this had been nothing more than a setup. She, George, Felix, and Lisa had simply been used as lab rats and that truly bothered her. She was a UFB woman after all, and this was an intolerable abuse in her view.

Chapter 17—Repercussions

The group first returned to the Shining Star. They wanted to pay a visit to their friends, some of whom had become victims again, while Emil and Anne wanted to visit their parents and his sister. They agreed to come by GE headquarters after supper. At last, Elsa drove Beth home. Neither of the two anticipated what they found as they entered the city, though Elsa later felt that she should have.

High pitched screams of shock, fright, and terror streamed seemingly out of nearly every home they drove past. As they approached GE headquarters, the din lessened considerably, for there was few homes this close to the heart of the city, the business district, and home to the alien headquarters and two of the ancient baron's castles. Once parked, Elsa helped Beth out and into the elevators, but as the doors opened onto the top floor, they heard two women screaming, utterly terror-stricken.

Beth whispered, "George? Felix?" Elsa merely nodded, and the two continued at Beth's slow, careful pace, entering her suite, where the screaming became mixed with loud sobbing. As they moved into the living room, Felix and George were sitting on the sofa, sobbing, screaming, and gasping for breath, an incredible mixture, as though they couldn't decide which to do. Lisa sat opposite them on a chair, frightened out of her wits, her body shaking quite visibly. The two newly hired young servants cowered in a corner, holding their hands over their ears in fright.

Beth snapped loudly and forcefully, "George! Felix! Get with it! You aren't dead. Snap out of this. I've just had to handle the most critical situation yet. You both were duped, betrayed by your bosses. Now snap out of this wailing this very instant!"

Slowly, the two men ceased screaming, though they continued to gasp and sob. "Come on. Snap out of it! If you value your CEO position in the slightest, snap out of it this *instant*! The world is about to come *down* around us. If you both don't take action *immediately*, all will be *lost*, and I do mean *all!*" Beth continued barking angrily at the two men.

"But look at us! We're, we're. . ." George tried to say, still fighting against the restriction of the corset to breathe.

"Well of course, look at what you've become. Nothing new there. Now George, Felix, you've got to listen to me and take immediate action, immediate action!" Beth continued to force the two men to let go of their victim emotions and at least to listen to her.

"What? What could be worse?" George said, still gasping, but he stopped sobbing.

"All right, listen fellows," Beth said in a softer tone. She outlined everything that had happened, pointing out just who had done what and how the Mind Control machine had been used as an extremely effective weapon. "So Ivan is seeing to the machine's dismantling. It will be brought to GE. Your own regional bosses have betrayed you fellows. We knew there had to be a catch to this assignment. Well, there obviously was. You two and thousands of others in Thromstead have paid the price for you two failing to figure this out. If it weren't for Elsa and me, no one would ever have found out about the treachery of your regional corporations. So what are you boys going to do about it? The brigade commanders are blowing up the bunker, but they will need new orders. Decide what is to be done and soon or I will!"

"But we're completely helpless," Felix complained.

"Felix, we've been betrayed! By our own bosses! I won't stand for this," George declared, finally finding an outlet for his suppressed anger.

"You're right. Betrayed. Sucker punched. I won't stand for this either, George," Felix finally began to allow a bit of anger come to the fore. "If those bastards at the regional headquarters think they can get away with this, they have another think coming. We're pulling out of the corporation's rule. Independence, George, Blackwell-C is going to be free and independent of the corporations! That's what we're going to do, pull out. Let them lose face, lose another world from their dominations, just like Ragnar-B. Hey, have they got the planetary defense shield up and running yet, George?"

"I think so. Main controls are at the spaceport. I like that idea, free and independent. Ha, so the corporations lose another world. Serves those sadistic bastards right. We'll show them," George replied.

A muffled explosion broke the silence between words. Both men looked startled, though it must have been a quite distant explosion. Beth spoke up, "That would be the brigade commander demolishing the secret bunker. So you two should meet with the brigade commander, see this Mind Control machine, send a message to the regional headquarters, and for heaven's sake, make a public address to the people of Thromstead. Oh, and start getting those cures that our heroines brought back duplicated in quantity. Thousands of women are going to need it."

"But we can't do any of that, Beth. We're helpless," George complained, slipping down from anger again.

"George, Felix, you two have a choice to make right now. Either you stop whining and complaining, and start acting like our CEOs or I will. I assure you if I do all this, then this world will recognize me as their top CEO and leader, and not you two. Your choice, boys," Beth chided them again.

"Beth, honey. Be reasonable," George complained. "We're, we're helpless freaks. We can't go before the reporters. Not looking like this. We simply can't. Maybe once we get some of the cures, maybe."

Felix added, "He's right. Think of us. We're freaks. Think of our humiliation. We can't do all that. We're helpless right now. Can't walk. Can't hardly talk." He kept his sentences short, gasping between each one.

"Okay. You've made your decisions. Now live with them. Lisa, you with me?" Beth declared.

"So that Mind Control thing was making me allow all those women to become UFB women? I won't stand for that either, Beth. If our pathetic husbands won't act, we certainly will. After all, I'm a duly elected queen around here," Lisa declared forcefully.

"Good. Elsa, call the brigade commander and have him report here for further orders." To one of the servant girls, she said, "Go find the doctor. Have him take our Bert Custer traitor to the infirmary, turn him into a UFBMD man, and send him over to Blackwoods when he revives. Lisa, you go and make arrangements for a public broadcast in say two hours from now. That should be enough time."

Lisa said forcefully, "You got it. I can't wait to see the faces of their bosses when we tell them we've destroyed their plot against us, captured their machine, and are declaring our independence from them. Should be a treasured moment, Beth."

A flurry of action followed, lasting up until the time the press arrived with their cameras, though no women were among the press, understandably so, Beth thought. The brigade commander arrived first. "Okay sir. Here's what we are going to do," she explained they were severing all ties to the regional corporate rule, making Blackwell-C an independent world. "This means they well could launch a counterattack against us. We need the planetary defense shield up and running from now on. Please station at least a regiment of your forces at the spaceport. If they try to retaliate against us, that's the place they will strike first in order to knock out the defense shield by landing a disguised transport ship filled with soldiers. We can't let them take down our shields or they could well destroy the entire world. Vital mission, brigade commander."

"The shields will be up in thirty minutes, Beth. I'll see security is tighter than a sealed drum," he replied, pleased with the forceful action she was taking.

"Good. Round up Colonel Achima and the others. Lisa and I will hold a press conference in about an hour. I want you to be there as well. I will be explaining everything that has happened and just those of us who are our heroes, saving all the world from these monster men," Beth declared. He saluted and left to round the others up.

"Now then, Lisa, it is time to make that call to the regional offices. We should record it as well," Beth suggested. "Elsa, little help with this, please." A few minutes later, Elsa hit the record button as Beth and Lisa, sitting side by side, each got their respective regional CEO on a secure channel.

"Lisa and I are now in control of GD and GE here on

Blackwell-C. We have discovered your vile treachery with the Mind Control machine, have captured it, and are studying it in our GE research labs. The bunker has been blown up. We have put an end to your vile, treasonous, and sadistic human experimentations here on Blackwell-C. Over."

"That's telling them," Lisa declared, watching the shocked reactions from both CEOs.

"You have no right to do that! This is a vital experiment designed to help save all the corporation-controlled Federation worlds," screamed the GE CEO.

"We won't let you get away with this. Send that machine back here immediately. That's a direct order!" the GD CEO screamed back.

Calmly, Beth replied, "Sorry. As of now, Blackwell-C is a free and independent Federation world. Corporations no longer rule this world, though we will continue acceptable trading arrangements. Our planetary defense shields are now fully operational. You blew it and have lost another world from your greedy paws."

Lisa added, "As soon as we have learned all about the Mind Control machine, we may well use it against you and your corporations, you fiends."

"That's telling them," Beth whispered, signaling Elsa to break the connections and terminate the recordings. "Now we need to get over to your castle for the news conference. I suppose we can send them down to the research labs so they can photograph the Mind Control device, unless they don't mind going there at our snail pace."

An hour later, three reporters were filming the news conference in Castle Berthold's throne room. They'd heard rumors of something major happening, including the distant explosion and eagerly awaited Beth's starting signal. Many others were lined up behind the thrones, including the brigadier himself. Thus, the reporters were certain this was going to make news. When everyone was situated, Beth nodded and after the brief introductory remarks by one of the reporters, Beth began outlining what had been going on.

"Hello. I'm Beth Gebberly, the current head of Galactic Electronics here in Thromstead. George and Felix are currently indisposed and will not be present. If you will recall, when we first arrived, we explained unless drastic action was taken with the UFB woman situation, in thirty years, there would be no normal women left, forcing many men to have to care for their needs, resulting in a disastrous crash in production. We saw this in the food shortage last winter. Thanks to our heroes who went in search of cures and brought them back to us, the disaster was alleviated earlier this year."

"Why am I bringing past history? Because as everyone knows, at this point in time, nearly every adult woman in Thromstead has undergone the transformation into a UFB woman, as well as a number of men. Why was this allowed? How could this happen? Already, we are putting children to work as women's assistants."

"Unknown to any of us, the regional Galactic Electronics CEO has been conducting a secret and terrible experiment on everyone in Thromstead. They were testing their newest weapon, a Mind Control machine. It beamed very high frequency waves down on our town from a secret bunker on the side of Mount Hoft. The insidiousness of this new weapon is that the operator sends a subliminal message out with these waves. The message was simple. Every woman had to become beautiful and perfect, a UFB woman."

"At first, using low power, only a few women began to request this from the queens, who were slightly reluctant to consent. As the power levels rose, the queens were also impacted and had no choice but to agree to the request. They raised the power levels higher and higher. Eventually, each of the ten queens was getting more than a hundred requests a day for the genetic mutation. The Mind Control is so powerful only a handful of women were able to resist its commands. I was one of those as well as Lisa's servant, Elsa. However, in resisting it, I suffered severe headaches all the time."

"Elsa brought this to my attention. She suspected our city was being bombarded with some kind of unknown energy waves. They were also directly aimed at the top two floors of GD and GE headquarters. Thus, our husbands were also forced to get the genetic modifications, as well as a number of others who worked on those floors. Elsa and I had one of our

GE electronics men create a detector, based on the theory that the mysterious and unknown energies would also have lower frequency harmonics. This proved to be the case. Yesterday, using Ivan's new device at my request, Elsa and Ivan traveled all around Thromstead and triangulated the signal, discovering it came from high on the side of Mount Hoft. They found the antenna arrays there and signs of an underground bunker."

"I had to act. However, knowing that nearly everyone in Thromstead was under the effects of this Mind Control machine, I made use of our previous heroes who were on their honeymoons. We called them back, and Colonel Achima and Captain Hedda, who were on a long-term secret assignment, took charge and led us to the bunker. Thanks to their skill and weapons, we captured the bunker, killing one security guard and capturing the scientist who was running the Mind Control machine doing these hideous things to all of us in Thromstead. Under my orders, Ivan got the machine safely turned off."

"I then called in the northern brigade commander, and he and his soldiers took charge. I ordered this awful device dismantled and brought to GE research labs. After this news conference, you are invited to go there and inspect it for yourselves. I also ordered the brigadier to blow up that secret bunker, which was huge and held enough provisions for those two evil men to stay there undetected for a year or more. Many of you may have heard that dull explosion earlier this afternoon."

"The regional corporation CEOs have demonstrated beyond any doubt that they are the enemies of every man, woman, and child on Blackwell-C. That being the case, Queen Lisa and I have called them up, telling them we discovered their wicked machine and dismantled it. We told them as of now, Blackwell-C is a free and independent Federation world. It is no longer under the control of any corporation CEO, myself included, though I will remain on post until you decide how you want the world to be governed. We will, of course, honor any and all fair trading agreements with other words and the corporations."

"Anticipating massive retaliation, I have ordered the

new planetary defense shield to be raised and kept up at all times. An entire regiment of our soldiers is garrisoning the control tower. Thus, there is nothing these evil, sadistic CEOs can do to harm our world, as long as the shield stays up. Of course, it can locally be lowered so space ships can land and depart. However, I have given orders to execute anyone who knowingly lowers the shield for any other reason, for that will endanger the entire world."

"Now then, with our security safeguarded, we must turn our attention to handling the terrible disaster these alien men caused to the women and few men of our capital city. Beginning tomorrow, soldiers will visit every home in the city and determine how many women desire the currently known cures. With only a few exceptions, anyone wishing the cures will have them and at no expense to themselves. GE will defray the costs of everyone's cures."

"However, unlike the genetic bio agent that creates the UFB women and men, the cures regrow arms and thus while in the coma, the person must be properly nourished with many vitamins and minerals that are used in bone and muscle creation. Calcium is needed in a large quantity, for example. So what I'm saying is that each person receiving the cure must be carefully monitored at all times and properly nourished. Thus, our infirmaries can only handle ten patients at a time. In the very near future, GD's infirmary will also be up and running, ready to deliver these cures, making twenty patients at one time. The process takes four days to complete."

"Bottom line: this will not be a rapid process. We will eventually get to everyone who wishes a cure. The last unofficial count I was able to put together from medical reports suggests we have close to a million who were recently turned into UFB women. At twenty women every four or five days, you can see it will take quite some time to get to everyone. Please be patient. We will get to you. In the meantime, I will be checking with the local medical centers to see if they can also be trained to deliver these cures and thus service more women each week. Remember, be patient, and you'll get your necessary cures."

"In the meantime, you need to determine the nature

and form of government that you desire to run Blackwell-C. Since we already have the local queens handling local business, it makes sense to utilize them in this process. Thus, beginning on Monday, anyone who has ideas or opinions on just how you want your world to be run are to pay a visit to your local queen and fully brief her. Later this spring, all the queens will meet and discuss the suggestions you have presented. We'll work this out; just give us time. However, in the interim, someone has to be in charge, so I will do so until this process is concluded and the new government takes control. Mind you, it should allow for free and open elections."

"That is all that I have for now. I will hold another press conference tomorrow at one. I will attempt to take your questions at that time. Again, if you wish to see this terrible new weapon, you are invited to visit the GE research labs now. Thank you." Beth nodded and the cameras and lights turned off.

The reporters wanted to interview Colonel Achima, Captain Hedda, and the brigadier, along with Emil and several others, and Beth decided to let them do so, since she wisely figured the others wouldn't want to return tomorrow. Colonel Achima described how they actually took the bunker, but she and the others refused to answer personal questions, particularly Emil. They wanted to know how he felt about being a UFBMD man with the cures. After that, they headed down to view the Mind Control machine.

"Back to my place," Beth suggested to Lisa and Elsa. "Thanks everyone for coming. Now the truth is out there. Thanks for saving the world too." Emil nodded, as did Colonel Achima. It was a long walk for the two UFB women to go from the throne room down to the tunnels, along them past GD headquarters and on to GE headquarters. By the time that they reached the elevators, the reporters had finished filming the Mind Control device and were just leaving.

"Good thing you didn't insist we tag along," Lisa whispered as they spotted the crew leaving GE's main entrance. Beth chuckled.

The smells of supper greeted them as they entered George and Beth's suite on the top floor of GE headquarters.

The two men were just where the women had left them. "You guys haven't practiced or anything?" Beth asked accusatively.

One of the twelve-year-old girls answered, "No, they just sat there and cried a lot. Supper came up, and we've got the table set. Smells good."

"Excellent. I'm starving. Fellows, get up and come to the table on your own if you want any supper," Beth ordered.

"But we can't manage that on our own," George pleaded. "We're helpless now, haven't you noticed?"

"We manage just fine, so can you, if you try," Beth countered. "Don't forget to toss your hair out of the way of your feet. Standing on it is painful." Beth, Lisa, and Elsa got to the table and seated. Meanwhile, the men were starving too and did their best to get themselves up and to the table. Both very nearly fell over as they lunged to their feet. Wild contortions kept them from falling. Their walk to the table was anything but graceful, but gasping for breath, both made it. Elsa kindly moved the chairs out for them, while Beth nodded to the two servant girls to take their positions and feed the men. Elsa did double duty, handling the two women.

After dinner, Beth had them turn on the news. The special news conference was just being rebroadcast again, and they listened to it. The men moaned and groaned, as they again saw just how they had been played and used by their bosses. However, Beth watched them closely. Not once, did either man compliment her or Elsa on taking the initiative and doing what they'd done. *That settles that,* Beth thought. *Time they learned their lessons.*

With supper done and the news watched, Beth and Lisa headed back into the living room. "You men can come too or you can just sit there on the chairs until bed time," Beth declared.

"But we need help, honey," George whined. "Have pity on us." Beth didn't and later watched the two men's wild movements, as they somehow managed to get up, walk into the living room, and mostly fall down onto the second sofa.

Again gasping for breath from that bit of exertion, George said, "So get us the cures tomorrow morning, please!"

"Right. First thing," Felix added.

Beth smiled. "Sorry fellows. You don't deserve to be the first ones to be cured. In fact, you, as former CEOs and allowing this to happen, will graciously forgo your cures until the last person who wants them has theirs completed."

"But you can't do that to us. We're helpless. We have to have the cures. Now, right away. We can't live like this," Felix protested. Lisa gave him a very dirty stare.

"Look," Beth shot back, "you men believe the way we and you are now is the ultimate in feminine beauty. So it is high time you both truly understand what you make your UFB women endure. You won't be getting your cures for quite some time, probably at least a year or more. So you're simply going to have to learn to do everything on your own that you make us UFB women do. You think we like our intense restrictions just to look beautiful for you fellows? Well, after enduring this for a year or so, I think you will have a definite change in your viewpoints of UFB women. Frankly, it's sadistic and certainly not the ultimate in beauty. Now if we had normal feet, normal arms, normal waists, normal boobs, then yes, we would be incredibly beautiful and perhaps even the ultimate, but not like we are. So stuff it. I'm in charge, and I've given the doctors strict orders not to give you two the cures until the last person has had theirs and that's final. So stop your whining and practice. Lisa and I do quite well in spite of our limitations, and you can too."

Elsa fought hard to keep from laughing aloud. Beth went on, "Look, Emil is like you two, though admittedly he's had the cures, but still he played an integral role in stopping that madman and even went before the cameras today. He has a lovely wife and she's expecting soon. So you two simply have to experience life fully as a UFB woman. Only then will you true appreciate the immense value of the cures Emil and the others went to such lengths to bring back for this world."

"But we love you, and we have always been there to help you two," Felix continued to protest.

"Of course, you have. Felix, if you hadn't, why, we would likely just ship you both off to Blackwoods and be done with you. No, you must learn what life is really like for what you desire to be your ultimate women," Beth remained adamant. "Don't worry. Lisa and I will teach you how we do things, since you've probably never really paid any attention to such things. The key is to practice a whole lot. This is final, fellows. Protest and whine all you want, but it won't do you any good."

Lisa giggled. "If you have half the guts that Emil has, you will buckle up and get to work learning how to survive. We thought we were marrying men who knew how to lead, strong men. Right now, you're proving you're the complete opposite of that."

"She's right," Beth added, "it is easy to play the big shot when you have the power, the money, and the influence. Anyone can play the big shot with that backing. But what happens when you hit a little adversity? Okay a big adversity. Your mettle is being put to the test, guys. Lisa and I want you to live up to our expectations of your mettle. You'll probably never have as big a test of your spirit, your resilience, your courage than this. We are behind you, and we want you to succeed, but it must be up to you to do it. We can't do it for you."

Felix sighed. He knew she had very valid points. He ventured, "You know, you should set up some kind of priority scheme for the cures. Some women hold or did hold more critical positions than others. Those should be cured first."

Beth smiled. "Excellent point. Now you are starting to act like a leader again. I'll look into that in the morning."

George ventured to ask, "Could you ask Emil to pay us a visit soon? I, we'd like to talk with him about this."

"Sure. I think he will be willing to come by," Beth replied. "Crap! I'm getting horny again. All the excitement of the day has worn off, and I can't seem to keep that at bay. Elsa, we should go to bed early tonight."

Chapter 18—Epilogue

Elsa's new orders were to get a complete copy of the plans, construction details, and methods of operation of the Mind Control machine and send them on up the line. It took her a week to obtain her own copies of these, primarily because Ivan had an enormous amount of material to sort through and study to determine what was what. Once she sent off her electronic copies, she waited for new orders to arrive. Two days later, they came: Monitor until new government is stable. She sent off an acknowledgment.

The following morning, Beth did more research into the affected women and discovered that Felix was correct. Some women simply had to be handled or cured as soon as possible. With Elsa's assistance, she formulated the guidelines to be followed. Additionally, within a week four other medical centers began delivering the cures. Two dozen patients could be fully handled in a week, with a few days for the staff to prepare for the next batch. That was too slow, so more beds were added, and women, who volunteered to be nurses, were cured and put to work. Within two weeks, the number being handled increased to well over a hundred. Still, Beth calculated that it would take several centuries to get to everyone. She continued to enlarge the facilities, adding more beds and medical equipment and nurses. Finally, she was able to reduce the total time to project completion down to three years and decided that was the best that could reasonably be hoped for. Their husbands didn't like that, but were unable to do anything about it.

One year into this lengthy process, Beth and Lisa began their families. Beth had a son, while Lisa had a daughter. Two years later, Beth had a daughter, while Lisa had a son. If there was any doubt about genetic inheritance, they were dispelled. Both their sons and daughters were born armless. They would grow up to look like UFB women and UFBMD men, at least until they received their cures. Nevertheless, both the new mothers and the fathers were extremely proud of their new children and growing families.

Beth held true to her declarations, and after three years of handing out cures, the last ones were scheduled. At this point, Felix and George insisted their children get the cures first, and then taking Beth and Lisa by surprise, they insisted their wives get the cures before they did, an action that took both women by surprise and pleasing them. After the two women came out of their comas, finally Felix and George entered theirs. When they were finished, there were very few true UFB women still on Blackwell-C, mostly in the exotic escort and bordellos, where once more they began earning a hefty salary, only this time, the new laws of the queens demanded they were paid in cash each year and not cheated out of their life's earnings.

As far as their choice of government, after lengthy discussions and two votes, Blackwell-C decided upon a president, electing him or her every five years, but with the stipulation no one could hold the office more than three times, whether consecutive or not. They did decide to keep the queens, though they also voted to allow them to have their cures as well, which in time they all received.

History books say Beth Gebberly was the father of their democracy and was their duly elected president for three terms. When she left office, Thromstead unveiled a life size bronze statue of her in Freedom Park, the renamed Central Park.

Once Felix and George had their cures, Elsa's assistance was no longer needed. She quietly retired from her position and vanished from Blackwell-C, heading off to her next assignment.

Thus, during the span of some twenty years, the vice grip that the corporations had held on the many worlds of the Federation crumbled. No one world's story is identical to the next, but the result was always the independence of such worlds. More critical was the loss of around half of the offensive space fleets of the combined Federation of Planets, as well as a sizable portion of their armed forces. Some claimed all this was inevitable. Some claimed it was all a monstrous conspiracy by the "tin cans." Regardless of the reasons, the breakdown of the Federation of Planets played a significant role in what was to come. However, one additional fallout from the disaster on Blackwell-C must be told.

Chapter 19—Fallout

Twenty-five year old Hans Becker used to work at Galactic Electronics as a research technician, before being promoted to a manager and moved up to the second floor of GE headquarters. His life was going along splendidly, money rolling in, promotions, and his longtime girlfriend had just said yes to his marriage proposal. Then came the terrible Mind Control attack on those working on the top two floors. Strange ideas formed in his head, but for days, he fought against them, resulting in severe headaches, forcing him to go to bed early, sometimes before supper. Then somehow, Hans woke up to a living nightmare, but claiming he was perfect and beautiful, though completely helpless.

"It wasn't me," he later tried to explain what ensued. "It was as if I went asleep, and something else woke up in this body. They wanted it to be a UFB woman, not me. God, I'd never want to be this—this freakish thing. And no, I had no deep down, hidden desire to change my sex. This other person did it to my body, as though they put me to sleep and took it over. Now here I'm awake again, only to find my body is ruined, a hideous freak."

Had it been months since it happened? Hans had no memories of that period, though the calendar said it must have been. The other person had gotten what they wanted from his body that much was clear. His body was one of the usual UFB women, fabulously beautiful, monster breasts, tiny waist, feet with a ninety-degree arch forcing him to wear the tiny toe shoes, hardly shoes at all, and lush, thick, shiny, wavy, raven hair falling to his knees, each strand of which had an amazing sense of touch or feel. But it was a body that lacked arms, and that turned the whole thing into a living nightmare of utter helplessness, at least at the beginning as far as Hans was concerned.

His aging parents refused to take him in, since his father was hard pressed to take care of his mother who had also become a victim weeks before Hans had. His girlfriend called him a total freak and ended their relationship. Hans found himself shipped off to Blackwoods Assisted Living, where at least someone fed him, though he was treated more like some child's doll. However, all this was merely a role played by the other person, the one who had stolen his body and put him to sleep, a role that apparently they had greatly desired.

Then came that terrible day, the day he had awakened from his long slumber, somewhere inside the body. Later, he learned Beth had ordered the Mind Control machine powered down. That had forced this other person out of his mind and body, and awakened him. Hans awoke to the nightmare that was now his life. He screamed louder than he imagined anyone could, but it wasn't even his own voice that was screaming. His tenor voice was replaced by a woman's high-pitched soprano. The impossibly tight corset that helped his back support the enormous weight of the two basketballs called breasts prevented him from breathing properly. Hans fainted, revived, screamed, and fainted, repeatedly—for hours some said.

The sudden waves of stark terror finally subsided, and he stopped screaming. Like so many others, Hans slumped into heavy grief, sobbing his life away, but then so were others in this facility. Later, he discovered about half of those who were here were recent victims, like himself. The others, well they didn't even have voices and were always silent, though their misery was far greater than his was.

Somehow, during that blur of a day, someone had him sitting in front of a big screen TV. Another UFB woman was speaking. Vaguely, he recognized her. Beth. His boss's wife. Slowly, his mind, like those around him, began to duplicate what was being said. Thankfully several times, the station replayed the interview and subsequent footage of the disassembled Mind Control machine, and understanding of what had happened sunk into his mind. Hans finally understood what had happened to him and to many, many as he now was, the supposed ultimate in feminine beauty as everyone claimed—he should know, since he'd taken some of Carsten's fabulous escorts out on dates before he met the love of his life, but it wasn't right that he too looked like a UFB woman. He was a man. *No, I'm a helpless freak.* He corrected his conclusion. Anger replaced his grief.

As the helpless days passed, his anger seethed and slipped into an utter hatred against those who had done this to him, turning him into a useless and monstrous freak, unwanted by all. His was a precisely focused hatred, directed towards the corporation behind this, the very one he had worked so long and hard for—Galactic Electronics. No, not GE in Thromstead, but GE's corporate headquarters on Zeta Minor-C, the regional corporation that oversaw GE on Blackwell-C and several other worlds. Vitriolic hatred filled Hans and became his sole driving force, his sole ambition, and his sole goal: to destroy them on Zeta Minor-C.

While Blackwoods did care for his physical needs, he spent all his awake hours sitting in the community center with all the others like him. However, they did have a language-learning machine there, one of the very few things he could do, and Hans constantly sat beside it learning to speak the dialect of English spoken on Zeta Minor-C. *One day I will go there and destroy them all, but I must be able to speak and understand them. Learn, Hans, learn.*

Unexpectedly came miracle day, as Hans later referred to it. His name had come up as the next to receive the known cures, again thanks to Beth and her unrelenting program to provide the cures to everyone who desired it, expect for a few criminals of course. Hans awoke from his second coma a new person, sort of. At least, he was no longer the helpless vegetable he had been. He had arms! The basketball breasts were now just overly large ones, half their previous size, though still far above the norm for women. His feet arches were lower, but he still couldn't place his feet flat on the floor and was told that he now had to wear at least six-inch heels, but walking was drastically easier now, and the restrictive corset, a thing of the nightmare past. His hair was untouched, still knee-length and with its remarkable sense of touch. As he looked at his body's modified form in the mirror, he realized he was still a freak. He looked and sounded like a very beautiful young woman, a super model perhaps, but he still had his maleness intact, making him a freak of nature, now and until the end of his days.

From GE, he received a nice financial award to help compensate for his on the job *accident*, as they called it, once more compliments of Beth, who was now running the corporation. Returning finally to his old apartment, he stared at his old suits, clothes, and shoes, none of which he could ever wear again. The vitriolic hatred seethed and boiled. He boxed up all his former apparel and donated them to a local charity. Then, he took a deep breath and headed to the recommended women's apparel store to purchase new clothing. He only had the single outfit he was given when he awoke from the curing coma.

His embarrassment knew no bounds as he entered the unfamiliar store, filled with unfamiliar clothing and heels, but he had no choice. He couldn't keep wearing this same garish gown. The saleswoman believe he was a woman and treated him as one. "Oh dearie, you simply should look your best. What about this elegant strapless gown? See, it is form fitting to bring out your magnificent curves. Men will go nuts seeing you in this."

Red-faced, he said meekly, "I'm conservative." More embarrassment. She continued to try to sell him all manner of fancy gowns and dresses, all of which only added to him embarrassment and humiliation. Finally, Hans saw an outfit on a mannequin that he could tolerate.

"Oh, I see, yes, a professional woman's outfit. That would be perfect for you. I think you would look conservative enough in it and yet still allow your beautiful aspects to show a little," she chatted gaily, convinced at last she'd found this young woman's tastes in fashionable apparel. She was right. Hans bought a dozen outfits and heels, all quite similar in color and fabrics—various shades of white, silk blouses and simple knee-length skirts in shades of greys and blacks, along with matching, leather heels with the requisite six-inch, spiked heels.

Once the many packages were delivered to his apartment, Hans tried one on and decided that of all the possibilities, this was the most acceptable to him. He did look like a professional woman, a very stunning one at that, though those thoughts only added to his humiliation and embarrassment. The next day, dressed as a professional woman, he fought down his intense feelings of embarrassment and headed over to his former company, GE, seeking employment as an electronics technician, the original job he had with them. He was surprised Beth hired him, and he was allowed to assist Ivan who was working on analyzing the captured Mind Control machine.

Instantly, Hans realized God must be on his side. Here he was in close contact with the very machine the evil, wicked corporations had used against him and so many others! The means of his revenge was now in his hands! For the next few months, Hans studied every aspect of the machine, including the extensive experimentation logs that Bert Custer had kept.

He even tried to contact his former fiancé. She too had undergone the UFB women mutation and had her cures. When he visited her, he was quite humiliated. "Oh Hans, I'm now a *gorgeous* woman myself. I've got many men asking me out on dates now. At one *time*, Hans, you were an interesting man, but look at you now. Why, you are a gorgeous woman yourself. I certainly am not attracted to beautiful women. Surely, you can understand that." His face hot and probably crimson, Hans quietly left her doorstep and headed home, crushed yet again, the vitriolic hatred further fueled.

During the next weeks, Hans purchased electronic components. He intended to build his own Mind Control machine, but not here on Blackwell-C, rather on Zeta Minor-C. He knew he dared not take a completed machine with him, for surely, it would be recognized and confiscated when he landed and went through customs. But parts, now those would pass inspection, since he was an electronics technician.

Based upon his experience with his ex-girlfriend, he knew he had to change his name and ID card somehow. While he could be called Hans Becker here in Thromstead—a male name but with what was seen as a gorgeous female body—off-world, no one would even remotely understand. Hans—he knew his name meant God is gracious. His revenge would be gracious, divine retribution in fact. So he chose the feminine version, Hanne and set about getting a new ID card identifying him as Hanne Becker, female. No one questioned his request, since it seemed obvious he was a woman.

As spring ended, Hans packed up three shipping crates, two with his clothing and sundries, and one with his precious electronic components. He packed his own coded construction and operational specifications, taken from the extensive documentation of the Mind Control machine, and encoded such that only he knew what the strange symbols and seeming gibberish words actually meant. Satisfied he had everything he needed, Hans booked a commercial flight to Zeta Minor-C, specifically to its capital city, Athens, where the regional headquarters for many of the corporations were located, particularly GE and GD.

Slightly nervous, Hanne Becker walked up to the customs agent at the spaceport in Athens, her heels clicking on the granite floor, attracting attention her way, which she found continually embarrassing, to say nothing of the many men who stared at her. To her amazement, the customs agent asked few questions and stamped her ID card with the requisite visitor's stamp, allowing her complete freedom of movement on this world. One thing she soon learned was that the men she came in contact with all bent over backwards to *assist* her, carrying her crates to a cart, pushing the cart for her, even loading them into the public transport, all so they could get a good look at this raven haired beauty. By the time the public transport departed, she'd managed to deflect a dozen passes men had tossed at her, embarrassing her as well as humiliating her, though that only further steeled her will to extract total revenge.

Unlike the hilly world of Blackwell-C, Zeta Minor-C was a fully modern world. Here, again corporation standards were in full force. Their headquarters were hundred story skyscrapers of concrete, steel, and glass, nearly all built from the same mold. Athens was a thriving city of ten million with the corporation headquarters dominating the central city skyline. She rode the public transport around the heart of the city several times, until she spotted the ideal location and finally pulled the cord to be dropped off in front of the Grant Hotel, three blocks from the GE skyscraper and four from

GD's.

As she walked into the spacious entrance of the hotel, she could see that this was a rather rundown hotel, one long past its glory days. The once plush carpeting was traffic worn; the many chairs and sofas were stained in spots. Making use of the bellboy to bring her three crates and whose eyes followed her every curve and wiggle as she walked, Hanne walked up to the registration desk, where an older man stepped up to the his side of the desk, again looking her over. "May I help you, madam," he said as she reached the sign in book.

"I wish a room on the east side, preferably on the highest floor available," Hanne explained.

"7042 is available. And how long will the madam be staying?"

"Months, if that is acceptable," she replied. His lecherous grin told her t it was. This hotel wasn't as expensive as she'd anticipated, and she paid for meals as well. Rather like some puppy, the bellhop insisted on carrying her three crates up to the room for her, and she remembered to tip the lad, though she would have rather slapped him. Humiliation knows no bounds, Hanne thought.

After he left, she checked the view from the windows. Perfect, clear line of sight to GE and to GD from here. Perfect. Hanne then spent the rest of the day unpacking her many professional woman's outfits and then opened her electronics parts crate, smiling at them. Hanne settled down to work, building her own version of the Mind Control machine. She knew it would likely take weeks of work, but she was patient. *I will have my revenge on these men!*

As she headed down to the dining room, which had once been elegant and fancy but now had long ago seen better days, a new and unforeseen problem arose, one which only exacerbated her humiliation and embarrassment. Various men constantly hit on her, trying to pick her up, asking her for dates, and even far less subtle actions. She soon discovered the hotel ran an escort service out of the lower three floors! *Well, she concluded, as rundown as this place is, I can see why they need to pull in extra cash. Still, this is getting unbearable. They think I'm a hooker!*

After a week of constant harassment, Hanne got a brilliant idea, a way to defuse and snuff out all these men hounding her. Hire an escort herself and show them she was only interested in other women! They would see her as a lesbian and finally leave her alone in peace. Brilliant, she thought.

Later that evening, she made inquiries about the service at the main desk, and received instructions to pay a visit to Room 101, on the second floor. She entered the room and found a well-dressed man in an expensive black suit sitting behind a desk. On the side walls were photographs of fifty women, most either erotically dressed or wearing elegant gowns, provocative for sure. They were all attractive women. "May I help the madam?"

"Yes, I was told that I could hire an escort for the evening here," Hanne didn't waste time. This was cutting into her construction time, but had to be done if only to stop men from constantly trying to pick her up as though she was one of these women for sale.

"Ah, but of course, madam." He pointed to the wall, "Here are our beauties. Each can be dressed to suit your tastes and needs, whether that be an elegant night out, a maid, a fetish queen, or even kinky school girls. We even have an assortment of the truly ultimate in exotic women, the UFB women, as you can see there on the right side. Of course, those women will need quite a bit of assistance with everything, but they are the ultimate in beauty, though I must say that you are nearly so yourself, madam. Now if you would consider working for me, I can guarantee you a tidy profit."

"Sorry, I'm not interested in men, not remotely, so I'm afraid you'd lose money that way. Might I see some of these UFB women?" Hanne asked, figuring these women would be more readily satisfied than all the normal women who would certainly ask far too many questions of her.

"Of course, of course, madam. If you will follow me, they are on the second floor in the choosing room, as we call it. There you may cast your eyes on the finest women Athens has to offer, all for your pleasure," he said smoothly.

A few minutes later, Hanne began to believe this was

yet another mistake. The room was filled with gorgeous UFB women, all elegantly dressed, sitting stiffly on love seats around the choosing room. As she walked past them, each did her best to flirt with Hanne, trying to get her to pick them. At the very end of the rows of soft seats, she spotted a lovely blonde woman, but she had obviously been crying. Her cheeks were wet, and the man chided her as they walked up. "Mary Beth! Stop this childish behavior. You know you're here to please the clientele not sob. No one will want you if you cannot control your emotions."

Turning to Hanne, he explained, "Mary Beth is our newest addition and hasn't yet gotten accustomed to all of this. I'm sure in a short while she will adapt and become a productive member of our service. So have you decided upon your pick for this evening?"

Afterwards, Hanne couldn't say what motivated her pick or why, only that she felt a kinship with the woman. "I'd like Mary Beth, if that's acceptable."

"What? But she isn't—but of course. The client is always right. Mary Beth, this is your first client. Stand up and go out with her. Make sure she has a delightful time." The young woman had no choice but to attempt to get up. Unlike these other experienced women, Hanne suspected Mary Beth had only recently become a UFB woman. She wobbled and wiggled wildly as she lunged upwards, nearly falling over before she stabilized herself. Hanne charged it to her room and slipped an arm around Mary Beth, steadying her, just as many assistants had done for her before she received her cures.

Slowly, the pair walked out of the room, but Hanne noticed the man was shaking his head in disbelief. If looks could kill, Hanne's would have. Once free from the room, Hanne decided to take her down to the dining room where they could talk and take tea. Ever since her conversion, Hanne found her tolerance for alcoholic beverages had become minimal. Somehow, alcohol affected her rapidly, and she'd forgone her favorite ales long ago.

After helping Mary Beth get seated and having moved her hair out of the way so young, inexperienced woman didn't sit on it, she ordered tea and a straw for her escort. "Thank you. I really am supposed to please you, but I don't know how," Mary Beth said softly, trying hard to keep from crying again.

"That's all right. So why don't you tell me what happened to you? How did you end up in there with that lecherous man?"

Over tea, Mary Beth was very willing to share her sad tale. "I was a secretary for Harry Eagles, one of the top executives at GE. Their building isn't far from here. I was making good wages too, but then his wife—she's a UFB woman herself, she accused me of having an affair with Harry. Honestly, I didn't do that. I was just his secretary. He never even made a pass at me, but I guess Harry had to listen to her. She wanted me out of there and insisted I become a UFB woman. I protested and told them I was innocent, but that didn't matter. When I woke up, I found myself here in this hotel. They told me I had been sold, and I was now one of his escorts."

"That was two weeks ago. I sobbed, cried, and protested, but they just laughed at me. I still can't walk much, but I know I don't have any choice but to do what they say. I'm completely helpless and will be forever. I can't do anything about it. I can't even call my parents, but then I know they won't take me in. They are against UFB women, you see. I don't know what I'll do. What am I supposed to do with you tonight? They just told me to do what I have to do to please you."

"You just keep me company, Mary Beth. What they did to you is criminal. Somehow, you need to get justice from them."

"Oh how I want to do that, Hanne, but I'm completely helpless now. I can barely breathe. I almost fall down every time I try to stand up. It's all I can manage to walk a little bit. I don't see how I can ever give you pleasure or anything, but I do like you and the tea. This is nice for a change. I've been cooped up in that place since I got here."

"Well, I'll keep on taking you out so maybe they will go easier on you. I do understand what you are going through, Mary Beth, I really do," Hanne replied, hesitant to say more.

"He said that if I didn't earn my keep, he'd sell me to one of the filthy bordellos." Just saying that brought on another round of crying, embarrassing the young woman even further. Hanne didn't say anything but inwardly fumed. This wasn't right, not remotely. Then, something she'd just said gave Hanne an idea.

After allowing a number of the men hanging around the area, some of which had tried several times to pick her up, Hanne decided it was time to return Mary Beth, though she hated to do that. She rather wished she could shoot the man with a d-gun instead. The poor woman was right though. She could just barely walk and needed all the support Hanne gave her.

When she returned her to the room, she struck up another conversation with the owner, who asked, "Well, did she perform acceptable? Or did she sob the whole time?"

Hanne refused to answer him, saying instead, "I take it that she has been more trouble for you than she's worth."

The man sneered, "Damned observant, madam. That she has. I took her on as a favor to a gentlemen, but I should have known better. These new ones need a year to adjust. She's costing me a fortune. Why?"

"Well, what would you sell her for?" Hanne asked, the words sticking in her throat. She was talking as if the young woman was little more than a thing to be bought and sold like a book.

"You interested, eh?" he sneered. "Well, I'll tell you what I'll do. I'll make you a good deal on that one." The two haggled over the price until Hanne got it down to five hundred credits.

"Okay deal. Charge it to my room now. Does she come with clothes and shoes?"

"I'll throw in a couple outfits, but that's all for this price." Hanne agreed and watched as he billed her room and the charge went through. "I'll send some clothes up to your room in the morning. If you will please take what sobbing woman with you now, we'd all be a whole lot happier. I sure don't see what you see in her, but then I guess *certain* women's tastes are different than ours," he jeered.

"Of course, I'll take her now." Hanne moved over to where Mary Beth had finally managed to fall back down on the love seat. Carefully, she helped the young woman get back up without all the terrified wobbling. Slipping an arm around her, she again led her to the door. Once outside, Hanne whispered, "Now you are free forever from him and this kind of life."

"I don't understand. I now belong to you? Why? What must I do?" Mary Beth whispered back, very confused, but that was nothing new. She'd been confused for weeks now.

"You will stay with me. I can help you learn to get by fairly well. You are free, Mary Beth. I'll explain more when we get to my room."

Once there, Mary Beth was gasping and quite tired. All this had been far too taxing, so Hanne simply got her undressed and tucked into bed, where she fell asleep almost at once. Hanne went back into the main room and continued to work on her machine until late at night, before undressing and crawling in beside Mary Beth.

In the morning, Mary Beth's motions roused Hanne. The poor woman was trying desperately to pleasure herself. At this point, Hanne recalled forgotten details from her days at Blackwoods. UFB men and women had very powerful sexual drives. The women who were not married wore special panties that kept a vibrator inserted in them, which automatically activated several times a day, giving the women their desperately needed relief. Compounding the problem, Hanne still had her own intense sex drives. Mary Beth's wiggling had totally aroused her, and Hanne was just as unable to control her drives as Mary Beth was.

Before either knew what was happening, they were passionately kissing and more. A half hour later, amid a tangle of blonde and raven hair, super sensitive to touch, the pair finished, Mary Beth lying against Hanne. She said timidly, "Thank you. I was so desperate. This never happened before I was changed, but now I can't help myself, and they didn't put those special panties on me last night. What did you use? One of those things women use?"

"I've a confession to make, Mary Beth. I've not been completely honest with you. I am a man."

"No you are not. You are a very beautiful woman. I can see that. They didn't harm my eyes. You are a beautiful professional woman."

"I'm not. Look," Hanne pulled back the covers.

"Oh!" exclaimed a very confused Mary Beth.

"I was a man, an electronics technician working for GE back on my world," Hanne began. She outlined in some detail what had happened to her and how she'd come to be here in Athens.

"So I'll make you a deal. You play along with me and keep my secrets. I promise you we'll get our revenge on these beasts. After that, I'll take you back to my world and get you your cures too. You can have your life back too, Mary Beth. Meantime, I'll teach you all I learned about surviving as you are now. Together, we can get by, but you must keep our secrets. Okay?" Mary Beth agreed, and the two rose to begin facing another day. The room had an electrostatic hair machine, which they both used. Before breakfast, a porter delivered two additional outfits for Mary Beth, enough for the moment, though Hanne knew they would have to go out shopping for more.

Part of each day, Hanne spent with Mary Beth, showing her how to manage the very few things that were possible for a UFB woman. After then leaving her to practice them on her own, Hanne spent the rest working on her version of the Mind Control machine.

The subterfuge worked incredibly well. Since Hanne was always seen escorting Mary Beth around, men quickly began ignoring them, presumably believing Hanne was a lesbian with her new lover. The hardest challenge was the outing they made a week later to get Mary Beth some new clothing. The poor girl was constantly gasping for breath, but they were successful, much to both women's relief.

Three weeks later, Hanne finished the machine. After satisfying each other in bed, Hanne, with Mary Beth beside her, turned on the machine, focusing it on the top floors of the GE building, though GD was also in the path of the energy beams. Lacking any other inspiration, Hanne used the same script Bert Custer had used on her and the thousands in

Thromstead. However, unlike Bert, she set it to its maximum power setting. She wasn't about to dilly dally around. After that, the two headed down for breakfast. When they got back to the room, Hanne gave Mary Beth an assignment: watch the news channels and report on any results, while she kept watch on the machine and began working out other potential scripts to use.

They left the machine running constantly. On the third day, Mary Beth called out, "Hanne, come quick! It's working. It's really working! Harry Eagles has gone and done it! Hurray!"

Hanne joined her and watched the coverage. That fifty of the top executives of both GE and GD corporations had ordered their doctors to turn them into UFBMD men and UFB women was the top story that day. After that, Hanne lowered the angle and focused on the middle floors and by the end of the week, she had it trained on the lower ones too.

On Sunday, Mary Beth reported the newscaster said for unknown reasons, everyone who worked at GE and GD corporate headquarters had gotten themselves converted. Speculation ran rampant upon the reasons. However, those who had come out of their comas, were jubilant, claiming that now they were absolutely beautiful and utterly perfect in all ways, completely ignoring the fact that all operations at these two corporation headquarters servicing several other worlds beyond Zeta Minor-C had come to a complete and total halt.

Curiously, the world's largest battleship, the Indestructible, had just been ordered to land and conduct a full investigation into the seemingly utterly bazaar behavior. The giant ship was due to land at Athens' spaceport later this morning. That gave Hanne another idea.

From their tall skyscraper windows, she could see the sprawling, busy spaceport far off in the distance. She recorded a different script and focused it roughly where she thought the giant ship might be descending and fired it up, again at maximum power. Mary Beth made her slow way to stand beside her lover, looking out at the wonderful view of the city.

"Say, what's that low, huge building way over there?" Hanne asked, pointing it out to Mary Beth.

"Oh that's the barracks for the infantry division that is supposed to guard Athens from attacks. Why?"

"Interesting. I wonder if it will have any effect on the battleship?" The two watched the world going by outside their seventieth floor windows for some time.

Suddenly, Mary Beth cried, "There, I see it. It's huge."

"Where?"

Mary Beth broke down and began sobbing, unable to point it out to Hanne. "It's okay, Mary Beth. I see it now. Look, its landing, bringing thousands of soldiers." As the pair watched, suddenly the giant ship accelerated and smashed into the ground, exploding in a ball of flames a mile high. Both women gasped.

"How very interesting. Okay, one more target, and we will be heading to my world and your cure, my love." Hanne pointed the device to the army barracks, activating it with the UFB woman script. That done, she packed up their things, which now occupied four shipping crates. After making sure they were leaving nothing behind, Hanne places an explosive device with a timer on the machine. Based on the frequency of housekeeping, she set it for three hours and called for the porter, who carried their crates down to the lobby desk. Their crates arrived long before the two slow moving women did. After checking out, they took a public bus to Northampton's spaceport, some fifty miles away, where they boarded a commercial flight that made a stop on Blackwell-C.

Their flight was on time, and the deep space transport lifted off just as the timer went off. The explosion destroyed the Mind Control machine, bits scattered all over the main room of that hotel suite. Later on, when the authorities attempted to track down the woman Hanne Becker of Blackwell-C, they discovered no such woman existed, but there was a man called Hans Becker. They dropped the investigation, failing utterly to ask for a photograph of the man. Obviously from all accounts, a beautiful woman had been staying at the hotel and was responsible for the mess she left behind. No one had a clue about what had happened at the corporate headquarters or the army barracks, but decided the loss of their largest battleship was due to a terrible accident.

Corporate control on Zeta Minor-C never recovered from these disasters, and the outer worlds they oversaw took this opportunity to rebel themselves.

Back in Thromstead, Hans took Mary Beth to the hospital and paid for her cures. Four days later, Mary Beth's life was restored. Not surprising, she and Hans married a few days after that. A few weeks later, Hans was rehired at GE and brought Mary Beth along with him, insisting she be his secretary. From this point on, the two continued to appear to the world as a lesbian couple, greatly reducing the humiliation and embarrassment that Hans had been facing. Alone in their new home, both knew otherwise and soon began their own family, satisfied that they had their revenge.

The End.

A Favor to Other Readers

How about helping other readers? Many readers rely on reviews to make the decision whether to buy a book. You can help them make their decision by leaving your opinions and viewpoint in a short review of the positive things of this book. Writing the review and expressing your opinion only takes a few minutes, and other readers will appreciate your efforts.

Click this link: Slow Comes the Dark Volume 4 Perversion Incarnate
.   http://www.amazon.com/dp/B00NZGNW6U
scroll down to Customer Reviews; click on Write a Review, and enter your review. Thank you.

Author Information

Visit My Amazon.com Author Page
Vic Broquard Author Page
http://amazon.com/author/vic-broquard

Follow My Blog:
http://www.broquard-ebooks.com/blog/

Follow Me on Social Media

Facebook
http://www.facebook.com/vic.broquard/

Google+
http://plus.google.com/102242823668960002176/

LinkedIn
http://www.linkedin.com/profile/view?id=297732151

YouTube
http://www.youtube.com/channel/UCQWcs-WAX2YqViIiafUqJuw

Other Books by Vic Broquard

The Return of the Wizards: Twelve Companions – The Making of Wizards (fantasy)

Slow Comes the Dark Series: (science fiction)

www.ingramcontent.com/pod-product-compliance
Lightning Source LLC
Chambersburg PA
CBHW070658180626
46817CB00006B/2431